The Time of the Sword Rulers

*In those days there were oceans of light and cities
in the skies. It was a time of gods, a time of giants.
It was a rich time and a dark time. It was the time
of the Sword Rulers . . . .*

*For upstart man was beginning to spread like a
pestilence across the Earth, striking down the Old
Races wherever he found them. And it was not
only death that man brought, but terror too. He
made of the Older Earth nothing but ruins and
bones.*

*By creating man, the universe had betrayed the
Old Races. Those who curse the universe curse
that which is deaf, they shake their fists at blind
stars. But there will always be such beings, sometimes beings of great wisdom. The last of the
Vadhagh Race, Prince Corum Jhaelen Irsei, was
one of those.*

This chronicle concerns him.

THE SWORDS TRILOGY

MICHAEL MOORCOCK

BERKLEY BOOKS, NEW YORK

Originally published in three separate volumes as THE KNIGHT
OF THE SWORDS, THE QUEEN OF THE SWORDS, and
THE KING OF THE SWORDS.

THE SWORDS TRILOGY

A Berkley Book / published by arrangement with
the author

PRINTING HISTORY
Berkley edition / August 1977
Twelfth printing / March 1986

ISBN: 0-425-08848-0

A BERKLEY BOOK ® TM 757,375
Berkley Books are published by The Berkley Publishing Group,
200 Madison Avenue, New York, NY 10016.
The name "BERKLEY" and the stylized "B" with design
are trademarks belonging to Berkley Publishing Corporation.

PRINTED IN THE UNITED STATES OF AMERICA

Contents

THE KNIGHT OF THE SWORDS

THE QUEEN OF THE SWORDS

BOOK ONE

BOOK TWO

THE BOOKS OF

CORUM

Being a History in Three Volumes Concerning the Quests and Adventures of Corum Jhaelen Irsei of the Vadhagh Folk, who is also called the Prince in the Scarlet Robe

---

Volume the First

THE KNIGHT OF THE SWORDS

This book is for Wendy Fletcher

INTRODUCTION

In those days there were oceans of light and cities in the skies and wild flying beasts of bronze. There were herds of crimson cattle that roared and were taller than castles. There were shrill, viridian things that haunted bleak rivers. It was a time of gods, manifesting themselves upon our world in all her aspects; a time of giants who walked on water; of mindless sprites and misshapen creatures who could be summoned by an ill-considered thought but driven away only on pain of some fearful sacrifice; of magics, phantasms, unstable nature, impossible events, insane paradoxes, dreams come true, dreams gone awry, of nightmares assuming reality.

It was a rich time and a dark time. The time of the Sword Rulers. The time when the Vadhagh and the Nhadragh, age-old enemies, were dying. The time when Man, the slave of fear, was emerging, unaware that much of the terror he experienced was the result of nothing else but the fact that he, himself, had come into existence. It was one of many ironies connected with Man, who, in those days, called his race "Mabden."

The Mabden lived brief lives and bred prodigiously. Within a few centuries they rose to dominate the westerly continent on which they had evolved. Superstition stopped them from sending many of their ships toward Vadhagh and Nhadragh lands for another century or two, but gradually they gained courage when no resistance was offered. They began to feel jealous of the older races; they began to feel malicious.

The Vadhagh and the Nhadragh were not aware of this. They had dwelt a million or more years upon the planet which now, at last, seemed at rest. They knew of the Mabden but considered them not greatly different from other beasts. Though continuing to indulge their traditional hatreds of one another, the Vadhagh and the

3

Nhadragh spent their long hours in considering abstractions, in the creation of works of art and the like. Rational, sophisticated, at one with themselves, these older races were unable to believe in the changes that had come. Thus, as it almost always is, they ignored the signs.

There was no exchange of knowledge between the two ancient enemies, even though they had fought their last battle many centuries before.

The Vadhagh lived in family groups occupying isolated castles scattered across a continent called by them Bro-an-Vadhagh. There was scarcely any communication between these families, for the Vadhagh had long since lost the impulse to travel. The Nhadragh lived in their cities built on the islands in the seas to the northwest of Bro-an-Vadhagh. They, also, had little contact, even with their closest kin. Both races reckoned themselves invulnerable. Both were wrong.

Upstart Man was beginning to breed and spread like a pestilence across the world. This pestilence struck down the old races wherever it touched them. And it was not only death that Man brought, but terror, too. Willfully, he made of the older world nothing but ruins and bones. Unwittingly, he brought psychic and supernatural disruption of a magnitude which even the Great Old Gods failed to comprehend.

And the Great Old Gods began to know Fear.

And Man, slave of fear, arrogant in his ignorance, continued his stumbling progress. He was blind to the huge disruptions aroused by his apparently petty ambitions. As well, Man was deficient in sensitivity, had no awareness of the multitude of dimensions that filled the universe, each plane intersecting with several others. Not so the Vadhagh nor the Nhadragh, who had known what it was to move at will between the dimensions they termed the Five Planes. They had glimpsed and understood the nature of the many planes, other than the Five, through which the Earth moved.

Therefore it seemed a dreadful injustice that these wise races should perish at the hands of creatures who were still little more than animals. It was as if vultures feasted on and squabbled over the paralyzed body of the youthful poet who could only stare at them with puzzled eyes as they slowly robbed him of an exquisite existence they would never appreciate, never know they were taking.

"If they valued what they stole, if they knew what they were destroying," says the old Vadhagh in the story, "The Only Autumn Flower," "then I would be consoled."

It was unjust.

By creating Man, the universe had betrayed the old races.

4

But it was a perpetual and familiar injustice. The sentient may perceive and love the universe, but the universe cannot perceive and love the sentient. The universe sees no distinction between the multitude of creatures and elements which comprise it. All are equal. None is favored. The universe, equipped with nothing but the materials and the power of creation, continues to create: something of this, something of that. It cannot control what it creates and it cannot, it seems, be controled by its creations (though a few might deceive themselves otherwise). Those who curse the workings of the universe curse that which is deaf. Those who strike out at those workings fight that which is inviolate. Those who shake their fists, shake their fists at blind stars.

But this does not mean that there are some who will not try to do battle with and destroy the invulnerable.

There will always be such beings, sometimes beings of great wisdom, who cannot bear to believe in an insouciant universe.

Prince Corum Jhaelen Irsei was one of these. Perhaps the last of the Vadhagh race, he was sometimes known as The Prince in the Scarlet Robe.

This chronicle concerns him.

—*The Book of Corum*

BOOK ONE

In which Prince Corum learns a lesson and loses a limb

The First Chapter

AT CASTLE ERORN

At Castle Erorn dwelt the family of the Vadhagh prince, Khlonskey. This family had occupied the castle for many centuries. It loved, exceedingly, the moody sea that washed Erorn's northern walls and the pleasant forest that crept close to her southern flank.

Castle Erorn was so ancient that it seemed to have fused entirely with the rock of the huge eminence that overlooked the sea. Outside, it was a splendor of time-worn turrets and salt-smoothed stones. Within, it had moving walls which changed shape in tune with the elements and changed color when the wind changed course. And there were rooms full of arrangements of crystals and fountains, playing exquisitely complicated fugues composed by members of the family, some living, some dead. And there were galleries filled with paintings brushed on velvet, marble, and glass by Prince Khlonskey's artist ancestors. And there were libraries filled with manuscripts written by members of both the Vadhagh and the Nhadragh races. And elsewhere in Castle Erorn were rooms of statues, and there were aviaries and menageries, observatories, laboratories, nurseries, gardens, chambers of meditation, surgeries, gymnasia, collections of martial paraphernalia, kitchens, planetaria, museums, conjuratoria, as well as rooms set aside for less specific purposes, or rooms forming the apartment of those who lived in the castle.

● ● ●

Twelve people lived in the castle now, though once five hundred had occupied it. The twelve were Prince Khlonskey, himself, a very ancient being; his wife Colatalarna, who was, in appearance, much younger than her husband; Ilastru and Pholhinra, his twin daughters; Prince Rhanan, his brother; Sertreda, his niece; Corum, his son. The remaining five were retainers, distant cousins of the prince. All had characteristic Vadhagh features: narrow, long skulls; ears that were almost without lobes and tapered flat alongside the head; fine hair that a breeze would make rise like flimsy clouds about their faces; large almond eyes that had yellow centers and purple surrounds; wide, full-lipped mouths; and skin that was a strange, gold-flecked rose-pink. Their bodies were slim and tall and well proportioned and they moved with a leisurely grace that made the human gait seem like the shambling of a crippled ape.

Occupying themselves chiefly with remote, intellectual pastimes, the family of Prince Khlonskey had had no contact with other Vadhagh folk for two hundred years and had not seen a Nhadragh for three hundred. No news of the outside world had come to them for over a century. Only once had they seen a Mabden, when a specimen had been brought to Castle Erorn by Prince Opash, a naturalist and first cousin to Prince Khlonskey. The Mabden—a female—had been placed in the menageries where it was cared for well, but it lived little more than fifty years and when it died was never replaced. Since then, of course, the Mabden had multiplied and were, it appeared, even now inhabiting large areas of Bro-an-Vadhagh. There were even rumors that some Vadhagh castles had been infested with Mabden who had overwhelmed the inhabitants and eventually destroyed their homes altogether. Prince Khlonskey found this hard to believe. Besides, the speculation was of little interest to him or his family. There were so many other things to discuss, so many more complex sources of speculation, pleasanter topics of a hundred kinds.

Prince Khlonskey's skin was almost milk-white and so thin that all the veins and muscles were clearly displayed beneath. He had lived for over a thousand years and only recently had age begun to enfeeble him. When his weakness became unbearable, when his eyes began to dim, he would end his life in the manner of the Vadhagh, by going to the Chamber of Vapors and laying himself on the silk quilts and cushions and inhaling the various sweet-smelling gases until he died. His hair had turned a golden brown with age and the color of his eyes had mellowed to a kind of reddish-purple with pupils of a dark orange. His robes were now rather too large for his body, but, although he carried a staff of plaited platinum in which ruby metal had been woven, his bearing was still proud and his back was not bent.

One day he sought his son, Prince Corum, in a chamber where music was formed by the arranging of hollow tubes, vibrating wires, and shifting stones. The very simple, quiet music was almost drowned by the sound of Khlonskey's feet on the tapestries, the tap of his staff, and the rustle of the breath in his thin throat.

Prince Corum withdrew his attention from the music and gave his father a look of polite inquiry.

"Father?"

"Corum. Forgive the interruption."

"Of course. Besides, I was not satisfied with the work." Corum rose from his cushions and drew his scarlet robe about him.

"It occurs to me, Corum, that I will soon visit the Chamber of Vapors," said Prince Khlonskey, "and, in reaching this decision, I had it in mind to indulge a whim of mine. However, I will need your help."

Now Prince Corum loved his father and respected his decision, so he said gravely, "That help is yours, Father. What can I do?"

"I would know something of the fate of my kinsmen. Of Prince Opash, who dwells at Castle Sarn in the East. Of Princess Lorim, who is at Castle Crachah in the South. And of Prince Faguin of Castle Gal in the North."

Prince Corum frowned. "Very well, Father, if . . ."

"I know, Son, what you think—that I could discover what I wish to know by occult means. Yet this is not so. For some reason it is difficult to achieve intercourse with the other planes. Even my perception of them is dimmer than it should be, try as I might to enter them with my senses. And to enter them physically is almost impossible. Perhaps it is my age . . ."

"No, Father," said Prince Corum, "for I, too, have found it difficult. Once it was easy to move through the Five Planes at will. With a little more effort the Ten Planes could be contacted, though, as you know, few could visit them physically. Now I am unable to do more than see and occasionally hear those other four planes which, with ours, form the spectrum through which our planet directly passes in its astral cycle. I do not understand why this loss of sensibility has come about."

"And neither do I," agreed his father. "But I feel that it must be portentous. It indicates some major change in the nature of our Earth. That is the chief reason why I would discover something of my relatives and, perhaps, learn if they know why our senses become bound to a single plane. It is unnatural. It is crippling to us. Are we to become like the beasts of this plane, which are aware only

9

of one dimension and have no understanding that the others exist at all? Is some process of devolution at work? Shall our children know nothing of our experiences and slowly return to the state of those aquatic mammals from which our race sprang? I will admit to you, my son, that there are traces of fear in my mind.''

Prince Corum did not attempt to reassure his father. "I read once of the Blandhagna," he said thoughtfully. "They were a race based on the Third Plane. A people of great sophistication. But something took hold of their genes and of their brains and, within five generations, they had reverted to a species of flying reptile still equipped with a vestige of their former intelligence—enough to make them mad and, ultimately, destroy themselves completely. What is it, I wonder, that produces these reversions?''

"Only the Sword Rulers know," his father said.

Corum smiled. "And the Sword Rulers do not exist. I understand your concern, Father. You would have me visit these kinsmen of yours and bring them our greetings. I should discover if they fare well and if they have noticed what we have noticed at our Castle Erorn.''

His father nodded. "If our perception dims to the level of a Mabden, then there is little point in continuing our race. Find out, too, if you can, how the Nhadragh fare—if this dullness of the senses comes to them.''

"Our races are of more or less equal age," Corum murmured. "Perhaps they are similarly afflicted. But did not your kinsman Shulag have something to say, when he visited you some centuries back?''

"Aye. Shulag had it that the Mabden had come in ships from the West and subjugated the Nhadragh, killing most and making slaves of those remaining. Yet I find it hard to believe that the Mabden half-beasts, no matter how great their numbers, would have the wit to defeat Nhadragh cunning.''

Prince Corum pursed his lips reflectively. "Possibly they grew complacent," he said.

His father turned to leave the chamber, his staff of ruby and platinum tapping softly on the richly embroidered cloth covering the flagstones, his delicate hand clutching it more tightly than usual. "Complacency is one thing," he said, "and fear of an impossible doom is another. Both, of course, are ultimately destructive. We need speculate no more, for on your return you may bring us answers to these questions. Answers that we can understand. When would you leave?''

"I have it in mind to complete my symphony," Prince Corum

said. "That will take another day or so. I will leave on the morning after the day I finish it."

Prince Khlonskey nodded his old head in satisfaction. "Thank you, my son."

When he had gone, Prince Corum returned his attention to his music, but he found that it was difficult for him to concentrate. His imagination began to focus on the quest he had agreed to undertake. A certain emotion took hold of him. He believed that it must be excitement. When he embarked on the quest, it would be the first time in his life that he had left the environs of Castle Erorn.

He attempted to calm himself, for it was against the customs of his people to allow an excess of emotion.

"It will be instructive," he murmured to himself, "to see the rest of this continent. I wish that geography had interested me more. I scarcely know the outlines of Bro-an-Vadhagh, let alone the rest of the world. Perhaps I should study some of the maps and travelers' tales in the library. Yes, I will go there tomorrow, or perhaps the next day."

No sense of urgency filled Prince Corum, even now. The Vadhagh being a long-lived people, they were used to acting at leisure, considering their actions before performing them, spending weeks or months in meditation before embarking on some study or creative work.

Prince Corum then decided to abandon his symphony, on which he had been working for the past four years. Perhaps he would take it up again on his return, perhaps not. It was of no great consequence.

The Second Chapter

PRINCE CORUM SETS FORTH

And so, with the hooves of his horse hidden by the white mist of the morning, Prince Corum rode out from Castle Erorn to begin his quest.

The pale light softened the lines of the castle so that it seemed, more than ever, to merge with the great high rock on which it stood, and the trees that grew beside the path down which Corum rode also appeared to melt and mingle with the mist so that the landscape was a silent vision of gentle golds and greens and grays tinged with the pink rays of a distant, hidden sun. And, from beyond the rock, the sea, cloaked by the mist, could be heard retreating from the shore.

As Corum reached the sweet-smelling pines and birches of the forest a wren began to sing, was answered by the croak of a rook, and both fell silent as if startled by the sounds their own throats had made.

Corum rode on through the forest until the whisper of the sea dimmed behind him and the mist began to give way before the warming light of the rising sun. This ancient forest was familiar to him and he loved it, for it was here he had ridden as a boy and had been taught the obsolete art of war, which had been considered by his father as useful a way as any of making his body strong and quick. Here, too, he had lain through whole days watching the small animals that inhabited the forest—the tiny horselike beast of gray and yellow which had a horn growing from its forehead and was no bigger than a dog; the fan-winged gloriously colored bird that could soar higher than the eye could see and yet which built its nests in abandoned fox and badger sets underground; the large, gentle pig with thick, curly black hair that fed on moss; and many others.

Prince Corum realized that he had almost forgotten the pleasures of the forest, he had spent so long inside the castle. A small smile touched his lips as he looked about him. The forest, he thought, would endure forever. Something so beautiful could not die.

But this thought put him, for some reason, in a melancholy mood and he urged his horse to a somewhat faster gait.

The horse was glad to gallop as fast as Corum desired, for it also knew the forest and was enjoying the exercise. It was a red Vadhagh horse with a blue-black mane and tail, and it was strong, tall, and graceful, unlike the shaggy, wild ponies that inhabited the forest. It was mantled in yellow velvet and hung about with panniers; two spears; a plain, round shield made of different thicknesses of timber, brass, leather and silver; a long bone bow; and a quiver holding a good quantity of arrows. In one of the panniers were provisions for the journey, and in another were books and maps for guidance and entertainment.

Prince Corum himself wore a conical silver helm which had his full name carved in three characters above the short peak—Corum Jhaelen Irsei—which meant Corum, the Prince in the Scarlet Robe. It was the custom of the Vadhagh to choose a robe of a distinctive color and identify themselves by means of it, as the Nhadragh used crests and banners of greater complication. Corum wore the robe now. It had long, wide sleeves, a full skirt that was spread back over his horse's rump, and it was open at the front. At the shoulders was fixed a hood large enough to go over his helmet. It had been made from the fine, thin skin of a creature that was thought to dwell in another plane, forgotten even by the Vadhagh. Beneath the coat was a double byrnie made up of a million tiny links. The upper layer of this byrnie was silver and the lower layer was of brass.

For weapons other than bow and lance, Corum bore a long-hafted Vadhagh war-axe of delicate and intricate workmanship, a long, strong sword of a nameless metal manufactured on a different plane of the Earth, with pommel and guard worked in silver and both red and black onyx. His shirt was of blue samite and his breeks and boots were of soft brushed leather, as was his saddle, which was finished in silver.

From beneath his helm, some of Prince Corum's fine, silvery hair escaped and his youthful face now bore an expression that was half introspection, half excited anticipation at the prospect of his first sight of the ancient lands of his kinfolk.

He rode alone because none of the castle's retainers could be spared, and he rode on horseback rather than in a carriage because he wished to make the fastest possible speed.

It would be days before he would reach the first of the several castles he must visit, but he tried to imagine how different these dwelling places of his kinfolk would be and how the people themselves would strike him. Perhaps he would even find a wife among them. He knew that, while his father had not mentioned this, it had been an extra consideration in Prince Khlonskey's mind when the old man had begged him to go on this mission.

Soon Corum had left the forest and had reached the great plain called Broggfythus where once the Vadhagh and the Nhadragh had met in bloody and mystical battle.

It had been the last battle ever fought between the two races and, at its height, it had raged through all five planes. Producing neither victor nor defeated, it had destroyed more than two thirds of each of their races. Corum had heard that there were many empty castles across Bro-an-Vadhagh now, and many empty cities in the Nhadragh Isles which lay across the water from Castle Erorn.

Toward the middle of the day Corum found himself in the center of Broggfythus and he came to the spot that marked the boundaries of the territories he had roamed as a boy. Here was the weed-grown wreckage of the vast sky city that, during the month-long battle of his ancestors, had careered from one plane to another, rupturing the fine fabric that divided the different dimensions of the Earth until, crashing at last upon the gathered ranks of the Vadhagh and the Nhadragh, it had destroyed them. Being of a different plane, the tangled metal and stone of the sky city still retained that peculiar shifting effect. Now it had the appearance of a mirage, though the weeds, gorse, and birch trees that twined around it looked solid enough.

On other, less urgent, occasions, Prince Corum had enjoyed shifting his perspective out of this plane and into another, to see different aspects of the city, but the effort took too much energy these days and at the present moment the diaphanous wreckage represented nothing more than an obstacle around which he was forced to make various detours, for it stretched in a circumference of more than twenty miles.

But at last he reached the edge of the plain called Broggfythus and the sun set and he left behind him the world he knew and rode on toward the Southwest, into lands he knew only from the maps he carried.

He rode steadily for three more days without pause until the red horse showed signs of tiredness and, in a little valley through which a cold stream flowed, he made camp and rested for a while.

Corum ate a slice of the light, nourishing bread of his people and sat with his back against the bole of an old oak while his horse cropped the grass of the river bank.

Corum's silver helm lay beside him, together with his axe and sword. He breathed the leafy air and relaxed as he contemplated the peaks of the mountains, blue, gray, and white in the distance. This was pleasant, peaceful country and he was enjoying his journey through it. Once, he knew, it had been inhabited by several Vadhagh estates, but there was no trace of them now. It was as if they had grown into the landscape or been engulfed by it. Once or twice he had seen strangely shaped rocks where Vadhagh castles had stood, but they had been no more than rocks. It occurred to him that these rocks were the transmogrified remains of Vadhagh dwellings, but his intellect rejected such an impossibility. Such imaginings were the stuff of poetry, not of reason.

He smiled at his own foolishness and settled himself more comfortably against the tree. In another three days he would be at Castle Crachah, where his aunt the Princess Lorim lived. He watched as his horse folded its legs and lay down beneath the trees to sleep, and he wrapped his scarlet coat about him, raised the hood, and slept also.

The Third Chapter

THE MABDEN HERD

Toward the middle of the following morning Prince Corum was
awakened by sounds that somehow did not fit the forest. His horse
had heard them too, for it was up and sniffing at the air, showing
small signs of agitation.

Corum frowned and went to the cool water of the river to wash his
face and hands. He paused, listening again. A thump. A rattle. A
clank. He thought he heard a voice shouting further down the valley
and he peered in that direction and thought he saw something
moving.

Corum strode back to where he had left his gear and he picked up
his helmet, settling it on his head, fixed his sword's scabbard to his
belt, looped the axe onto his back. Then he began to saddle the horse
as it drank from the river.

The sounds were stronger now and, for some reason, Corum felt
disquiet touch his mind. He mounted his horse but continued to
watch.

Up the valley came a tide of beasts and vehicles. Some of the
creatures were clothed in iron, fur, and leather. Corum guessed that
this was a Mabden herd. From the little he had read of Mabden
habits, he knew the breed to be for the most part a migratory
species, constantly on the move; as it exhausted one area it would
move on, seeking fresh game and wild crops. He was surprised to
note how much like Vadhagh arms and armor were the swords,
shields, and helmets worn by some of the Mabden.

Closer they came and still Corum observed them with intense
curiosity, as he would study any unusual beast he had not previously
seen.

This was a large group, riding in barbarically decorated chariots

16

of timber and beaten bronze, drawn by shaggy horses with harness of leather painted in dull reds, yellows, and blues. Behind the chariots came wagons, some open and some with awnings. Perhaps these carried females, Corum thought, for there were no females to be seen elsewhere.

The Mabden had thick, dirty beards, long sweeping moustaches, and matted hair flowing out from under their helmets. As they moved, they yelled at each other and passed wineskins from hand to hand. Astonished, Corum recognized the language as the common tongue of the Vadhagh and the Nhadragh, though much corrupted and harshened. So the Mabden had learned a sophisticated form of speech.

Again came the unaccountable sense of disquiet. Corum backed his horse into the shadows of the trees, continuing to watch.

And now he could see why so many of the helmets and weapons were familiar.

They were Vadhagh helmets and Vadhagh weapons.

Corum frowned. Had these been looted from some old abandoned Vadhagh castle? Were they gifts? Or had they been stolen?

The Mabden also bore arms and armor of their own crude manufacture, obviously copies of Vadhagh workmanship, as well as a few Nhadragh artifacts. A few had clothes of stolen samite and linen, but for the most part they wore wolfskin cloaks, bearskin hoods, sealskin jerkins and breeks, sheepskin jackets, goatskin caps, rabbitskin kilts, pigskin boots, shirts of deerskin or wool. Some had chain of gold, bronze, and iron hanging round their necks or wound about their arms or legs, or even woven into their filthy hair.

Now, as Corum watched, they began to pass him. He stifled a cough as their smell reached his nose. Many were so drunk they were almost falling out of their chariots. The heavy wheels rumbled and the hooves of the horses plodded on. Corum saw that the wagons did not contain females, but booty. Much of it was Vadhagh treasure, there was no mistaking it.

The evidence was impossible to interpret in any other way. This was a party of warriors—a raiding party or a looting party, Corum could not be sure. But he found it hard to accept that these creatures had lately done battle with Vadhagh warriors and won.

Now the last chariots of the caravan began to pass and Corum saw that a few Mabden walked behind, tied to the chariots by ropes attached to their hands. These Mabden bore no weapons and were hardly clothed at all. They were thin, their feet were bare and bleeding, they moaned and cried out from time to time. Often the response of the charioteer to whose chariot they were attached would be to curse or laugh and tug at the ropes to make them stumble.

One did stumble and fall and desperately tried to regain his feet as he was dragged along. Corum was horrified. Why did the Mabden treat their own species in such a way? Even the Nhadragh, who were counted more cruel than the Vadhagh, had not caused such pain to their Vadhagh prisoners in the old days.

"These are peculiar brutes, in truth," mused Corum, half-aloud.

One of the Mabden at the head of the caravan called out loudly and brought his chariot to a halt beside the river. The other chariots and wagons began to stop. Corum saw that they intended to make camp here.

Fascinated, he continued to observe them, stock still on his horse, hidden by the trees.

The Mabden removed the yokes from the horses and led them to the water. From the wagons they took cooking pots and poles and began to build fires.

By sunset they were eating, though their prisoners, still tied to the chariots, were given nothing.

When they were done with eating, they began to drink again and soon more than half the herd was insensible, sprawled on the grass and sleeping where they fell. Others were rolling about on the ground engaged in mock fights, many of which increased in savagery so that knives and axes were drawn and some blood spilled.

The Mabden who had originally called for the caravan to stop roared at the fighting men and began to stagger amongst them, a wineskin clutched in one hand, kicking them and plainly ordering them to stop. Two refused to heed him and he drew the huge bronze war-axe from his belt and smashed it down on the skull of the nearest man, splitting his helmet and his head. A silence came to the camp and Corum, with an effort, made out the words the leader spoke:

"By the Dog! I'll have no more squabbling of this sort. Why spend your energies on each other. There is sport to be had yonder!" He pointed with his axe to the prisoners, who were now sleeping.

A few of the Mabden laughed and nodded and rose up, moving through the faint light of the evening to where their prisoners lay. They kicked them awake, cut the ropes attached to the chariots, and forced them toward the main encampment, where the warriors who had not succumbed to the wine were arranging themselves in a circle. The prisoners were pushed into the center of this circle and stood there staring in terror at the warriors.

The leader stepped into the circle and confronted the prisoners.

"When we took you with us from your village I promised you that we Denledhyssi hated only one thing more than we hated Shefanhow. Do you remember what that was?"

One of the prisoners mumbled, staring at the ground. The Mabden leader moved quickly, pushing the head of his axe under the man's chin and lifting it up.

"Aye, you have learned your lesson well, friend. Say it again."

The prisoner's tongue was thick in his mouth. His broken lips moved again and he turned his eyes to the darkening skies and tears fell down his cheeks and he yelled in a wild, cracked voice, "Those who lick Shefanhow urine!"

And a great groan shuddered from him and then he screamed.

The Mabden leader smiled, drew back his axe, and rammed the haft into the man's stomach so that the scream was cut short and he doubled over in agony.

Corum had never witnessed such cruelty and his frown deepened as he saw the Mabden begin to tie down their prisoners, staking them out on the ground and bringing brands and knives to their limbs, burning and cutting them so that they did not die but writhed in pain.

The leader laughed as he watched, taking no part in the torture itself.

"Oh, your spirits will remember me as they mingle with the Shefanhow demons in the Pits of the Dog!" he chuckled. "Oh, they will remember the Earl of the Denledhyssi, Glandyth-a-Krae, the Doom of the Shefanhow!"

Corum found it difficult to work out what these words meant. *Shefanhow* could be a corruption of the Vadhagh word *Sefano*, which roughly meant "fiend". But why did these Mabden call themselves "Denledhyssi"—a corruption, almost certainly, of *Donledyssi* meaning "murderers"? Were they proud that they were killers? And was *Shefanhow* a term used in general to describe their enemies? And were, as seemed unquestionably the case, their enemies other Mabden?

Corum shook his head in puzzlement. He understood the motives and behavior of less developed animals better than he understood the Mabden. He found it difficult to retain a clinical interest in their customs and was becoming quickly disturbed by them. He turned his horse into the depths of the forest and rode away.

The only explanation he could find, at present, was that the Mabden species had undergone a process of evolution and devolution more rapid than most. It was possible that these were the mad

19

remnants of the race. If so, then that was why they turned on their own kind, as rabid foxes did.

A greater sense of urgency filled him now and he rode as fast as his horse could gallop, heading for Castle Crachah. Princess Lorim, living in closer proximity to Mabden herds, might be able to give him clearer answers to his questions.

The Fourth Chapter

THE BANE OF BEAUTY:
THE DOOM OF TRUTH

Save for dead fires and some litter, Prince Corum saw no further
signs of Mabden before he breasted the high green hills that enclosed Valley Crachah and searched with his eyes for the castle of
Princess Lorim.

The valley was full of poplars, elms, and birch and looked
peaceful in the gentle light of the early afternoon. But where was the
castle, he wondered.

Corum drew his map again from within his byrnie and consulted
it. The castle should be almost in the center of the valley, surrounded by six rings of poplars and two outer rings of elms. He
looked again.

Yes, there were the rings of poplars and elms. And near the
center, no castle, just a cloud of mist.

But there should be no mist on such a day. It could only be smoke.

Prince Corum rode rapidly down the hill.

He rode until he reached the first of the rings of trees and he
peered through the other rings but could, as yet, see nothing. He
sniffed the smoke.

He passed through more rings of trees and now the smoke stung
his eyes and throat and he could see a few black shapes in it.

He passed through the final ring of poplars and he began to choke
as the smoke filled his lungs and his watering eyes made out the
shapes. Sharp crags, tumbled rocks, blistered metal, burned beams.

Prince Corum saw a ruin. It was without a doubt the ruin of Castle
Crachah. A smoldering ruin. Fire had brought Castle Crachah
down. Fire had eaten her folk, for now Corum, as he rode his
snorting horse around the perimeter of the ruins, made out blackened skeletons. And beyond the ruins were signs of battle. A

broken Mabden chariot. Some Mabden corpses. An old Vadhagh woman, chopped into several pieces.

Even now the crows and the ravens were beginning to sidle in, risking the smoke.

Prince Corum began to understand what sorrow must be. He thought that the emotion he felt was that.

He called out once, in the hope that some inhabitant of Castle Crachah lived, but there was no reply. Slowly, Prince Corum turned away.

He rode toward the East. Toward Castle Sarn.

He rode steadily for a week, and the sense of sorrow remained and was joined by another nagging emotion. Prince Corum began to think it must be a feeling of trepidation.

Castle Sarn lay in the middle of a dense elder forest and was reached by a pathway down which the weary Prince in the Scarlet Robe and his weary horse moved. Small animals scampered away from them and a thin rain fell from a brooding sky. No smoke rose here. And when Corum came to the castle he saw that it was no longer burning. Its black stones were cold, and the crows and ravens had already picked the corpses clean and gone away in search of other carrion.

And then tears came to Corum's eyes for the first time, and he dismounted from his dusty horse and clambered over the stones and the bones and sat down and looked about him.

For several hours Prince Corum sat thus until a sound came from his throat. It was a sound he had not heard before and he could not name it. It was a thin sound that could not express what was within his stunned mind. He had never known Prince Opash, though his father had spoken of him with great affection. He had never known the family and retainers who had dwelt in Castle Sarn. But he wept for them until at length, exhausted, he stretched out upon the broken slab of stone and fell into a gloomy slumber.

The rain continued to fall on Corum's scarlet coat. It fell on the ruins and it washed the bones. The red horse sought the shelter of the elder trees and lay down. For a while it chewed the grass and watched its prone master. Then it, too, slept.

When he eventually awoke and clambered back over the ruins to where his horse still lay, Corum's mind was incapable of speculation. He knew now that this destruction must be Mabden work, for it was not the custom of the Nhadragh to burn the castles of their enemies. Besides, the Nhadragh and the Vadhagh had been at peace for centuries. Both had forgotten how to make war.

It had occurred to Corum that the Mabden might have been inspired to their destruction by the Nhadragh, but even this was unlikely. There was an ancient code of war to which both races had, no matter how fierce the fighting, always adhered. And with the decline in their numbers, there had been no need for the Nhadragh to expand their territories or for the Vadhagh to defend theirs.

His face thin with weariness and strain, coated with dust and streaked with tears, Prince Corum aroused his horse and mounted him, riding on toward the North, where Castle Gal lay. He hoped a little. He hoped that the Mabden herds moved only in the South and the East, that the North would still be free of their encroachments, as the West was.

A day later, as he stopped to water his horse at a small lake, he looked across the gorse moor and saw more smoke curling. He took out his map and consulted it. No castle was marked there.

He hesitated. Was the smoke coming from another Mabden camp? If so, they might have Vadhagh prisoners whom Corum should attempt to rescue. He decided to ride toward the source of the smoke.

The smoke came from several sources. This was, indeed, a Mabden camp, but it was a permanent camp, not unlike the smaller settlements of the Nhadragh, though much cruder. A collection of stone huts built close to the ground, with thatched roofs and chimneys of slate from which the smoke came.

Around this camp were fields that had evidently contained crops, though there were no crops now, and others which had a few cows grazing in them.

For some reason Corum did not feel wary of this camp as he had felt wary of the Mabden caravan, but he nonetheless approached it cautiously, stopping his horse a hundred yards away and studying the camp for signs of life.

He waited an hour and saw none.

He moved his horse in closer until he was less than fifty yards away from the nearest single-story building.

Still no Mabden emerged from any of the low doorways.

Corum cleared his throat.

A child began to scream and the scream was muffled suddenly.

"Mabden!" Corum called, and his voice was husky with weariness and sorrow. "I would speak with you. Why do you not come out of your dens?"

From the nearby hovel a voice replied. The voice was a mixture of fear and anger.

"We have done no harm to the Shefanhow. They have done no

23

harm to us. But if we speak to you the Denledhyssi will come back and take more of our food, kill more of our menfolk, rape more of our women. Go away, Shefanhow Lord, we beg you. We have put the food in a sack by the door. Take it and leave us.''

Corum saw the sack now. So, it had been an offering to him. Did they not know that their heavy food would not settle in a Vadhagh stomach?

"I do not want food, Mabden," he called back.

"What do you want, Shefanhow Lord? We have nothing else but our souls."

"I do not know what you mean. I seek answers to questions."

"The Shefanhow know everything. We know nothing."

"Why do you fear the Denledhyssi? Why do you call me a fiend? We Vadhagh have never harmed you."

"The Denledhyssi call you Shefanhow. And because we dwelt in peace with your folk, the Denledhyssi punish us. They say that Mabden must kill the Shefanhow—the Vadhagh and the Nhadragh—that you are evil. They say our crime is to let evil live. They say that the Mabden are put upon this Earth to destroy the Shefanhow. The Denledhyssi are the servants of the great Earl, Glandyth-a-Krae, whose own liege is our liege, King Lyr-a-Brode whose stone city called Kalenwyr is in the high lands of the Northeast. Do you not know all this, Shefanhow Lord?''

"I did not know it," said Prince Corum softly, turning his horse away. "And now that I know it, I do not understand it." He raised his voice. "Farewell, Mabden. I'll give you no further cause for fear . . ." And then he paused. "But tell me one last thing."

"What is that, Lord?" came the nervous voice.

"Why does a Mabden destroy another Mabden?"

"I do not understand you, Lord."

"I have seen members of your race killing fellow members of that race. Is this something you often do?''

"Aye, Lord. We do it quite often. We punish those who break our laws. We set an example to those who might consider breaking those laws.''

Prince Corum sighed. "Thank you, Mabden. I ride away now.''

The red horse trotted off over the moor, leaving the village behind.

Now Prince Corum knew that Mabden power had grown greater than any Vadhagh would have suspected. They had a primitively complicated social order, with leaders of different ranks. Permanent settlements of a variety of sizes. The larger part of Bro-an-Vadhagh seemed ruled by a single man—King Lyr-a-Brode. The name meant as much as, or something like, in their coarsened dialect, King of All the Land.

Corum remembered the rumors. That Vadhagh castles had been taken by these half-beasts. That the Nhadragh Isles had fallen completely to them.

And there were Mabden who devoted their whole lives to seeking out members of the older races and destroying them. Why? The older races did not threaten Man. What threat could they be to a species so numerous and fierce? All that the Vadhagh and the Nhadragh had was knowledge. Was it knowledge that the Mabden feared?

For ten days, pausing twice to rest, Prince Corum rode north, but now he had a different vision of what Castle Gal would look like when he reached it. But he must go there to make sure. And he must warn Prince Faguin and his family of their danger, if they still lived.

The settlements of the Mabden were seen often and Prince Corum avoided them. Some were of the size of the first he had seen, but many were larger, built around grim stone towers. Sometimes he saw bands of warriors riding by and only the sharper senses of the Vadhagh enabled him to see them before they sighted him.

Once, by a huge effort, he was forced to move both himself and his horse into the next dimension to avoid confrontation with Mabden. He watched them ride past him, less than ten feet away, completely unable to observe him. Like the others he had seen, these did not ride horses, but had chariots drawn by shaggy ponies. As Corum saw their faces, pocked with disease, thick with grease and filth, their bodies strung with barbaric ornament, he wondered at their powers of destruction. It was still hard to believe that such insensitive beasts as these, who appeared to have no second sight at all, could bring to ruin the great castles of the Vadhagh.

And at last the Prince in the Scarlet Robe reached the bottom of the hill on which Castle Gal stood and saw the black smoke billowing and the red flames leaping and knew from what fresh destruction the Mabden beasts had been riding.

But here there had been a much longer siege, by the look of it. A battle had raged here that had lasted many days. The Vadhagh had been more prepared at Castle Gal.

Hoping that he would find some wounded kinsmen whom he could help, Corum urged his horse to gallop up the hill.

But the only thing that lived beyond the blazing castle was a groaning Mabden, abandoned by his fellows. Corum ignored him.

He found three corpses of his own folk. Not one of the three had died quickly or without what the Mabden would doubtless consider humiliation. There were two warriors who had been stripped of their arms and armor. And there was a child. A girl of about six years.

Corum bent and picked up the corpses one by one, carrying them to the fire to be consumed. He went back to his horse.

The wounded Mabden called out. Corum paused. It was not the usual Mabden accent.

"Help me, Master!"

This was the liquid tongue of the Vadhagh and the Nhadragh. Was this a Vadhagh who had disguised himself as a Mabden to escape death? Corum began to walk back, leading his horse through the billowing smoke.

He looked down at the Mabden. He wore a bulky wolfskin coat covered by a half-byrnie of iron links and a helmet that covered most of his face, which had slipped to blind him. Corum tugged at the helmet until it was free, tossed it aside, and then gasped.

This was no Mabden. Nor was it a Vadhagh. It was the bloodied face of a Nhadragh, dark with flat features and hair growing down to the ridge of the eye sockets.

"Help me, Master," said the Nhadragh again. "I am not too badly hurt. I can still be of service."

"To whom, Nhadragh?" said Corum softly. He tore off a piece of the man's sleeve and wiped the blood free of the eyes. The Nhadragh blinked, focusing on him.

"Who would you serve, Nhadragh? Would you serve me?"

The Nhadragh's dazed eyes cleared and then filled with an emotion Corum could only surmise was hatred.

"*Vadhagh!*" snarled the being. "A Vadhagh lives!"

"Aye. I live. Why do you hate me?"

"All Nhadragh hate the Vadhagh. They have hated them through eternity! Why are you not dead? Have you been hiding?"

"I am not from Castle Gal."

"So I was right. This was not the last Vadhagh castle." The being tried to stir, tried to draw his knife, but he was too weak. He fell back.

"Hatred was not what the Nhadragh had once," Corum said. "You wanted our lands, yes. But you fought us without this *hatred*, and we fought you without it. You have learned hatred from the Mabden, Nhadragh, not from your ancestors. They knew honor. You did not. How could one of the older races make himself a Mabden slave?"

The Nhadragh's lips smiled slightly. "All the Nhadragh that remain are Mabden slaves and have been for two hundred years. They only suffer us to live in order to use us like dogs, to sniff out

26

those beings they call Shefanhow. We swore oaths of loyalty to them in order to continue living.''

''But could you not escape? There are other planes.''

''The other planes were denied to us. Our historians held that the last great battle of the Vadhagh and the Nhadragh so disrupted the equilibrium of those planes that they were closed to us by the Gods . . .''

''So you have relearnt superstition, too,'' mused Corum. ''Ah, what do these Mabden do to us?''

The Nhadragh began to laugh and the laugh turned into a cough and blood came out of his mouth and poured down his chin. As Corum wiped away the blood, he said, ''They supersede us, Vadhagh. They bring the darkness and they bring the terror. They are the bane of beauty and the doom of truth. The world is Mabden now. We have no right to continue existing. Nature abhors us. We should not be here!''

Corum sighed. ''Is that your thinking, or theirs?''

''It is a fact.''

''You said you thought this the last of our castles . . .''

''Not I. I sensed there was another one. I told them.''

''And they have gone to seek it?''

''Yes.''

Corum gripped the being's shoulder. ''Where?''

The Nhadragh smiled. ''Where? Where else but in the West?''

Corum ran to his horse.

''Stay!'' croaked the Nhadragh. ''Slay me, I pray you, Vadhagh! Do not let me linger!''

''I do not know how to kill,'' Corum replied as he mounted the horse.

''Then you must learn, Vadhagh. You must learn!'' cackled the dying being as Corum frantically forced his horse to gallop down the hill.

The Fifth Chapter

A LESSON LEARNED

And here was Castle Erorn, her tinted towers entwined with greedy fires. And still the surf boomed in the great black caverns within the headland on which Erorn was raised and it seemed that the sea protested, that the wind wailed its anger, that the lashing foam sought desperately to drench the victorious flame.

Castle Erorn shuddered as she perished and the bearded Mabden laughed at her downfall, shaking the brass and gold trappings of their chariots, casting triumphant glances at the little row of corpses lying in a semicircle before them.

They were Vadhagh corpses.

Four women and eight men.

In the shadows on the far side of the natural bridge of rock that led to the headland, Corum saw glimpses of the bloody faces and he knew them all: Prince Khlonskey, his father. Colatalarna, his mother. His twin sisters, Ilastru and Pholhinra. His uncle, Prince Rhanan. Sertreda, his cousin. And the five retainers, all second and third cousins.

Three times Corum counted the corpses as the cold grief transformed itself to fury and he heard the butchers yell to one another in their coarse dialect.

Three times he counted, and then he looked at them and his face really was the face of a *Shefanhow*.

Prince Corum had discovered sorrow and he had discovered fear. Now he discovered rage.

For two weeks he had ridden almost without pause, hoping to get ahead of the Denledhyssi and warn his family of the barbarians' coming. And he had arrived a few hours too late.

The Mabden had ridden out in their arrogance born of ignorance and destroyed those whose arrogance was born of wisdom. It was the way of things. Doubtless Corum's father, Prince Khlonskey, had thought as much as he was hacked down with a stolen Vadhagh war-axe. But now Corum could find no such philosophy within his own heart.

His eyes turned black with anger, save for the irises, which turned bright gold, and he drew his tall spear and urged his weary horse over the causeway, through the flame-lit night, toward the Denledhyssi.

They were lounging in their chariots and pouring sweet Vadhagh wine down their faces and into their gullets. The sounds of the sea and the blaze hid the sound of Corum's approach until his spear pierced the face of a Denledhyssi warrior and the man shrieked.

Corum had learned how to kill.

He slid the spear's point free and struck the dead man's companion through the back of the neck as he began to pull himself upright. He twisted the spear.

Corum had learned how to be cruel.

Another Denledhyssi raised a bow and pulled back an arrow on the string, but Corum hurled the spear now and it struck through the man's bronze breastplate, entered his heart, and knocked him over the side of the chariot.

Corum drew his second spear.

But his horse was failing him. He had ridden it to the point of exhaustion and now it could barely respond to his signals. Already the more distant charioteers were whipping their ponies to life, turning their great, groaning chariots around to bear down on the Prince in the Scarlet Robe.

An arrow passed close and Corum sought the archer and urged his tired horse forward to get close enough to drive his spear through the archer's unprotected right eye and slip it out in time to block a blow from his comrade's sword.

The metal-shod spear turned the blade and, using both hands, Corum reversed the spear to smash the butt into the swordsman's face and knock him out of the chariot.

But now the other chariots were bearing down on him through the tumbling shadows cast by the roaring fires that ate at Castle Erorn.

They were led by one whom Corum recognized. He was laughing and yelling and whirling his huge war-axe about his head.

"By the Dog! Is this a Vadhagh who knows how to fight like a Mabden? You have learned too late, my friend. You are the last of your race!"

It was Glandyth-a-Krae, his gray eyes gleaming, his cruel mouth snarling back over yellow fangs.

Corum flung his spear.

The whirling axe knocked it aside and Glandyth's chariot did not falter.

Corum unslung his own war-axe and waited and, as he waited, the legs of his horse buckled and the beast collapsed to the ground.

Desperately Corum untangled his feet from the stirrups, gripped his axe in both hands, and leapt backward and aside as the chariot came at him. He aimed a blow at Glandyth-a-Krae, but struck the brass edge of the chariot. The shock of the blow numbed his hands so that he almost dropped the axe. He was breathing harshly now and he staggered. Other chariots raced by on both sides and a sword struck his helmet. Dazed, he fell to one knee. A spear hit his shoulder and he fell in the churned mud.

Then Corum learned cunning. Instead of attempting to rise, he lay where he had fallen until all the chariots had passed. Before they could begin to turn, he pulled himself to his feet. His shoulder was bruised, but the spear had not pierced it. He stumbled through the darkness, seeking to escape the barbarians.

Then his feet struck something soft and he glanced down and saw the body of his mother and he saw what had been done to her before she died and a great moan escaped him and tears blinded him and he took a firmer grip on the axe in his left hand and painfully drew his sword, screaming, "Glandyth-a-Krae!"

And Corum had learned the lust for revenge.

The ground shook as the hooves of the horses beat upon it, hauling the returning chariots toward him. The tall tower of the castle suddenly cracked and crumbled into the flames, which leapt higher and brightened the night to show Earl Glandyth whipping the horses as he bore down on Corum once again.

Corum stood over the corpse of his mother, the gentle Princess Colatalarna. His first blow split the forehead of the leading horse and it fell, dragging the others down with it.

Earl Glandyth was flung forward, almost over the edge of the chariot, and he cursed. Behind him two other charioteers hastily tried to rein in their horses to stop from crashing into their leader. The others, not understanding why they were stopping, also hauled at their reins.

Corum clambered over the bodies of the horses and swung his sword at Glandyth's neck, but the blow was blocked by a gorget and the huge, hairy head turned and the pale gray eyes glared at Corum. Then Glandyth leapt from the chariot and Corum leapt too, to come face to face with the destroyer of his family.

They confronted each other in the firelight, panting like foxes, crouching and ready to spring.

Corum moved first, lunging with his sword at Glandyth-a-Krae and swinging his axe at the same time.

Glandyth jumped away from the sword and used his own axe to parry the blow, kicking out at Corum's groin, but missing.

They began to circle, Corum's black-and-gold eyes locked on the pale gray ones of the Mabden earl.

For several minutes they circled, while the other Mabden looked on. Glandyth's lips moved and began to voice a word, but Corum sprang in again, and this time the alien metal of his slender sword pierced Glandyth's armor at the shoulder join and slid in. Glandyth hissed and his axe swung round to strike the sword with such a blow that it was wrenched from Corum's aching hand and fell to the ground.

"Now," murmured Glandyth, as if speaking to himself. "Now, Vadhagh. It is not my fate to be slain by a Shefanhow."

Corum swung his axe.

Again Glandyth dodged the blow.

Again his axe came down.

And this time Corum's weapon was struck from his hand and he stood defenseless before the grinning Mabden.

"But it is my fate to slay Shefanhow!" He twisted his mouth in a snarling grin.

Corum flung himself at Glandyth, trying to wrest the axe from him. But Corum had spent the last of his strength. He was too weak.

Glandyth cried out to his men. "By the Dog, Lads, get this demon off me. Do not slay him. We'll take our time with him. After all, he is the last Vadhagh we shall ever have the chance to sport with!"

Corum heard them laugh and he struck out at them as they seized him. He was shouting as a man shouts in a fever and he could not hear his own words.

Then one Mabden plucked off his silver helm and another hit him on the back of the head with a sword pommel, and Corum's body went suddenly limp and he sank down into welcome darkness.

The Sixth Chapter

THE MAIMING OF CORUM

The sun had risen and set twice before Corum awoke to find himself
trussed in chains in the back of a Mabden wagon. He tried to raise
his head and see through the gap in the awning, but he saw nothing,
save that it was daytime.

Why had they not killed him? he wondered. And then he shuddered as he understood that they were waiting for him to awake so
that they could make his death both long and painful.

Before he had set off on his quest, before he had witnessed what
had happened to the Vandagh castles, before he had seen the blight
that had come to Bro-an-Vadhagh, he might have accepted his fate
and prepared himself to die as his kinfolk had died, but the lessons
he had learned remained with him. He hated the Mabden. He
mourned for his relatives. He would avenge them if he could. And
this meant that he would have to live.

He closed his eyes, conserving his strength. There was one way
to escape the Mabden and that was to ease his body into another
plane where they could not see him. But to do this would demand
much energy and there was little point in doing it while he remained
in the wagon.

The guttural Mabden voices drifted back to the wagon from time
to time, but he could not hear what they said. He slept.

He stirred. Something cold was striking his face. He blinked. It
was water. He opened his eyes and saw the Mabden standing over
him. He had been removed from the wagon and was lying on the
ground. Cooking fires burned nearby. It was night.

"The Shefanhow is with us again, Master," called the Mabden
who had thrown the water. "He is ready for us, I think."

Corum winced as he moved his bruised body, trying to stand

upright in the chains. Even if he could escape to another plane, the chains would come with him. He would be little better off. Experimentally, he tried to see into the next plane, but his eyes began to ache and he gave up.

Earl Glandyth-a-Krae appeared now, pushing his way through his men. His pale eyes regarded Corum triumphantly. He put a hand to his beard, which had been plaited into several strands and strung with rings of stolen gold, and he smiled. Almost tenderly, he reached down and pulled Corum upright. The chains and the cramped space of the wagon had served to cut off the circulation of blood to his legs—they began to buckle.

"Rodlik! Here, Lad!" Earl Glandyth called behind him.

"Coming, Master!" A red-headed boy of about fourteen trotted forward. He was dressed in soft Vadhagh samite, both green and white, and there was an ermine cap on his head, soft deerskin boots on his feet. He had a pale face, spotted with acne, but was otherwise handsome for a Mabden. He knelt before Earl Glandyth. "Aye, Lord?"

"Help the Shefanhow to stand, Lad." Glandyth's low, harsh voice contained something like a note of affection as he addressed the boy. "Help him stand, Rodlik."

Rodlik sprang up and took Corum's elbow, steadying him. The boy's touch was cold and nervous.

All the Mabden warriors looked expectantly at Glandyth. Casually, he took off his heavy helmet and shook out his hair, which was curled and heavy with grease.

Corum, too, watched Glandyth. He studied the man's red face, decided that the gray eyes showed little real intelligence, but much malice and pride.

"Why have you destroyed all the Vadhagh?" said Corum quietly. His mouth moved painfully. "Why, Earl of Krae?"

Glandyth looked at him as if in surprise, and he was slow to reply. "You should know. We hate your sorcery. We loathe your superior airs. We desire your lands and those goods of yours which are of use to us. So we kill you." He grinned. "Besides, we have not destroyed *all* the Vadhagh. Not yet. One left."

"Aye," promised Corum. "And one that will avenge his people if he is given the opportunity."

"No." Glandyth put his hands on his hips. "He will not be."

"You say you hate our sorcery. But we have no sorcery. Just a little knowledge, a little second sight . . ."

"Ha! We have seen your castles and the evil contraptions they contain. We saw that one, back there—the one we took a couple of nights ago. Full of sorcery!"

33

Corum wetted his lips. "Yet even if we did have such sorcery, that would be no reason for destroying us. We have offered you no harm. We have let you come to our land without resisting you. I think you hate us because you hate something in yourselves. You are—unfinished—creatures."

"I know. You call us half-beasts. I care not what you think now, Vadhagh. Not now that your race is gone." Glandyth spat on the ground and waved his hand at the youth. "Let him go."

The youth sprang back.

Corum swayed, but did not fall. He continued to stare in contempt at Glandyth-a-Krae.

"You and your race are insane, Earl. You are like a canker. You are a sickness suffered by this world."

Earl Glandyth spat again. This time he spat straight into Corum's face. "I told you—I know what the Vadhagh think of us. I know what the Nhadragh thought before we made them our hunting dogs. It's your pride that has destroyed you, Vadhagh. The Nhadragh learned to do away with pride and so some of them were spared. They accepted us as their masters. But you Vadhagh could not. When we came to your castles, you ignored us. When we demanded tribute, you said nothing. When we told you that you served us now, you pretended you did not understand us. So we set out to punish you. And you would not resist. We tortured you and, in your pride, you would not give us an oath that you would be our slaves, as the Nhadragh did. We lost patience, Vadhagh. We decided that you were not fit to live in the same land as the great King Lyr-a-Brode, for you would not admit to being his subjects. That is why we set out to slay you all. You have earned this doom."

Corum looked at the ground. So it was complacency that had brought down the Vadhagh race.

He lifted his head again and stared back at Glandyth.

"I hope, however," said Corum, "that I will be able to show you that the last of the Vadhagh can behave in a different way."

Glandyth shrugged and turned to address his men.

"He hardly knows what he will show us soon, will he, Lads?"

The Mabden laughed.

"Prepare the board!" Earl Glandyth ordered. "I think we shall begin."

Corum saw them bring up a wide plank of wood. It was thick and pitted and stained. Near its four corners were fixed lengths of chain. Corum began to guess at the board's function.

Two Mabden grasped his arms and pushed him toward the board.

34

Another brought a chisel and an iron hammer. Corum was pushed with his back against the board, which now rested on the trunk of a tree. Using the chisel, a Mabden struck the chains from him, then his arms and legs were seized and he was spread-eagled on the board while new rivets were driven into the links of chain, securing him there. Corum could smell stale blood. He could see where the board was scored with the marks of knives, swords, and axes, where arrows had been shot into it.

He was on a butcher's block.

The Mabden bloodlust was rising. Their eyes gleamed in the firelight, their breath steamed and their nostrils dilated. Red tongues licked thick lips and small, anticipatory smiles were on several faces.

Earl Glandyth had been supervising the pinning of Corum to the board. Now he came up and stood in front of the Vadhagh and he drew a slim sharp blade from his belt.

Corum watched as the blade came toward his chest. Then there was a ripping sound as the knife tore the samite shirt away from his body.

Slowly, his grin spreading, Glandyth-a-Krae worked at the rest of Corum's clothing, the knife only occasionally drawing a thin line of blood from his body, until at last Corum was completely naked.

Glandyth stepped back.

"Now," he said, panting, "you are doubtless wondering what we intend to do with you."

"I have seen others of my people whom you have slain," Corum said. "I think I know what you intend to do."

Glandyth raised the little finger of his right hand while he tucked his dagger away with his left.

"Ah, you see. You do not know. Those other Vadhagh died swiftly—or relatively so—because we had so many to find and to kill. But you are the last. We can take our time with you. We think, in fact, that we will give you a chance to live. If you *can* survive with your eyes gone, your tongue put out, your hands and feet removed, and your genitals taken away, then we will let you so survive."

Corum stared at him in horror.

Glandyth burst into laughter. "I see you appreciate our joke!" He signaled to his men.

"Bring the tools! Let's begin."

A great brazier was brought forward. It was full of red-hot charcoal and from it poked irons of various sorts. These were instruments especially designed for torture, thought Corum. What sort of race could conceive such things and call itself sane?

Glandyth-a-Krae selected a long iron from the brazier and turned it this way and that, inspecting the glowing tip.

"We will begin with an eye and end with an eye," he said. "The right eye, I think."

If Corum had eaten anything in the last few days, he would have vomited then. As it was, bile came into his mouth and his stomach trembled and ached.

There were no further preliminaries.

Glandyth began to advance with the heated iron. It smoked in the cold night air.

Now Corum tried to forget the threat of torture and concentrate on his second sight, trying to see into the next plane. He sweated with a mixture of terror and the effort of his thought. But his mind was confused. Alternately, he saw glimpses of the next plane and the ever-advancing tip of the iron coming closer and closer to his face.

The scene before him shivered, but still Glandyth came on, the gray eyes burning with an unnatural lust.

Corum twisted in the chains, trying to avert his head. Then Glandyth's left hand shot out and tangled itself in his hair, forcing the head back, bringing the iron down.

Corum screamed as the red-hot tip touched the lid of his closed eye. Pain filled his face and then his whole body. He heard a mixture of laughter, his own shouts, Glandyth's rasping breathing . . .

. . . and Corum fainted.

Corum wandered through the streets of a strange city. The buildings were high and seemed but recently built, though already they were grimed and smeared with slime.

There was still pain, but it was remote, dull. He was blind in one eye. From a balcony a woman's voice called him. He looked around. It was his sister, Pholhinra. When she saw his face, she cried out in horror.

Corum tried to put his hand to his injured eye, but he could not.

Something held him. He tried to wrench his left hand free from whatever gripped it. He pulled harder and harder. Now the wrist began to pulse with pain as he tugged.

Pholhinra had disappeared, but Corum was now absorbed in trying to free his hand. For some reason, he could not turn to see what it was that held him. Some kind of beast, perhaps, holding on to his hand with its jaws.

Corum gave one last, huge tug and his wrist came free.

He put up the hand to touch the blind eye, but still felt nothing.
He looked at the hand.
There was no hand. Just a wrist. Just a stump.
Then he screamed again . . .

. . . and he opened his eyes and saw the Mabden holding the arm
and bringing down white-hot swords on the stump to seal it.

They had cut off his hand.

And Glandyth was still laughing, holding Corum's severed hand
up to show his men, with Corum's blood still dripping from the
knife he had used.

Now Corum saw the other plane distinctly, superimposed, as it
were, over the scene before him. Summoning all the energy born of
his fear and agony, he shifted himself into that plane.

He saw the Mabden clearly, but their voices had become faint.
He heard them cry out in astonishment and point at him. He saw
Glandyth wheel, his eyes widening. He heard the Earl of Krae call
out to his men to search the woods for Corum.

The board was abandoned as Glandyth and his men lumbered off
into the darkness seeking their Vadhagh captive.

But their captive was still chained to the board, for it, like him,
existed on several planes. And he still felt the pain they had caused
him and he was still without his right eye and his left hand.

He could stay away from further mutilation for a little while, but
eventually his energy would give out completely and he would
return to their plane and they would continue their work.

He struggled in the chains, waving the stump of his left wrist in a
futile attempt to free himself of those manacles still holding his
other limbs.

But he knew it was hopeless. He had only averted his doom for a
short while. He would never be free—never be able to exercise his
vengeance on the murderer of his kin.

The Seventh Chapter

THE BROWN MAN

Corum sweated as he forced himself to remain in the other plane, and he watched nervously for the return of Glandyth and his men.

It was then that he saw a shape move cautiously out of the forest and approach the board.

At first Corum thought it was a Mabden warrior, without a helmet and dressed in a huge fur jerkin. Then he realized that this was some other creature.

The creature moved cautiously toward the board, looked about the Mabden camp, and then crept closer. It lifted its head and stared directly at Corum.

Corum was astonished. The beast could see him! Unlike the Mabden, unlike the other creatures of the plane, this one had second sight.

Corum's agony was so intense that he was forced to screw up his eye at the pain. When he opened it again, the creature had come right up to the board.

It was a beast not unlike the Mabden in general shape, but it was wholly covered in its own fur. Its face was brown and seamed and apparently very ancient. Its features were flat. It had large eyes, round like a cat's, and gaping nostrils and a huge mouth filled with old, yellowed fangs.

Yet there was a look of great sorrow on its face as it observed Corum. It gestured at him and grunted, pointing into the forest as if it wanted Corum to accompany it. Corum shook his head, indicating the manacles with a nod.

The creature stroked the curly brown fur of its own neck thoughtfully, then it shuffled away again, back into the darkness of the forest.

Corum watched it go, almost forgetful of his pain in his astonishment.

Had the creature witnessed his torture? Was it trying to save him?

Or perhaps this was an illusion, like the illusion of the city and his sister, induced by his agonies.

He felt his energy weakening. A few more moments and he would be returning to the plane where the Mabden would be able to see him. And he knew that he would not find the strength again to leave the plane.

Then the brown creature reappeared and it was leading something by one of its hands, pointing at Corum.

At first Corum saw only a bulky shape looming over the brown creature—a being that stood some twelve feet tall and was some six feet broad, a being that, like the furry beast, walked on two legs.

Corum looked up at it and saw that it had a face. It was a dark face and the expression on it was sad, concerned, doomed. The rest of its body, though in outline the same as a man's, seemed to refuse light—no detail of it could be observed. It reached out and it picked up the board as tenderly as a father might pick up a child. It bore Corum back with it into the forest.

Unable to decide if this were fantasy or reality, Corum gave up his efforts to remain on the other plane and merged back into the one he had left. But still the dark-faced creature carried him, the brown beast at its side, deep into the forest, moving at great speed until they were far away from the Mabden camp.

Corum fainted once again.

He awoke in daylight and he saw the board lying some distance away. He lay on the green grass of a valley and there was a spring nearby and, close to that, a little pile of nuts and fruit. Not far from the pile of food sat the brown beast. It was watching him.

Corum looked at his left arm. Something had been smeared on the stump and there was no pain there anymore. He put his right hand to his right eye and touched a sticky stuff that must have been the same salve as that which was on his stump.

Birds sang in the nearby woods. The sky was clear and blue. If it were not for his injuries, Corum might have thought the events of the last few weeks a black dream.

Now the brown, furry creature got up and shambled toward him. It cleared its throat. Its expression was still one of sympathy. It touched its own right eye, its own left wrist.

"How—pain?" it said in a slurred tone, obviously voicing the words with difficulty.

"Gone," Corum said. "I thank you, Brown Man, for your help in rescuing me."

The brown man frowned at him, evidently not understanding all the words. Then it smiled and nodded its head and said, "Good."

"Who are you?" Corum said. "Who was it you brought last night?"

The creature tapped its chest. "Me Serwde. Me friend of you."

"Serwde," said Corum, pronouncing the name poorly. "I am Corum. And who was the other being?"

Serwde spoke a name that was far more difficult to pronounce than his own. It seemed a complicated name.

"Who was he? I have never seen a being like him. I have never seen a being like yourself, for that matter. Where do you come from?"

Serwde gestured about him. "Me live here. In forest. Forest called Laahr. My master live here. We live here many, many, many days—since before Vadhagh, you folk."

"And where is your master now?" Corum asked again.

"He gone. Not want be seen folk."

And now Corum dimly recalled a legend. It was a legend of a creature that lived even further to the west than the people of Castle Erorn. It was called by the legend the Brown Man of Laahr. And this was the legend come to life. But he remembered no legend concerning the other being whose name he could not pronounce.

"Master say place nearby will tend you good," said the Brown Man.

"What sort of place, Serwde?"

"Mabden place."

Corum smiled crookedly. "No, Serwde. The Mabden will not be kind to me."

"This different Mabden."

"All Mabden are my enemies. They hate me." Corum looked at his stump. "And I hate them."

"These *old* Mabden. *Good* Mabden."

Corum got up and staggered. Pain began to nag in his head, his left wrist began to ache. He was still completely naked and his body bore many bruises and small cuts, but it had been washed.

Slowly it began to dawn on him that he was a cripple. He had been saved from the worst of what Glandyth had planned for him, but he was now less of a being than he had been. His face was no longer pleasing for others to look at. His body had become ugly.

And the wretch that he had become was all that was left of the noble Vadhagh race. He sat down again and he began to weep.

Serwde grunted and shuffled about. He touched Corum's shoulder with one of his handlike paws. He patted Corum's head, trying to comfort him.

Corum wiped his face with his good hand. "Do not worry, Serwde. I must weep, for if I did not I should almost certainly die. I weep for my kin. I am the last of my line. There are no more Vadhagh but me . . ."

"Serwde too. Master too," said the Brown Man of Laahr. "We have no more people like us."

"Is that why you saved me?"

"No. We helped you because Mabden were hurting you."

"Have the Mabden ever hurt you?"

"No. We hide from them. Their eyes bad. Never see us. We hide from Vadhagh, the same."

"Why do you hide?"

"My master know. We stay safe."

"It would have been well for the Vadhagh if they had hidden. But the Mabden came so suddenly. We were not warned. We left our castles so rarely, we communicated amongst ourselves so little, we were not prepared."

Serwde only half understood what Corum was saying, but he listened politely until Corum stopped, then he said, "You eat. Fruit good. You sleep. Then we go to Mabden place."

"I want to find arms and armor, Serwde. I want clothes. I want a horse. I want to go back to Glandyth and follow him until I see him alone. Then I want to kill him. After that, I will wish only to die."

Serwde looked sadly at Corum. "You kill?"

"Only Glandyth. He killed my people."

Serwde shook his head. "Vadhagh not kill like that."

"I do, Serwde. I am the last Vadhagh. And I am the first to learn what it is to kill in malice. I will be avenged on those who maimed me, on those who took away my family."

Serwde grunted miserably.

"Eat. Sleep."

Corum stood up again and realized he was very weak. "Perhaps you are right there. Perhaps I should try to restore my strength before I carry on." He went to the pile of nuts and fruits and began to eat. He could not eat much at first and lay down again to sleep, confident that Serwde would rouse him if danger threatened.

For five days Corum stayed in the valley with the Brown Man of Laahr. He hoped that the dark-faced creature would come back and tell him more of his and Serwde's origin, but this did not happen.

At last his wounds had healed completely and he felt well enough to set off on a journey. On that morning, he addressed Serwde.

"Farewell, Brown man of Laahr. I thank you for saving me. And I thank your master. Now I go."

Corum saluted Serwde and began to walk up the valley, heading toward the east. Serwde came shambling after him. "Corum! Corum! You go wrong way."

"I go back to where I shall find my enemies," Corum said. "That is not the wrong way."

"My master say, me take you that way . . ." Serwde pointed toward the west.

"There is only sea that way, Serwde. It is the far tip of Bro-an-Vadhagh."

"My master say that way," insisted Serwde.

"I am grateful for your concern, Serwde. But I go this way—to find the Mabden and take my revenge."

"You go that way." Serwde pointed again and put his paw on Corum's arm. "That way."

Corum shook the paw off. "No. This way." He continued to walk up the valley toward the west.

Then, suddenly, something struck him on the back of the head. He reeled and turned to see what had struck him. Serwde stood there, holding another stone ready.

Corum cursed and was about to berate Serwde when his senses left him once again and he fell full length on the grass.

He was awakened by the sound of the sea.

At first he could not decide what was happening to him and then he realized that he was being carried, face down, over Serwde's shoulder. He struggled, but the Brown Man of Laahr was much stronger than he appeared to be. He held Corum firmly.

Corum looked to one side. There was the sea, green and foaming against the shingle. He looked to the other side, his blind side, and managed to strain his head round to see what lay there.

It was the sea again. He was being carried along a narrow piece of land that rose out of the water. Eventually, though his head was bumping up and down as Serwde jogged along, he saw that they had left the mainland and were moving along some kind of natural causeway that stretched out into the ocean.

Seabirds called. Corum shouted and struggled, but Serwde remained deaf to his curses and entreaties, until the Brown Man stopped at last and dumped him to the ground.

Corum got up.

"Serwde, I . . ."

He paused, looking about him.

They had come to the end of the causeway and were on an island that rose steeply from the sea. At the peak of the island was a castle of a kind of architecture Corum had never seen before.

Was this the Mabden place Serwde had spoken of?

But Serwde was already trotting back down the causeway. Corum called to him. The Brown Man only increased his pace. Corum began to follow, but he could not match the creature's speed. Serwde had reached the land long before Corum had crossed halfway—and now his path was blocked, for the tide was rising to cover the causeway.

Corum paused in indecision, looking back at the castle. Serwde's misguided help had placed him, once again, in danger.

Now he saw mounted figures coming down the steep path from the castle. They were warriors. He saw the sun flash on their lances and on their breastplates. Unlike other Mabden, these did know how to ride horses, and there was something in their bearing that made them look more like Vadhagh than Mabden.

But, nonetheless, they were enemies and Corum's choice was to face them naked or try to swim back to the mainland with only one hand.

He made up his mind and waded into the brine, the cold water making him gasp, heedless of the shouts of the riders behind him.

He managed to swim a little way until he was in deeper water, and then the current seized him. He fought to swim free of it, but it was useless.

Rapidly, he was borne out to sea.

The Eighth Chapter

THE MARGRAVINE OF ALLOMGLYL

Corum had lost much blood during the Mabden torturings and had by no means recovered his original strength. It was not long before he could fight the current no more and the cramps began to set in his limbs.

He began to drown.

Destiny seemed determined that he should not live to take his vengeance on Glandyth-a-Krae.

Water filled his mouth and he fought to keep it from entering his lungs as he twisted and thrashed in the water. Then he heard a shout from above and tried to peer upward through his good eye to locate the source of the voice.

"Stay still, Vadhagh. You'll frighten my beasts. They're nervous monsters at the best of times."

Now Corum saw a dark shape hovering over him. It had great wings that spread four times the length of the largest eagle's. But it was not a bird and, though its wings had a reptilian appearance, it was not a reptile. Corum recognized it for what it was. The ugly, apelike face with its white, thin fangs was the face of a gigantic bat. And the bat had a rider on it.

The rider was a lithe, young Mabden who appeared to have little in common with the Mabden warriors of Glandyth-a-Krae. He was actually climbing down the side of the creature and making it flap lower so that he could extend a hand to Corum.

Corum automatically stretched out his nearest arm and realized that it was the one without a hand. The Mabden was unconcerned. He grabbed the limb near the elbow and hauled Corum up so that Corum could use his single hand to grasp a tethering strap which secured a high saddle on the back of the great bat.

Unceremoniously, Corum's dripping body was hauled up and

draped in front of the rider, who called something in a shrill voice and made the bat climb high above the waves and turn back in the direction of the island castle.

The beast was evidently hard to control, for the rider constantly corrected course and continued to speak to it in the high-pitched language to which it responded. But at length they had reached the island and were hovering over the castle.

Corum could hardly believe that this was Mabden architecture. There were turrets and parapets of delicate workmanship, roof walks and balconies covered in ivy and flowers, all fashioned from a fine, white stone that shone in the sunshine.

The bat landed clumsily and the rider got off quickly, pulling Corum with him. Almost instantly, the bat was up again, wheeling in the sky and then diving toward a destination on the other side of the island.

"They sleep in caves," the rider exclaimed. "We use them as little as possible. They're hard things to control, as you saw."

Corum said nothing.

For all that the Mabden had saved his life and seemed both cheerful and courteous, Corum had learned, as an animal learns, that the Mabden were his enemies. He glowered at the Mabden.

"What have you saved me *for*, Mabden?"

The man looked surprised. He dusted down his tunic of scarlet velvet and adjusted his swordbelt on his hips. "You were drowning," he said. "Why did you run away from our men when they came to get you?"

"How did you know I was coming?"

"We were told by our Margravine to expect you."

"And who told your Margravine?"

"I know not. You are somewhat ungracious, sir. I thought the Vadhagh a courteous folk."

"And I thought the Mabden vicious and mad," Corum replied. "But you . . ."

"Ah, you speak of the folk of the South and the East, eh? You have met them then?"

With his stump, Corum tapped his ruined eye. "They did this."

The young man nodded his head sympathetically. "I suppose I would have guessed. Mutilation is one of their favorite sports. I am surprised you escaped."

"I, too."

"Well, sir," said the youth, spreading his hand in an elaborate gesture toward a doorway in a tower, "would you go in?"

Corum hesitated.

"We are not your Mabden of the East, sir, I assure you."

"Possibly," Corum said harshly, "but Mabden you are. There are so many of you. And now, I find, there are even varieties. I suspect you share common traits, however . . ."

The young man showed signs of impatience. "As you like, Sir Vadhagh. I, for one, will go in. I trust you will follow me at your leisure."

Corum watched him enter the doorway and disappear. He remained on the roof, watching the sea birds drift, dive, and climb. With his good hand, he stroked the stump of his left hand and shivered. A strong wind was beginning to blow and it was cold and he was naked. He glanced toward the doorway.

A woman stood there. She seemed quiet and self-contained and had a gentleness about her. Her long black hair was soft and fell below her shoulders. She was wearing a gown of embroidered samite containing a multitude of rich colors. She smiled at him.

"Greetings," she said. "I am Rhalina. Who are you, sir?"

"I am Corum Jhaelen Irsei," he replied. Her beauty was not that of a Vadhagh, but it affected him nonetheless. "The Prince in the—"

"—Scarlet Robe?" She was plainly amused. "I speak the old Vadhagh tongue as well as the common speech. You are misnamed, Prince Corum. I see no robe. In fact, I see no . . ."

Corum turned away. "Do not mock me, Mabden. I am resolved to suffer no further at the hands of your kind."

She moved nearer. "Forgive me. Those who did this to you are not our kind, though they be of the same race. Have you never heard of Lywm-an-Esh?"

His brow furrowed. The name of the land was familiar, but meant nothing.

"Lywm-an-Esh," she continued, "is the name of the country whence my people come. That people is an ancient one and has lived in Lywm-an-Esh since well before the Great Battles of the Vadhagh and the Nhadragh shook the Five Planes . . ."

"You know of the Five Planes?"

"We once had seers who could look into them. Though their skills never matched those of the Old Folk—your folk."

"How do you know so much of the Vadhagh?"

"Though the sense of curiosity atrophied in the Vadhagh many centuries ago, ours did not," she said. "From time to time Nhadragh ships were wrecked on our shores and, though the Nhadragh themselves vanished away, books and tapestries and other artifacts were left behind. We learned to read those books and interpret those tapestries. In those days, we had many scholars."

"And now?"

"Now, I do not know. We receive little news from the mainland."

"What? And it so close?"

"Not that mainland, Prince Corum," said she with a nod in the direction of the shore. She pointed out to sea. "That mainland—Lywm-an-Esh—or, more specifically, the Duchy of Bedwilral-nan-Rywm, on whose borders this Margravate once lay."

Prince Corum watched the sea as it foamed on the rocks at the base of the island. "What ignorance was ours," he mused, "when we thought we had so much wisdom."

"Why should such a race as the Vadhagh be interested in the affairs of a Mabden land?" she said. "Our history was brief and without color compared with yours."

"But why a Margrave here?" he continued. "What do you defend your land against?"

"Other Mabden, Prince Corum."

"Glandyth and his kind?"

"I know of no Glandyth. I speak of the Pony Tribes. They occupy the forests of yonder coast. Barbarians, they have ever represented a threat to Lywm-an-Esh. The Margravate was made as a bastion between those tribes and our land."

"Is the sea not a sufficient bastion?"

"The sea was not here when the Margravate was established. Once this castle stood in a forest and the sea lay miles away to the north and the south. But then the sea began to eat our land away. Every year it devours more of our cliffs. Towns, villages, and castles have vanished in the space of weeks. The people of the mainland retreat ever further back into the interior . . ."

"And you are left behind? Has not this castle ceased to fulfill its function? Why do you not leave and join your folk?"

She smiled and shrugged, walking to the battlements and leaning out to watch the seabirds gather on the rocks. "This is my home," she said. "This is where my memories are. The Margrave left so many mementos. I could not leave."

"The Margrave?"

"Earl Moidel of Allomglyl. My husband."

"Ah." Corum felt a strange twinge of disappointment.

The Margravine Rhalina continued to stare out to sea. "He is dead," she said. "Killed in a shipwreck. He took our last ship and set off for the mainland seeking news of the fate of our folk. A storm blew up shortly after he had gone. The ship was barely seaworthy. It sank."

Corum said nothing.

As if the Margravine's words had reminded it of its temper, the

47

wind suddenly blew stronger, plucking at her gown and making it swirl about her body. She turned to look at him. It was a long, thoughtful stare.

"And now, Prince," she said. "Will you be my guest?"

"Tell me one more thing, Lady Rhalina. How did you know of my coming? Why did the Brown Man bring me here?"

"He brought you at the behest of his master."

"And his master?"

"Told me to expect you and let you rest here until your mind and your body were healed. I was more than willing to agree. We have no visitors, normally—and certainly none of the Vadhagh race."

"But who is that strange being, the Brown Man's master? I saw him only briefly. I could not distinguish his shape too well, though I knew he was twice my size and had a face of infinite sadness."

"That is he. He comes to the castle at night, bringing sick domestic animals that have escaped our stables at some time or another. We think he is a being from another plane, or perhaps another Age, before even the Age of the Vadhagh and the Nhadragh. We cannot pronounce his name, so we call him simply the Giant of Laahr."

Corum smiled for the first time. "Now I understand better. To him, perhaps, I was another sick beast. This is where he always brings sick beasts."

"You could be right, Prince Corum." She indicated the doorway. "And if you are sick, we should be happy to help you mend . . ."

A shadow passed over Corum's face as he followed her inside. "I fear that nothing can mend my sickness now, Lady. It is a disease of the Mabden and there are no cures known to the Vadhagh."

"Well," she said with forced lightness, "perhaps we Mabden can devise something."

Bitterness filled him then. As they descended the steps into the main part of the castle he held up his stump and touched his eyeless socket. "But can the Mabden give me back my hand and my eye?"

She turned and paused on the steps. She gave him an oddly candid look. "Who knows?" she said quietly. "Perhaps they can."

The Ninth Chapter

CONCERNING LOVE AND HATRED

Although doubtless magnificent by Mabden standards, the Margravine's castle struck Prince Corum as simple and pleasant. At her invitation, he allowed himself to be bathed and oiled by castle servants and was offered a selection of clothing to wear. He chose a samite shirt of dark blue, embroidered in a design of light blue, and a pair of brown linen breeks. The clothes fitted him well.

"They were the Margrave's," a girl servant told him shyly, not looking at him directly.

None of the servants had seemed at ease with him. He guessed that his appearance was repellent to them.

Reminded of this, he asked the girl, "Would you bring me a mirror?"

"Aye, Lord." She ducked her head and left the chamber.

But it was the Margravine herself who returned with the mirror. She did not hand it to him immediately.

"Have you not seen your face since it was injured?" she asked.

He shook his head.

"You were handsome?"

"I do not know."

She looked at him frankly. "Yes," she said. "You were handsome." Then she gave him the mirror.

The face he saw was framed by the same light golden hair, but it was no longer youthful. Fear and agony had left their marks. The face was lined and hard and the set of the mouth grim. One eye of gold and purple stared bleakly back at him. The other socket was an ugly hole made up of red, scarred tissue. There was a small scar on his left cheek and another on his neck. The face was still characteristically a Vadhagh face, but it had suffered abuse never suffered by a

49

Vadhagh before. From the face of an angel it had been transformed by Glandyth's knives and irons into the face of a demon.

Silently, Corum gave her back the mirror.

He passed his good hand over the scars of his face and he brooded. "If I was handsome, I am ugly now."

She shrugged. "I have seen much worse."

Then the rage began to fill him again and his eye blazed and he shook the stump of his hand and he shouted at her. "Aye—and you will see much worse when I have done with Glandyth-a-Krae!"

Surprised, she recoiled from him and then regained her composure. "If you did not know you were handsome, if you were not vain, then why has this affected you so much?"

"I need my hands and my eyes so that I may kill Glandyth and watch him perish. With only half of these, I lose half the pleasure!"

"That is a childish statement, Prince Corum. It is not worthy of a Vadhagh. What else has this Glandyth done?"

Corum realized that he had not told her, that she would not know, living in this remote place, as cut off from the world as any Vadhagh had been.

"He has slain all the Vadhagh," he said. "Glandyth has destroyed my race and would have destroyed me if it had not been for your friend, the Giant of Laahr."

"He has done what . . . ?" Her voice was faint. She was plainly shocked.

"He has put all my folk to death."

"For what reason? Have you been warring with this Glandyth?"

"We did not know of his existence. It did not occur to us to guard against the Mabden. They seemed so much like brutes, incapable of harming us in our castles. But they have razed all our castles. Every Vadhagh save me is dead and most of the Nhadragh, I learned, who are not their cringing slaves."

"Are these the Mabden whose king is called Lyr-a-Brode of Kalenwyr?"

"They are."

"I, too, did not know they had become so powerful. I had assumed that it was the Pony Tribes who had captured you. I wondered why you were traveling alone so far from the nearest Vadhagh castle."

"What castle is that?" For a moment Corum hoped that there were Vadhagh still alive, much further west than he had guessed.

"It is called Castle Eran—Erin—some such name."

"Erorn?"

"Aye. That sounds the right name. It is over five hundred miles from here . . ."

"Five hundred miles? Have I come so far? The Giant of Laahr must have carried me much further than I suspected. That castle you mention, my lady, was our castle. The Mabden destroyed it. It will take me longer than I thought to return and find Earl Glandyth and his Denledhyssi."

Suddenly Corum realized just how alone he was. It was as if he had entered another plane of Earth where everything was alien to him. He knew nothing of this world. A world in which the Mabden ruled. How proud his race had been. How foolish. If only they had concerned themselves with knowledge of the world around them instead of seeking after abstractions.

Corum bowed his head.

The Margravine Rhalina seemed to understand his emotion. She lightly touched his arm. "Come, Prince of the Vadhagh. You must eat."

He allowed her to lead him from the room and into another where a meal had been laid out for them both. The food—mainly fruit and forms of edible seaweed—was much closer to his taste than any Mabden food he had seen previously. He realized that he was very hungry and that he was deeply tired. His mind was confused and his only certainty was the hatred he still felt for Glandyth and the vengeance he intended to take as soon as possible.

As they ate, they did not speak, but the Margravine watched his face the whole time and once or twice she opened her lips as if to say something, but then seemed to decide against it.

The room in which they ate was small and hung with rich tapestries covered in fine embroidery. As he finished his food and began to observe the details of the tapestry, the scenes thereon began to swim before his eyes. He looked questioningly at the Margravine, but her face was expressionless. His head felt light and he had lost the use of his limbs.

He tried to form words, but they would not come.

He had been drugged.

The woman had poisoned his food.

Once again he had allowed himself to become a victim of the Mabden.

He rested his head on his arms and fell, unwillingly, into a deep sleep.

Corum dreamed again.

He saw Castle Erorn as he had left it when he had first ridden out. He saw his father's wise face speaking and strained to hear the words, but could not. He saw his mother at work, writing her latest

51

*treatise on mathematics. He saw his sisters dancing to his uncle's
new music.*

The atmosphere was joyful.

*But now he realized that he could not understand their activities.
They seemed strange and pointless to him. They were like children
playing, unaware that a savage beast stalked them.*

He tried to cry out—to warn them—but he had no voice.

*He saw fires begin to spring up in rooms—saw Mabden warriors
who had entered the unprotected gates without the inhabitants'
being in the least aware of their presence. Laughing amongst
themselves, the Mabden put the silk hangings and the furnishings to
the torch.*

*Now he saw his kinfolk again. They had become aware of the
fires and were rushing to seek their source.*

*His father came into a room in which Glandyth-a-Krae stood,
hurling books onto a pyre he had erected in the middle of the
chamber. His father watched in astonishment as Glandyth burned
the books. His father's lips moved and his eyes were questioning—
almost polite surprise.*

*Glandyth turned and grinned at him, drawing his axe from his
belt. He raised the axe . . .*

*Now Corum saw his mother. Two Mabden held her while an-
other heaved himself up and down on her naked body.*

Corum tried to enter the scene, but something stopped him.

*He saw his sisters and his cousin suffering the same fate as his
mother. Again his path to them was blocked by something invisible.*

*He struggled to get through, but now the Mabden were slitting
the girls' throats. They quivered and died like slain fawns.*

Corum began to weep.

He was still weeping, but he lay against a warm body and from
somewhere in the distance came a soothing voice.

His head was being stroked and he was being rocked back and
forth in a soft bed by the woman on whose breast he lay.

For a moment he tried to free himself, but she held him tight.

He began to weep again, freely this time, great groans racking
his body, until he slept again. And now the sleep was free from
dreams . . .

He awoke feeling anxious. He felt that he had slept for too long,
that he must be up and doing something. He half raised himself in
the bed and then sank down again into the pillows.

It slowly came to him that he was much refreshed. For the first time since he had set off on his quest, he felt full of energy and well-being. Even the darkness in his mind seemed to have retreated.

So the Margravine had drugged him, but now, it seemed, it had been a drug to make him sleep, to help him regain his strength.

But how many days had he slept?

He stirred again in the bed and felt the soft warmth of another beside him, on his blind side. He turned his head and there was Rhalina, her eyes closed, her sweet face at peace.

He recalled his dreaming. He recalled the comfort he had been given as all the misery in him poured forth.

Rhalina had comforted him. He reached out with his good hand to stroke the tumbled hair. He felt affection for her—an affection almost as strong as he had felt for his own family.

Reminded of his dead kin, he stopped stroking her hair and contemplated, instead, the puckered stump of his left hand. It was completely healed now, leaving a rounded end of white skin. He looked back at Rhalina. How could she bear to share her bed with such a cripple?

As he looked at her, she opened her eyes and smiled at him.

He thought he detected pity in that smile and was immediately resentful. He began to climb from the bed, but her hand on his shoulder stopped him.

"Stay with me, Corum, for I need your comforting now."

He paused, looked back at her suspiciously.

"Please, Corum. I believe that I love you."

He frowned. "Love? Between Vadhagh and Mabden? Love of that kind?" He shook his head. "Impossible. There could be no issue."

"No children, I know. But love gives birth to other things . . ."

"I do not understand you."

"I am sorry," she said. "I was selfish. I am taking advantage of you." She sat up in bed. "I have slept with no one else since my husband went away. I am not . . ."

Corum studied her body. It moved him and yet it should not have. It was unnatural for one species to feel such emotion for another . . .

He reached down and kissed her breast. She clasped his head. They sank, again, into the sheets, making gentle love, learning of one another as only those truly in love may.

After some hours, she said to him, "Corum, you are the last of your race. I will never see my people again, save for those retainers who are here. It is peaceful in this castle. There is little that would disturb that peace. Would you not consider staying here with me—at least for a few months?"

"I have sworn to avenge the deaths of my folk," he reminded her softly, and kissed her cheek.

"Such oaths are not true to your nature, Corum. You are one who would rather love than hate, I know."

"I cannot answer that," he replied, "for I will not consider my life fulfilled unless I destroy Glandyth-a-Krae. This wish is not so hate-begotten as you might think. I feel, perhaps, like one who sees a disease spreading through a forest. One hopes to cut out the diseased plants so that the others may grow straight and live. That is my feeling concerning Glandyth-a-Krae. He has formed the habit of killing. Now that he has killed all the Vadhagh, he will want to kill others. If he finds no more strangers, he will begin to kill those wretches who occupy the villages ruled by Lyr-a-Brode. Fate has given me the impetus I need to pursue this attitude of mine to its proper conclusion, Rhalina."

"But why go from here now? Sooner or later we will receive news concerning this Glandyth. When that moment arrives, then you can set forth to exact your vengeance."

He pursed his lips. "Perhaps you are right."

"And you must learn to do without your hand and your eye," she said. "That will take much practice, Corum."

"True."

"So stay here, with me."

"I will agree to this much, Rhalina. I will make no decision for a few more days."

And Corum made no decision for a month. After the horror of his encounters with the Mabden raiders, his brain needed time to heal and this was difficult with the constant reminder of his injuries every time he automatically tried to use his left hand or glimpsed his reflection.

When not with him, Rhalina spent much of her time in the castle's library, but Corum had no taste for reading. He would walk about the battlements of the castle or take a horse and ride over the causeway at low tide (though Rhalina was perturbed by this for fear that he would fall prey to one of the Pony Tribes, which occasionally ranged the area) and ride for a while among the trees.

And though the darkness in his mind became less noticeable as the pleasant days passed, it still remained. And Corum would sometimes pause in the middle of some action or stop when he witnessed some scene that reminded him of his home, the Castle Erorn.

The Margravine's castle was called simply Moidel's Castle and was raised on an island called Moidel's Mount, after the name of the family that had occupied it for centuries. It was full of interesting things. There were cabinets of porcelain and ivory figurines, rooms filled with curiosities taken at different times from the sea, chambers in which arms and armor were displayed, paintings (crude by Corum's standards) depicting scenes from the history of Lywm-an-Esh, as well as scenes taken from the legends and folktales of that land, which was rich in them. Such strange imaginings were rare amongst the Vadhagh, who had been a rational people, and they fascinated Corum. He came to realize that many of the stories concerning magical lands and weird beasts were derived from some knowledge of the other planes. Obviously the other planes had been glimpsed and the legend makers had speculated freely from the fragments of knowledge thus gained. It amused Corum to trace a wild folktale back to its rather more mundane source, particularly where these folktales concerned the Old Races—the Vadhagh and the Nhadragh—to whom were attributed the most alarming range of supernatural powers. He was also, by this study, offered some insight concerning the attitudes of the Mabden of the East, who seemed to have lived in awe of the Old Races before they had discovered that they were mortal and could be slain easily. It seemed to Corum that the vicious genocide engaged upon by these Mabden was partly caused by their hatred of the Vadhagh for *not* being the great seers and sorcerers the Mabden had originally thought them to be.

But this line of thought brought back the memories and the sorrow and the hatred, and Corum would become depressed, sometimes for days, and even Rhalina's love could not console him then.

But then one day he inspected a tapestry in a room he had not previously visited and it absorbed his attention as he looked at the pictures and studied the embroidered text.

This was a complete legend telling of the adventures of Mag-an-Mag, a popular folk hero. Mag-an-Mag had been returning from a magical land when his boat had been set upon by pirates. These pirates had cut off Mag-an-Mag's arms and legs and thrown him overboard, then they had cut off the head of his companion, Jhakor-Neelus, and tossed his body after that of his master, but kept the head, apparently to eat. Eventually Mag-an-Mag's limbless body had been washed up on the shore of a mysterious island and Jhakor-Neelus's headless body had arrived at a spot a little further up the beach. These bodies were found by the servants of a magician who, in return for Mag-an-Mag's services against his enemies, offered to put back his limbs and make him as good as new. Mag-an-Mag had accepted on condition that the sorcerer find

55

Jhakor-Neelus a new head. The sorcerer had agreed and furnished Jhakor-Neelus with the head of a crane, which seemed to please everyone. The pair then left the island loaded down with the sorcerer's gifts and went on to fight his enemies.

Corum could find no origin for this legend in the knowledge of his own folk. It did not seem to fit with the others.

At first he dismissed his obsession with the legend as being fired by his own wish to get back the hand and the eye he had lost, but he remained obsessed.

Feeling embarrassed by his own interest, he said nothing of the legend to Rhalina for several weeks.

Autumn came to Moidel's Castle and with it a warm wind that stripped the trees bare and lashed the sea against the rocks and drove many of the birds away to seek a more restful clime.

And Corum began to spend more and more time in the room where hung the tapestry concerning Mag-an-Mag and the wonderful sorcerer. Corum began to realize that it was the text that chiefly interested him. It seemed to speak with an authority that was elsewhere lacking in the others he had seen.

But he still could not bring himself to tax Rhalina with questions concerning it.

Then, on one of the first days of winter, she sought for him and found him in the room and she did not seem surprised. However, she did show a certain concern, as if she had feared that he would find the tapestry sooner or later.

"You seem absorbed by the amusing adventures of Mag-an-Mag," she said. "They are only tales. Something to entertain us."

"But this one seems different," Corum said.

He turned to look at her. She was biting her lip.

"So it is different, Rhalina," Corum murmured. "You do know something about it!"

She began to shake her head, then changed her mind. "I know only what the old tales say. And the old tales are lies, are they not? Pleasing lies."

"Truth is somewhere in this tale, I feel. You must tell me what you know, Rhalina."

"I know more than is on this tapestry," she said quietly. "I have been lately reading a book that relates to it. I knew I had seen the book some years ago and I sought it out. I find quite recent reports concerning an island of the kind described. And there is, according to this book, an old castle there. The last person to see that island was an emissary of the Duchy, sailing here with supplies and greetings. And that was the last emissary to visit us . . . ."

"How long ago? How long ago?"

"Thirty years."

And then Rhalina began to weep and shake her head and cough and try to control her tears.

He embraced her.

"Why do you weep, Rhalina?"

"I weep, Corum, because this means you will leave me. You will go away from Moidel's Castle in the wintertime and you will seek that island and perhaps you, too, will be wrecked. I weep because nothing I love stays with me."

Corum took a step back. "Has this thought been long in your mind?"

"It has been long in my mind."

"And you have not spoken it."

"Because I love you so much, Corum."

"You should not love me, Rhalina. And I should not have allowed myself to love you. Though this island offers me the faintest of hopes, I must seek it out."

"I know."

"And if I find the sorcerer and he gives me back my hand and my eye—"

"Madness, Corum! He cannot exist!"

"But if he does and if he can do what I ask, then I will go to find Glandyth-a-Krae and I will kill him. Then, if I live, I will return. But Glandyth must die before I can know complete peace of mind, Rhalina."

She said softly, "There is no boat that is seaworthy."

"But there are boats in the harbor caves that can be made seaworthy."

"It will take several months to make one so."

"Will you lend me your servants to work on the boat?"

"Yes."

"Then I will speak to them at once."

And Corum left her, hardening his heart to the sight of her grief, blaming himself for letting himself fall in love with the woman.

With all the men he could muster who had some knowledge of shipcraft, Corum descended the steps that led from below the castle floor down through the rock to the sea caves where the ships lay. He found one skiff that was in better repair than the others and he had it hauled upright and inspected.

Rhalina had been right. There was a great deal of work to be done before the skiff would safely ride the waters.

He would wait impatiently, though now that he had a goal—no

matter how wild—he began to feel a lessening of the weight that had been upon him.

He knew that he would never tire of loving Rhalina, but that he could never love her completely until his self-appointed task had been accomplished.

He rushed back to the library to consult the book she had mentioned. He found it and discovered the name of the island.

Svi-an-Fanla-Brool. Not a pleasant name. As far as Corum could make out it meant "Hope of the Gorged God." What could that mean? He inspected the text for an answer, but found none.

The hours passed as he copied out the charts and reference points given by the captain of the ship that had visited Moidel's Mount thirty years before. And it was very late when he sought his bed and found Rhalina there.

He looked down at her face. She had plainly wept herself to sleep.

He knew that it was his turn to offer her comfort.

But he had no time . . .

He undressed. He eased himself into the bed, between the silks and the furs, trying not to disturb her. But she stirred.

"Corum?"

He did not reply.

He felt her body tremble for a moment, but she did not speak again.

He sat up in bed, his mind full of conflict. He loved her. He should not love her. He tried to settle back, to go to sleep, but he could not.

He reached out and stroked her shoulder.

"Rhalina?"

"Yes, Corum?"

He took a deep breath, meaning to explain to her how strongly he needed to see Glandyth dead, to repeat that he would return when his vengeance was taken.

Instead he said, "Storms blow strongly now around Moidel's Castle. I will set aside my plans until the spring. I will stay until the spring."

She turned in the bed and peered through the darkness at his face. "You must do as you desire. Pity destroys true love, Corum."

"It is not pity that moves me."

"Is it your sense of justice? That, too, is . . ."

"I tell myself that it is my sense of justice that makes me stay, but I know otherwise."

"Then why would you stay?"

"My resolve to go has weakened."

"What has weakened it, Corum?"

"Something quieter in me, yet something, perhaps, that is stronger. It is my love for you, Rhalina, that has conquered my desire to have immediate revenge on Glandyth. It is love. That is all I can tell you."

And she began to weep again, but it was not from sorrow.

The Tenth Chapter

A THOUSAND SWORDS

Winter reached its fiercest. The towers seemed to shake with the force of the gales that raged around them. The seas smashed against the rocks of Moidel's Mount and sometimes the waves seemed to rise higher than the castle itself.

Days became almost as dark as night. Huge fires were lit in the castle, but they could not keep out the chill that was everywhere. Wool and leather and fur had to be worn at all times and the inhabitants of the castle lumbered about like bears in their thick garments.

Yet Corum and Rhalina, a man and a woman of alien species, hardly noticed the winter's brawling. They sang songs to each other and wrote simple sonnets concerning the depth and passion of their love. It was a madness that was upon them (if madness is that which denies certain fundamental realities) but it was a pleasant madness, a sweet madness.

Yet madness it was.

When the worst of the winter had gone, but before spring elected to show herself; when there was still snow on the rocks below the castle and few birds sang in the gray skies above the bare and distant forests of the mainland; when the sea had exhausted itself and now washed sullen and dark around the cliffs; that was when the strange Mabden were seen riding out of the black trees in the late morning, their breath steaming and their horses stumbling on the icy ground, their harness and their arms rattling.

It was Beldan who saw them first as he went onto the battlements to stretch his legs.

Beldan, the youth who had rescued Corum from the sea, turned and went hastily back into the tower and began to run down the steps until a figure blocked his way, laughing at him.

"The privy is above, Beldan, not below!"

Beldan drew a breath and spoke slowly. "I was on the way to your apartments, Prince Corum. I have seen them from the battlements. There is a large force."

Corum's face clouded and he seemed to be thinking a dozen thoughts at once. "Do you recognize the force? Who are they? Mabden?"

"Mabden, without doubt. I think they might be warriors of the Pony Tribes."

"The folk against whom this Margravate was built?"

"Aye. But they have not bothered us for a hundred years."

Corum smiled grimly. "Perhaps we all, in time, succumb to the ignorance that killed the Vadhagh. Can we defend the castle, Beldan?"

"If it is a small force, Prince Corum. The Pony Tribes are normally disunited and their warriors rarely move in bands of more than twenty or thirty."

"And do you think it is a small force?"

Beldan shook his head. "No, Prince Corum, I fear it is a large one."

"You had best alert the warriors. What about the bat creatures?"

"They sleep in winter. Nothing will wake them."

"What are your normal methods of defense?"

Beldan bit his lip.

"Well?"

"We have none to speak of. It has been so long since we needed to consider such things. The Pony Tribes still fear the power of Lywm-an-Esh—their fear is even superstitious since the land retreated beyond the horizon. We relied on that fear."

"Then do your best, Beldan, and I'll join you shortly, when I've taken a look at these warriors first. They may not come in war, for all we know."

Beldan raced away down the steps and Corum climbed the tower and opened the door and went out onto the battlements.

He saw that the tide was beginning to go out and that when it did the natural causeway between the mainland and the castle would be exposed. The sea was gray and chill, the shore was bleak. And the warriors were there.

They were shaggy men on shaggy ponies and they had helmets of iron with visors of brass beaten into the form of savage and evil faces. They had cloaks of wolfskin or wool, byrnies of iron, jackets of leather, trews of blue, red, or yellow cloth bound around the feet and up to the knees with thongs. They were armed with spears, bows, axes, clubs. And each man had a sword strapped to the saddle

61

of his pony. They were all new swords, Corum judged, for they glinted as if freshly forged, even in the dull light of that winter's day.

There were several ranks of them already on the beach and more were trotting from the forest.

Corum drew his sheepskin coat about him with his good hand and he kicked thoughtfully at one of the battlement stones, as if to reassure himself that the castle was solid.

He looked at the warriors on the beach again.

He counted a thousand.

A thousand riders with a thousand new-forged swords.

He frowned.

A thousand helmets of iron were turned toward Moidel's Castle. A thousand brass masks glared at Corum across the water as the tide slowly receded and the causeway began to appear below the surface.

Corum shivered. A gannet flew low over the silent throng and it shrieked as if in startled terror and climbed high into the clouds.

A deep drum began to sound from the forest. The metallic note was measured and slow and it echoed across the water.

It seemed that the thousand riders did not come in peace.

Beldan came out and joined Corum.

Beldan looked pale. "I have spoken to the Margravine and I have alerted our warriors. We have a hundred and fifty able men. The Margravine is consulting her husband's notes. He wrote a treatise on the best way to defend the castle in case of an attack of this kind. He knew that the Pony Tribes would unite one day, it seems."

"I wish I had read that treatise," said Corum. He swallowed a deep breath of the freezing air. "Are there none here with actual experience of war?"

"None, Prince."

"Then we must learn rapidly."

"Aye."

There was a noise on the steps within the tower and brightly armored men came out. Each was armed with a bow and many arrows. Each had a helmet on his head that was made from the curly-spined pink shell of a giant murex. Each controlled his fear.

"We will try to parley with them," murmured Corum, "when the causeway is clear. We will attempt to continue the conversation until the tide comes in again. This will give us a few more hours in which to prepare ourselves."

"They will suspect such a ruse, surely," Beldan said.

Corum nodded and rubbed at his cheek with his stump. "True.

But if we—if we *lie* to them, regarding our strength, perhaps we shall be able to disconcert them a little.''

Beldan gave a wry smile, but he said nothing. His eyes began to shine with an odd light. Corum thought he recognized it as battle fever.

"I'll see what the Margravine has learned from her husband's texts," Corum said. "Stay here and watch, Beldan. Let me know if they begin to move."

"That damned drum!" Beldan pressed his hand to his temple. "It makes my brains shiver."

"Try to ignore it. It is meant to weaken our resolve."

Corum entered the tower and ran down the steps until he came to the floor where he and Rhalina had their apartments.

She was seated at a table with manuscripts spread out before her. She looked up as he entered and she tried to smile. "We are paying a price for the gift of love, it seems."

He looked at her in surprise. "That's a Mabden conception, I think. I do not understand it . . .''

"And I am a fool to make so shallow a statement. But I wish they had not chosen this time to come against us. They have had a hundred years to choose from . . .''

"What have you learned from your husband's notes?"

"Where our weakest positions are. Where our ramparts are best defended. I have already stationed men there. Cauldrons of lead are being heated."

"For what purpose?"

"You really do know little of war!" she said. "Less than do I. The molten lead will be poured on the heads of the invaders when they try to storm our walls."

Corum shuddered. "Must we be so crude?"

"We are not Vadhagh. We are not fighting Nhadragh. I believe you can expect these Mabden to have certain crude battle practices of their own . . .''

"Of course. I had best cast an eye over the Margrave's manuscripts. He was evidently a man who understood the realities."

"Aye," she said softly, handing him a sheet, "certain kinds of reality, at any rate."

It was the first time he had heard her offer an opinion of her husband. He stared at her, wanting to ask more, but she waved a delicate hand. "You had best read swiftly. You will understand the writing easily enough. My husband chose to write in the old High Speech we learned from the Vadhagh."

Corum looked at the writing. It was well formed but without any individual character. It seemed to him that it was a somewhat soulless imitation of Vadhagh writing, but it was, as she had said, easy enough to understand.

There was a knock on the main door to their apartments. While Corum read, Rhalina went to answer it. A soldier stood there.

"Beldan sent me, Lady Margravine. He asked Prince Corum to join him on the battlements."

Corum put down the sheets of manuscript. "I will come immediately. Rhalina, will you see that my arms and armor are prepared?"

She nodded. He left.

The causeway was almost clear of water now. Beldan was yelling something across to the warriors on the bank, speaking of a parley.

The drum continued its slow but steady beat.

The warriors did not reply.

Beldan turned to Corum. "They might be dead men for all they'll respond. They seem singularly well ordered for barbarians. I think there is some extra element to this situation that has not revealed itself as yet."

Corum had the same feeling. "Why did you send for me, Beldan?"

"I saw something in the trees. A flash of gold. I am not sure. Vadhagh eyes are said to be sharper than Mabden eyes. Tell me, Prince, if you can make anything out. Over there." He pointed.

Corum's smile was bitter. "Two Mabden eyes are better than one Vadhagh . . ." But nonetheless he peered in the direction Beldan indicated. Sure enough there was something hidden by the trees. He altered the angle of his vision to see if he could make it out more clearly.

And then he realized what it was. It was a gold-decorated chariot wheel.

As he watched, the wheel began to turn. Horses emerged from the forest. Four shaggy horses, slightly larger than those ridden by the Pony Tribes, drawing a huge chariot in which stood a tall warrior.

Corum recognized the driver of the chariot. The Mabden was dressed in fur and leather and iron and had a winged helmet and a great beard and held himself proudly.

"It is Earl Glandyth-a-Krae, my enemy," said Corum softly.

Beldan said, "Is that the one who took off your hand and put out your eye?"

Corum nodded.

"Then perhaps it is he who has united the Pony Tribes and given them those bright, new swords they carry, and drilled them to the order they now hold."

"I think it likely. I have brought this upon Moidel's Castle, Beldan."

Beldan shrugged. "It would have come. You made our Margravine happy. I have never known her happy before, Prince."

"You Mabden seem to think that happiness must be bought with misery."

"I suppose we do."

"It is not easy for a Vadhagh to understand that. We believe—believed—that happiness was a natural condition of reasoning beings."

Now from the forest emerged another twenty chariots. They arranged themselves behind Glandyth so that the Earl of Krae was between the silent, masked warriors and his own followers, the Denledhyssi.

The drum stopped its beating.

Corum listened to the tide drawing back. Now the causeway was completely exposed.

"He must have followed me, learned where I was, and spent the winter recruiting and training those warriors," Corum said.

"But how did he discover your hiding place?" Beldan said.

For answer, the ranks of the Pony Tribes opened and Glandyth drove his chariot down toward the causeway. He bent and picked something from the floor of his chariot, raised it above his head, and flung it over the backs of his horses to fall upon the causeway.

Corum shuddered when he recognized it.

Beldan stiffened and stretched out his hand to grasp the stone of the battlement, lowering his head.

"Is it the Brown Man, Prince Corum?"

"It is."

"The creature was so innocent. So kind. Could not its master save it? They must have tortured it to get the information concerning your whearabouts . . ."

Corum straightened his back. His voice was soft and cold when he spoke next. "I once told your mistress that Glandyth was a disease that must be stopped. I should have sought him out sooner, Beldan."

"He would have killed you."

"But he would not have killed the Brown Man of Laahr. Serwde would still be serving his sad master. I think there is a doom upon me, Beldan. I think I am meant to be dead and that all those who help me to continue living are doomed, also. I will go out now and fight Glandyth alone. Then the castle will be saved."

65

Beldan swallowed and spoke hoarsely. "We chose to help you. You did not ask for that help. Let us choose when we shall take back that help."

"No. For if you do, the Margravine and all her people will surely perish."

"They will perish anyway," Beldan told him.

"Not if I let Glandyth take me."

"Glandyth must have offered the Pony Tribes this castle as a prize if they would assist him," Beldan pointed out. "They do not care about you. They wish to destroy and loot something that they have hated for centuries. Certainly it is likely that Glandyth would be content with you—he would go away—but he would leave his thousand swords behind. We must all fight together, Prince Corum. There is nothing else for it now."

The Eleventh Chapter

THE SUMMONING

Corum returned to his apartments where his arms and his armor had been laid out for him. The armor was unfamiliar, consisting of breastplate, backplate, greaves, and a kilt, all made from the pearly blue shells of a sea creature called the *anufec*, which had once inhabited the waters of the West. The shell was stronger than the toughest iron and lighter than any byrnie. A great, spined helmet with a jutting peak had, like the helmets of the other warriors of Moidel's Castle, been manufactured from the shell of the giant murex. Servants helped Corum don his gear and they gave him a huge iron broadsword that was so well balanced that he could hold it in his one good hand. His shield, which he had them strap to his handless arm, was the shell of a massive crab which had once lived, the servants told him, in a place far beyond even Lywm-an-Esh and known as the Land of the Distant Sea. This armor had belonged to the dead Margrave, who had inherited it from his ancestors, who had owned it long before it had been considered necessary to establish a Margravate at all.

Corum called to Rhalina as he was prepared for battle, but, although he could see her through the doors dividing the chambers, she did not look up from her papers. It was the last of the Margrave's manuscripts and it seemed to absorb her more than the others.

Corum left to return to the battlements.

Save for the fact that Glandyth's chariot was now on the approach to the causeway, the ranks of the warriors had not shifted. The little broken corpse of the Brown Man of Laahr still lay on the causeway.

The drum had begun to beat again.

"Why do they not advance?" Beldan said, his voice sharp with tension.

"Perhaps for a twofold reason," Corum replied. "They are hoping to terrify us and banish the terror in themselves."

"They are terrified of us?"

"The Pony Tribesmen probably are. After all, they have, as you told me yourself, lived in superstitious fear of the folk of Lywm-an-

67

Esh for centuries. They doubtless suspect we have supernatural means of defense."

Beldan gestured toward Glandyth-a-Krae. "There is the Mabden who gave me my first lesson."

"He seems without fear, at least."

"He does not fear swords, but he fears himself. Of all Mabden traits, I would say that that was the most destructive."

Now Glandyth was raising a gauntleted hand.

Again silence fell.

"Vadhagh!" came the savage voice. "Can you see who it is who has come to call on you in this castle of vermin?"

Corum did not reply. Hidden by a battlement, he watched as Glandyth scanned the ramparts, seeking him out.

"Vadhagh! Are you there?"

Beldan looked questioningly at Corum, who continued to remain silent.

"Vadhagh! You see we have destroyed your demon familiar! Now we are going to destroy you—and those most despicable of Mabden who have given you shelter. Vadhagh! Speak!"

Corum murmured to Beldan. "We must stretch this pause as far as it will go. Every second brings the tide back to cover our causeway."

"They will strike soon," Beldan said. "Well before the tide returns."

"Vadhagh! Oh, you are the most cowardly of a cowardly race!"

Corum now saw Glandyth begin to turn his head back toward his men, as if to give the order to attack. He emerged from his cover and raised his voice.

His speech, even in cold anger, was liquid music compared with Glandyth's rasping tones.

"Here I am, Glandyth-a-Krae, most wretched and pitiable of Mabden!"

Disconcerted, Glandyth turned his head back. Then he burst into raucous laughter. "I am not the wretch!" He reached inside his furs and drew something out that was on a string round his neck. "Would you come and fetch this back from me?"

Corum felt bile come when he saw what Glandyth sported. It was Corum's own mummified hand, still bearing the ring that his sister had given him.

"And look!" Glandyth took a small leather bag from his furs and waved it at Corum. "I have also saved your eye!"

Corum controlled his hatred and his nausea and called, "You may have the rest, Glandyth, if you will turn back your horde and depart from Moidel's Castle in peace."

Glandyth flung his chin toward the sky and roared with laughter. "Oh, no, Vadhagh! They would not let me rob them of a fight—let alone their prize. They have waited many months for this. They are going to slay all their ancient enemies. And I am going to slay you. I had planned to spend the winter in the comfort of Lyr-an-Brode's court. Instead I have had to camp in skin tents with our friends here. I intend to slay you quickly, Vadhagh, I promise you. I have no more time to spend on a crippled piece of offal, such as yourself." He laughed again. "Who is the 'half-thing' now?"

"Then you would not be afraid to fight me alone," Corum called. "You could do battle on this causeway with me and doubtless kill me very quickly. Then you could leave the castle to your friends and return to your own land the faster."

Glandyth frowned, debating this with himself.

"Why should you sacrifice your life a little earlier than you need to?"

"I am tired of living as a cripple. I am tired of fearing you and your men."

Glandyth was not convinced. Corum was trying to buy time with his talk and his suggestion, but on the other hand it did not matter to Glandyth how much trouble the Pony Tribesmen would be forced to go to to take the castle after he had killed Corum.

Eventually he nodded, shouting back, "Very well, Vadhagh, come down to the causeway. I will tell my men to stand off until we have had our fight. If you kill me, I will have my charioteers leave the battle to the others . . ."

"I do not believe that part of your bargain," Corum replied. "I am not interested in it, either. I will come down."

Corum took his time descending the steps. He did not want to die at Glandyth's hand and he knew that if Glandyth did, by some luck, fall to him, the Earl of Krae's men would swiftly leap to their master's assistance. All he hoped for was to gain a few hours for the defenders.

Rhalina met him outside their apartments.

"Where go you, Corum?"

"I go to fight Glandyth and most probably to die," he said. "I shall die loving you, Rhalina."

Her face was a mask of terror. "Corum! No!"

"It is necessary, if this castle is to have a chance of withstanding those warriors."

"No, Corum! There may be a way to get help. My husband speaks of it in his treatise. A last resort."

"What help?"

"He is vague on that score. It is something passed on to him by his forefathers. A summoning. Sorcery, Corum."

Corum smiled sadly. "There is no such thing as sorcery, Rhalina. What you call sorcery is a handful of half-learned scraps of Vadhagh wisdom."

"This is not Vadhagh wisdom—it is something else. A summoning."

He made to move past her. She held his arm. "Corum, let me try the summoning!"

He pulled his arm away and, sword in hand, continued down the steps. "Very well, try what you will, Rhalina. Even if you are right, you will need the time I can gain for you."

He heard her shout wordlessly and he heard her sob, and then he had reached the hall and was walking toward the great main gates of the castle.

A startled warrior let him through and he stood at last upon the causeway. At the other end, his chariot and horses led away, the body of the Brown Man kicked to one side, stood Earl Glandyth-a-Krae. And beside Glandyth-a-Krae, holding his war-axe for him, was the gawky figure of the youth, Rodlik.

Glandyth reached out and tousled his page's hair and bared his teeth in a wolfish grin. He took the axe from the youth's hand and began to advance along the causeway.

Corum walked to meet him.

The sea slapped against the rocks of the causeway. Sometimes a seabird cried out. There was no sound from the warriors of either side. Both defenders and attackers watched tensely as the two approached each other and then, in the middle, stopped. About ten feet separated them.

Corum saw that Glandyth had grown a little thinner. But the pale, gray eyes still contained that strange, unnatural glint and the face was just as red and unhealthy as the last time Corum had seen it. He held his war-axe down in front of him, in his two hands, his helmeted head on one side.

"By the Dog," he said, "you have become hugely ugly, Vadhagh."

"We make a fine pair, then, Mabden, for you have changed not at all."

Glandyth sneered. "And you are hung all about with pretty shells, I see, like some sea god's daughter going to be wed to her fishy husband. Well, you may become their nuptial feast when I throw your body into the sea."

Corum wearied of these heavy insults. He leapt forward and swung his great broadsword at Glandyth, who brought his metal-

70

shod axe haft up swiftly and blocked the blow, staggering a little. He kept his axe in his right hand and drew his long knife, dropped to a crouch, and aimed the axe at Corum's knees.

Corum jumped high and the axe blade whistled under his feet. He stabbed out at Glandyth and the blade scraped the Mabden's shoulder plate but did not harm him.

Nonetheless Glandyth cursed and tried the same trick again. Again Corum jumped and the axe missed him. Glandyth sprang back and brought the axe down on the crab-shell shield, which creaked with the strain of the blow, but did not shatter, though Corum's arm was numb from wrist to shoulder. He retaliated with an overarm blow which Glandyth blocked.

Corum kicked out at Glandyth's legs, hoping to knock him off balance, but the Mabden ran backward several paces before standing his ground again.

Corum advanced cauriously toward him.

Then Glandyth cried out, "I'm tired of this. We have him now. Archers—shoot!"

And then Corum saw the charioteers, who had moved quietly down to the forefront of the ranks and were aiming their bows at him. He raised his shield to protect himself against their arrows.

Glandyth was running back down the causeway.

Corum had been betrayed. There was still an hour before the tide came in. It seemed he was going to die for nothing.

Now another shout, this time from the castle's battlements, and a wave of arrows swept down. Beldan's archers had shot first.

The Denledhyssi arrows rattled on Corum's shield and against his greaves. He felt something bite into his leg just above the knee, where he had scant protection. He looked down. It was an arrow. It had passed completely through his leg, and now half of it stuck out behind his knee. He tried to stumble backward, but it was hard to run with the arrow in him. To pull it out with his only hand would mean he would have to drop his sword. He glanced toward the shore.

As he had known they would, the first of the horsemen were beginning to cross.

He began to drag himself back along the causeway for a few more yards and then knew he would never reach the gates in time. Quickly he knelt on his good leg, put his sword on the ground, snapped off part of the arrow at the front, and drew the rest through his leg, flinging it to one side.

He picked up his sword again and prepared to stand his ground.

The warriors in the brass war masks were galloping along the causeway two abreast, their new swords in their hands.

71

Corum struck at the first rider and his blow was a lucky one, for it hurled the man from his saddle. The other rider had tried to strike at Corum but had missed and overshot.

Corum swung himself up into the pony's primitive saddle. For stirrups there were just two leather loops hanging from the girth strap. Painfully, Corum managed to get his feet into these and block the sword blow from the returning rider. Another rider came up now and his sword clanged on Corum's shield. The horses were snorting and trying to rear, but the causeway was so narrow there was little room for maneuver and neither Corum nor the other two could use their swords effectively as they tried to control their half-panicked horses.

The rest of the masked riders were forced to rein in their beasts for fear of toppling off the causeway into the sea and this gave Beldan's archers the opportunity they required. Dark sheets of arrows sped from the battlements and into the ranks of the Pony Tribesmen. More ponies went down than men, but it added further to the confusion.

Slowly Corum retreated down the causeway until he was almost at the gate. His shield arm was completely paralyzed and his sword arm aching dreadfully, but he still managed to continue defending himself against the riders.

Glandyth was screaming at the pony barbarians, trying to force them to retreat and regroup. Evidently his plans of attack had not been followed. Corum managed to grin. At least that was something he had gained.

Now the gates of the castle suddenly opened behind him. Beldan stood there with fifty archers poised to shoot.

"In, Corum, quickly!" Beldan cried.

Understanding Beldan's intention, Corum flung himself from the back of the pony and bent double, running toward the gate as the first flight of arrows rushed over his head. Then he was through the gates and they had closed.

Corum leaned panting against a pillar. He felt he had failed in his intention. But now Beldan was slapping his shoulder.

"The tide's coming in, Corum! We succeeded!"

The slap was enough to topple Corum. He saw Beldan's surprised expression as he fell to the flagstones and for a moment he was amused by the situation before he passed out completely.

As he awoke, in his own bed with Rhalina sitting at the table nearby, still reading from the manuscripts, Corum realized that no matter how well he trained himself to fight, no matter how well he had survived during the battle of the causeway, he would not survive long in the Mabden world with both a hand and an eye gone.

"I must have a new hand," he said, sitting upright. "I must have a new eye, Rhalina."

Rhalina did not appear to hear him at first. Then she looked up. Her face was tired and drawn in lines of heavy concentration. Absently, she said, "Rest," and returned to her reading.

There was a knock. Beldan came in quickly. Corum began to get out of bed. He winced as he moved. His wounded leg was stiff and his whole body was bruised.

"They lost some thirty men in that encounter," Beldan said. "The tide goes out again just before sunset. I'm not sure if they'll try another attack then. I would say they will wait until morning."

Corum frowned. "It depends on Glandyth, I'd say. He would judge that we wouldn't expect an evening attack and would therefore try to make one. But if those Pony Tribesmen are as superstitious as we think, they might be reluctant to fight at night. We had best prepare for an attack on the next tide. And guard all sides of the castle. How does that match with the Margrave's treatise, Rhalina?"

She looked up vaguely, nodding. "Well enough."

Corum began painfully to buckle on his armor. Beldan helped him. They left for the battlements.

The Denledhyssi had regrouped on the shore. The dead men and their ponies, as well as the corpse of the Brown Man of Laahr, had been washed away by the sea. A few corpses bobbed among the rocks below the castle.

They had formed the same ranks as earlier. The mounted masked riders were massed some ten ranks deep with Glandyth behind them and the charioteers behind Glandyth.

Cauldrons of lead bubbled on fires built on the battlements; small catapults had been erected, with piles of stone balls beside them, for ammunition; extra arrows and javelins were heaped by the far wall.

Again the tide was retreating.

The metallic drum began to beat again. There was the distant jingle of harness. Glandyth was speaking to some of the horsemen.

"I think he will attack," said Corum.

The sun was low and all the world seemed turned to a dark, chill gray. They watched as the causeway gradually became exposed until only a foot or two of water covered it.

Then the beat of the drum became more rapid. There was a howl from the riders. They began to move forward and splash onto the causeway.

The real battle for Moidel's Castle had begun.

Not all the horsemen rode along the causeway. About two thirds of the force remained on the shore. Corum guessed what this meant.

"Are all points of the castle guarded now, Beldan?"

"They are, Prince Corum."

"Good. I think they'll try to swim their horses round and get a hold on the rocks so that they can attack from all sides. When darkness falls, have flare arrows shot regularly from all quarters."

Then the horsemen were storming the castle. The cauldrons of lead were upended and beasts and riders screamed in pain as the white-hot metal flooded over them. The sea hissed and steamed as the lead hit it. Some of the riders had brought up battering rams, slung between their mounts. They began to charge the gates. Riders were shot from their saddles, but the horses ran wildly on. One of the rams struck the gates and smashed into them and through them, becoming jammed. The riders strove to extricate it, but could not. They were struck by a wave of boiling lead, but the ram remained.

"Get archers to the gates," Corum commanded. "And have horses ready in case the main hall is breached."

It was almost dark, but the fight continued. Some of the barbarians were riding round the lower parts of the hill. Corum saw the next rank leave the shore and begin to swim their horses through the shallow waters.

But Glandyth and his charioteers remained on the beach, taking no part in the battle. Doubtless Glandyth planned to wait until the castle defenses were breached before he crossed the causeway.

Corum's hatred of the Earl of Krae had increased since the betrayal earlier that day and now he saw him using the superstitious barbarians for his own purposes, Corum knew that his judgment of Glandyth was right. The man would corrupt anything with which he came in contact.

All around the castle now, the defenders were dying from spear and arrow wounds. At least fifty were dead or badly hurt and the remaining hundred were spread very thinly.

Corum made a rapid tour of the defenses, encouraging the warriors to greater efforts, but now the boiling lead was finished and arrows and spears were running short. Soon the hand-to-hand fighting would begin.

Night fell. Flare arrows revealed bands of barbarians all around the castle. Beacons burned on the battlements. The fighting continued.

The barbarians reconcentrated on the main gates. More rams were brought up. The gates began to groan and give way.

Corum took all the men he could spare into the main hall. There they mounted their horses and formed a semicircle behind the archers, waiting for the barbarians to come through.

More rams pierced the gates and Corum heard the sound of swords and axes beating on the splintered timbers outside.

Suddenly they were through, yelling and howling. Firelight glinted on their masks of brass, making them look even more evil and terrifying. Their ponies snorted and reared.

There was time for only one wave of arrows, then the archers retreated to make way for Corum and his cavalry to charge the disconcerted barbarians.

Corum's sword smashed into a mask, sheared through it, and destroyed the face beneath. Blood splashed high and a nearby brand fizzed as the liquid hit it.

Forgetful of the pain of his wounds, Corum swung the sword back and forth, knocking riders from their mounts, striking heads from shoulders, limbs from bodies. But slowly he and his remaining men were retreating as fresh waves of Pony Tribesmen surged into the castle.

Now they were at the far end of the hall, where a stone stairway curled up to the next floor. The archers were positioned here, along the stairs, and began to shoot their arrows into the barbarians. The barbarians not directly engaged with Corum's men retaliated with javelins and arrows, and slowly Moidel's archers fell.

Corum glanced around him as he fought. There were few left with him—perhaps a dozen—and there were some fifty barbarians in the hall. The fight was nearing its conclusion. Within moments he and his friends would all be dead.

He saw Beldan begin to descend the stairs. At first Corum thought he was bringing up reinforcements, but he had only two warriors with him.

"Corum! Corum!"

Corum was pressed by two barbarians. He could not reply.

"Corum! Where is the Lady Rhalina?"

Corum found extra strength now. He delivered a blow to the first barbarian's skull, which killed him. He kicked a man from his saddle, then stood on the back of his horse and jumped to the stairs. "What? Is the Lady Rhalina in danger?"

"I do not know, Prince. I cannot discover where she is. I fear . . ."

Corum raced up the stairs.

From below the noise of the battle was changing. There seemed to be disconcerted shouts coming from the barbarians. He paused and looked back.

The barbarians were beginning to retreat in panic.

Corum could not understand what was happening, but he had no more time to watch.

He reached his apartments. "Rhalina! Rhalina!"

No reply.

Here and there were the bodies of their own warriors and barbarians who had managed to sneak into the castle through poorly defended windows and balconies.

Had Rhalina been taken by a party of barbarians?

Then, from the balcony of her apartment, he heard a strange sound.

It was a singing sound, like nothing he had experienced before. He paused, then approached the balcony cautiously.

Rhalina stood there and she was singing. The wind caught her garments and spread them about her like strange, multicolored clouds. Her eyes were fixed on the far distance and her throat vibrated with the sounds she made.

She seemed to be in a trance and Corum made no sound, but watched. The words she sang were in no language he knew. Doubtless it was an ancient Mabden language. It made him shudder.

Then she stopped and turned in his direction. But she did not see him. Still in the trance, she walked straight past him and back into the room.

Corum peered around a buttress. He had seen an odd green light shining in the direction of the mainland.

He saw nothing more, but heard the yells of the barbarians as they splashed about near the causeway. There was no doubt now but they were retreating.

Corum entered the apartments. Rhalina was sitting in her chair by the table. She was stiff and could not hear him when he murmured her name. Hoping that she would succumb no further to the peculiar trance, he left the room and ran for the main battlements.

Beldan was already there, his jaw slack as he watched what was taking place.

There was a huge ship rounding the headland to the north. It was the source of the strange green light and it sailed rapidly, though there was no wind at all now. The barbarians were scrambling onto their horses, or plunging on foot through the water that was beginning to cover the causeway. They seemed mad with fear. From the darkness on the shore, Corum heard Glandyth cursing them and trying to make them go back.

The ship flickered with many small fires, it seemed. Its masts and its hull seemed encrusted with dull jewels. And Corum saw what the

76

barbarians had seen. He saw the crew. Flesh rotted on their faces and limbs.

The ship was crewed by corpses.

"What is it, Beldan?" he whispered. "Some artful illusion?"

Beldan's voice was hoarse. "I do not think it is an illusion, Prince Corum."

"Then what?"

"It is a summoning. That is the old Margrave's ship. It has been drawn up to the surface. Its crew has been given something like life. And see—" he pointed to the figure on the poop, a skeletal creature in armor which, like Corum's, was made from great shells, whose sunken eyes flickered with the same green fire that covered the ship like weed—"there is the Margrave himself. Returned to save his castle."

Corum forced himself to watch as the apparition drew closer.

"And what else has he returned for, I wonder?" he said.

The Twelfth Chapter

THE MARGRAVE'S BARGAIN

The ship reached the causeway and stopped. It reeked of ozone and of decay.

"If it be an illusion," Corum murmured grimly, "it is a good one."

Beldan made no reply.

In the distance they heard the barbarians blundering off through the forest. They heard the sound of the chariots turning as Glandyth pursued his allies.

Though all the corpses were armed, they did not move, but simply turned their heads, as one, toward the main gate of the castle.

Corum was transfixed in astonished horror. The events he was witnessing were like something from the superstitious mind of a Mabden. They could have no existence in actuality. Such images were those created by ignorant fear and morbid imagination. They were something from the crudest and most barbaric of the tapestries he had looked at in the castle.

"What will they do now, Beldan?"

"I have no understanding of the occult, Prince. The Lady Rhalina is the only one of us who has made some study of such things. It was she who made this summoning. I only know that there is said to be a bargain involved . . ."

"A bargain?"

Beldan gasped. "The Margravine!"

Corum saw that Rhalina, still walking in a trance, had left the gates and was moving, calf-deep, along the causeway toward the ship. The head of the dead Margrave turned slightly and the green fire in his eye sockets seemed to burn more deeply.

"NO!"

Corum raced from the battlements, leapt down the stairway, and stumbled through the main hall over the corpses of the fallen.

"NO! Rhalina! NO!"

He reached the causeway and began to wade after her, the stench from the ship of the dead choking him.

"Rhalina!"

It was a dream worse than any he had had since Glandyth's destruction of Castle Erorn.

"Rhalina!"

She had almost reached the ship when Corum caught up with her and seized her by the arm with his good hand.

She seemed oblivious of him, continued to try to reach the ship.

"Rhalina! What bargain did you make to save us? Why did this ship of the dead come here?"

Her voice was cold, toneless. "I will join my husband now."

"No, Rhalina. Such a bargain cannot be honored. It is obscene. It is evil. It—it . . ." He tried to express his knowledge that such things as this could not exist, that they were all under some peculiar hallucination. "Come back with me, Rhalina. Let the ship return to the depths."

"I must go with it. Those were the terms of our bargain."

He clung to her, trying to drag her back, and then another voice spoke. It was a voice that seemed without substance and yet which echoed in his skull and made him pause.

"She sails with us, Prince of the Vadhagh. This must be."

Corum looked up. The dead Margrave had raised his hand in a commanding gesture. The eyes of fire burned deeply into Corum's single eye.

Corum tried to alter his perspective, to see into the other dimensions around him. At last he succeeded.

But it made no difference. The ship was in each of the five dimensions. He could not escape it.

"I will not let her sail with you," Corum replied. "Your bargain was unjust. Why should she die?"

"She does not die. She will awaken soon."

"What? Beneath the waves?"

"She has given this ship life. Without it, we shall sink again. With her on board, we live."

"Live? You do not live."

"It is better than death."

"Then death must be something more awful than I imagined."

"For us it is, Prince of the Vadhagh. We are the slaves of Shool-an-Jyvan, for we died in the waters he rules. Now, let us be rejoined, my wife and myself."

"No." Corum took a firmer grip on Rhalina's arm. "Who is this Shool-an-Jyvan?"

"He is our master. He is of Svi-an-Fanla-Brool."

"The Home of the Gorged God!" The place where Corum had meant to go before Rhalina's love had kept him at Moidel's Castle. "Now. Let my wife come aboard."

"What can you do to make me? You are dead! You have only the power to frighten away barbarians."

"We saved your life. Now give us the means to live. She must come with us."

"The dead are selfish."

The corpse nodded and the green fire dimmed a little. "Aye. The dead are selfish."

Now Corum saw that the rest of the crew were beginning to move. He heard the slithering of their feet on the slime-grown deck. He saw their rotting flesh, their glowing eye sockets. He began to move backward, dragging Rhalina with him. But Rhalina would not go willingly and he was completely exhausted. Panting, he paused, speaking urgently to her. "Rhalina. I know you never loved him, even in life. You love me. I love you. Surely that is stronger than any bargain!"

"I must join my husband."

The dead crew had descended to the causeway and were moving toward them. Corum had left his sword behind. He had no weapons.

"Stand back!" he cried. "The dead have no right to take the living!"

On came the corpses.

Corum cried up to the figure of the Margrave, still on the poop. "Stop them! Take me instead of her! Make a bargain with me!"

"I cannot."

"Then let me sail with her. What is the harm in that? You will have two living beings to warm your dead souls!"

The Margrave appeared to consider this.

"Why should you do it? The living have no liking for the dead."

"I love Rhalina. It is love, do you understand?"

"Love? The dead know nothing of love."

"Yet you want your wife with you."

"She proposed the bargain. Shool-an-Jyvan heard her and sent us."

The shuffling corpses had completely surrounded them now. Corum gagged at their stench.

"Then I will come with you."

The dead Margrave inclined his head.

Escorted by the shuffling corpses, Corum allowed himself and

Rhalina to be led aboard the ship. It was covered in scum from the bottoms of the sea. Weed draped it, giving off the strange green fire. What Corum had thought were dull jewels were colored barnacles which encrusted everything. Slime lay on all surfaces.

While the Margravine watched from his poop, Corum and Rhalina were taken to a cabin and made to enter. It was almost pitch-black and it stank of decay.

He heard the rotting timbers creak and the ship began to move.

It sailed rapidly, without wind or any other understandable means of propulsion.

It sailed for Svi-an-Fanla-Brool, the island of the legends, the Home of the Gorged God.

BOOK TWO

In which Prince Corum receives a gift and makes a pact

The First Chapter

THE AMBITIOUS SORCERER

As they sailed through the night, Corum made many attempts to waken Rhalina from her trance, but nothing worked. She lay amongst the damp and rotting silks of a bunk and stared at the roof. Through a porthole too small to afford escape came a faint green light. Corum paced the cabin, still barely able to believe his predicament.

These were plainly the dead Margrave's own quarters. And if Corum were not here now, would the Margrave be sharing the bunk with his wife . . . ?

Corum shuddered and pressed his hand to his skull, certain that he was insane or had been entranced—certain that none of this could be.

As a Vadhagh he was prepared for many events and situations that would have seemed strange to the Mabden. Yet this was something that seemed completely unnatural to him. It defied all he knew of science. If he were sane and all was as it seemed, then the Mabden's powers were greater than anything the Vadhagh had known. Yet they were dark and morbid powers, unhealthy powers that were quintessentially evil . . .

Corum was tired, but he could not sleep. Everything he touched was slimy and made him feel ill. He tested the lock on the cabin door. Although the wood was rotten, the door seemed unusually strong. Some other force was at work here. The timbers of the ship were bound by more than rivets and tar.

The weariness did not help his head to clear. His thoughts remained confused and desperate. He peered frequently through the porthole, hoping to get some sort of bearing, but it was impossible to see anything more than the occasional wave and a star in the sky.

Then, much later, he noticed the first line of gray on the horizon and he was relieved that morning was coming. This ship was a ship of the night. It would disappear with the sun and he and Rhalina would awake to find themselves in their own bed.

But what had frightened the barbarians? Or was that part of the dream? Perhaps his collapse within the gates after his fight with Glandyth had induced a feverish dream? Perhaps his comrades were still fighting for their lives against the Pony Tribesmen. He rubbed at his head with the stump of his hand. He licked his dry lips and tried to peer, once again, into the dimensions. But the other dimensions were closed to him. He paced the cabin, waiting for the morning.

But then a strange droning sound came to his ears. It made his brain itch. He wrinkled his scalp. He rubbed his face. The droning increased. His ears ached. His teeth were on edge. The volume grew.

He put his good hand to one ear and covered the other with his arm. Tears came into his eye. In the socket where the other eye had been a huge pain pulsed.

He stumbled from side to side of the rotting cabin and even attempted to break through the door.

But his senses were leaving him. The scene grew dim . . .

. . . He stood in a dark hall with walls of fluted stone which curved over his head and touched to form the roof, high above. The workmanship of the hall was equal to anything the Vadhagh had created, but it was not beautiful. Rather, it was sinister.

His head ached.

The air before him shimmered with a pale blue light and then a tall youth stood there. The face was young, but the eyes were ancient. He was dressed in a simple flowing gown of yellow samite. He bowed, turned his back, walked a little way, and then sat down on a stone bench that had been built into the wall.

Corum frowned.

"You believe you dream, Master Corum?"

"I am Prince Corum in the Scarlet Robe, last of the Vadhagh race."

"There are no other princes here but me," said the youth softly. "I will allow none. If you understand that, there will be no tension between us."

Corum shrugged. "I believe I dream, yes."

"In a sense you do, of course. As we all dream. For some while, Vadhagh, you have been trapped in a Mabden dream. The rules of the Mabden control your fate and you resent it."

"Where is the ship that brought me here. Where is Rhalina?"

"The ship cannot sail by day. It has returned to the depths."

"Rhalina?"

The youth smiled. "She has gone with it, of course. That was the bargain she made."

"Then she is dead?"

"No. She lives."

"How can she live when she is below the surface of the ocean!"

"She lives. She always will. She cheers the crew enormously."

"Who are you?"

"I believe you have guessed my name."

"Shool-an-Jyvan."

"Prince Shool-an-Jyvan, Lord of All That Is Dead in the Sea—one of my several titles."

"Give me back Rhalina."

"I intend to."

Corum looked suspiciously at the sorcerer. "What?"

"You do not think I would bother to answer such a feeble attempt at a Summoning as the one she made, do you, if I did not have other motives in mind?"

"Your motive is clear. You relished the horror of her predicament."

"Nonsense. Am I so childish? I have outgrown such things. I see you are beginning to argue in Mabden terms. It is just as well for you, if you wish to survive in this Mabden dream."

"It is a dream . . . ?"

"Of sorts. Real enough. It is what you might call the dream of a God. There again you might say that it is a dream that a God has allowed to become reality. I refer of course to the Knight of the Swords who rules the Five Planes."

"The Sword Rulers! They do not exist. It is a superstition once entertained by the Vadhagh and the Nhadragh."

"The Sword Rulers do exist, Master Corum. You have one of them, at least, to thank for your misfortunes. It was the Knight of the Swords who decided to let the Mabden grow strong and destroy the Old Races."

"Why?"

"Because he was bored by you. Who would not be? The world has become more interesting now, I'm sure you will agree."

"Chaos and destruction is 'interesting'?" Corum made an impatient gesture. "I thought you had outgrown such childish ideas."

Shool-an-Jyvan smiled. "Perhaps I have. But has the Knight of the Swords?"

"You do not speak plainly, Prince Shool."

"True. A vice I find impossible to give up. Still, it enlivens a dull conversation sometimes."

"If you are bored with this conversation, return Rhalina to me and I will leave."

Shool smiled again. "I have it in my power to bring Rhalina back to you and to set you free. That is why I let Master Moidel answer her Summoning. I wished to meet you, Master Corum."

"You did not know I would come."

"I thought it likely."

"Why did you wish to meet me?"

"I have something to offer you. In case you refused my gift, I thought it wise to have Mistress Rhalina on hand."

"And why should I refuse a gift?"

Shool shrugged. "My gifts are sometimes refused. Folk are suspicious of me. The nature of my calling disturbs them. Few have a kind word for a sorcerer, Master Corum."

Corum peered around him in the gloom. "Where is the door? I will seek Rhalina myself. I am very weary, Prince Shool."

"Of course you are. You have suffered much. You thought your own sweet dream a reality and you thought reality a dream. A shock. There is no door. I have no need of them. Will you not hear me out?"

"If you choose to speak in a less elliptical manner, aye."

"You are a poor guest, Vadhagh. I thought your race a courteous one."

"I am no longer typical."

"A shame that the last of a race should not typify its virtues. However, I am, I hope, a better host and I will comply with your request. I am an ancient being. I am not of the Mabden and I am not of the folk you call the Old Races. I came before you. I belonged to a race which began to degenerate. I did not wish to degenerate and so I concerned myself with the discovery of scientific ways in which I could preserve my mind in all its wisdom. I discovered the means to do such a thing, as you see. I am, essentially, pure mind. I can transfer myself from one body to another, with some effort, and thus am immortal. Efforts have been made to extinguish me, over

86

the millenia, but they have never been successful. It would have involved the destruction of too much. Therefore I have, generally speaking, been allowed to continue my existence and my experiments. My wisdom has grown. I control both Life and Death. I can destroy and I can bring back to life. I can give other beings immortality, if I choose. By my own mind and my own skill I have become, in short, a God. Perhaps not the most powerful of the Gods—but that will come eventually. Now you will understand that the Gods who simply"—Shool spread his hands—"*popped* into existence—who exist only through some cosmic fluke—why, they resent me. They refuse to acknowledge my Godhood. They are jealous. They would like to have done with me for I disturb their self-esteem. The Knight of the Swords is my enemy. He wishes me dead. So, you see, we have much in common, Master Corum."

"I am no 'God,' Prince Shool. In fact, until recently, I had no belief in gods, either."

"The fact that you are not a God, Master Corum, is evident from your obtuseness. That is not what I meant. What I did mean was this—we are both the last representatives of races whom, for reasons of their own, the Sword Rulers decided to destroy. We are both, in their eyes, anachronisms which must be eradicated. As they replaced my folk with the Vadhagh and the Nhadragh, so they are replacing the Vadhagh and the Nhadragh with the Mabden. A similar degeneration is taking place in your people—forgive me if I associate you with the Nhadragh—as it did in mine. Like me, you have attempted to resist this, to fight against it. I chose science— you chose the sword. I will leave it to you to decide which was the wisest choice . . ."

"You seem somewhat petty for a God," Corum said, losing his patience. "Now . . ."

"I am a petty God at the moment. You will find me more lordly and benign when I achieve the position of a greater God. Will you let me continue, Master Corum? Can you not understand that I have acted, so far, out of fellow feeling for you?"

"Nothing you have done so far seems to indicate your friendship."

"I said fellow feeling, not friendship. I assure you, Master Corum, I could destroy you in an instant—and your lady, too."

"I would feel more patience if I knew you had released her from that dreadful bargain she made and brought her here so that I could see for myself that she still lives and is capable of being saved."

"You will have to take my word."

"Then destroy me."

Prince Shool got up. His gestures were the testy gestures of a very old man. They did not match the youthful body at all and made the sight of him even more obscene. "You should have greater respect for me, Master Corum."

"Why is that? I have seen a few tricks and heard a great deal of pompous talk."

"I am offering you much, I warn you. Be more pleasant to me."

"What are you offering me?"

Prince Shool's eyes narrowed.

"I am offering you your life. I could take it."

"You have told me that."

"I am offering you a new hand and a new eye."

Corum's interest evidently betrayed itself, for Prince Shool chuckled.

"I am offering you the return of this Mabden female you have such a perverse affection for." Prince Shool raised his hand. "Oh, very well. I apologize. Each to his own pleasures, I suppose. I am offering you the opportunity to take vengeance on the cause of your ills . . ."

"Glandyth-a-Krae?"

"No, no, no! The Knight of the Swords! The Knight of the Swords! The one who allowed the Mabden to take root in the first place in this plane!"

"But what of Glandyth? I have sworn his destruction."

"You accuse *me* of pettiness. Your ambitions are tiny. With the powers I offer you, you can destroy any number of Mabden earls!"

"Continue . . ."

"Continue? Continue? Have I not offered you enough?"

"You do not say how you propose to make these offers into something more than so much breath."

"Oh, you are insulting! The Mabden fear me! The Mabden gibber when I materialize myself. Some of them die of terror when I make my powers manifest!"

"I have seen too much horror of late," Prince Corum said.

"That should make no difference. Your trouble is, Vadhagh, that these horrors I employ are Mabden horrors. You associate with Mabden, but you are still a Vadhagh. The dark dreams of the Mabden frighten you less than they frighten the Mabden themselves. If you had been a Mabden, I should have had an easier task of convincing you . . ."

"But you could not use a Mabden for the task you have in mind," Corum said grimly. "Am I right?"

"Your brains are sharpening. That is exactly the truth. No Mabden could survive what you must survive. And I am not sure that even a Vadhagh . . ."

"What is the task?"

"To steal something I need if I am to develop my ambitions further."

"Could you not steal it yourself?"

"Of course not. How could I leave my island? They would destroy me then, of a certainty."

"Who would destroy you?"

"My rivals, of course—the Sword Rulers and the rest! I only survive because I protect myself with all manner of devices and spells which, though they have, at this moment, the power to break, they dare not do so for fear of the consequences. To break my spells might lead to the very dissolution of the Fifteen Planes—and the extinction of the Sword Rulers themselves. No, you must do the thieving for me. No other, in this whole plane, would have the courage—or the motivation. For if you do this thing, I will restore Rhalina to you. And, if you still wish it, you will have the power to take your vengeance on Glandyth-a-Krae. But, I assure you, the real one to blame for the very existence of Glandyth is the Knight of the Swords, and by stealing this thing from him, you will be thoroughly avenged."

Corum said, "What must I steal?"

Shool chuckled. "His heart, Master Corum."

"You wish me to kill a God and take his heart . . ."

"Plainly you know nothing of Gods. If you killed the Knight, the consequences would be unimaginable. He does not keep his heart in his breast. It is better guarded than that. His heart is kept on this plane. His brain is kept on another—and so on. This protects him, do you see?"

Corum sighed. "You must explain more later. Now. Release Rhalina from that ship and I will try to do what you ask of me."

"You are excessively obstinate, Master Corum!"

"If I am the only one who can help you further your ambitions, Prince Shool, then I can surely afford to be."

The young lips curled in a growl that was almost Mabden. "I am glad you are not immortal, Master Corum. Your arrogance will only plague me for a few hundred years at most. Very well, I will show you Rhalina. I will show that she is safe. But I will not release her. I will keep her here and deliver her to you when the heart of the Knight of the Swords is brought to me."

"What use is the heart to you?"

"With it, I can bargain very well."

"You may have the ambitions of a God, Master Shool, but you have the methods of a peddler."

"*Prince* Shool. Your insults do not touch me. Now . . ."

* * *

Shool disappeared behind a cloud of milky green smoke that came from nowhere. A scene formed in the smoke. Corum saw the ship of the dead and he saw the cabin. He saw the corpses of the Margrave embracing the living flesh of his wife, Rhalina, the Margravine. And Corum saw that Rhalina was shouting with horror but unable to resist.

"You said she would be unharmed! Shool! You said she would be safe!"

"So she is—in the arms of a loving husband," came an offended voice from nowhere.

"Release her, Shool!"

The scene dissolved. Rhalina stood panting and terrified in the chamber that had no door. "Corum?"

Corum ran forward and held her, but she drew away with a shudder. "Is it Corum? Are you some phantom? I made a bargain to save Corum . . ."

"I am Corum. In turn, I have made a bargain to save you, Rhalina."

"I had not realized it would be so foul. I did not understand the terms. . . . He was going to . . ."

"Even the dead have their pleasures, Mistress Rhalina." An anthropoid creature in a green coat and breeks stood behind them. It noted Corum's astonishment with pleasure. "I have several bodies I can utilize. This was an ancestor of the Nhadragh, I think. One of those races."

"Who is it, Corum?" Rhalina asked. She drew closer to him and he held her comfortingly now. Her whole body shook. Her skin was oddly damp.

"This is Shool-an-Jyvan. He claims to be a God. It was he who saw that your Summoning was answered. He has suggested that I perform an errand for him and in return he will allow you to live safely here until I return. Then we will leave together."

"But why did he . . . ?"

"It was not you I wanted but your lover," Shool said impatiently. "Now that I have broken my promise to your husband I have lost my power over him! It is irritating."

"You have lost your power over Moidel, the Margrave?" Rhalina asked.

"Yes, yes. He is completely dead. It would be far too much effort to revive him again."

"I thank you for releasing him," Rhalina said.

"It was no wish of mine. Master Corum made me do it." Prince

Shool sighed. "However, there are plenty more corpses in the sea. I shall have to find another ship, I suppose."

Rhalina fainted. Corum supported her with his good hand.

"You see," Shool said, with a trace of triumph, "the Mabden fear me excellently."

"We will need food, fresh clothing, beds, and the like," Corum said, "before I will discuss anything further with you, Shool."

Shool vanished.

A moment later the large room was full of furniture and everything else Corum had desired.

Corum could not doubt Shool's powers, but he did doubt the being's sanity. He undressed Rhalina and washed her and put her into bed. She awoke then and her eyes were still full of fear, but she smiled at Corum. "You are safe now," he said. "Sleep."

And she slept.

Now Corum bathed himself and inspected the clothes that had been laid out for him. He pursed his lips as he picked up the folded garments and looked at the armor and weapons that had also been provided. They were Vadhagh clothes. There was even a scarlet robe that was almost certainly his own.

He began to consider the implications of his alliance with the strange and amoral sorcerer of Svi-an-Fanla-Brool.

The Second Chapter

THE EYE OF RHYNN
AND THE HAND OF KWLL

Corum had been asleep.

Now, suddenly, he was standing upright. He opened his eyes.

"Welcome to my little shop." Shool's voice came from behind him. He turned. This time he confronted a beautiful girl of about fifteen. The chuckle that came from the young throat was obscene.

Corum looked around the large room. It was dark and it was cluttered. All manner of plants and stuffed animals filled it. Books and manuscripts teetered on crazily leaning shelves. There were crystals of a peculiar color and cut, bits of armor, jeweled swords, rotting sacks from which treasure, as well as other, nameless, substances, spilled. There were paintings and figurines, an assortment of instruments and gauges, including balances, and what appeared to be clocks with eccentric divisions marked in languages Corum did not know. Living creatures scuffled amongst the piles or chittered in corners. The place stank of dust and mold and death.

"You do not, I think, attract many customers," Corum said.

Shool sniffed. "There are not many I should desire to serve. Now . . ." In his young girl's form, he went to a chest that was partially covered by the shining skins of a beast that must have been large and fierce in life. He pushed away the skins and muttered something over the chest. Of its own accord, the lid flew back. A cloud of black stuff rose from within and Shool staggered away a pace or two, waving his hands and screaming in a strange speech. The black cloud vanished. Cautiously, Shool approached the chest and peered in. He smacked his lips in satisfaction. ". . . here we are!"

He drew out two sacks, one smaller than the other. He held them up, grinning at Corum. "Your gifts."

"I thought you were going to restore my hand and my eye."

"Not 'restore,' exactly. I am going to give you a much more useful gift than that. Have you heard of the Lost Gods?"

"I have not."

"The Lost Gods who were brothers? Their names were Lord Rhynn and Lord Kwll. They existed even before I came to grace the universe. They became involved in a struggle of some kind, the nature of which is now obscured. They vanished, whether voluntarily or involuntarily, I do not know. But they left a little of themselves behind." He held up the sacks again. "These."

Corum gestured impatiently.

Shool put out his girl's tongue and licked his girl's lips. The old eyes glittered at Corum. "The gifts I have here, they once belonged to those warring Gods. I heard a legend that they fought to the death and only these remained to mark the fact that they had existed at all." He opened the smaller sack. A large object fell into his hand. He held it out for Corum to see. It was jeweled and faceted. The jewels shone with somber colors, deep reds and blues and blacks.

"It is beautiful," said Corum, "but I . . ."

"Wait." Shool emptied the larger sack on the lid of the chest, which had closed. He picked up the object and displayed it.

Corum gasped. It seemed to be a gauntlet with room for five slender fingers and a thumb. It, too, was covered with strange, dark jewels.

"That gauntlet is of no use to me," Corum said. "It is for a left hand with six fingers. I have five fingers and no left hand."

"It is not a gauntlet. It is Kwll's hand. He had four, but he left one behind. Struck off by his brother, I understand . . ."

"Your jokes do not appeal to me, Sorcerer. They are too ghoulish. Again, you waste time."

"You had best get used to my jokes, as you call them, Master Vadhagh."

"I see no reason to."

"These are the gifts. To replace your missing eye—I offer you the Eye of Rhynn. To replace your missing hand—the Hand of Kwll!"

Corum's mouth curved with nausea. "I'll have nothing of them! I want no dead being's limbs! I thought you would give me back my own! You have tricked me, sorcerer!"

"Nonsense. You do not understand the properties these things possess. They will give you greater powers than any of your race or the Mabden has ever known! The eye can see into areas of time and space never observed before by a mortal. And the hand—the hand

93

can summon aid from those areas. You do not think I would send you into the lair of the Knight of the Swords without some supernatural aid, do you?''

"What is the extent of their powers?"

Shool shrugged his young girl's shoulders. "I have not had the opportunity to test them."

"So there could be danger in using them?"

"Why should there be?"

Corum became thoughtful. Should he accept Shool's disgusting gifts and risk the consequences in order to survive, slay Glandyth, and rescue Rhalina? Or should he prepare to die now and end the whole business?

Shool said, "Think of the knowledge these gifts will bring you. Think of the things you will see on your travels. No mortal has ever been to the domain of the Knight of the Swords before! You can add much to your wisdom, Master Corum. And remember—it is the Knight who is ultimately responsible for your doom and the deaths of your folk . . .''

Corum drew deeply of the musty air. He made up his mind.

"Very well, I will accept your gifts."

"I am honored," Shool said sardonically. He pointed a finger at Corum and Corum reeled backward, fell amongst a pile of bones, and tried to rise. But he felt drowsy. "Continue your slumbers, Master Corum," Shool said.

He was back in the room in which he had originally met Shool. There was a fierce pain in the socket of his blind eye. There was a terrible agony in the stump of his left hand. He felt drained of energy. He tried to look about him, but his vision would not clear.

He heard a scream. It was Rhalina.

"Rhalina! Where are you?"

"I—I am here—Corum. What has been done to you? Your face—your hand . . .''

With his right hand he reached up to touch his blind socket. Something warm shifted beneath his fingers. It was an eye! But it was an eye of an unfamiliar texture and size. He knew then that it was Rhynn's eye. His vision began to clear.

He saw Rhalina's horrified face. She was sitting up in the bed, her back stiff with horror.

He looked down at his left hand. It was of similar proportions to the old, but it was six-fingered and the skin was like that of a jeweled snake.

He staggered as he strove to accept what had happened to him. "They are Shool's gifts," he murmured inanely. "They are the Eye

94

of Rhynn and the Hand of Kwll. They were Gods—the Lost Gods, Shool said. Now I am whole again, Rhalina.''

''Whole? You are something more and something less than whole, Corum. Why did you accept such terrible gifts? They are evil. They will destroy you!''

''I accepted them so that I might accomplish the task that Shool has set me, and thus gain the freedom of us both. I accepted them so that I might seek out Glandyth and, if possible, strangle him with this alien hand. I accepted them because if I did not accept them, I would perish.''

''Perhaps,'' she said softly, ''it would be better for us to perish.''

The Third Chapter

BEYOND THE FIFTEEN PLANES

"What powers I have, Master Corum! I have made myself a God and I have made you a demi-God. They will have us in their legends soon."

"You are already in their legends." Corum turned to confront Shool, who had appeared in the room in the guise of a bearlike creature wearing an elaborate plumed helmet and trews. "And for that matter so are the Vadhagh."

"We'll have our own cycle soon, Master Corum. That is what I meant to say. How do you feel?"

"There is still some pain in my wrist and in my head."

"But no sign of a join, eh? I am a master surgeon! The grafting was perfect and accomplished with the minimum of spells!"

"I see nothing with the Eye of Rhynn, however," Corum said. "I am not sure it works, sorcerer."

Shool rubbed his paws together. "It will take time before your brain is accustomed to it. Here, you will need this, too." He produced something resembling a miniature shield of jewels and enamelwork with a strap attached to it. "It is to put over your new eye."

"And blind myself again!"

"Well, you do not want to be forever peering into those worlds beyond the Fifteen Planes, do you?"

"You mean the eye only sees there?"

"No. It sees here, too, but not always in the same kind of perspective."

Corum frowned suspiciously at the sorcerer. The action made him blink. Suddenly, through his new eye, he saw many new images, while still staring at Shool with his ordinary eye. They were

96

dark images and they shifted until eventually one predominated.

"Shool! What is this world?"

"I am not sure. Some say there are another Fifteen Planes which are a kind of distorted mirror image of our own planes. That could be such a place, eh?"

Things boiled and bubbled, appeared and disappeared. Creatures crept upon the scene and then crept back again. Flames curled, land turned to liquid, strange beasts grew to huge proportions and shrank again, flesh seemed to flow and reform.

"I am glad I do not belong to that world," Corum murmured. "Here, Shool, give me the shield."

He took the thing from the sorcerer and positioned it over the eye. The scenes faded and now he saw only Shool and Rhalina—but with both eyes.

"Ah, I did not point out that the shield protects you from visions of the other worlds, not of this one."

"What did you see, Corum?" Rhalina asked quietly.

He shook his head. "Nothing I could easily describe."

Rhalina looked at Shool. "I wish you would take back your gifts, Prince Shool. Such things are not for mortals."

Shool grimaced. "He is not a mortal now. I told you, he is a demi-God."

"And what will the Gods think of that?"

"Well, naturally, some of them will be displeased if they ever discover Master Corum's new state of being. I think it unlikely, however."

Rhalina said grimly, "You talk of these matters too lightly, Sorcerer. If Corum does not understand the implications of what you have done to him, I do. There are laws which mortals must obey. You have transgressed those laws and you will be punished— as your creations will be punished and destroyed!"

Shool waved his bear's arm dismissively. "You forget that I have a great deal of power. I shall soon be in a position to defy any God upstart enough to lock swords with me."

"You are insane with pride," she said. "You are only a mortal sorcerer!"

"Be silent, Mistress Rhalina! Be silent for I can send you to a far worse fate than that which you have just escaped! If Master Corum here were not useful to me, you would both be enjoying some foul form of suffering even now. Watch your tongue. Watch your tongue!"

"We are wasting time again," Corum put in. "I wish to get my task over with so that Rhalina and I can leave this place."

Shool calmed down, turned and said, "You are a fool to give so much for this creature. She, like all her kind, fears knowledge, fears the deep, dark wisdom that brings power."

"We'll discuss the heart of the Knight of the Swords," Corum said. "How do I steal it?"

"Come," said Shool.

They stood in a garden of monstrous blossoms that gave off an almost overpoweringly sweet scent. The sun was red in the sky above them. The leaves of the plants were dark, near-black. They rustled.

Shool had returned to his earlier form of a youth dressed in a flowing blue robe. He led Corum along a path.

"This garden I have cultivated for millenia. It has many peculiar plants. Filling most of the island not filled by my castle, it serves a useful purpose. It is a peaceful place in which to relax, it is hard for any unwanted guests to find their way through."

"Why is the island called the Home of the Gorged God?"

"I named it that—after the being from whom I inherited it. Another God used to dwell here, you see, and all feared him. Looking for a safe place where I could continue with my studies, I found the island. But I had heard that a fearsome God inhabited it and, naturally, I was wary. I had only a fraction of my present wisdom then, being little more than a few centuries old, so I knew that I did not have the power to destroy a God."

A huge orchid reached out and stroked Corum's new hand. He pulled it away.

"Then how did you take over his island?" he asked Shool.

"I heard that the God ate children. One a day was sacrificed to him by the ancestors of those you call the Nhadragh. Having plenty of money it occurred to me to buy a good number of children and feed them to him all at once, to see what would happen."

"What did happen?"

"He gobbled them all and fell into a gorged slumber."

"And you crept up and killed him!"

"No such thing! I captured him. He is still in one of his own dungeons somewhere, though he is no longer the fine being he was when I inherited his palace. He was only a little God, of course, but some relative to the Knight of the Swords. That is another reason why the Knight, or any of the others, does not trouble me too much, for I hold Pliproth prisoner."

"To destroy your island would be to destroy their brother?"

"Quite."

"And that is another reason why you must employ me to do this piece of thievery. You are afraid that if you leave they will be able to extinguish you."

"Afraid? Not at all. But I exercise a reasonable degree of caution. That is why I still exist."

"Where is the heart of the Knight of the Swords?"

"Well, it lies beyond the Thousand League Reef, of which you have doubtless heard."

"I believe I read a reference to it in some old Geography. It lies to the north, does it not?" Corum untangled a vine from his leg.

"It does."

"Is that all you can tell me?"

"Beyond the Thousand-League Reef is a place called Urde that is sometimes land and sometimes water. Beyond that is the desert called Dhroonhazat. Beyond the desert are the Flamelands where dwells the Blind Queen, Ooresé. And beyond the Flamelands is the Ice Wilderness, where the Brikling wander."

Corum paused to peel a sticky leaf from his face. The thing seemed to have tiny red lips which kissed him. "And beyond that?" he asked sardonically.

"Why, beyond that is the domain of the Knight of the Swords."

"These strange lands. On which plane are they situated?"

"On all five where the Knight has influence. Your power to move through the planes will be of no great use to you, I regret."

"I am not sure I still have that power. If you speak truth, the Knight of the Swords has been taking that power away from the Vadhagh."

"Worry not, you have powers that are just as good." Shool reached over and patted Corum's strange new hand.

That hand was now responding like any ordinary limb. From curiosity, Corum used it to lift the jeweled patch that covered his jeweled eye. He gasped and lowered the patch again quickly.

Shool said, "What did you see?"

"I saw a place."

"Is that all?"

"A land over which a black sun burned. Light rose from the ground, but the black sun's rays almost extinguished it. Four figures stood before me. I glimpsed their faces and . . ." Corum licked his lips. "I could look no longer."

"We touch on so many planes," Shool mused. "The horrors that exist and we only sometimes catch sight of them—in dreams, for instance. However, you must learn to confront those faces and all the other things you see with your new eye, if you are to use your powers to the full."

"It disturbs me, Shool, to know that those dark, evil planes do exist and that around me lurk so many monstrous creatures, separated only by some thin, astral fabric.''

"I have learned to live knowing such things—and using such things. You become used to almost everything in a few millenia.''

Corum pulled a creeper from around his waist. ''Your garden plants seem overfriendly.''

"They are affectionate. They are my only real friends. But it is interesting that they like you. I tend to judge a being on how my plants react to him. Of course, they are hungry, poor things. I must induce a ship or two to put in to the island soon. We need meat. We need meat. All this preparation has made me forgetful of my regular duties.''

"You still have not described very closely how I may find the Knight of the Swords.''

"You are right. Well, the Knight lives in a palace on top of a mountain that is in the very center of both this planet and the five planes. In the top-most tower of that palace he keeps his heart. It is well guarded, I understand.''

"And is that all you know? You do not know the nature of his protection?''

"I am employing you, Master Corum, because you have a few more brains, a jot more resilience, and a fraction more imagination and courage than the Mabden. It will be up to you to discover what is the nature of his protection. You may rely upon one thing, however.''

"What is it, Master Shool?''

"Prince Shool. You may rely upon the fact that he will not be expecting any kind of attack from a mortal such as yourself. Like the Vadhagh, Master Corum, the Sword Rulers grow complacent. We all climb up. We all fall down.'' Shool chuckled. ''And the planes go on turning, eh?''

"And when you have climbed up, will you not fall down?''

"Doubtless—in a few billenia. Who knows? I could rise so high I could control the whole movement of the multiverse. I could be the first truly omniscient and omnipotent God. Oh, what games I could play!''

"We studied little of mysticism amongst the Vadhagh folk,'' Corum put in, ''but I understood all Gods to be omniscient and omnipotent.''

"Only on very limited levels. Some Gods—the Mabden patheon, such as the Dog and the Horned Bear—are more or less omniscient concerning the affairs of Mabden, and they can, if they wish, control those affairs to a large degree. But they know nothing of my affairs and even less of those of the Knight of the Swords, who knows most things, save those that happen upon my well-protected island. This is an Age of Gods, I am afraid, Master Corum. There are many, big and small, and they crowd the universe. Once it was not so. Sometimes, I suspect, the universe manages with none at all!"

"I had thought that."

"It would come to pass. It is thought," Shool tapped his skull, "that creates Gods and Gods who create thought. There must be periods when thought—which I sometimes consider overrated—does not exist. Its existence or lack of it does not concern the universe, after all. But if I had the power—I would *make* the universe concerned!" Shool's eyes shone. "I would alter its very nature! I would change all the conditions! You are wise to aid me, Master Corum."

Corum jerked his head back as something very much like a gigantic mauve tulip, but with teeth, snapped at him.

"I doubt it, Shool. But then I have no choice."

"Indeed, you have not. Or, at least, your choice is much limited. It is the ambition I hold not to be forced to make choices, on however large a scale, which drives me on, Master Corum."

"Aye," nodded Corum ironically. "We are all mortal."

"Speak for yourself, Master Corum."

BOOK THREE

*In Which Prince Corum achieves that
which is both impossible and unwelcome*

The First Chapter

THE WALKING GOD

Corum's leavetaking from Rhalina had not been easy. It had been full of tension. There had been no love in her eyes as he had embraced her, only concern for him and fear for both of them.

This had disturbed him, but there had been nothing he could do.

Shool had given him a quaintly shaped boat and he had sailed away. Now sea stretched in all directions. With a lodestone to guide him, Corum sailed north for the Thousand-League Reef.

Corum knew that he was mad, in Vadhagh terms. But he supposed that he was sane enough in Mabden terms. And this was, after all, now a Mabden world. He must learn to accept its peculiar disorders as the norm, if he were to survive. And there were many reasons why he wished to survive, Rhalina not least among them. He was the last of the Vadhagh, yet he could not believe it. The powers available to sorcerers like Shool might be controlled by others. The nature of time could be tampered with. The circling planes could be halted in their course, perhaps reversed. The events of the past year could be changed, perhaps eradicated completely. Corum proposed to live and, in living, to learn.

And if he learned enough, perhaps he would gain sufficient power to fulfill his ambitions and restore a world to the Vadhagh and the Vadhagh to the world.

It would be just, he thought.

● ● ●

The boat was of beaten metal on which were many raised and assymetrical designs. It gave off a faint glow which offered Corum both heat and light during the nights, for the sailing was long. Its single mast bore a single square sail of samite smeared with a strange substance that also shone and turned, without Corum's guidance, to catch any wind. Corum sat in the boat wrapped in his scarlet robe, his war gear laid beside him, his silver helm upon his head, his double byrnie covering him from throat to knee. From time to time he would hold up his lodestone by its string. The stone was shaped like an arrow and the head pointed always north.

He thought much of Rhalina and his love for her. Such a love had never before existed between a Vadhagh and a Mabden. His own folk might have considered his feelings for Rhalina degenerate, much as a Mabden would suspect such feelings in a man for his mare, but he was attracted to her more than he had been attracted to any Vadhagh woman and he knew that her intelligence was a match for his. It was her moods he found hard to understand—her intimations of doom—her superstition.

Yet Rhalina knew this world better than he. It could be that she was right to entertain such thoughts. His lessons were not yet over.

On the third night, Corum slept, his new hand on the boat's tiller, and in the morning he was awakened by bright sunshine in his eyes.

Ahead lay the Thousand-League Reef.

It stretched from end to end of the horizon and there seemed to be no gap in the sharp fangs of rock that rose from the foaming sea.

Shool had warned him that few had ever found a passage through the reef and now he could understand why. The reef was unbroken. It seemed not of natural origin at all, but to have been placed there by some entity as a bastion against intruders. Perhaps the Knight of the Swords had built it.

Corum decided to sail in an easterly direction along the reef, hoping to find somewhere where he could land the boat and perhaps drag it overland to the waters that lay beyond the reef.

He sailed for another four days, without sleep, and the reef offered neither a passage through nor a place to land.

A light mist, tinged pink by the sun, now covered the water in all directions and Corum kept away from the reef by using his lodestone and by listening for the sounds of the surf on the rocks. He drew out his maps, pricked out on skin, and tried to judge his position. The maps were crude and probably inaccurate, but they were the best Shool had had. He was nearing a narrow channel between the reef and a land marked on the map as Khoolocrah. Shool had been unable to tell him much about the land, save that a race called the Ragha-da-Kheta lived thereabouts.

In the light from the boat, he peered at the maps, hoping to distinguish some gap in the reef marked there, but there was none.

Then the boat began to rock rapidly and Corum glanced about him, seeking the source of this sudden eddy. Far away, the surf boomed, but then he heard another sound, to the south of him, and he looked there.

The sound was a regular rushing and slapping noise, like that of a man wading through a stream. Was this some beast of the sea? The Mabden seemed to fear many such monsters. Corum clung desperately to the sides, trying to keep the boat on course away from the rocks, but the waves increased their agitation.

And the sound came closer.

Corum picked up his long, strong sword and readied himself.

He saw something in the mist then. It was a tall, bulky shape—the outline of a man. And the man was dragging something behind him. A fishing net! Were the waters so shallow, then? Corum leaned over the side and lowered his sword, point downward, into the sea. It did not touch bottom. He could make out the ocean floor a long way below him. He looked back at the figure. Now he realized that his eyes and the mist had played tricks on him. The figure was still some distance from him and it was gigantic—far huger than the Giant of Laahr. This was what made the waves so large. This was why the boat rocked so.

Corum made to call out, to ask the gigantic creature to move away lest he sink the boat, then he thought better of it. Beings like this were considered to think less kindly of mortals than did the Giant of Laahr.

Now the giant, still cloaked in mist, changed his course, still fishing. He was behind Corum's boat and he trudged on through the water, dragging his nets behind him.

The wash sent the boat flying away from the Thousand-League Reef, heading almost due east, and there was nothing Corum could do to stop it. He fought with the sail and the tiller, but they would not respond. It was as if he was borne on a river rushing toward a chasm. The giant had set up a current which he could not fight.

There was nothing for it but to allow the boat to bear him where it would. The giant had long since disappeared in the mist, heading toward the Thousand-League Reef, where perhaps he lived.

Like a shark pouncing on its prey, the little boat moved, until suddenly it broke through the mist into hot sunshine.

And Corum saw a coast. Cliffs rushed at him.

The Second Chapter

TEMGOL-LEP

Desperately Corum tried to turn the boat away from the cliffs. His six-fingered left hand gripped the tiller and his right hand tugged at the sail.

Then there was a grinding sound. A shudder ran through the metal boat and it began to keel over. Corum grabbed at his weapons and managed to seize them before he was flung overboard and carried on by the wash. He gasped as water filled his mouth. He felt his body scrape on shingle and he tried to stagger upright as the current began to retreat. He saw a rock and grasped it, dropping his bow and his quiver of arrows, which were instantly swept away.

The sea retreated. He looked back and saw that his upturned boat had gone with it. He let go of the rock and climbed to his feet, buckling his swordbelt around his waist, straightening his helmet on his head, a sense of failure gradually creeping through him.

He walked a few paces up the beach and sat down beneath the tall, black cliff. He was stranded on a strange shore, his boat was gone and his goal now lay on the other side of an ocean.

At that moment Corum did not care. Thoughts of love, of hatred, of vengeance disappeared. He felt that he had left them all behind in the dream world that was Svi-an-Fanla-Brool. All he had left of that world was the six-fingered hand and the jeweled eye.

Reminded of the eye and what it had witnessed, he shivered. He reached up and touched the patch that covered it.

And then he knew that by accepting Shool's gifts, he had accepted the logic of Shool's world. He could not escape from it now.

Sighing, he got up and peered at the cliff. It was unscalable. He began to walk along the gray shingle, hoping to discover a place where he could climb to the top of the cliff and inspect the land in which he found himself.

He took a gauntlet given him by Shool and drew it over his hand. He remembered what Shool had told him, before he left, about the powers of the hand. He still only half-believed Shool's words and he was unwilling to test their veracity.

For more than an hour he trudged along the shore until he moved round a headland and saw a bay whose sides sloped gently upward and would be easily scaled. The tide was beginning to come in and would soon cover the beach. He began to run.

He reached the slopes and paused, panting. He had found safety in time. The sea had already covered the largest part of the beach. He climbed to the top of the slope and he saw the city.

It was a city of domes and minarets that blazed white in the light of the sun, but as he inspected it more closely Corum saw that the towers and domes were not white, but comprised of a multicolored mosaic. He had seen nothing like it.

He debated whether to avoid the city or approach it. If the people of the city were friendly, he might be able to get their help to find another boat. If they were Mabden, then they were probably unfriendly.

Were these the Rhaga-da-Kheta people mentioned on his maps? He felt for his pouch, but the maps had gone with the boat, as had his lodestone. Despair returned.

He set off toward the city.

Corum had traveled less than a mile before the bizarre cavalry came racing toward him—warriors mounted on long-necked speckled beasts with curling horns and wattles like those of a lizard. The spindly legs moved swiftly, however, and soon Corum could see that the warriors were also very tall and extremely thin, but with small, rounded heads and round eyes. These were not Mabden, but they were like no race he had ever heard of.

He stopped and waited. There was nothing else he could do until he discovered if they were his enemies or not.

Swiftly, they surrounded him, peering down at him through their huge, staring eyes. Their noses and their mouths were also round and their expressions were ones of permanent surprise.

"Olanja ko?" said one wearing an elaborate cloak and hood of bright feathers and holding a club fashioned like the claw of a giant bird. "Olanja ko, drajer?"

Using the Low Speech of the Vadhagh and the Nhadragh, which was the common tongue of the Mabden, Corum replied, "I do not understand this language."

The creature in the feather cloak cocked his head to one side and closed his mouth. The other warriors, all dressed and armed similarly, though not as elaborately, muttered amongst themselves.

Corum pointed roughly southward. "I come from across the sea." Now he used Middle Speech, which Vadhagh and Nhadragh had spoken, but not Mabden.

The rider leaned forward as if this sound was more familiar to him, but then he shook his head, understanding none of the words.

"Olanja ko?"

Corum also shook his head. The warrior looked puzzled and made a delicate scratching gesture at his cheek. Corum could not interpret the gesture.

The leader pointed at one of his followers. "Mor naffa!" The man dismounted and waved one of his spindly arms at Corum, gesturing that he climb on the long-necked beast.

With some difficulty, Corum managed to swing himself into the narrow saddle and sit there, feeling extreme discomfort.

"Hoj!" The leader waved to his men and turned his mount back toward the city. "Hoj—ala!"

The beasts jogged off, leaving the remaining warrior to make his way back to the city on foot.

The city was surrounded by a high wall patterned with many geometric designs of a thousand colors. They entered it through a tall, narrow gate, moved through a series of walls that were probably designed as a simple maze, and began to ride along a broad avenue of blooming trees toward a palace that lay at the center of the city.

Reaching the gates of the palace, they all dismounted, and servants, as thin and tall as the warriors, with the same astonished round faces, took away the mounts. Corum was led through the gates, up a staircase of more than a hundred steps, into an enclave. The designs on the walls of the palace were less colorful but more elaborate than those on the outer walls of the city. These were chiefly in gold, white, and pale blue. Although faintly barbaric, the workmanship was beautiful and Corum admired it.

They crossed the enclave and entered a courtyard that was surrounded by an enclosed walk and had a fountain in its center.

Under an awning was a large chair with a tapering back. The chair was made of gold and a design was picked out upon it in rubies. The warriors escorting Corum came to a halt and almost immediately a figure emerged from the interior. He had a huge, high headdress of peacock feathers, a great cloak, also of many brilliant feathers, and a kilt of thin gold cloth. He took his place on the throne. This, then, was the ruler of the city.

The leader of the warriors and his monarch conversed briefly in their own language and Corum waited patiently, not wishing to behave in any way that these people would judge to be unfriendly.

At length the two creatures stopped conversing. The monarch addressed Corum. He seemed to speak several different tongues until at length Corum heard him say, in a strange accent:

"Are you of the Mabden race?"

It was the old speech of the Nhadragh, which Corum had learned as a child.

"I am not," he replied haltingly.

"But you are not Nhedregh."

"Yes—I am not—'Nhedregh.' You know of that folk?"

"Two of them lived amongst us some centuries since. What race are you?"

"The Vadhagh."

The king sucked at his lips and smacked them. "The enemy, yes, of the Nhedregh?"

"Not now."

"Not now?" The king frowned.

"All the Vadhagh save me are dead," Corum explained. "And what is left of those you call Nhedregh have become degenerate slaves of the Mabden."

"But the Mabden are barbarians!"

"Now they are very powerful barbarians."

The king nodded. "This was predicted." He studied Corum closely. "Why are you not dead?"

"I chose not to die."

"No choice was yours if Arioch decided."

"Who is 'Arioch'?"

"The God."

"Which God?"

"The God who rules our destinies. Duke Arioch of the Swords."

"The Knight of the Swords?"

"I believe he is known by that title in the distant south." The king seemed deeply disturbed now. He licked his lips. "I am King Temgol-Lep. This is my city, Arke." He waved his thin hand. "These are my people, the Ragha-da-Kheta. This land is called Khoolocrah. We, too, soon shall die."

"Why so?"

"It is Mabden time. Arioch decides." The king shrugged his narrow shoulders. "Arioch decides. Soon the Mabden will come and destroy us."

"You will fight them, of course."

"No. It is Mabden time. Arioch commands. He lets the Ragha-

109

da-Kheta live longer because they obey him, because they do not resist him. But soon we shall die."

Corum shook his head. "Do you not think that Arioch is unjust to destroy you thus?"

"Arioch decides."

It occurred to Corum that these people had not been so fatalistic once. Perhaps they, too, were in a process of degeneration, caused by the Knight of the Swords.

"Why should Arioch destroy so much beauty and learning as you have here?"

"Arioch decides."

King Temgol-Lep seemed to be more familiar with the Knight of the Swords and his plans than anyone Corum had yet met. Living so much closer to his domain, perhaps they had seen him.

"Has Arioch told you this himself?"

"He has spoken through our wise ones."

"And the wise ones—they are certain of Arioch's will?"

"They are certain."

Corum sighed. "Well, I intend to resist his plans. I do not find them agreeable!"

King Temgol-Lep drew his lids over his eyes and trembled slightly. The warriors looked at him nervously. Evidently they recognized that the king was displeased.

"I will speak no more about Arioch," King Temgol-Lep said. "But as our guest we must entertain you. You will drink some wine with us."

"I will drink some wine. I thank you." Corum would have preferred food to begin with, but he was still cautious of giving offense to the Ragha-da-Kheta, who might yet supply him with the boat he needed.

The king spoke to some servants who were waiting in the shadows near the door into the palace. They went inside.

Soon they returned with a tray on which were tall, thin goblets and a golden jug. The king reached out and took the tray in his own hands, balancing it on his knee. Gravely, he poured wine into one of the cups and handed it to Corum.

Corum stretched out his left hand to receive the goblet.

The hand quivered.

Corum tried to control it, but it knocked the goblet away. The king looked startled and began to speak.

The hand plunged forward and its six fingers seized the king's throat.

King Temgol-Lep gurgled and kicked as Corum tried to pull the

110

Hand of Kwll away. But the fingers were locked on the throat. Corum could feel himself squeezing the life from the king.

Corum shouted for help before he realized that the warriors thought that he was attacking the king on his own volition. He drew his sword and hacked around him as they attacked with their oddly wrought clubs. They were plainly unused to battle, for their actions were clumsy and without proper coordination.

Suddenly the hand released King Temgol-Lep and Corum saw that he was dead.

His new hand had murdered a kindly and innocent creature! And it had ruined his chances of getting help from the Ragha-da-Kheta. It might even have killed him, for the warriors were very numerous.

Standing over the corpse of the king, he swept his sword this way and that, striking limbs from bodies, cutting into heads. Blood gushed everywhere and covered him, but he fought on.

Then, suddenly, there were no more living warriors. He stood in the courtyard while the gentle sun beat down and the fountain played and he looked at all the corpses. He raised his gauntleted alien hand and spat on it.

"Oh, evil thing! Rhalina was right! You have made me a murderer!"

But the hand was his again, it had no life of its own. He flexed the six fingers. It was now like any ordinary limb.

Save for the splashing of the water from the fountain, the courtyard was silent.

Corum looked back at the dead king and he shuddered. He raised his sword. He could cut the Hand of Kwll from him. Better to be crippled than to be the slave of so evil a thing!

And then the ground fell away from him and he plunged downward to fall with a crash upon the back of a beast that spit and clawed at him.

The Third Chapter

THE DARK THINGS COME

Corum saw daylight above and then the flagstone slid back and he was in darkness with the beast that dwelled in the pit beneath the courtyard. It was snarling in a corner somewhere. He prepared to defend himself against it.

Then the snarling stopped and there was silence for a moment. Corum waited.

He heard a shuffling. He saw a spark. The spark became a flame. The flame came from a wick that burned in a clay vessel full of oil.

The clay vessel was held by a filthy hand. And the hand belonged to a hairy creature whose eyes were full of anger.

"Who are you?" Corum said.

The creature shuffled again and placed the crude lamp on a niche on the wall. Corum saw that the chamber was covered in dirty straw. There was a pitcher and a plate and, at the far end, a heavy iron door. The place reeked of human excrement.

"Can you understand me?" Corum still spoke the Nhadragh tongue.

"Stop your gabbling." The creature spoke distantly, as if he did not expect Corum to know what he was saying. He had spoken in the Low Speech. "You will be like me soon."

Corum made no reply. He sheathed his sword and walked about the cell, inspecting it. There seemed no obvious way of escape. Above him he heard footsteps on the flagstones of the courtyard. He heard, quite clearly, the voices of the Rhaga-da-Kheta. They were agitated, almost hysterical.

The creature cocked his head and listened.

"So that is what happened," he mused, staring at Corum and grinning to himself. "You killed the feeble little coward, eh? Hm,

112

well I don't resent your company nearly so much. Though your stay will be short, I fear. I wonder how they will destroy you . . ."

Corum listened in silence, still not revealing that he understood the creature's words. He heard the sound of the corpses being dragged away overhead. More voices came and went.

"Now they are in a quandary," chuckled the creature. "They are only good at killing by stealth. What did they try to do to you, my friend, poison you? That's the way they usually get rid of those they fear."

Poison? Corum frowned. Had the wine been poisoned? He looked at the hand. Had it—*known?* Was it in some way sentient?

He decided to break his silence. "Who are you?" he said in the Low Speech.

The creature began to laugh. "So you can understand me! Well, since you are my guest, I feel you should answer my questions first. You look like a Vadhagh to me, yet I thought all the Vadhagh had perished long since. Name yourself and your folk, Friend."

Corum said, "I am Corum Jhaelen Irsei—the Prince in the Scarlet Robe. And I am the last of the Vadhagh."

"And I am Hanafax of Pengarde, something of a soldier, something of a priest, something of an explorer—and something of a wretch, as you see. I hail from a land called Lywm-an-Esh—a land far to the west where . . ."

"I know of Lywm-an-Esh. I have been a guest of the Margravine of the East."

"What? Does that Margravate still exist? I had heard it had been washed away by the encroaching seas long since!"

"It may be destroyed by now. The Pony Tribes . . ."

"By Urleh! Pony Tribes! It is something from the histories."

"How come you to be so far from your own land, Sir Hanafax?"

"It's a long tale, Prince Corum. Arioch—as he is called here—does not smile on the folk of Lywm-an-Esh. He expects all the Mabden to do his work for him—chiefly in the reduction of the older races, such as your own. As you doubtless know, our folk have had no interest in destroying these races, for they have never harmed us. But Urleh is a kind of vassal deity to the Knight of the Swords. It was Urleh that I served as a priest. Well, it seems that Arioch grows impatient (for reasons of his own) and commands Urleh to command the people of Lywm-an-Esh to embark on a crusade, to travel far to the west where a seafolk dwell. These folk are only about fifty in all and live in castles built into coral. They are called the Shalafen. Urleh gave me Arioch's command. I decided to believe that this was a false command—coming from another entity un-

113

friendly to Urleh. My luck, which was never of the best, changed greatly then. There was a murder. I was blamed. I fled my lands and stole a ship. After several somewhat dull adventures, I found myself amongst this twittering people who so patiently await Arioch's destruction. I attempted to band them together against Arioch. They offered me wine, which I refused. They seized me and placed me here, where I have been for more than a few months."

"What will they do with you?"

"I cannot say. Hope that I die eventually, I suppose. They are a misguided folk and a little stupid, but they are not by nature cruel. Yet their terror of Arioch is so great that they dare not do anything that might offend him. In this way they hope he will let them live a year or two longer."

"And you do not know how they will deal with me? I killed their king, after all."

"That is what I was considering. The poison has failed. They would be very reluctant to use violence on you themselves. We shall have to see."

"I have a mission to accomplish," Corum told him. "I cannot afford to wait."

Hanafax grinned. "I think you will have to, Friend Corum! I am something of a sorcerer, as I told you. I have a few tricks, but none will work in this place, I know not why. And if sorcery cannot aid us, what can?"

Corum raised his alien hand and stared at it thoughtfully.

Then he looked into the hairy face of his fellow prisoner. "Have you ever heard of the Hand of Kwll?"

Hanafax frowned. "Aye . . . I believe I have. The sole remains of a God, one of two brothers who had some sort of feud. . . . A legend, of course, like so many—"

Corum held up his left hand. "This is the Hand of Kwll. It was given me by a sorcerer, along with this eye—the Eye of Rhynn—and both have great powers, I am told."

"You do not know?"

"I have had no opportunity to test them."

Hanafax seemed disturbed. "Yet such powers are too great for a mortal, I would have thought. The consequences of using them would be monstrous . . ."

"I do not believe I have any choice. I have decided. I will call upon the powers of the Hand of Kwll and the Eye of Rhynn!"

"I trust you will remind them that I am on your side, Prince Corum."

Corum stripped the gauntlet from his six-fingered hand. He was

114

shivering with the tension. Then he pushed the patch up to his forehead.

He began to see the darker planes. Again he saw the landscape on which a black sun shone. Again he saw the four cowled figures.

And this time he stared into their faces.

He screamed.

But he could not name the reason for his terror.

He looked again.

The Hand of Kwll stretched out toward the figures. Their heads moved as they saw the hand. Their terrible eyes seemed to draw all the heat from his body, all the vitality from his soul. But he continued to look at them.

The Hand beckoned.

The dark figures moved toward Corum.

He heard Hanafax say, "I see nothing. What are you summoning? What do you see?"

Corum ignored him. He was sweating now and every limb save the Hand of Kwll was shaking.

From beneath their robes the four figures drew huge scythes.

Corum moved numbed lips. "Here. Come to this plane. Obey me."

They came nearer and seemed to pass through a swirling curtain of mist.

Then Hanafax cried out in terror and disgust. "Gods! They are things from the Pits of the Dog! Shefanhow!" He jumped behind Corum. "Keep them off me, Vadhagh! Aah!"

Hollow voices issued from the strangely distorted mouths: "Master. We will do your will. We will do the will of Kwll."

"Destroy that door!" Corum commanded.

"Will we have our prize, master?"

"What prize is that?"

"A life for each of us, Master."

Corum shuddered. "Aye, very well, you'll have your prize."

The scythes rose up and the door fell down and the four creatures that were truly "Shefanhow" led the way into a narrow passage.

"My kite!" Hanafax murmured to Corum. "We can escape on that."

"A kite?"

"Aye. It flies and can take both of us."

The Shefanhow marched ahead. From them radiated a force that froze the skin.

They mounted some steps and another door was burst by the scythes of the cloaked creatures. There was daylight.

They found themselves in the main courtyard of the palace.

From all sides came warriors. This time they did not seem so reluctant to kill Corum and Hanafax, but they paused when they saw the four cloaked beings.

"There are your prizes," Corum said. "Take as many as you will and then return to whence you came."

The scythes whirled in the sunshine. The Rhaga-da-Kheta fell back screaming.

The screaming grew louder.

The four began to titter. Then they began to roar. Then they began to echo the screams of their victims as their scythes swung and heads sprang from necks.

Sickened, Corum and Hanafax ran through the corridors of the palace. Hanafax led the way and eventually stopped outside a door.

Everywhere now the screams sounded and the loudest screams of all were those of the four.

Hanafax forced the door open. It was dark within. He began to rummage about in the room. "This is where I was when I was their guest. Before they decided that I had offended Arioch. I came here in my kite. Now . . ."

Corum saw more soldiers rushing down the corridor toward them.

"Find it quickly, Hanafax," he said. He leapt out to block the corridor with his sword.

The spindly beings came to a halt and looked at his sword. They raised their own bird-claw clubs and began cautiously to advance.

Corum's sword darted out and cut a warrior's throat. He collapsed in a tangle of legs and arms. Corum struck another in the eye.

The screams were dying now. Corum's foul allies were returning to their own plane with their prizes.

Behind Corum, Hanafax was dragging forth a dusty arrangment of rods and silk. "I have it, Prince Corum. Give me a short while to remember the spell I need."

Rather than being frightened by the deaths of their comrades, the Rhaga-da-Kheta seemed spurred on to fight more fiercely. Partly protected by a little mound of the slain, Corum fought on.

Hanafax began to call out something in a strange tongue. Corum felt a wind rise that ruffled his scarlet robe. Something grabbed him from behind and then he was rising into the air, over the heads of the Rhaga-da-Kheta, speeding along the corridor and into the open.

He looked down nervously.

The city was rushing past below them.

Hanafax dragged him into the box of yellow and green silk. Corum was sure he would fall, but the kite held.

The ragged, unkempt figure beside him was grinning.

"So the will of Arioch can be denied," Corum said.

"Unless we are his instruments in this," said Hanafax, his grin fading.

The Fourth Chapter

IN THE FLAMELANDS

Corum got used to the flight, though he still felt uncomfortable.
Hanafax hummed to himself while he chopped at his hair and
whiskers until a handsome, youngish face was revealed. Apparently without concern, he discarded his rags and drew on a clean
doublet and pair of breeks he had brought with him in his bundle.

"I feel a thousand times improved. I thank you, Prince Corum,
for visiting the City of Arke before I had entirely rotted away!"
Corum had discovered that Hanafax could not sustain his moods of
introspection but was naturally of a cheerful disposition.

"Where is this flying thing taking us, Sir Hanafax?"

"Ah, there's the problem," Hanafax said. "It is why I have
found myself in more trouble than I sought. I cannot—um—*guide*
the kite. It flies where it will."

They were over the sea now.

Corum clung to the struts and fixed his eyes ahead of him while
Hanafax began a song which was not complementary either to
Arioch or to the Dog God of the Eastern Mabden folk.

Then Corum saw something below and he said drily, "I would
advise you to forget the insults to Arioch. We appear to be flying
over the Thousand-League Reef. As I understand it, his domain lies
somewhere beyond that."

"A fair distance, though. I hope the kite brings us down soon."

They reached the coast. Corum screwed up his eyes as he tried
to make it out. Some of the time it seemed to consist of water alone
—a kind of huge inland sea—and some of the time the water vanished completely and only land could be seen. It was shifting all the
time.

"Is that Urde, Sir Hanafax?"

"I think it must be the place 'Urde' by its position and appearance. Unstable matter, Prince Corum, created by the Chaos Lords.''

"The Chaos Lords? I have not heard that term used before.''

"Have you not? Well, it is their will that rules you. Arioch is one of them. Long since there was a war between the forces of Order and the forces of Chaos. The forces of Chaos won and came to dominate the Fifteen Planes and, as I understand it, much that lies beyond them. Some say that Order was defeated completely and all her Gods vanished. They say the Cosmic Balance tipped too far in one direction and that is why there are so many arbitrary events taking place in the world. They say that once the world was *round* instead of dish-shaped. It is hard to accept, I agree.''

"Some Vadhagh legends say it was once round.''

"Aye. Well, the Vadhagh began their rise just before Order was banished. That is why the Sword Rulers hate the old races so much. They are not their creation at all. But the Great Gods are not allowed to interfere too directly in mortal affairs, so they have worked through the Mabden, chiefly . . .''

"Is this the truth?''

"It is *a* truth,'' Hanafax shrugged. "I know other versions of the same tale. But I am inclined to believe this one.''

"These Great Gods—you speak of the Sword Rulers?''

"Aye, the Sword Rulers and others. Then there are the Great Old Gods, to whom all the myriad planes of Earth are merely a tiny fragment in a greater mosaic.'' Hanafax shrugged. "This is the cosmology I was taught when I was a priest. I cannot vouch for its truth.''

Corum frowned. He looked below and now they were crossing a bleak yellow and brown desert. It was the desert called Dhroonhazat and it seemed entirely waterless. By an accident of fate he was being borne toward the Knight of the Swords faster than he had expected.

Or was it an accident of fate?

Now the heat was increasing and the sand below shimmered and danced. Hanafax licked his lips. "We're getting dangerously close to the Flamelands, Prince Corum. Look.''

On the horizon Corum saw a thin, flickering line of red light. The sky above it was also tinged red.

The kite sped nearer and the heat increased. To his astonishment, Corum saw that they were approaching a wall of flame that stretched as far as he could see in both directions.

"Hanafax, we shall be burned alive," he said softly.

"Aye, it seems likely.''

"Is there no means of turning this kite of yours?''

119

"I have tried, in the past. It is not the first time it has taken me away from one danger and into a worse one . . ."

The wall of fire was now so close that Corum could feel its direct heat burning his face. He heard it rumble and crackle and it seemed to feed on nothing but the air itself.

"Such a thing defies nature!" he gasped.

"Is that not a fair definition of all sorcery?" Hanafax said. "This is the Chaos Lords' work. The disruption of the natural harmony is, after all, their pleasure."

"Ah, this sorcery. It wearies my mind. I cannot grasp its logic."

"That is because it has none. It is arbitrary. The Lords of Chaos are the enemies of Logic, the jugglers of Truth, the molders of Beauty. I should be surprised if they had not created these Flame-lands out of some aesthetic impulse. Beauty—an ever-changing beauty—is all they live for."

"An evil beauty."

"I believe that such notions as 'good' and 'evil' do not exist for the Chaos Lords."

"I should like to make it exist for them." Corum mopped his sweating head with his coat sleeve.

"And destroy all their beauty?"

Corum darted an odd look at Hanafax. Was the Mabden on the side of the Knight? Had he, in fact, trapped Corum into accompanying him?

"There are other, quieter kinds of beauty, Sir Hanafax."

"True."

Everywhere below them now the flame yelled and leaped. The kite began to increase its height as its silk started to smolder. Corum was certain it would soon be destroyed by the fire and they would be plunged into the depths of the flame wall.

But now they were above it and, in spite of the silk's suddenly springing alive with little fires and Corum's feeling he was being roasted in his armor like a turtle in its shell, they now saw the other side of the wall.

A piece of the kite fell blazing away.

Hanafax, his face a bright red, his body running with sweat, clung to a strut and gasped, "Grasp a beam, Prince Corum! Grasp a beam!"

Corum took hold of one of the beams beneath his body as the burning silk was ripped from the frame and fluttered into the fires below. The kite dipped and threatened to follow the silk. It was losing height rapidly. Corum coughed as the burning air entered his

120

lungs. Blisters appeared on his right hand, though his left hand seemed immune.

The kite lurched and began to fall.

Corum was flung back and forth during the crazy descent, but he managed to keep his hold on the strut. Then there was a cracking sound, a mighty thump, and he lay amidst the wreckage on a surface of flat obsidian, the wall of flame behind him.

He raised his bruised body upright. It was still unbearably hot and the flames sang close to his back, rising a hundred feet or more into the air. The fused rock on which he stood was green and glistened and reflected the flame, seeming to writhe beneath his feet. A little distance to his left ran a sluggish river of molten lava, a few flames fluttering on its surface. Everywhere Corum looked was the same shining rock, the same red rivers of fire. He inspected the kite. It was completely useless. Hanafax was lying amongst its struts cursing it. He got up.

"Well," he kicked at the blackened, broken frame, "you'll never fly me into any more dangers!"

"I think this danger is all we need," Corum said. "It could be the last one we'll ever face."

Hanafax picked up his swordbelt from the wreckage and tied it round his waist. He found a singed cloak and put it on to protect his shoulders. "Aye, I think you could speak truth, Prince Corum. A poor place to meet one's end, eh?"

"According to some Mabden legends," Corum said, "we might already have met our ends and been consigned here. Are not certain Mabden netherworlds said to be made of eternally burning flame?"

Hanafax snorted. "In the East, perhaps. Well, we cannot go back, so I suppose we must go forward."

"I was told that an Ice Wilderness lay toward the north," Corum said. "Though how it does not melt being so near to the Flamelands, I do not know."

"Another quirk of the Lords of Chaos, doubtless."

"Doubtless."

They began to make their way over the slippery rock that burned their feet with every step, leaving the wall of flame behind them, leaping over rivulets of lava, moving so slowly and so circuitously that they were soon exhausted and paused to rest, look back at the distant flame wall, mop their brows, exchange daunted looks. Thirst now plagued them and their voices were hoarse.

"I think we are doomed, Prince Corum."

Corum nodded wearily. He looked up. Red clouds boiled above, like a dome of fire. It seemed that all the world burned.

121

"Have you no spells for bringing on rain, Sir Hanafax?"

"I regret not. We priests scorn such primitive tricks."

"Useful tricks. Sorcerers seem to enjoy only the spectacular."

"I am afraid it is so." Hanafax sighed. "What about your own powers? Can you not," he shuddered, "summon some kind of aid from whatever netherworld it is your horrid allies came?"

"I fear those allies are only useful in battle. I have no true conception of what they are or why they come. I have come to believe that the sorcerer who fitted me with this hand and this eye had no clearer idea himself. His work was something of an experiment, it seems."

"You have noticed, I take it, that the sun does not appear to set in the Flamelands. We can expect no night to come to relieve us."

Corum was about to reply when he saw something move on a rise of black obsidian a short distance away. "Hush, Sir Hanafax . . ."

Hanafax peered through the smoky heat. "What is it?"

And then they revealed themselves.

There were about a score of them, mounted on beasts whose bodies were covered in thick, scaly skin resembling plate armor. They had four short legs and cloven feet, a nest of horns jutted on heads and snouts, and small, red eyes gleamed at them. The riders were covered from head to foot in red garments of some shining material which hid even their faces and hands. They had long, barbed lances for weapons.

Silently, they surrounded Corum and Hanafax.

For a few moments there was silence, and then one of the riders spoke. "What do you in our Flamelands, Strangers?"

"We are not here from choice," replied Corum. "An accident brought us to your country. We are peaceful."

"You are not peaceful. You bear swords."

"We did not know there were any inhabitants to these lands," Hanafax said. "We seek help. We wish to leave."

"None may leave the Flamelands save to suffer a mighty doom." The voice was sonorous, even sad. "There is only one gateway and that is through the Lion's Mouth."

"Can we not . . . ?"

The riders began to close in. Corum and Hanafax drew their swords.

"Well, Prince Corum, it seems we are to die."

Corum's face was grim. He pushed up his eye patch. For a moment his vision clouded and then he saw into the netherworld once again. He wondered for a moment if it would not be better to die at the hands of the Flameland dwellers but now he was looking at a cavern in which tall figures stood as if frozen.

With a shock Corum recognized them as the dead warriors of the Ragha-da-Kheta, their wounds now bloodless, their eyes glazed, their clothes and armor torn, their weapons still in their hands. They began to move toward him as his hand stretched out to summon them.

"NO! These, too, are my enemies!" Corum shouted.

Hanafax, unable to see what Corum saw, turned his head in astonishment.

The dead warriors came on. The scene behind them faded. They materialized on the obsidian rock of the Flamelands.

Corum backed away, gesticulating wildly. The Flameland warriors drew their mounts to a stop in surprise. Hanafax's face was a mask of fear.

"No! I . . ."

From the lips of the dead King Temgol-Lep came a whispering voice. "We serve you, Master. Will you give us our prizes?"

Corum controlled himself. Slowly, he nodded. "Ay. You may take your prizes."

The long-limbed warriors turned to face the mounted warriors of the Flamelands. The beasts snorted and tried to move back but were forced to stand their ground by their riders. There were about fifty of the Ragha-da-Kheta. Dividing into groups of two or three, their clawed clubs raised, they flung themselves at the mounted beings.

Barbed lances came up and stabbed down at the Ragha-da-Kheta. Many were struck, but it did not deter them. They began to drag the struggling riders from their saddles.

Pale-faced, Corum watched. He knew now that he was consigning the Flamelands warriors to the same netherworld from which he had summoned the Ragha-da-Kheta. And his actions had sent the Ragha-da-Kheta to that netherworld in the first place.

On the gleaming rock, around which ran rivers of red rock, the ghastly battle continued. The clawed clubs ripped the cloaks from the riders, revealing a people whose faces were familiar.

"Stop!" Corum cried. "Stop! That is enough. Kill no more!"

Temgol-Lep turned his glazed eyes on Corum. The dead king had a barbed spear sticking completely through his body, but he seemed unaware of it. His dead lips moved. "These are our prizes, Master. We cannot stop."

"But they are Vadhagh! They are like me! They are my own people!"

Hanafax put an arm on Corum's shoulder. "They are all dead now, Prince Corum."

Sobbing, Corum ran toward the corpses, inspecting the faces.

They had the same long skulls, the same huge, almond eyes, the same tapering ears.

"How came Vadhagh here?" Hanafax murmured.

Now Temgol-Lep was dragging one of the corpses away, aided by two of his minions. The scaled beasts scattered, some of them splashing through the lava uncaringly.

Through the Eye of Rhynn, Corum saw the Ragha-da-Kheta pull the corpses into their cave. With a shudder, he replaced the eye patch. Save for a few weapons and tatters of armor and clothing, save for the disappearing mounts, nothing remained of the Vadhagh of the Flamelands.

"I have destroyed my own folk!" Corum screamed. "I have consigned them to a frightful doom in that netherworld!"

"Sorcery has a way of recoiling suddenly upon its user," Hanafax said quietly. "It is an arbitrary power, as I said."

Corum wheeled on Hanafax. "Stop your prattling, Mabden! Do you not realize what I have done?"

Hanafax nodded soberly. "Aye. But it *is* done, is it not? Our lives are saved."

"Now I add fratricide to my crimes." Corum fell to his knees, dropping his sword on the rock. And he wept.

"Who weeps?"

It was a woman's voice. A sad voice.

"Who weeps for Cira-an-Venl, the Lands That Are Now Flame? Who remembers her sweet meadows and her fair hills?"

Corum raised his head and got to his feet. Hanafax was already staring at the apparition on the rock above them.

"Who weeps, there?"

The woman was old. Her face was handsome and grim and white and lined. Her gray hair swirled about her and she was dressed in a red cloak such as the warriors had worn, mounted on a similar horned beast. She was a Vadhagh woman and very frail. Where her eyes had been were white, filmy pools of pain.

"I am Corum Jhaelen Irsei, Lady. Why are you blind?"

"I am blind through choice. Rather than witness what had become of my land, I plucked my eyes from my head. I am Ooresé, Queen of Cira-an-Venl, and my people number twenty."

Corum's lips were dry. "I have slain your people, Lady. That is why I weep."

Her face did not alter. "They were doomed," she said, "to die. It is better that they are dead. I thank you, Stranger, for releasing them. Perhaps you would care to release me, also. I only live so that the memory of Cira-an-Venl may live." She paused. "Why do you use a Vedragh name?"

"I am of the Vadhagh—the Vedragh, as you call them—I am from the lands far to the south."

"So Vedragh did go south. And is their land sweet?"

"It is very sweet."

"And are your folk happy, Prince Corum in the Scarlet Robe?"

"They are dead, Queen Ooresé. They are dead."

"All dead, then, now? Save you?"

"And save yourself, my queen."

A smile touched her lips. "He said we should all die, wherever we were, on whichever plane we existed. But there was another prophecy—that when we died, so would he. He chose to ignore it, as I remember."

"Who said that, Lady?"

"The Knight of the Swords. Duke Arioch of Chaos. He who inherited these five planes for his part in that long-ago battle between Order and Chaos. Who came here and willed that smooth rock cover our pretty hills, that boiling lava run in our gentle streams, that flame spring where green forests had been. Duke Arioch, Prince, made that prediction. But, before he departed to the place of his banishment, Lord Arkyn made another."

"Lord Arkyn?"

"Lord of Law, who ruled here before Arioch ousted him. He said that by destroying the old races, he would destroy his own power over the five planes."

"A pleasant wish," murmured Hanafax, "but I doubt if that is true."

"Perhaps we do deceive ourselves with happy lies, you who speak with the accent of a Mabden. But then you do not know what we know, for you are Arioch's children."

Hanafax drew himself up. "His children we may be, Queen Ooresé, but his slaves we are not. I am here because I defied Arioch's will."

Again she smiled her sad smile. "And some say that the Vedragh doom was of their own doing. That they fought the Nhadragh and so defied Lord Arkyn's scheme of things."

"The Gods are vengeful," Hanafax murmured.

"But I am vengeful, too, Sir Mabden," the queen said.

"Because we killed your warriors?"

She waved an ancient hand in a gesture of dismissal. "No. They attacked you. You defended yourselves. That is what that is. I speak of Duke Arioch and his whim—the whim that turned a beautiful land into this dreadful wasteland of eternal flame."

"You would be revenged, then, on Duke Arioch?" Corum said.

"My people once numbered hundreds. One after the other I sent them through the Lion's Mouth to destroy the Knight of the Swords. None did so. None returned."

"What is the Lion's Mouth?" Hanafax asked. "We heard it was the only escape from the Flamelands."

"It is. And it is no escape. Those who survive the passage through the Lion's Mouth do not survive what lies beyond it—the palace of Duke Arioch himself."

"Can none survive?"

The Blind Queen's face turned toward the rosy sky. "Only a great hero, Prince in the Scarlet Robe. Only a great hero."

"Once the Vadhagh had no belief in heroes and such," Corum said bitterly.

She nodded. "I remember. But then they needed no beliefs of that kind."

Corum was silent for a moment. Then he said, "Where is this Lion's Mouth, Queen?"

"I will lead you to it, Prince Corum."

The Fifth Chapter

THROUGH THE LION'S MOUTH

The queen gave them water from the cask that rested behind her saddle and called up two of the lumbering mounts for Corum and Hanafax to ride. They climbed onto the beasts, clasped the reins, and then began to follow her over the black and green obsidian slabs, between the rivers of flame.

Though blind, she guided her beast skillfully, and she talked all the while of what had been here, what had grown there, as if she remembered every tree and flower that had once grown in her ruined land.

After a good space of time she stopped and pointed directly ahead. "What do you see there?"

Corum peered through the rippling smoke. "It looks like a great rock . . ."

"We will ride closer," she said.

And as they rode closer, Corum began to see what it was. It was, indeed, a gigantic rock. A rock of smooth and shining stone that glowed like mellowed gold. And it was fashioned, in perfect detail, to resemble the head of a huge lion with its sharp-fanged mouth wide open in a roar.

"Gods! Who made such a thing?" Hanafax murmured.

"Arioch created it," said Queen Ooresé. "Once our peaceful city lay there. Now we live—lived—in caves below the ground where water runs and it is a little cooler."

Corum stared at the enormous lion's head and he looked at Queen Ooresé. "How old are you, Queen?"

"I do not know. Time does not exist in the Flamelands. Perhaps ten thousand years."

Far away another wall of flame danced. Corum remarked upon it.

"We are surrounded by flame on all sides. When Arioch first created it, many flung themselves into it rather than look upon what had become of their land. My husband died in that manner and thus did my brothers and all my sisters perish."

Corum noticed that Hanafax was not his usual talkative self. His head was bowed and he rubbed at it from time to time as if puzzled.

"What is it, Friend Hanafax?"

"Nothing, Prince Corum. A pain in my head. Doubtless the heat causes it."

Now a singular moaning sound came to their ears. Hanafax looked up, his eyes wide and uncomprehending. "What is it?"

"The Lion sings," said the Queen. "He knows we approach."

Then from Hanafax's throat a similar sound issued, as a dog will imitate another's howling.

"Hanafax, my friend!" Corum rode his beast close to the other's. "Is something ailing you?"

Hanafax stared at him vaguely. "No. I told you, the heat . . ." His face twisted. "Aah! The pain! I will not! I will not!"

Corum turned to Queen Ooresé. "Have you known this to happen before?"

She frowned, seeming to be thinking rather than displaying concern for Hanafax. "No," she said at last. "Unless . . ."

"Arioch! I will not!" Hanafax began to pant.

Then Corum's borrowed hand leapt up from the saddle where it had held the reins.

Corum tried to control it, but it shot straight toward Hanafax's face, its fingers extended. Fingers drove into the Mabden's eyes. They pierced the head, plunging deep into the brain. Hanafax screamed. "No, Corum, please do not . . . I can fight it . . . *aaaah!*"

And the Hand of Kwll withdrew itself, the fingers dripping with Hanafax's blood and brains, while the lifeless body of the Mabden fell from the saddle.

"What is happening?" Queen Ooresé called.

Corum stared at the mired hand, now once again his. "It is nothing," he murmured. "I have killed my friend."

He looked up suddenly.

Above him, on a hill, he thought he saw the outline of a figure watching him. Then smoke drifted across the scene and he saw nothing.

"So you guessed what I guessed, Prince in the Scarlet Robe," said the queen.

"I guessed nothing. I have killed my friend, that is all I know. He helped me. He showed me . . ." Corum swallowed with difficulty.

"He was only a Mabden, Prince Corum. Only a Mabden servant of Arioch."

"He hated Arioch!"

"But Arioch found him and entered him. He would have tried to kill us. You did right to destroy him. He would have betrayed you, Prince."

Corum stared at her through brooding eyes. "I should have let him kill me. Why should I live?"

"Because you are of the Vedragh. The last of the Vedragh who can avenge our race."

"Let it perish, unavenged! Too many crimes have been committed so that that vengeance might be won! Too many unfortunates have suffered frightful fates! Will the Vadhagh name be recalled with love—or muttered in hatred?"

"It is already spoken with hatred. Arioch has seen to that. There is the Lion's Mouth. Farewell, Prince in the Scarlet Robe!" and Queen Ooresé spurred her beast into a gallop and went plunging past the great rock, on toward the vast wall of flame beyond.

Corum knew what she would do.

He looked at the body of Hanafax. The cheerful fellow would smile no more and his soul was now doubtless suffering at the whim of Arioch.

Again, he was alone.

He gave a shuddering sigh.

The strange, moaning sound once again began to issue from the Lion's Mouth. It seemed to be calling him. He shrugged. What did it matter if he perished? It would only mean that no more would die because of him.

Slowly, he began to ride toward the Lion's Mouth. As he drew nearer, he gathered speed and then, with a yell, plunged through the gaping jaws and into the howling darkness beyond!

The beast stumbled, lost its footing, fell. Corum was thrown clear, got up, sought the reins with his groping hands. But the beast had turned and was galloping back toward the daylight that flickered red and yellow at the entrance.

For an instant Corum's mind cooled and he made to follow it. Then he remembered the dead face of Hanafax and he turned and began to trudge into the deeper darkness.

He walked thus for a long while. It was cool within the Lion's Mouth and he wondered if Queen Ooresé had been voicing nothing more than a superstition, for the interior seemed to be just a large cave.

Then the rustling sounds began.

He thought he glimpsed eyes watching him. Accusing eyes? No. Merely malevolent. He drew his sword. He paused, looking about him. He took another step forward.

He was in whirling nothingness. Colors flashed past him, something shrieked, and laughter filled his head. He tried to take another step.

He stood on a crystal plain, and imbedded in it, beneath his feet, were millions of beings—Vadhagh, Nhadragh, Mabden, Ragha-da-Kheta, and many others he did not recognize. There were males and females and all had their eyes open; all had their faces pressed against the crystal; all stretched out their hands as if seeking aid. All stared at him. He tried to hack at the crystal with his sword, but the crystal would not crack.

He moved forward.

He saw all the Five Planes, one superimposed upon the other, as he had seen them as a child—as his ancestors had known them. He was in a canyon, a forest, a valley, a field, another forest. He made to move into one particular plane, but he was stopped.

Screaming things came at him and pecked at his flesh. He fought them off with his sword. They vanished.

He was crossing a bridge of ice. It was melting. Fanged, distorted things waited for him below. The ice creaked. He lost his footing. He fell.

He fell into a whirlpool of seething matter that formed shapes and then destroyed them instantly. He saw whole cities brought into existence and then obliterated. He saw creatures, some beautiful, some disgustingly ugly. He saw things that made him love them and things that made him scream with hatred.

And he was back in the blackness of the great cavern where things tittered at him and scampered away from beneath his feet.

And Corum knew that anyone who had not experienced the horrors that he had experienced would have been quite mad by now. He had gained something from Shool the sorcerer besides the Eye of Rhynn and the Hand of Kwll. He had gained an ability to face the most evil of apparitions and be virtually unmoved.

And, he thought, this meant that he had lost something, too . . .

He moved on another step.

He stood knee deep in slithering flesh that was without shape but which lived. It began to suck him down. He struck about him with his sword. Now he was waist deep. He gasped and forced his body through the stuff.

He stood beneath a dome of ice and with him stood a million Corums. There he was, innocent and gay before the coming of the

Mabden, there he was moody and grim, with his jeweled eye and his murderous hand, there he was dying . . .

Another step.

Blood flooded over him. He tried to regain his feet. The heads of foul reptilian creatures rose from the stuff and snapped at his face with their jaws.

His instinct was to draw back. But he swam toward them.

He stood in a tunnel of silver and gold. There was a door at the end and he could hear movement behind it.

Sword in hand, he stepped through.

Strange, desperate laughter filled the immense gallery in which he found himself.

He knew that he had reached the Court of the Knight of the Swords.

The Sixth Chapter

THE GOD FEASTERS

Corum was dwarfed by the hugeness of the hall. Suddenly he saw his past adventures, his emotions, his desires, his guilts as utterly inconsequential and feeble. This mood was increased by the fact that he had expected to confront Arioch the moment he reached his court.

But Corum had entered the palace completely unnoticed. The laughter came from a gallery high above where two scaled demons with long horns and longer tails were fighting. As they fought, they laughed, though both seemed plainly near death.

It was on this fight that Arioch's attention seemed fixed.

The Knight of the Swords—the Duke of Chaos—lay in a heap of filth and quaffed some ill-smelling stuff from a dirty goblet. He was enormously fat and the flesh trembled on him as he laughed. He was completely naked and formed in all details like a Mabden. There seemed to be scabs and sores on his body, particularly near his pelvis. His face was flushed and it was ugly, and his teeth, when he opened his mouth, seemed decayed.

Corum would not have known he was the God at all if it had not been for his size, for Arioch was as large as a castle and his sword, the symbol of his power, if it had been placed upright, would have stood as high as the tallest tower of Castle Erorn.

The sides of the hall were tiered. Uncountable tiers stretched high toward the distant dome of the ceiling, which, itself, was wreathed in greasy smoke. These tiers were occupied, mainly with Mabden of all ages. Corum saw that most were naked. In many of the tiers they were copulating, fighting, torturing each other. Elsewhere were other beings—mainly scaly Shefanhow somewhat smaller than the two who were fighting together.

Arioch's sword was jet black and carved with many peculiar

patterns. Mabden were at work on the sword. They knelt on the blade and polished part of a design, or they climbed the hilt and washed it, or they sat astride the handgrip and mended the gold wire which bound it.

And other beings were busy, too. Like lice, they scampered and crawled over the God's huge bulk, picking at his skin, feeding off his blood and his flesh. Of all these activities, Arioch seemed oblivious. His interest continued to be in the fight to the death in the gallery above.

Was this, then, the all-powerful Arioch, living like a drunken farmer in a pigsty? Was this the malevolent creature which had destroyed whole nations, which pursued a vendetta upon all the races to spring up on the Earth before his coming?

Arioch's laughter shook the floor. Some of the parasitic Mabden fell off his body. A few were unhurt, while others lay with their backs or their limbs broken, unable to move. Their comrades ignored their plight and patiently climbed again upon the God's body, tearing tiny pieces from him with their teeth.

Arioch's hair was long, lank, and oily. Here, too, Mabden searched for and fought over the bits of food that clung to the strands. Elsewhere in the God's body hair Mabden crept in and out, hunting for scraps and crumbs or tender portions of his flesh.

The two demons fell back. One of them was dead, the other almost dead but still laughing weakly. Then the laughter stopped.

Arioch slapped his body, killing a dozen or so Mabden, and scratched his stomach. He inspected the bloody remains in his palm and absently wiped them on his hair. Living Mabden seized the scraps and devoured them.

Then a huge sigh issued from the God's mouth and he began to pick his nose with a dirty finger that was the size of a tall poplar.

Corum saw that there were openings beneath the galleries and stairways twisting upward, but he had no notion where the highest tower of the palace might be. He began to move, soft-footed, around the hall.

Arioch's ears caught the sound and the God became alert. He bent his head and peered about the floor. The huge eyes fixed on Corum and a monstrously large hand reached out to grasp him.

Corum raised his sword and hacked at the hand, but Arioch laughed and drew the Vadhagh prince toward him.

"What's this?" the voice boomed. "Not one of mine. Not one of mine."

Corum continued to strike at the hand and Arioch continued to seem unaware of the blows, though the sword raised deep cuts in the flesh. From over his shoulders, from behind his ears, and from

133

within his filthy hair, Mabden eyes regarded Corum with terrified curiosity.

"Not one of mine," Arioch boomed again. "One of his. One of his."

"Whose?" Corum shouted, still struggling.

"The one whose castle I recently inherited. The dour fellow. Arkyn. Arkyn of Law. One of his. I thought they were all gone by now. I cannot keep an eye on little beings not of my own manufacture. I do not understand their ways."

"Arioch! You have destroyed all my kin!"

"Ah, good. All of them, you say? Good. Is that the message you bring to me? Why did I not hear before, from one of my own little creatures?"

"Let me go!" Corum screamed.

Arioch opened his hand and Corum staggered free, gasping. He had not expected Arioch to comply.

And then the full injustice of his fate struck him. Arioch bore no malice toward the Vadhagh. He cared for them no more nor less than he cared for the Mabden parasites feeding off his body. He was merely wiping his palette clean of old colors as a painter will before he begins a fresh canvas. All the agony and the misery he and his had suffered was on behalf of the whim of a careless God who only occasionally turned his attention to the world that he had been given to rule.

Then Arioch vanished.

Another figure stood in his place. All the Mabden were gone.

The other figure was beautiful and looked upon Corum with a kind of haughty affection. He was dressed all in black and silver, with a miniature version of the black sword at his side. His expression was quizzical. He smiled. He was the quintessence of evil.

"Who are you?" Corum gasped.

"I am Duke Arioch, your master. I am the Lord of Hell, a Noble of the Realm of Chaos, the Knight of the Swords. I am your enemy."

"So you are my enemy. The other form was not your true form!"

"I am anything you please, Prince Corum. What does 'true' mean in this context? I can be anything I choose—or anything you choose, if you prefer. Consider me evil and I will don the appearance of evil. Consider me good—and I will take on a form that fits the part. I care not. My only wish is to exist in peace, you see. To while away my time. And if you wish to play a drama, some game of your own devising, I will play it until it begins to bore me."

"Were your ambitions ever thus?"

"What? What? Ever? No, I think not. Not when I was embattled

134

with those Lords of Law who ruled this plane before. But now I have won, why, I deserve what I fought for. Do not all beings require the same?''

Corum nodded. ''I suppose they do.''

''Well,'' Arioch smiled. ''What now, Little Corum of the Vadhagh? You must be destroyed soon, you know. For my peace of mind, you understand, that is all. You have done well to reach my Court. I will give you hospitality as a reward and then, at some stage, I will flick you away. You know why now.''

Corum glowered. ''I will *not* be 'flicked' away, Duke Arioch. Why should I be?''

Arioch raised a hand to his beautiful face and he yawned. ''Why should you not be? Now. What can I do to entertain you?''

Corum hesitated. Then he said, ''Will you show me all your castle? I have never seen anything so huge.''

Arioch raised an eyebrow. ''If that is all . . . ?''

''All for the moment.''

Arioch smiled. ''Very well. Besides, I have not seen all of it myself. Come.'' He placed a soft hand on Corum's shoulder and led him through a doorway.

As they walked along a magnificent gallery with walls of coruscating marble, Arioch spoke reasonably to Corum in a low, hypnotic voice. ''You see, Friend Corum, these Fifteen Planes were stagnating. What did you Vadhagh and the rest do? Nothing. You hardly moved from your cities and your castles. Nature gave birth to poppies and daisies. The Lords of Law made sure that all was properly ordered. Nothing was happening at all. We have brought so much more to your world, my brother Mabelode and my sister Xiombarg.''

''Who are the others?''

''You know them, I think, as the Queen of the Swords and the King of the Swords. They each rule five of the other ten planes. We won them from the Lords of Law a little while ago.''

''And began your destruction of all that is truthful and wise.''

''If you say so, Mortal.''

Corum paused. His understanding was weakening to Arioch's persuasive voice. He turned. ''I think you are lying to me, Duke Arioch. There must be more to your ambition than this.''

''It is a matter of perspective, Corum. We follow our whims. We are powerful now and nothing can harm us. Why should we be vindictive?''

''Then you will be destroyed as the Vadhagh were destroyed. For the same reasons.''

Arioch shrugged. ''Perhaps.''

"You have a powerful enemy in Shool of Svi-an-Fanla-Brool! You should fear him, I think."

"You know of Shool, then?" Arioch laughed musically. "Poor Shool. He schemes and plots and maligns us. He is amusing, is he not?"

"He is merely amusing?" Corum was disbelieving.

"Aye—merely amusing."

"He says you hate him because he is almost as powerful as yourself."

"We hate no one."

"I mistrust you, Arioch."

"What mortal does not mistrust a God?"

Now they were walking up a spiral ramp that seemed comprised entirely of light.

Arioch paused. "I think we will explore some other part of the palace. This leads only to a tower." Ahead Corum saw a doorway on which pulsed a sign—eight arrows arranged around a circle.

"What is that sign, Arioch?"

"Nothing at all. The arms of Chaos."

"Then what lies beyond the door?"

"Just a tower." Arioch became impatient. "Come. There are more interesting sights elsewhere."

Reluctantly, Corum followed him back down the ramp. He thought he had seen the place where Arioch kept his heart.

For several more hours they wandered through the palace, observing its wonders. Here all was light and beauty, and there were no sinister sights. This fact disturbed Corum. He was sure that Arioch was deceiving him.

They returned to the hall.

The Mabden lice had vanished. The filth had disappeared. In its place was a table laden with food and wine. Arioch gestured toward it.

"Will you dine with me, Prince Corum?"

Corum's grin was sardonic. "Before you destroy me?"

Arioch laughed. "If you wish to continue your existence a while longer, I have no objection. You cannot leave my palace, you see. And while your naiveté continues to entertain me, why should I destroy you?"

"Do you not fear me at all?"

"I fear you not at all."

"Do you not fear what I represent?"

"What do you represent?"

"Justice."

Again Arioch laughed. "Oh, you think so narrowly. There is no such thing!"

"It existed when the Lords of Law ruled here."

"Everything may exist for a short while—even justice. But the true state of the universe is anarchy. It is the mortal's tragedy that he can never accept this."

Corum could not reply. He seated himself at the table and began to eat. Arioch did not eat with him, but sat on the other side of the table and poured himself some wine. Corum stopped eating. Arioch smiled.

"Do not fear, Corum. It is not poisoned. Why should I resort to such things as poisons?"

Corum resumed eating. When he had finished he said, "Now I would rest, if I am to be your guest."

"Ah," Arioch seemed perplexed. "Yes—well, sleep, then." He waved his hand and Corum fell face forward upon the table.

And slept.

The Seventh Chapter

THE BANE OF THE SWORD RULERS

Corum stirred and forced his eyes open. The table had gone. Gone, too, was Arioch. The vast hall was in darkness, illuminated only by faint light issuing from a few of the doorways and galleries.

He stood up. Was he dreaming? Or had he dreamed everything that had happened earlier? Certainly all the events had had the quality of dreams become reality. But that was true of the entire world now, since he had left the sanity of Castle Erorn so long ago.

But where had Duke Arioch gone? Had he left on some mission in the world? Doubtless he had thought his influence over Corum would last longer. After all, that was why he wished the Vadhagh all destroyed, because he could not understand them, could not predict everything they would do, could not control their minds as he controlled those of the Mabden.

Corum realized suddenly that he now had an opportunity, perhaps his only opportunity, to try to reach the place where Arioch kept his heart. Then he might escape while Arioch was still away, get back to Shool and reclaim Rhalina. Vengeance now no longer motivated him. All he sought was an end to his adventure, peace with the woman he loved, security in the old castle by the sea.

He ran across the floor of the hall and up the stairway to the gallery with the walls of coruscating marble until he came to the ramp that seemed made of nothing but light. The light had dimmed to a glow now, but high above was the doorway with the pulsating orange sign—the eight arrows radiating from a central hub—the Sign of Chaos.

Breathing heavily, he ran up the spiral ramp. Up and up he ran, until the rest of the palace lay far below him, until he reached the door which dwarfed him, until he stopped and looked and wondered, until he knew he'd reached his goal.

The huge sign pulsed regularly, like a living heart itself, and it bathed Corum's face and body and armor in its red-gold light. Corum pushed at the door, but it was like a mouse pushing at the door of a sarcophagus. He could not move it.

He needed aid. He contemplated his left hand—the Hand of Kwll. Could he summon help from the dark world? Not without a "prize" to offer them.

But then the Hand of Kwll bunched itself into a fist and began to glow with a light that blinded Corum and made him stretch his arm away as far as it would go, flinging his other arm over his eyes. He felt the Hand of Kwll rise into the air and then strike at the mighty door. He heard a sound like the tolling of bells. He heard a crack as if the Earth herself had split. And then the Hand of Kwll was limp by his side and he opened his eyes and saw that a crack had appeared in the door. It was a small crack in the bottom of the right corner, but it was large enough for Corum to wriggle through.

"Now you are aiding me as I would wish to be aided," he murmured to the hand. He got down on his knees and crawled through the crack.

Another ramp stretched upward over a gulf of sparkling emptiness. Strange sounds filled the air, rising and dying, coming close and then falling away. There were hints of menace here, hints of beauty, hints of death, hints of everlasting life, hints of terror, hints of tranquility. Corum made to draw his sword and then realized the uselessness of such an action. He set foot on the ramp and began to climb again.

A wind seemed to spring up and his scarlet robe flew out behind him. Cool breezes wafted him and hot winds scoured his skin. He saw faces all around him and many of the faces he thought he recognized. Some of the faces were huge and some were infinitely tiny. Eyes watched him. Lips grinned. A sorrowful moaning came and went. A dark cloud engulfed him. A tinkling as of glass bells ringing filled his ears. A voice called his name and it echoed and echoed and echoed away forever. A rainbow surrounded him, entered him, and made his whole body flash with color. Steadily he continued his walk up the long ramp.

And now he saw he was coming to a platform that was at the end of the ramp but which hung over the gulf. There was nothing beyond it.

On the platform was a dais. On the dais was a plinth and on the plinth was something that throbbed and gave forth rays.

Transfixed by these rays were several Mabden warriors. Their bodies were frozen in attitudes of reaching for the source of the rays, but their eyes moved as they saw Corum approach the dais. Pain was in those eyes, and curiosity, and a warning.

Corum stopped.

The thing on the plinth was a deep, soft blue and it was quite small and it shone and it looked like a jewel that had been fashioned into the shape of a heart. At every pulse, tubes of light shot forth from it.

This could only be the heart of Arioch.

But it protected itself, as was evident from the frozen warriors surrounding it.

Corum took a pace nearer. A beam of light struck his cheek and it tingled.

Another pace nearer and two more beams of light hit his body and made it shiver, but he was not frozen. And now he was past the Mabden warriors. Two more paces and the beams bombarded his whole head and body, but the sensation was only pleasant. He stretched out his right hand to seize the heart, but his left hand moved first and the Hand of Kwll gripped the heart of Arioch.

"The world seems full of fragments of Gods," Corum murmured. He turned and saw that the Mabden warriors were no longer frozen. They were rubbing at their faces, sheathing their swords.

Corum spoke to the nearest. "Why did you seek the heart of Arioch?"

"Through no choice of my own. A sorcerer sent me, offering me my life in return for stealing the heart from Arioch's palace."

"Was this Shool?"

"Aye—Shool. Prince Shool."

Corum looked at the others. They were all nodding. "Shool sent me!" "And me!"

"And Shool sent me," said Corum. "I had not realized he had tried so many times before."

"It is a game Arioch plays with him," murmured one of the Mabden warriors. "I learned that Shool has little power of his own at all. Arioch gives Shool the power he thinks is his own, for Arioch enjoys the sport of having an enemy with whom he can play. Every action Arioch makes is inspired by nothing but boredom. And now you have his heart. Plainly he did not expect the game to get so out of hand."

"Aye," Corum agreed. "It was only Arioch's carelessness that allowed me to reach this place. Now, I return. I must find a way from the palace before he realizes what has happened."

"May we come with you?" the Mabden asked.

Corum nodded. "But hurry."

They crept back down the ramp.

Halfway down, one of the Mabden screamed, flailed at the air, staggered to the edge of the ramp, and went drifting down into the sparkling emptiness.

Their pace increased until they reached the tiny crack at the bottom of the huge door and crawled through it, one by one.

Down the ramp of light they went. Through the gallery of coruscating marble. Down the stairway into the darkened hall.

Corum sought the silver door through which he had entered the palace. He made one complete circuit of the hall and his feet were aching before he realized that the door had vanished.

The hall was suddenly alive with light again and the vast, fat figure Corum had originally seen was laughing on the floor, lying amidst filth, with the Mabden parasites peering from out of the air beneath his arms, from his navel, from his ears.

"Ha, ha! You see, Corum, I am kind! I have let you have almost everything you desired of me. You even have my heart! But I cannot let you take it away from me, Corum. Without my heart, I could not rule here. I think I will restore it into this flesh of mine."

Corum's shoulders slumped. "He has tricked us," he said to his terrified Mabden companions.

But one Mabden said, "He has used you, Sir Vadhagh. He could never have taken his heart himself. Did you not know that?"

Arioch laughed and his belly shook and Mabden fell to the floor. "True! True! You have done me a service, Prince Corum. The heart of each Sword Ruler is kept in a place that is banned to him, so that the others may know that he dwells only in his own domain and may travel to no other, thus he cannot usurp some rival ruler's power. But you, Corum, with your ancient blood, with your peculiar characteristics, were able to do that which I am unable to do. Now I have my heart and I may extend my domain wherever I choose. Or not, of course, if I choose not to."

"Then I have helped you," Corum said bitterly, "when I wished to hinder you . . ."

Arioch's laughter filled the hall. "Yes. Exactly. A fine joke, eh? Now, give me my heart, little Vadhagh."

Corum pressed his back to the wall and drew his blade. He stood there with the heart of Arioch in his left hand and his sword in his right. "I think I will die first, Arioch."

"As you please."

The monstrous hand reached out for Corum. He dodged it. Arioch bellowed with laughter again and plucked two of the Mabden warriors from the floor. They screamed and writhed as he drew them toward his great, wet mouth, full of blackened teeth. Then he

141

popped them into his maw and Corum heard their bones crunch. Arioch swallowed and spat out a sword. Then he returned his gaze to Corum.

Corum jumped behind a pillar. Arioch's hand came round it, feeling for him. Corum ran.

More laughter, and the hall reverberated. The God's mirth was echoed by the tittering voices of his Mabden parasites. A pillar crashed as Arioch struck at it, seeking Corum.

Corum dashed across the floor of the hall, leaping over the broken bodies of the Mabden who had fallen from the corpulent body of the God.

And then Arioch saw him, seized him, and his chuckles subsided.

"Give me my heart now."

Corum gasped for breath and freed his two hands from the soft flesh that enclosed him. The giant's great hand was warm and filthy. The nails were broken.

"Give me my heart, Little Being."

"No!" Corum drove his sword deep into the thumb, but the God did not notice. Mabden clung to the hair of the chest and watched, their grins blank.

Corum's ribs were near to breaking, but still he would not release the Heart of Arioch that lay in his left fist.

"No matter," said Arioch, his grip relaxing a trifle, "I can absorb both you and the heart at the same time."

Now Arioch began to carry his great hand toward his open mouth. His breath came out in stinking blasts and Corum choked on it, but still he stabbed and stabbed. A grin spread over the gigantic lips. All Corum could see now was that mouth, the scabrous nostrils, the huge eyes. The mouth opened wider to swallow him. He struck at the upper lip, staring into the red darkness of the God's throat.

Then his left hand contracted. It squeezed the heart of Arioch. Corum's own strength could not have done it, but once again the Hand of Kwll was possessed of a power of its own. It squeezed.

Arioch's laughter faded. The vast eyes widened and a new light filled them. A bellow came from the throat.

The Hand of Kwll squeezed tighter still.

Arioch shrieked.

The heart began to crumble in the hand. Rays of a reddish blue light sprang from between Corum's fingers. Pain flooded up his arm.

There was a high whistling sound.

Arioch began to weep. His grasp on Corum weakened. He staggered backward.

"No, Mortal. No . . ." The voice was pathetic. "Please, Mortal, we can . . ."

Corum saw the God's bloated form begin to melt into the air. The hand that held him began to lose its shape.

And then Corum was falling toward the floor of the hall, the broken pieces of Arioch's heart scattering as he fell. He landed with a crash, tried to rise, saw what was left of Arioch's body writhing in the air, heard a mournful sound, and then Corum lost consciousness, hearing, as he did so, Arioch's last whispered words:

"Corum of the Vadhagh. You have won the eternal bane of the Sword Rulers . . ."

The Eighth Chapter

A PAUSE IN THE STRUGGLE

Corum saw a procession passing him.

Beings of a hundred different races marched or rode or were carried in that procession and he knew that he watched all the mortal races that had ever existed since Law and Chaos had begun their struggle for domination over the multitudinous planes of the Earth.

In the distance, he saw the banners of Law and of Chaos raised, side by side, the one bearing the eight radiating arrows, the other bearing the single straight arrow of Law. And over all this hung a huge balance in perfect equilibrium. In each of the balance's cups were marshaled other beings, not mortal. Corum saw Arioch and the Lords of Chaos in one and he saw the Lords of Law in the other.

And Corum heard a voice which said, "This is as it should be. Neither Law nor Chaos must dominate the destinies of the mortal planes. There must be equilibrium."

Corum cried out, "But there is no equilibrium. Chaos rules All!"

The voice replied, saying, "The balance sometimes tips. It must be righted. And that is the power of mortals, to adjust the balance."

"How may I do that?"

"You have begun the work already. Now you must continue until it is finished. You may perish before it is complete, but some other will follow you."

Corum shouted, "I do not want this. I cannot bear such a burden!"

"YOU MUST!"

The procession marched on, not seeing Corum, not seeing the two banners flying, not seeing the Cosmic Balance that hung over them.

● ● ●

Corum hung in cloudy space and his heart was at peace. Shapes began to appear and then he saw that he was back in Arioch's hall. He sought for his sword, but it was gone.

"I will return your sword before you leave, Prince Corum of the Vadhagh."

The voice was level and it was clear.

Corum turned.

He drew a sudden breath. "The Giant of Laahr!"

The sad, wise face smiled down on him. "I was called that, when I was in exile. But now I am no longer exiled and you may address me by my true name. I am Lord Arkyn and this is my palace. Arioch has gone. Without his heart he cannot assume flesh on these planes. Without flesh, he cannot wield power. I rule here now, as I ruled before."

The being's substance was still shadowy, though not as formless as before.

Lord Arkyn smiled. "It will take time before I assume my old form. Only by a great power of will did I enable myself to remain on this plane at all. I did not know when I rescued you, Corum, that you would be the cause of my restoration. I thank you."

"I thank you, my lord."

"Good breeds good," Lord Arkyn said. "Evil breeds evil."

Corum smiled. "Sometimes, my lord."

Lord Arkyn chuckled quietly. "Aye, you are right—sometimes. Well, mortal, I must return you to your own plane."

"Can you transport me to a particular place, my lord?"

"I can, Prince in the Scarlet Robe."

"Lord Arkyn, you know why I embarked upon this course of mine. I sought the remnants of the Vadhagh race, my folk. Tell me, are they all gone now?"

Lord Arkyn lowered his head. "All, save you."

"And cannot you restore them?"

"The Vadhagh were always the mortals I loved most, Prince Corum. But I have not the power to reverse the very cycle of time. You are the last of the Vadhagh. And yet . . ." Lord Arkyn paused. "And yet there might come a moment when the Vadhagh will return. But I see nothing clearly and I must speak no more of that."

Corum sighed. "Well, I must be content. And what of Shool? Is Rhalina safe?"

"I think so. My senses are still not capable of seeing all that happens and Shool was a thing of Chaos and is therefore much harder for me to see. But I believe that Rhalina is in danger, though Shool's power has waned with the passing of Arioch."

"Then send me, I beg you, to Svi-an-Fanla-Brool, for I love the Margravine."

"It is your capacity for love that makes you strong, Prince Corum."

"And my capacity for hate?"

"That directs your strength."

Lord Arkyn frowned, as if there was something he could not understand.

"You are sad in your triumph, Lord Arkyn? Are you always sad?"

The Lord of Law looked at Corum, almost in surprise. "I suppose I am still sad, yes. I mourn for the Vadhagh as you mourn. I mourn for the one who was killed by your enemy, Glandyth-a-Krae—the one you called the Brown Man."

"He was a good creature. Does Glandyth still bring death across the land of Bro-an-Vadhagh?"

"He does. You will meet him again, I think."

"And then I will kill him."

"Possibly."

Lord Arkyn vanished. The palace vanished.

Sword in hand, Corum stood before the low, twisted door that was the entrance to Shool's dwelling. Behind him, in the garden, the plants craned up to drink the rain that fell from a pale sky.

A peculiar calm hung over the dark and oddly formed building, but without hesitation Corum plunged into it and began to run down eccentric corridors.

"Rhalina! Rhalina!" The house muffled his shouts no matter how loudly he uttered them.

"Rhalina!"

Through the murky dwelling he ran until he heard a whining voice he recognized. Shool!

"Shool! Where are you?"

"Prince Shool. I will be given my proper rank. You mock me now my enemies have beaten me."

Corum entered a room and there was Shool. Corum recognized only the eyes. The rest was a withered, decrepit thing that lay upon a bed, unable to move.

Shool whimpered. "You, too, come to torment me now that I am conquered. Thus it always is with mighty men brought low."

"You only rose because it suited Arioch's sense of humor to let you."

"Silence! I will not be deceived. Arioch has taken vengeance upon me because I was more powerful than he."

"You borrowed, without knowing it, a fraction of his power.

146

Arioch is gone from the Five Planes, Shool. You set events in motion which resulted in his banishment. You wanted his heart so that you might make him your slave. You sent many Mabden to steal it. All failed. You should not have sent me, Shool, for I did not fail and it resulted in your undoing."

Shool sobbed and shook his haggard head.

"Where is Rhalina, Shool? If she is harmed . . ."

"Harmed?" A hollow laugh from the wizened lips. "I harm her? It is she who placed me here. Take her away from me. I know she means to poison me."

"Where is she?"

"I gave you gifts. That new hand, that new eye. You would be crippled still if I had not been kind to you. But you will not remember my generosity, I know. You will—"

"Your 'gifts,' Shool, near crippled my soul! Where is Rhalina?"

"Promise you will not hurt me, if I tell you?"

"Why should I wish to hurt so pathetic a thing as you, Shool? Now, tell me."

"At the end of the passage is a stair. At the top of the stair is a room. She has locked herself in. I would have made her my wife, you know. It would have been magnificent to be the wife of a God. An immortal. But she . . ."

"So you planned to betray me?"

"A God may do as he chooses."

Corum left the room, ran down the passage and up the short flight of stairs, hammering with the hilt of his sword upon the door.

"Rhalina!"

A weary voice came from beyond the door. "So your power has returned, Shool. You will not trick me again by disguising yourself as Corum. Though he be dead, I shall give myself to no other, least of all . . ."

"Rhalina! This really is Corum. Shool can do nothing. The Knight of the Swords has been banished from this plane and with him went Shool's sorcery."

"Is it true?"

"Open the door, Rhalina."

Cautiously bolts were drawn back and there was Rhalina. She was tired, she had plainly suffered much, but she was still beautiful. She looked deeply into Corum's eyes and her face flushed with relief, with love. She fainted.

Corum picked her up and began to carry her down the stairway, along the passage. He paused at Shool's room.

The onetime sorcerer was gone.

Suspecting a trick, Corum hurried to the main door.

Through the rain, along a path between the swaying plants, hurried Shool, his ancient legs barely able to carry him.

He darted a look back at Corum and chittered with fear. He dived into the bushes.

There was a smacking sound. A hiss. A wail.

Bile rose in Corum's throat. Shool's plants were feeding for the last time.

Warily he carried Rhalina along the path, tugging himself free from the vines and blooms that sought to hold him and kiss him, and at last he reached the shore.

A boat was tied up there, a small skiff which, with careful handling, would bear them back to Moidel's Castle.

The sea was smooth beneath the gray rain that fell upon it. On the horizon, the sky began to lighten.

Corum placed Rhalina gently in the boat and set sail for Moidel's Mount.

She woke up several hours later, looked at him, smiled sweetly, then fell asleep again.

Toward nightfall, as the boat sailed steadily homeward, she came and sat beside him. He wrapped his scarlet robe around her and said nothing.

As the moon rose, she reached up and kissed him on the cheek.

"I had not hoped . . ." she began. And then she wept for a little while and he comforted her.

"Corum," she said at length, "how has our luck improved so?"

And he began to tell her of what had befallen him. He told her of the Ragha-da-Kheta, of the magical kite, of the Flamelands, of Arioch, and of Arkyn.

He told her all, save two things.

He did not tell her how he—or the Hand of Kwll—had murdered King Temgol-Lep, who had tried to poison him, or her countryman Hanafax, who had tried to help him.

When he had finished her brow was unclouded and she sighed with her happiness.

"So we have peace, at last. The conflict is over."

"Peace, if we are lucky, for a little while." The sun had begun to rise. He adjusted his course.

"You will not leave me again? Law rules now, surely, and . . ."

"Law rules only upon this plane. The Lords of Chaos will not be pleased with what has happened here. Arioch's last words to me were that I have incurred the bane of the Sword Rulers. And Lord Arkyn knows that much more must be done before Law is once again secure in the Fifteen Planes. And Glandyth-a-Krae will be heard of again."

"You still seek vengeance against him?"

"No longer. He was merely an instrument of Arioch. But he will not forget his hatred of me, Rhalina."

The sky cleared and was blue and golden. A warm breeze blew.

"Are we then, Corum, to have no peace?"

"We shall have some, I think. But it will be merely a pause in the struggle, Rhalina. Let us enjoy that pause while we may. We have won that much, at least."

"Aye." Her tone became merry. "And peace and love that are won are more greatly appreciated than if they are merely inherited!"

He held her in his arms.

The sun was strong in the sky. Its rays struck a jeweled hand and a jeweled eye and it made them burn brightly and flash like fire.

But Rhalina did not see them burning, for she slept again in Corum's arms.

Moidel's Mount came in sight. Its green slopes were washed by a gentle blue sea and the sun shone on its white stone castle. The tide was in, covering the causeway.

Corum looked down at Rhalina's sleeping face. He smiled and gently stroked her hair.

He saw the forest on the mainland. Nothing threatened.

He glanced up at the cloudless sky.

He hoped the pause would be a long one.

*This ends the First Book
of Corum*

THE BOOKS OF CORUM

*Being a History in Three Volumes
Concerning the Quests and Adventures
of Corum Jhaelen Irsei of the Vadhagh
Folk, Who Is also Called The Prince in
The Scarlet Robe*

Volume the Second

THE QUEEN OF THE SWORDS

This book is for Diane Boardman

INTRODUCTION

In those days there were oceans of light and cities in the skies and wild flying beasts of bronze. There were herds of crimson cattle that roared and were taller than castles. There were shrill, viridian things that haunted bleak rivers. It was a time of gods, manifesting themselves upon our world in all her aspects; a time of giants who walked on water; of mindless sprites and misshapen creatures who could be summoned by an ill-considered thought but driven away only on pain of some fearful sacrifice; of magics, phantasms, unstable nature, impossible events, insane paradoxes, dreams come true, dreams gone awry, of nightmares assuming reality.

It was a rich time and a dark time. The time of the Sword Rulers. The time when the Vadhagh and the Nhadragh, age-old enemies, were dying. The time when Man, the slave of fear, was emerging, unaware that much of the terror he experienced was the result of nothing else but the fact that he, himself, had come into existence. It was one of many ironies connected with Man (who, in those days, called his race Mabden).

The Mabden lived brief lives and bred prodigiously. Within a few centuries they rose to dominate the westerly continent on which they had evolved. Superstition stopped them from sending many of their ships toward Vadhagh and Nhadragh lands for another century or two, but gradually they gained courage when no resistance was offered. They began to feel jealous of the older races; they began to feel malicious.

The Vadhagh and the Nhadragh were not aware of this. They had dwelt a million or more years upon the planet, which now, at last, seemed at rest. They knew of the Mabden but considered them not greatly different from other beasts. Though continuing to indulge their traditional hatreds of one another, the Vadhagh and the Nhadragh spent their long hours in considering abstractions, in the creation of works of art and the like. Rational, sophisticated, at one with themselves, these older races were unable to believe in the changes that had come. Thus, as it almost always is, they ignored the signs.

There was no exchange of knowledge between the two ancient enemies, even though they had fought their last battle many centuries before.

The Vadhagh lived in family groups occupying isolated castles scattered across a continent called by them Bro-an-Vadhagh. There was scarcely any communication between these families, for the Vadhagh had long since lost the impulse to travel. The Nhadragh lived in their cities built on the islands in the seas to the northwest of Bro-an-Vadhagh. They, also, had little contact, even with their closest kin. Both races reckoned themselves invulnerable. Both were wrong.

Upstart Man was beginning to breed and spread like a pestilence across the world. This pestilence struck down the old races wherever it touched them. And it was not only death that Man brought, but terror, too. Willfully, he made of the older world nothing but ruins and bones. Unwittingly, he brought psychic and supernatural disruption of a magnitude which even the Great Old Gods failed to comprehend.

And the Great Old Gods began to know fear.

And Man, slave of fear, arrogant in his ignorance, continued his stumbling progress. He was blind to the huge disruptions aroused by his apparently petty ambitions. As well, Man was deficient in sensitivity, had no awareness of the multitude of dimensions that filled the universe, each plane intersecting with several others. Not so the Vadhagh and the Nhadragh, who had known what it was to move at will between the dimensions they termed the Five Planes. They had glimpsed and understood the nature of the many planes, other than the five, through which the Earth moved.

Therefore it seemed a dreadful injustice that these wise races should perish at the hands of creatures who were still little more than animals. It was as if vultures feasted on and squabbled over the paralyzed body of a youthful poet who could only stare at them with puzzled eyes as they slowly robbed him of an exquisite existence they would never appreciate, never know they were taking.

"If they valued what they stole, if they knew what they were destroying," says the old Vadhagh in the story, "The Only Autumn Flower," "then I would be consoled."

It was unjust.

By creating Man, the universe betrayed the old races.

But it was a perpetual and familiar injustice. The sentient may perceive and love the universe, but the universe cannot perceive and love the sentient. The universe sees no distinction between the multitude of creatures and elements which comprise it. All are equal. None is favored. The universe, equipped with nothing but the materials and the power of creation, continues to create: something of this, something of that. It cannot control what it creates and it cannot, it seems, be controlled by its creations (though a few might deceive themselves otherwise). Those who curse the workings of the universe curse that which is deaf. Those who strike out at those workings fight that which is inviolate. Those who shake their fists, shake their fists at blind stars.

But this does not mean that there are some who will not try to do battle with and destroy the invulnerable.

There will always be such beings, sometimes beings of great wisdom, who cannot bear to believe in an insouciant universe.

Prince Corum Jhaelen Irsei was one of these. Perhaps the last of the Vadhagh Race, he was sometimes known as the Prince in the Scarlet Robe.

This chronicle concerns him.

We have already learned how the Mabden followers of Earl Glandyth-a-Krae (who called themselves the Denledhyssi—or Murderers) killed Prince Corum's relatives and his nearest kin and thus taught the Prince in the Scarlet Robe how to hate, how to kill, and how to desire vengeance. We have heard how Glandyth tortured Corum and took away a hand and an eye and how Corum was rescued by the Giant of Laahr and taken to the castle of the Margravine Rhalina—a castle set upon a mount surrounded by the sea. Though Rhalina was a Mabden woman (of the gentler folk of Lywn-an-Esh), Corum and she fell in love. When Glandyth roused the Pony Tribes, the forest barbarians, to attack the Margravine's castle, she and Corum sought supernatural aid and thus fell into the hands of the sorcerer Shool, whose domain was the island called Svi-an-Fanla-Brool—Home of the Gorged God. And now Corum had direct experience of the morbid, unfamiliar powers at work in the world. Shool spoke of dreams and realities. ("I see you are beginning to argue in Mabden terms," he told Corum. "It is just as well for you, if you wish to survive in this Mabden dream."—"It is a dream. . . ?" says Corum.—"Of sorts. Real enough. It is what you might call the dream of a God. There again you might say that it is a dream that a God has allowed to become reality. I refer of course to the Knight of the Swords who rules the Five Planes.")

With Rhalina his prisoner Shool could make a bargain with

155

Corum. He gave him two gifts—the Hand of Kwll and the Eye of Rhynn—to replace his own missing organs. These jeweled and alien things were once the property of two brother gods, known as the Lost Gods since they had mysteriously vanished.

Now Shool told Corum what he must do if he wished to see Rhalina saved. Corum must go to the Realm of the Knight of the Swords—Duke Arioch of Chaos who had ruled the Five Planes since he had wrested them from the control of Lord Arkyn of Law. There Corum must find the heart of the Knight of the Swords—a thing which was kept in a tower of his castle and which enabled him to take material shape on Earth and thus wield power (without a material shape—or a number of them—the Lords of Chaos could not rule mortals).

With little hope Corum set off in a boat for the domain of Arioch but on his way was wrecked when a huge giant passed by him, merely fishing. In the land of the strange Ragha-da-Kheta he discovered that the Eye could see into frightful netherworlds and that the Hand could summon dreadful beings from those worlds to aid him—also the hand seemed to sense danger before it came and was ruthless in slaying even when Corum did not desire to slay. Then he realized that by accepting Shool's gifts, he had accepted the logic of Shool's world and could not escape from it.

During these adventures Corum learned of the eternal struggle between Law and Chaos. A cheerful traveler from Lywn-an-Esh enlightened him. It was, he said, "the Chaos Lords' will that rules you. Arioch is one of them. Long since there was a war between the forces of Order and the forces of Chaos. The forces of Chaos won and came to dominate the fifteen Planes and, as I understand it, much that lies beyond them. Some say that Order was defeated completely and all her Gods vanished. They say the Cosmic Balance tipped too far in one direction and that is why there are so many arbitrary events taking place in the world. They say that once the world was round instead of dish-shaped . . ."—"Some Vadhagh legends say it was once round," Corum informed him.—"Aye. Well, the Vadhagh began their rise before Order was banished. That is why the Sword Rulers hate the old races so much. They are not their creation at all. But the Great Gods are not allowed to interfere too directly in mortal affairs, so they have worked through the Mabden, chiefly . . ."—Corum said, "Is this the truth?"—Hanafax shrugged. "It is a truth . . ."

Later, in the Flamelands where the blind queen Ooresé lived, Corum saw a mysterious figure who almost immediately vanished after he had slain poor Hanafax with the Hand of Kwll (which knew Hanafax would betray him). He learned that Arioch was the Knight

156

of the Swords and that Xiombarg was the Queen of Swords ruling the next group of Five Planes, while the most powerful Sword Ruler of all ruled the last of the Five Planes—Mabelrode, King of the Swords. Corum learned that all the hearts of the Sword Rulers were hidden where even they could not touch them. But after further adventures in Arioch's castle, he at last succeeded in finding the heart of the Knight of Swords and, to save his life, destroyed it, thus banishing Arioch to limbo and allowing Arkyn of Law to return to occupy his old castle. But Corum had earned the Bane of the Sword Rulers and by destroying Arioch's heart had set a pattern of destiny for himself. A voice told him, "Neither Law nor Chaos must dominate the destinies of the mortal planes. There must be equilibrium." But it seemed to Corum that there was no equilibrium, that Chaos ruled all. "The balance sometimes tips," replied the voice. "It must be righted. And that is the power of mortals, to adjust the balance. You have begun the work already. Now you must continue until it is finished. You may perish before it is complete, but some other will follow you."

Corum shouted, "I do not want this. I cannot bear such a burden."

The voice replied:

"YOU MUST!"

And then Corum returned to find Shool's power gone and Rhalina free.

They returned to the lovely castle on Moidel's Mount, knowing that they were no longer in any sense in control of their own fates . . .

—*The Book of Corum*

BOOK ONE

In which Prince Corum meets a poet, hears a portent, and plans a journey

The First Chapter

WHAT THE SEA GOD DISCARDED

Now the skies of summer were pale blue over the deeper blue of the sea; over the golden green of the mainland forest; over the grassy rocks of Moidel's Mount and the white stones of the castle raised on its peak. And the last of the Vadhagh race, Prince Corum in the Scarlet Robe, was deep in love with the Mabden woman, Margravine Rhalina of Allomglyl.

Corum Jhaelen Irsei, whose right eye was covered by a patch encrusted with dark jewels so that it resembled the orb of an insect, whose left eye (the natural one) was large and almond-shaped with a yellow center and purple surround, was unmistakably Vadhagh. His skull was narrow and long and tapering at the chin and his ears were tapered, too. They had no lobes and were flat against the skull. The hair was fair and finer than the finest Mabden maiden's, his mouth was wide, full-lipped, and his skin was rose-pink and flecked with gold. He would have been handsome save for the baroque blemish that was now his right eye and for the somewhat grim twist to his lips. Then, too, there was the alien hand which strayed often to his sword hilt, visible when he pushed back his scarlet robe.

This left hand bore six fingers on it and seemed encased in a jeweled gauntlet (not so—the "jewels" were the hand's skin). It was a sinister thing and it had crushed the heart of the Knight of the Swords himself—my lord Arioch of Chaos—and allowed Arkyn, Lord of Law, to return.

159

Corum certainly seemed a being bent on vengeance and he was, indeed, pledged to avenge his murdered family by slaying Earl Glandyth of Krae, servant of King Lyr-a-Brode of Kalenwyr, who ruled the South and the East of the continent once ruled by the Vadhagh. And he was also pledged to the Cause of Law against the Cause of Chaos (whose servants Lyr and his subjects were). This knowledge made him sober and manly, but it also made his soul heavy. He was also unsettled by the thought of the power grafted to his flesh—the power of the Hand and the Eye.

The Margravine Rhalina was womanly and beautiful and her gentle face was framed by thick, black tresses. She had huge, dark eyes and red, loving lips. She, too, was nervous of the sorcerous gifts of the dead wizard Shool, but she tried not to brood upon them, just as earlier she had refused to brood upon the loss of her husband, the Margrave, when he had been drowned in a shipwreck while on his way to Lywn-an-Esh, the land he served, which was gradually being covered by the sea.

She found more to laugh at than did Corum and she was his comfort, for once he had been innocent and had laughed a great deal, and he remembered this innocence with longing. But the longing brought other memories—of his family lying dead, mutilated, dishonored on the sward outside Castle Erorn as it burned and Glandyth brandished his weapons, which were clothed in Vadhagh blood. Such violent images were stronger than the images of his earlier, peaceful life. They forever inhabited his skull, sometimes filling it, sometimes lurking in the darker corners and merely threatening to fill it. And when his revenge-lust seemed to wane, they would always bring it back to fullness. Fire, flesh, and fear; the barbaric chariots of the Denledhyssi—brass, iron, and crude gold. Short, shaggy horses and burly, bearded warriors in borrowed Badhagh armor—opening their red mouths and bellowing their insensate triumph, while the old stones of Castle Erorn cracked and tumbled in the yelling blaze and Corum discovered what hate and terror were . . .

Glandyth's brutal face would fill his dreams, dominating even the dead, tortured faces of his parents and his sisters, so that he would often awake in the middle of the night, fierce, tensed, and shouting.

Then only Rhalina could calm him, stroking his ruined face and holding his shaking body close to her own.

Yet, during those days of early summer, there were moments of peace and they could ride through the woods of the mainland without fear, now, of the Pony Tribes, who had fled at the sight of the ship Shool had sent on the night of their attack—a dead ship from the bottom of the sea, crewed by corpses and commanded by the dead Margrave himself, Rhalina's drowned husband.

The woods were full of sweet life, of little animals and bright flowers and rich scents. And though they never quite succeeded, they offered to heal the scars on Corum's soul; they offered an alternative to conflict and death and sorcerous horror, and they showed him that there were things in the universe which were calm and ordered and beautiful and that Law offered more than just a sterile order but sought to establish throughout the Fifteen Planes a harmony in which all things could exist in all their variety. Law offered an environment in which all the mortal virtues could flourish.

Yet while Glandyth and all he represented survived, Corum knew that Law would be under constant threat and that the corrupting monster Fear would destroy all virtue.

As they rode, one pretty day, through the woods, he cast about him with his mismatched eyes and he said to Rhalina, "Glandyth must die!"

And she nodded but did not question why he had made this sudden statement, for she had heard it many times in similar circumstances. She tightened the rein on her chestnut mare and brought the beast to a prancing halt in a glade of lupine and hollyhock. She dismounted and picked up her long skirts of embroidered samite as she waded gracefully through the knee-high grass. Corum sat his tawny stallion and watched her, taking pleasure in her pleasure as she had known he would. The glade was warm and shadowy, sheltered by kindly elm and oak and ash in which squirrels and birds had made their nests.

"Oh, Corum, if only we could stay here forever! We could build a cottage, plant a garden . . ."

He tried to smile. "But we cannot," he said. "Even this is but a respite. Shool was right. By accepting the logic of conflict I have accepted a particular destiny. Even if I forgot my own vows of vengeance, even if I had not agreed to serve Law against Chaos, Glandyth would still come and seek us out and make us defend this peace. And Glandyth is stronger than these gentle woods, Rhalina. He could destroy them overnight and, I think, would relish so doing if he knew we loved them."

She kneeled and smelled the flowers. "Must it always be so? Must hate always breed hate and love be powerless to proliferate?"

"If Lord Arkyn is right, it will not always be so. But those who believe that love should be powerful must be prepared to die to ensure its strength."

She raised her head suddenly and there was alarm in her eyes as they stared into his.

He shrugged. "It is true," he said.

Slowly, she got to her feet and went back to where her horse stood. She put a foot into the stirrup and pulled herself into the sidesaddle. He remained in the same position, staring at the flowers and at the grass, which was gradually springing back into the places it had occupied before she had walked through it.

"It is true."

He sighed and turned his horse toward the shore.

"We had best return," he murmured, "before the sea covers the causeway."

A little while later they emerged from the forest and trotted their steeds along the shore. Blue sea shifted on the white sand and, still some distance away, they saw the natural causeway leading through the shallows to the mount on which stood Castle Moidel, the farthest and forgotten outpost of the civilization of Lywn-an-Esh. Once the castle had stood among woods on the mainland of Lywn-an-Esh, but the sea now covered that land.

Seabirds called and wheeled in the cloudless sky, sometimes diving to spear a fish with their beaks and return with their catch to their nests amongst the rocks of Moidel's Mount. The hooves of the horses thumped the sand or splashed through the surf as they neared the causeway, which would soon be covered by the tide.

And then Corum's attention was caught by a movement far out to sea. He craned forward as he rode and peered into the distance.

"What is it?" she asked him.

"I am not sure. A big wave, perhaps. But this is not the season of heavy seas." He pointed. "Look."

"There seems to be a mist hanging over the water a mile or two out. It is hard to observe . . ." She gasped. "It is a wave!"

Now the water near the shore became slightly more agitated as the wave approached.

"It is as if some huge ship were passing by at great speed," Corum said. "It is familiar . . ."

Then he looked more sharply into the distant haze. "Do you see something—a shadow—the shadow of a man on the mist?"

"Yes, I do see it. It is enormous. Perhaps an illusion—something to do with the light . . ."

"No, he said. "I have seen that outline before. It is the giant—the great fisherman who was the cause of my shipwreck on the coast of Koolocrah!"

"The Wading God," she said. "I know of him. He is sometimes

162

also called the Fisher. Legends say that when he is seen it is an ominous portent."

"It was an ominous enough portent for me when I last saw him," Corum said with some humor. Now good-sized waves were rolling up the beach and they backed their horses off. "He comes closer. Yet the mist follows him."

It was true. The mist was moving nearer the shore as the waves grew larger and the gigantic fisherman waded closer. They could see his outline clearly now. His shoulders were bowed as he hauled his great net, walking backward through the water.

"What is he thought to catch?" whispered Corum. "Whales? Sea monsters?"

"Anything," she replied. "Anything that is upon or under the sea." She shivered.

The causeway was now completely covered by the artificial tide and there was no point in going forward. They were forced further back toward the trees as the sea rolled in, in massive breakers, crashing upon the sand and the shingle.

A little of the mist seemed to touch them and it became cold, though the sun was still bright. Corum drew his cloak about him. There came the steady sound of the giant's strides as he waded on. Somehow he seemed a doomed figure to Corum—a creature destined to drag his nets forever through the oceans of the world, never finding the thing he sought.

"They say he fishes for his soul," murmured Rhalina. "For his soul."

Now the silhouette straightened its back and hauled in its net. Many creatures struggled there—some of them unrecognizable. The Wading God inspected his catch carefully and then shook out the net, letting the things fall back into the water. He moved on slowly, once again fishing for something it seemed he would never find.

The mist began to leave the shore as the dim outline of the giant moved out to sea again. The waters began to subside until at last they were still and the mist vanished beyond the horizon.

Corum's horse snorted and pawed at the wet sand. The Prince in the Scarlet Robe looked at Rhalina. Her eyes were blank, fixed on the horizon. Her features were rigid.

"The danger is gone," he said, trying to comfort her.

"There was no danger," she said. "It is a warning of danger that the Wading God brings."

"It is only what the legends say."

Her eyes became alive again as she regarded him. "And have we not had cause to believe in legends of late?"

He nodded. "Come, let's get back to the castle before the causeway's flooded a second time."

Their horses were grateful to be moving toward the sanctuary of Moidel's Castle. The sea was rising swiftly on both sides of the rocky path as they began to cross and the horses broke spontaneously into a gallop.

At last they reached the great gates of the castle and these swung open to admit them. Rhalina's handsome warriors welcomed them back gladly, anxious for their own experiences to be confirmed.

"Did you see the giant, My Lady Margravine?" Beldan, her steward, sprang down the steps of the west tower. "I thought it another of Glandyth's allies." The young man's normally cheerful, open face was clouded. "What drove it off?"

"Nothing," she said, dismounting. "It was the Wading God. He was merely going about his business."

Beldan looked relieved. As with all the inhabitants of Castle Moidel, he ever expected a new attack. And he was right in his expectations. Sooner or later Glandyth would march again against the castle, bringing more powerful allies than the superstitious and easily frightened warriors of the Pony Tribes. They had heard that Glandyth, after his failure to take Castle Moidel, had returned in a rage to the court at Kalenwyr to ask King Lyr-a-Brode for an army. Perhaps next time he came he would also bring ships, which could attack from seaward while he attacked from the land. Such an assault would be successful, for Moidel's garrison was small.

The sun was setting as they made for the main hall of the castle to take their evening meal. Corum, Rhalina, and Beldan sat together to eat and Corum's mortal hand went often to the wine jug and far less frequently to the food. He was pensive, full of a sense of profound gloom which infected the others so that they did not even attempt to make conversation.

Two hours passed in this way and still Corum swallowed wine.

And then Beldan raised his head, listening. Rhalina, too, heard the sound and frowned. Only Corum appeared not to hear it.

It was a rapping noise—an insistent noise. Then there were voices and the rapping stopped for a moment. When the voices subsided the rapping began again.

Beldan got up. "I'll investigate . . ."

Rhalina glanced at Corum. "I'll stay."

Corum's head was lowered as he stared into his cup, sometimes fingering the patch covering his alien eye, sometimes raising the

Hand of Kwll and stretching the six fingers, flexing them, inspecting them, puzzling over the implications of the situation.

Rhalina listened. She heard Beldan's voice. Again the rapping died. There was a further exchange. Silence.

Beldan came back into the hall.

"We have a visitor at our gates," he informed her.

"Where is he from?"

"He says he is a traveler who has suffered some hardship and seeks sanctuary."

"A trick?"

"I know not."

Corum looked up. "A stranger?"

"Aye," Beldan said. "Some spy of Glandyth's possibly."

Corum rose unsteadily. "I'll come to the gate."

Rhalina touched his arm. "Are you sure . . . ?"

"Of course." He passed his hand over his face and drew a deep breath. He began to stride from the hall, Rhalina and Beldan following.

He came to the gates and as he did so the knocking started up once more.

"Who are you?" Corum called. "What business have you with the folk of Moidel's Castle?"

"I am Jhary-a-Conel, a traveler. I am here through no particular wish of my own, but I would be grateful for a meal and somewhere to sleep."

"Are you of Lywn-an-Esh?" Rhalina asked.

"I am of everywhere and nowhere. I am all men and no man. But one thing I am not—and that is your enemy. I am wet and I am shivering with cold."

"How came you to Moidel when the causeway is covered?" Beldan asked. He turned to Corum. "I have already asked him this once. He did not answer me."

The unseen stranger mumbled something in reply.

"What was that?" Corum said.

"Damn you! It's not a thing a man likes to admit. I was part of a catch of fish! I was brought here in a net and I was dumped offshore and I swam to this damned castle and I climbed your damned rocks and I knocked on your damned door and now I stand making conversation with damned fools. Have you no charity at Moidel?"

The three of them were astonished then—and they were convinced that the stranger was not in league with Glandyth.

Rhalina signed to the warriors to open the great gates. They creaked back a fraction and a slim, bedraggled fellow entered. He

165

was dressed in unfamiliar garb and had a sack over his back, a hat on his head whose wide brim was weighed down by water and hung about his face. His long hair was as wet as the rest of him. He was relatively young, relatively good looking, and, in spite of his sodden appearance, there was just a trace of amused disdain in his intelligent eyes. He bowed to Rhalina.

"Jhary-a-Conel at your service, ma'am."

"How came you to keep your hat while swimming so far through the sea?" Beldan asked. "And your sack for that matter?"

Jhary-a-Conel acknowledged the question with a wink. "I never lose my hat and I rarely lose my sack. A traveler of my sort learns to hold on to his few possessions—no matter what circumstances he finds himself in."

"You are just that?" Corum asked. "A traveler?"

Jhary-a-Conel showed some impatience. "Your hospitality reminds me somewhat of that I experienced some time since at a place called Kalenwyr . . ."

"You have come from Kalenwyr?"

"I have been *to* Kalenwyr. But I see I cannot shame you, even by that comparison . . ."

"I am sorry," said Rhalina. "Come. There is food already on the table. I'll have the servants bring you a change of clothing and so forth."

They returned to the main hall. Jhary-a-Conel looked about him. "Comfortable," he said.

They sat in their chairs and watched him as he casually stripped of his wet clothes and stood at last naked before them. He scratched his nose. A servant brought him towels and he began busily to dry himself. But the new clothes he refused. Instead he wrapped himself in another towel and seated himself at the table, helping himself to food and wine. "I'll take my own clothes when they're dry," he informed the servants. "I have a stupid habit concerning clothes not of my particular choosing. Take care when you dry the hat. The brim must be tilted just so."

These instructions given, he turned to Corum with a bright smile. "And what name is it in this particular time and place, my friend?"

Corum frowned. "I fail to understand you."

"Your name is all I asked. Yours changes as does mine. The difference is sometimes that you do not know that and I do—or vice versa. And sometimes we are the same creature—or, at least, aspects of the same creature."

Corum shook his head. The man sounded mad.

"For instance," continued Jhary as he ate heartily through a piled plate of seafood. "I have been called Timeras and Shalenak.

166

Sometimes I am the hero, but more often than not I am the companion to a hero."

"Your words make little sense, sir," Rhalina said gently. "I do not think Prince Corum understands them. Neither do we."

Jhary grinned. "Ah, then this is one of those times when the hero is aware of only one existence. For the best, I suppose, for it is often unpleasant to remember too many incarnations—particularly when they coexist. I recognize Prince Corum for an old friend, but he does not recognize me. It matters not." He finished his food, readjusted the towel about his waist, and leaned back.

"So you'd offer us a riddle and then will not give us the answer," Beldan said.

"I will explain," Jhary told him, "for I do not deliberately jest with you. I am a traveler of an unusual kind. It seems to be my destiny to move through all times and all planes. I do not remember being born and I do not expect to die—in the accepted sense. I am sometimes called Timeras and, if I am 'of' anywhere, then I suppose I am of Tanelorn."

"But Tanelorn is a myth," said Beldan.

"All places are a myth somewhere else—but Tanelorn is more constant than most. She can be found, if sought, from anywhere in the multiverse."

"Have you no profession?" Corum asked him.

"Well, I have made some poetry and plays in my time, but my main profession could be that I am a friend of heroes. I have traveled—under several names, of course, and in several guises— with Rackhir the Red Archer to Xerlerenes where the ships of the Boatmen sail the skies as your ships sail the seas—with Elric of Melniboné to the Court of the Dead God—with Asquiol of Pompeii into the deeper reaches of the multiverse where space is measured not in terms of miles but in terms of galaxies—with Hawkmoon of Köln to Londrah where the folk wear jeweled masks fashioned into the faces of beasts. I have seen the future and the past. I have seen a variety of planetary systems and I have learned that time does not exist and that space is an illusion."

"And the Gods?" Corum asked him eagerly.

"I think we create them, but I am not sure. Where primitives invent crude gods to explain the thunder, more sophisticated peoples created more elaborate gods to explain the abstractions which puzzle them. It has often been noted that gods could not exist without mortals and mortals could not exist without gods."

"Yet gods, it appears," said Corum, "can affect our destinies."

"And we can affect theirs, can we not?"

Beldan murmured to Corum, "Your own experiences are proof of that, Prince Corum."

"So you can wander at will amongst the Fifteen Planes," Corum said softly. "As some Vadhagh once could."

Jhary smiled. "I can wander nowhere 'at will'—or to very few places. I can sometimes return to Tanelorn, if I wish, but normally I am hurled from one existence to another without, apparently, rhyme or reason. I usually find that I am made to fulfill my role wherever I land—which is to be a companion to champions, the friend of heroes. That is why I recognized you at once for what you are—the Champion Eternal. I have known him in many forms, but he has not always known me. Perhaps, in my own periods of amnesia, I have not always known him."

"And you are never a hero yourself?"

"I have been heroic, I suppose, as some would see it. Perhaps I have even been a hero of sorts. And, there again, it is sometimes my fate to be one aspect of a particular hero—a part of another man or group of other men who together make up a single great hero. The stuff of our identities is blown by a variety of winds—all of them whimsical—about the multiverse. There is even a theory I have heard that all mortals are aspects of one single cosmic identity and some believe that even the gods are part of that identity, that all the planes of existence, all the ages which come and go, all the manifestations of space which emerge and vanish, are merely ideas in this cosmic mind, different fragments of its personality. Such speculation leads us nowhere and everywhere, but it makes no difference to our understanding of our immediate problems."

"I'd agree with that," Corum told him feelingly. "And now, will you explain in more detail how you came to Moidel?"

"I will explain what I can, friend Corum. It happened that I found myself at a grim place called Kalenwyr. How I came there I do not quite remember, but then I am used to that. This Kalenwyr—all granite and gloom—was not to my taste. I was there but a few hours before I came under suspicion of the inhabitants and, by means of a certain amount of climbing about on roofs, the theft of a chariot, the purloining of a boat on a nearby river, escaped them and reached the sea. Feeling it unsafe to land, I sailed along the coast. A mist closed in, the sea acted as if a storm had blown up, and suddenly my boat and myself were mixed up with a motley mixture of fish, snapping monsters, men, and creatures I would be hard put to describe. I managed to cling to the strands of the gigantic net which had trapped me and the rest as we were dragged along at great speed. How I found breath sometimes I do not remember. Then, at last, the net was upended and we were all released. My companions went their different ways and I was left alone in the water. I saw this island and your castle and I found a piece of driftwood which aided me to swim here . . .''

"Kalenwyr!'' Beldan said. "In Kalenwyr did you hear of a man called Glandyth-a-Krae?''

Jhary frowned. "An Earl Glandyth was mentioned in a tavern, I think—with some admiration. A mighty warrior, I gathered. The whole city seemed preparing for war, but I did not understand the issues or what they considered their enemies. I think they spoke of the land of Lywn-an-Esh with a certain amount of loathing. And they were expecting allies from across the sea.''

"Allies? From the Nhadragh Isles, perhaps?'' Corum asked him.

"No. I think they spoke of Bro-an-Mabden.''

"The continent in the West!'' Rhalina gasped. "I did not know many Mabden still inhabited it. But what moves them to plan war against Lywn-an-Esh?''

"Perhaps the same spirit which led them to destroy my race,'' Corum suggested. "Envy—and a hatred of peace. Your people, you told me, adopted many Vadhagh customs. That would be enough to win them the enmity of Glandyth and his kind.''

"It is true,'' Rhalina said. "Then this means that we are not the only ones who are in danger. Lywn-an-Esh has not fought a war for a hundred years or more. She will be unprepared for this invasion.''

A servant brought in Jhary's clothes. They were clean and dry. Jhary thanked him and began to don them, as unselfconsciously as he had taken them off. His shirt was of bright blue silk, his flared pantaloons were as bright a scarlet as Corum's robe. He tied a big yellow sash about his waist and over this buckled a sword belt from which hung a scabbarded saber and a long poniard. He pulled on soft boots which reached the knee and tied a scarf about his throat. His dark blue cloak he placed on the bench beside him, together with his hat (which he carefully creased to suit his taste) and his bundle. He seemed satisfied. "You had best tell me all you think I need to know,'' he suggested. "Then I may be able to help you. I have gathered a great deal of information in my travels—most of it useless . . .''

Corum told him of the Sword Rulers and the Fifteen Planes, of the struggle between Law and Chaos and the attempts to bring equilibrium to the Cosmic Balance. Jhary-a-Conel listened to all of this and seemed familiar with many of the things of which Corum spoke.

When Corum had finished, Jhary said, "It is plain that attempts to contact Lord Arkyn for help would, at this moment, be unsuccessful. Arioch's logic still prevails on these five planes and must be completely demolished before Arkyn and Law can know real power. It is ever the lot of mortals to symbolize these struggles between the Gods and doubtless this war which seems likely between King Lry-a-Brode and Lywn-an-Esh will mirror the war between Law and Chaos on other planes. If those who serve Chaos win—if King Lyr-a-Brode's army wins, in fact—then Lord Arkyn may yet again lose his power and Chaos will triumph. Arioch is not the most powerful of the Sword Rulers—Xiombarg has greater power on the planes she rules and Mabelrode has even more power than Xiombarg. I would say that you have hardly experienced the real manifestations of Chaos' rule here."

"You do not comfort me," said Corum.

"It is perhaps better, however, to understand these things," Rhalina said.

"Can the other Sword Rulers send aid to King Lyr?" Corum asked.

"Not directly. But there are ways of manipulating these things through messengers and agents. Would you know more of Lyr's plans?"

"Of course," Corum told him. "But that is impossible."

Jhary smiled. "I think you will discover that it is useful to have a companion to champions as experienced as myself in your employ." And he stooped and reached into his bag.

He brought something out of the sack which, to their astonishment was alive. It seemed unruffled by the fact that it had spent a day at least inside the sack. It opened its large, calm eyes and it purred.

It was a cat. Or, at least, it was a kind of cat, for this cat had resting on its back a pair of beautiful black wings tipped with white. Its other markings were black and white, like those of an ordinary cat, with white paws and a white muzzle and a white front. It seemed friendly and self-possessed. Jhary offered it food from the table and the cat ruffled its wings and began to eat hungrily.

Rhalina sent a servant for milk and when the little animal had finished drinking it sat beside Jhary on the bench and began to clean itself, first its face, paws, and body and then its wings.

"I have never seen such an animal!" Beldan muttered.

"And I have never seen another like it in all my travels," Jhary agreed. "It is a friendly creature and has often aided me. Sometimes our ways part and I do not see it for an age or two, but we are often together and he always remembers me. I call him Whiskers. Not an original name, I fear, but he seems to like it well enough. I think he will help us now."

"How can he help us?" Corum stared at the winged cat.

"Why, my friends, he can fly to Lyr's court and witness what takes place there. Then he can return with his news to us."

"He can speak?"

"Only to me—and even that is not speaking as such. Would you have me send him there?"

Corum was completely taken aback. He was forced to smile. "Why not?"

"Then Whiskers and I will go to your battlements, with your permission, and I will instruct him what to do."

In silence the three watched Jhary adjust his hat on his head, pick up his cat, bow to them, and mount the stairs that would take him to the battlements.

"I feel as if I dream," said Beldan when Jhary had disappeared.

"You do," said Corum. "A fresh dream is just beginning. Let us hope we survive it . . ."

The Second Chapter

THE GATHERING AT KALENWYR

The little winged cat flew swiftly eastward through the night and came at last to gloomy Kalenwyr.

The smoke of a thousand guttering brands rose up from Kalenwyr and seemed to smear out the light of the moon. Square blocks of dark granite made up the houses and the castles and nowhere was there a curve or a soft line. Dominating the rest of the city was the brooding pile of King Lyr-a-Brode and around its black battlements flickered oddly colored lights and there was a rumbling like thunder, though no clouds filled the night sky.

Toward this pile now flew the little cat, alighting on a tower of harsh angles and folding its wings. It turned its large, yellow eyes this way and that, as if deciding which way it would enter the castle.

The cat's fur prickled, the long whiskers for which it had been named twitched, the tail went stiff. The cat had become aware not only of sorcery and the presence of supernatural creatures in the castle, but of a particular creature which it hated more than all the rest. Its progress down the side of the tower became even more cautious. It reached a slotted window and squeezed in. It was in a darkened, circular room. An open door revealed steps winding down the inside of the tower. Tensely the cat made its way down the steps. There were plenty of shadows in which to hide, for Castle Kalenwyr was a shadowy place.

At last the cat saw brand light burning ahead and it paused, looking warily around the door frame. The brands illuminated a long, narrow passage and at the end of the passage were the sounds of many voices, the clatter of arms and of wine-cups. The cat spread its wings and flew into the shadows of the roof, finding a long, blackened beam down which it could walk. The beam passed through the wall with a little room to spare and the cat squeezed through to find itself looking down at a huge gathering of Mabden. It walked further along the beam and then settled itself to watch the proceedings.

In the center of Castle Kalenwyr's great hall was a dais carved from a single block of unpolished obsidian and upon this dais was a throne of granite studded with quartz. Some attempt had been made to carve gargoyles upon the stone, but the workmanship was crude and unfinished. Nonetheless, the half-shapes carved there were more sinister than if they had been fully realized.

Seated upon this throne were three people. On each asymmetrical arm sat a naked girl, with flesh tattooed in obscene designs. Each girl held a jug with which she replenished the wine cup of the man who sat on the throne itself. This man was big—more than seven feet tall—and a crown of pale iron was upon his matted hair. The hair was long, with short plaits clustered over the forehead. It had been yellow but was now streaked with white and it seemed that some attempt had been made to dye these streaks back to their original color. The beard, too, was yellow and flecked with areas of stained gray. The face was haggard, covered in broken veins, and from the deep eye sockets peered eyes that were bloodshot, faded blue, full of hatred, cunning, and suspicion. Robes clothed the body from neck to foot. These were plainly of Vadhagh origin—brocades and samite now covered in the marks of food and wine. Over them was thrown a dirty coat of tawny wolfskin—just as plainly made by the Mabden of the East, whom the man ruled. The hands were encrusted with stolen rings torn from the fingers of slain Vadhagh and Nhadragh. One of the hands rested upon the pommel of a great, battered iron sword. The other clutched a bronze, diamond-studded goblet from which slopped thick wine. Surrounding the dais, their backs to their master, were a guard of warriors, each as tall as or taller than the man on the throne. They stood rigidly shoulder to shoulder, swords drawn and placed across the rims of their great oval shields of leather and iron sheathed in brass. Their brass helms covered most of their faces and from the sides escaped the hair of their heads and beards. Their eyes seemed to contain a perpetual and controlled fury and they looked steadily into the middle distance. This was the Asper Guard—the Grim Guard which was unthinkingly loyal to the man who sat upon the throne.

King Lyr-a-Brode turned his massive head and surveyed his court.

Warriors filled it.

The only women were the tattooed, naked wenches who served the wine. Their hair was dirty, their bodies bruised, and they moved

173

like dead things with their heavy wine jugs balanced on their hips, squeezing themselves in and out of the ranks of the big, brutal Mabden men in their barbaric war gear, with their braided hair and beards.

These men stank of sweat and of the blood they had spilled. Their leather clothes creaked as they raised wine cups to their hard mouths, their harness rattled.

A feast had recently taken place here, but now the tables and the benches had been cleared away and, save for the few who had collapsed and been dragged into corners, all the warriors were standing, watching their king and waiting for him to speak.

The light from iron braziers suspended from the roof beams flung their huge shadows on the dark stone and made the warriors eyes shine red like the eyes of beasts.

Each warrior in the hall was a commander of other warriors. Here were earls and dukes and counts and captains who had ridden from all parts of Lyr's kingdom to attend this gathering. And some, dressed a little differently from the others—favoring fur to the stolen Vadhagh and Nhadragh samite—had come from across the sea as emissaries from Bro-an-Mabden, the rocky land of the Northwest in which the whole Mabden race had originated long ago.

Now King Lyr-a-Brode placed his hands on the arms of his throne and levered himself slowly to his feet. Instantly five hundred arms raised goblets in a toast.

"LYR OF THE LAND!"

Automatically he returned the toast, mumbling, "And the Land is Lyr . . ." He looked around him, almost disbelievingly, staring for a long second at one of the girls as if he recognized her for something other than she was. He frowned.

A burly noble with gray, unhealthy eyes, a red shiny face, his thick black hair and beard curled and braided, a cruel mouth which was partly closed over yellow fangs, stepped from the throng and positioned himself just the other side of the Grim Guard. This noble wore a tall, winged helmet of iron, brass, and gold, a huge bearskin cloak on his shoulders. There was a sense of authority about him, and, in many ways, he had more presence than did the tall king who looked down on him.

The king's lips moved. "Earl Glandyth-a-Krae?"

"My liege, I hight Glandyth, earl over the estates of Krae," the man assured him formally. "Captain of the Denledhyssi who had scoured your land free of the Vadhagh vermin and all who allied themselves with them, who helped conquer the Nhadragh Isles.

And I am a brother of the Dog, a son of the Horned Bear, a servant of the Lords of Chaos!''

King Lyr nodded. "I know thee, Glandyth. A loyal sword."

Glandyth bowed.

There was a pause.

Then, "Speak," said the king.

"There is one of the Shefanhow creatures who escapes your justice, my king. Just one Vadhagh who still lives." Glandyth tugged the thong of his jerkin, which showed over the top of his breastplate. He reached inside and brought out two things which hung by a string around his neck. One of the things was a withered, mummified hand. The other was a small leather pouch. He displayed them. "This is the hand I took from the Vadhagh and here, in this sack, is his eye. He took refuge in the castle which lies at the far western shore of your land—the castle called Moidel. A Mabden woman possessed that castle—she is the Margravine Rhalina-a-Allomglyl and she serves that land of traitors, Lywn-an-Esh—that land which you now plan to crush because it refuses to support our cause.''

"All this you have told me," King Lyr replied. "And you have told me of the monstrous sorcery used to thwart your attack upon that castle. Speak on."

"I would march again to Castle Moidel, for I have heard that the Shefanhow Corum and the traitoress Rhalina have returned there, thinking themselves safe from your justice."

"All our armies go westward," Lyr told him. "All our strength is aimed at the destruction of Lywn-an-Esh. Castle Moidel will fall in our passing."

"The boon I beg is that I be the instrument of that fall, my liege."

"You are one of our greatest captains, Earl Glandyth, we would use you and your Denledhyssi in a main engagement."

"While Corum lives, commanding sorcery, our cause is much threatened. I speak truly, great king. He is a powerful enemy—perhaps more powerful than the whole land of Lywn-an-Esh. It will take much time to destroy him."

"One maimed Shefanhow? How is this so?"

"He has made an alliance with Law. I have proof. One of my Nhadragh lackeys has used its second sight and seen clear."

"Where is the Nhadragh?"

"He is without, my liege. I would not bring the vile creature into your hall without your permission."

"Bring him now."

All the bearded warriors stared toward the door with a mixture of disgust and curiosity. Only the Grim Guard did not turn its gaze. King Lyr reseated himself on his throne and gestured with his cup for more wine.

The doors were opened and a dim shape was revealed. Though it had the outline of a man it was not a man. The ranks broke as it began to shuffle forward.

It had dark, flat features and the hair of its head grew down its forehead to meet at a peak just below the eyebrows. It was dressed in a jacket and breeks of sealskin. Its stance was servile, nervous, and it bowed frequently as it moved toward the waiting Glandyth.

King Lyr-a-Brode's lips curled in nausea. He gestured at Glandyth. "Make this thing speak and then make it leave."

Glandyth reached out and seized the Nhadragh by his coarse hair. "Now, filth, tell my king what you saw with your degenerate senses!"

The Nhadragh opened its mouth and stuttered.

"Speak! Quickly!"

"I—I saw into other planes than this . . ."

"You saw into Yffarn—into hell?" King Lyr murmured in horror.

"Into other planes . . ." The Nhadragh looked shiftily about him and agreed hastily. "Aye, then—into Yffarn. I saw a creature there which I cannot describe, but I spoke with it for a brief time. It—it told me that Duke Arioch of Chaos . . ."

"He means the Sword Ruler," Glandyth explained. "He means Arag the Great Old God."

"It told me that Arioch—Arag—had been slain by Corum Jhaelen Irsei of the Vadhagh and that Lord Arkyn of Law now ruled these five planes again . . ." The Nhadragh's voice trailed off.

"Tell my king the rest," Glandyth said fiercely, tugging again on the wretch's hair. "Tell him what you learned relating to us Mabden!"

"I was told that now Lord Arkyn has returned he will attempt to regain all the power he once had over the world. But he needs mortals as his agents and of these agents Corum is the most important—but it is certain that most of the folk of Lywn-an-Esh will serve Arkyn, too, for they learned the ways of the—the Shefanhow —long since . . ."

"So all our suspicions were correct," King Lyr said in quiet triumph. "We do well to ready for war against Lywn-an-Esh. We fight against that soft degeneration misnamed as Law!"

"And you would agree that it is my duty to destroy this Corum?" Glandyth asked.

The king frowned. The he raised his head and looked directly at

Glandyth. "Aye." He waved his hand. "Now take that stinking Shefanhow from this hall. It is time to summon the Dog and the Bear!"

High on the central roof beam the little cat felt its fur stiffen. It was inclined to leave the hall there and then, but made itself stay. It was loyal to its master, and Jhary-a-Conel had told it to witness all that passed during Lyr's gathering.

Now the warriors had packed themselves around the walls. The women had been dismissed. Lyr himself left his throne and the whole center of the hall was now bare of men.

A silence fell.

Lyr clapped his hands from where he stood, still surrounded by his Grim Guard.

The doors of the hall opened and prisoners were brought in. There were young children and women and some men of the peasant class. All were comely and all were terrified. They were wheeled into the hall in a great wicker cage and some of the children were wailing. The imprisoned adults made no attempt to comfort the children any longer, but clutched at the wicker bars and stared hopelessly out into the hall.

"Aha!" King Lyr cried. "Here is the food of the Dog and the Bear. Tender food! Tasty food!" He relished their misery. He stepped forward and the Grim Guard stepped forward too. He licked his lips as he inspected the prisoners. "Let the food be cooked," he commanded, "so that the smell will reach into Yffarn and whet the appetites of the gods and draw them to us."

One of the women began to scream and some of them fainted. Two of the young men bowed their heads and wept and the children looked out of their cage uncomprehendingly, merely frightened by the fact of their imprisonment, not of the fate which was to come.

Ropes were passed through loops at the top of the cage and men hauled on the ropes so that the entire contraption was raised toward the roof beams.

The little cat shifted its position, but continued to observe.

A huge brazier was wheeled in next and placed directly below the cage. The cage rocked and swayed as the prisoners struggled. The eyes of the watching warriors glowed in anticipation. The brazier was full of white-hot coals and now servants came with jars of oil and flung it upon the coals so that the flames roared high into the air and licked around the wicker cage. A horrid ululation came from the cage then—a dreadful, incoherent noise which filled the hall.

And King Lyr-a-Brode began to laugh.

Glandyth-a-Krae began to laugh.

The earls and the counts and the dukes and the captains of the court all began to laugh.

And soon the screams subsided and were replaced by the crackling of the fire, the smell of roasting, human flesh.

Then the laughter died and silence came again to the hall as the warriors waited tensely to see what would happen next.

Somewhere beyond the walls of Castle Kalenwyr—somewhere out beyond the town—beyond the darkness of the night—there came a howling.

The little cat drew itself further back along the beam, close to the opening which led into the passage beyond the hall.

The howling grew louder and the flames of the great brazier seemed to be chilled by it and went out.

Now there was pitch darkness in the hall.

The howling echoed everywhere, rising and falling, sometimes seeming to die and then rising to an even louder pitch.

And then it was joined by a peculiar roaring sound.

These were the sounds of the Dog and the Bear—the dark and dreadful gods of the Mabden.

The hall shuddered. A peculiar light began to manifest itself over the vacant throne.

And then, wreathed in radiance of unpleasant and unnameable colors, a being stood on the granite dais and it turned its muzzle this way and that, sniffing for the feast. It was huge and it stank and it stood upon its hind legs like parody of those who, quaking, observed it.

The Dog sniffed again. Noises came from its throat. It shook its hairy head.

Still from somewhere came the other sound—the sound of grunting and roaring. This now grew louder and louder and, hearing it, the Dog cocked its head on one side and paused in its sniffing.

A dark blue light appeared on the dais on the opposite side of the throne. It took a form and the Bear stood there—a great, black bear with long, black horns curling from its head. It opened its snout and grimaced, displaying its pointed fangs. It reached out toward the charred wicker cage and it ripped it down from where it hung.

The Dog and the Bear fell upon the contents of the cage, stuffing the roasted human flesh into their mouths, growling and snuffling and choking, crunching the bones with the bloody juices running down their snouts.

And then they were finished and they lounged on the dais and glared around them at the silent, fearful mortals.

Primitive gods for a primitive people.

For the first time King Lyr-a-Brode left his circle of guards and walked toward the throne. He lowered himself to his knees and raised his arms in supplication to the Dog and the Bear.

"Great lords, hear us!" he moaned. "We have learned that Duke Arag has been slain by our enemy the Shefanhow, who is in league with our enemies of Lywn-an-Esh, the Sinking Land. Our cause is threatened and thus is your own rule in danger. Will you aid us, lords?"

The Dog growled. The Bear snuffled.

"Will you aid us, lords?"

The Dog cast its fierce eyes about the hall and it seemed that the same feral glint was in every other eye there. It was pleased. It spoke.

"We know of the danger. It is greater than you think." The voice was clipped, harsh, and it did not come easily to the canine throat. "You will have to marshal your strength quickly and march swiftly upon our enemies if those we serve are to retain their power and make you, in turn, stronger."

"Our captains are already gathered, My Lord the Dog, and their armies come to join them at Kalenwyr."

"That is good. Then we shall send you the aid we can send." The Dog turned its huge head and regarded its brother, the Bear.

The Bear's voice was high-pitched but easier to understand.

"Our enemies will also seek aid, but they will have greater difficulty in finding it, for Arkyn of Law is still weak. Arioch—whom you call Arag—must be brought back to his rightful place to rule these planes again. But if he is to do this a new heart must be found for him and a new fleshy form. There is only one heart and one form which will serve—the heart and form of his banisher, Corum in the Scarlet Robe. Complicated sorcery will be required to prepare Corum once he is captured—but captured he must be."

"Not slain?"

These were Glandyth's disappointed tones.

"Why spare him?" said the Bear.

And even Glandyth shuddered.

"We leave now," said the Dog. "Our aid will arrive soon. It will be led by one who is a messenger to the Great Old Gods themselves —to the Sword Ruler of the next plane, Queen Xiombarg. He will tell you more than can we."

And then the Dog and the Bear were gone and the stink of the cooked human flesh hung in the black hall and King Lyr's quaking voice called through the darkness. "Bring brands! Bring brands!"

The doors were opened, and a dim, reddish light fell down the middle of the hall. It showed the dais, the throne, the torn wicker cage, the extinguished brazier, and the kneeling, shuddering king.

Lyr-a-Brode's eyes rolled as he was helped to his feet by two of his Grim Guards. He did not seem to relish the responsibility which his gods had inferred was his. He looked almost pleadingly at Glandyth.

And Glandyth was grinning and Glandyth was panting like a dog about to feast on fresh-caught prey.

The little cat crept down the beam, along the passage, up the stairs to the tower. And it went away on weary wings, back to Castle Moidel.

The Third Chapter

LYWN-AN-ESH

It was a still, warm afternoon in high summer and a few wisps of white cloud lay close to the horizon. Bright, gentle blossoms stretched across the sward for as far as the eye could see, growing right down to where the yellow sand divided the land from the flat, calm ocean. All the flowers were wild, but their profusion and variety gave the impression that they had once been planted as part of a vast garden which had been left untended for many years.

Just recently a small, trim schooner had beached on the sand and out of it had emerged a bright company, leading horses down makeshift gangplanks. Silks and steel flashed in the sunlight as the whole complement abandoned the craft, mounted its steeds, and began to move inland.

The four leading riders reached the sward and their horses moved knee-deep through wild tulips as soft and richly colored as velvet. The riders took deep breaths of the marvelously scented air.

All save one of the riders were armored. One, tall and strange-featured, wore a jeweled patch over his right eye and a six-fingered jeweled gauntlet upon his left hand. He had a high, conical helm, apparently of silver, with an aventail of tiny silver links suspended from staples round the lower edge of the helm. His byrnie was also of silver, although its second layer was of brass, and his shirt, breeks, and boots were of soft, brushed leather. He had a long sword at his side, its pommel and guard decorated with delicate silver-work as well as red and black onyx. In a saddle sheath was a long-hafted war-axe with decorations matching those on the sword. On his back was a coat of a peculiar texture and of brilliant scarlet and on this were crossed a quiver of arrows and a long bow. This was Prince Corum Jhaelen Irsei in the Scarlet Robe, caparisoned for war.

Next to Prince Corum rode one who also wore mail, though with an elaborate helm fashioned from the shell of the giant murex and with a shield which was also made from shell. A slender sword and a lance were the weapons of this rider and she was the beautiful Margravine Rhalina of Allomglyl, caparisoned for war.

At Rhalina's side rode a handsome young man with a helm and shield that matched hers, a tall lance and a short-hafted war-axe, a sword and a long, broad-bladed baselard. His long cloak was of orange samite and matched the sleek coat of his chestnut mare, whose jeweled harness was probably worth more than the rider's own gear. And this was Beldan-an-Allomglyl, caparisoned for war.

The fourth rider wore a broad-brimmed hat which was somewhat fastidiously tilted on his head and which now sported a long plume. His shirt was of bright blue silk and his pantaloons rivaled the scarlet of Corum's cloak, there was a broad yellow sash about his waist with a well-worn leather swordbelt supporting a saber and a poniard. His boots reached to the knee and his long, dark-blue cloak was so long that it stretched out to cover the whole of his horse's rump. A small, black-and-white cat was perched upon his shoulder, its wings folded. It was purring and seemed to be an animal of singularly pleasant disposition. The rider occasionally reached up to stroke its head and murmur to it. And this was the sometime traveler, sometime poet, sometime companion to champions Jhary-a-Conel and he was not seriously caparisoned for war.

Behind them came Rhalina's men-at-arms and their women. The soldiers wore the uniform of Allomglyl, with helms, shields, and breastplates made from the gigantic crustaceans that had once populated the sea.

It was a handsome company and it blended well with the landscape of the Duchy of Bedwilral-nan-Rywm, most easterly county in the land of Lywn-an-Esh.

They had left Castle Moidel behind them after a vain attempt had been made to awaken the huge bats that slept in the caves below the castle ("Chaos creatures," Jhary-a-Conel had murmured, "they'll be hard to press into our service now.") and Lord Arkyn, doubtless concerned with more pressing matters, had failed to answer their call to him. It had become plain that Castle Moidel could no longer be defended, when the winged cat had brought back its news, and they had decided to ride all together to the capital of Lywn-an-Esh which was called Halwygnan-Vake and warn the king of the coming of the barbarians from the East and the South.

As he looked around him Corum was impressed by the beauty of the landscape and thought he could understand how such a lovely land had produced in a Mabden race so many characteristics he would normally call Vadhagh.

It was not cowardice which had made them abandon Moidel's Mount but it was caution and the knowledge that Glandyth would waste days—perhaps weeks—by planning and launching an attack on the castle they no longer occupied.

The main city of the Duchy was called Llarak-an-Fol and it would be a good two days' ride before they reached it. Here they hoped to get fresh horses and some information concerning the present state of the country's defenses. The Duke himself lived in Llarak and had known Rhalina as a girl. She was certain he would help them and that he would believe the tale they brought. Halwyg-nan-Vake lay another week's ride, at least, beyond Llarak.

Corum, although he had suggested much of their present plan, could not rid from his head some sense that he was retreating from the object of his hatred, and part of him wanted to turn back to Moidel and wait for Glandyth's coming. He fought the impulse but the conflict in him often made him gloomy and a poor companion.

The others were more cheerful, delighting in the fact that they were able to help Lywn-an-Esh prepare for an attack which King Lyr-a-Brode thought would be unexpected. With superior weapons, there was every chance of the invasion's being completely thwarted.

Only Jhary-a-Conel sometimes had the task of reminding Rhalina and Beldan of the fact that the Dog and the Bear had promised aid to King Lyr, though none knew what form that aid would take and how powerful it would be.

They camped that night on the Plain of Blossoms and by the next morning had reached rolling downlands. Beyond the downs, sheltered by them, lay Llarak-an-Fol.

Then, in the afternoon, they came to a pleasant village built on both sides of a pretty stream and they saw that the village square was full of people who stood around a water trough upon which was balanced a man in dark robes who addressed them.

They reined in on the slope of the hill and watched from a distance, unable to make anything of the babble they heard.

Jhary-a-Conel frowned. "They seem rather agitated. Do you think we are late with our news?"

Corum fingered his eye patch and considered the scene. "Doubtless nothing more than some local village affair, Jhary. Let's you and I ride down there and ask them."

Jhary nodded and, after a word with the others, they rode rapidly toward the village.

Now the dark-robed man had seen them and their company and he was pointing and shouting. The villagers were plainly disturbed.

As they entered the village street and drew close to the crowd, the dark-robed man, whose face was full of madness, screamed at them. "Who are you? On which side do you fight? Do you come to destroy us? We have nothing for your army."

"Hardly an army," murmured Jhary. Then more loudly he called, "We mean you no harm, friend. We are passing this way on our journey to Llarak."

"To Llarak. So you are on the Duke's side! You will help bring disaster to us all!"

"By what means?" Corum called.

"By leaguing yourselves with the forces of weakness—with the soft, degenerate ones who speak of peace and who will bring terrible war to us."

"You are still not especially specific," Jhary said. "Who are you, sir?"

"I am Verenak and I am a priest of Urleh. Thus I serve this village and have its well-being at stake—not to say the well-being of our entire nation."

Corum whispered to Jhary, "Urleh is a local godling of these parts—a sort of vassal deity to Arioch. I should have thought that his power would have disappeared when Arioch was banished."

"Perhaps that is why this Verenak is so upset," suggested Jhary with a wink.

"Perhaps."

Verenak was now peering closely at Corum. "You are not human!"

"I am mortal," Corum told him equably, "but I am not of the Mabden race, it is true."

"You are Vadhagh!"

"That I am. The last."

Verenak put a trembling hand to his face. He turned again to the villagers. "Drive these two out from here lest the Lords of Chaos take their vengeance upon us! Chaos will soon come and you must be loyal to Urleh if you would survive!"

"Urleh no longer exists," said Corum. "He is banished from our planes with his master Arioch."

"It is a lie!" screamed Verenak. "Urleh lives!"

"It is not likely," Jhary told him.

Corum spoke to the villagers. "Lord Arkyn of Law rules the Five Planes now. He will bring peace to you and a greater security than you have ever previously known."

"Nonsense!" Verenak shouted. "Arkyn was defeated by Arioch ages since."

"And now Arioch is defeated," Corum said. "We must defend this new peace we are offered. Chaos in all its power brings destruction and terror. Your land is threatened by invaders of your own race who serve Chaos and plan to slay you all!"

"I say that you lie—you seek to turn us against the Great Lord Arioch and the Lord Urleh. We are loyal to Chaos!"

The villagers did not seem to be as certain of that statement as Verenak.

"Then you will bring only disaster to yourselves," Corum insisted. "I know that Arioch is banished—I am the one who sent him into limbo. I destroyed his heart."

"Blasphemy!" shrieked Verenak. "Begone from here. I will not let you corrupt these innocent souls."

The villagers glanced suspiciously at Corum and then bestowed the same suspicious looks upon Verenak. One of them stepped forward. "We have no particular interest in either Law or Chaos," he said. "We wish only to live our lives as we have always lived them. Until recently, Verenak, you did not interfere with us, save to offer us a little magical advice from time to time and receive payment in return. Now you speak of great causes and of struggles and terror. You say that we must arm ourselves and march against our liege, the Duke. Now this stranger, this Vadhagh, says we must ally ourselves with Law—also to save ourselves. And yet there is no threat that we can see. There have been no portents, Verenak . . ."

Verenak raged. "There have been signs. They have come to me in dreams. We must become warriors on the side of Chaos, attack Llarak, show that we are loyal to Urleh!"

Corum shrugged. "You must not side with Chaos," he said. "If you would side with no one, then Chaos will devour you, however. You call our little band an army—and that means you have no conception of what an army can be. Unless we prepare against your enemies your flowery hills will one day be black with riders who will trample you as easily as they trample the blossoms. I have suffered at their hands and I know that they torture and they rape before slaying. Nothing will be left of your village unless you come with us to Llarak and learn how to defend your lovely land."

"How came this dispute to begin?" Jhary asked, taking a different tack. "Why are you trying to arouse these people against the Duke, Sir Verenak?"

Verenak glowered. "Because the Duke has gone mad. Not a month since he banished all the priests of Urleh from his city but

185

allowed the priests of that milk-and-water godling Ilah to remain. Thus he put himself upon the side of Law and ceased to tolerate the adherents of Chaos. He will therefore bring Urleh's vengeance—aye, even Arioch's vengeance—upon himself. And that is why I seek to warn these poor, simple people and get them to take action.''

"The people seem considerably more intelligent than you, my friend," laughed Jhary.

Verenak raised his arms to the skies. "O, Urleh, destroy this grinning fool!''

He lost his footing on the water trough's sides. His arms began to wave. He fell backward into the water. The villagers laughed. The one who had spoken came up to Corum. "Worry not, my friend—we'll do no marching here. We've our crops to harvest, for one thing.''

"You'll harvest no crops if the Mabden of the East come this way," Corum warned him. "But I'll debate no longer with you save to warn you that we Vadhagh could not believe in the bloodlust of those Mabden and we ignored the warnings. That is why I saw my father and my mother and my sisters all slain. That is why I am the last of my race.''

The man drew his hand over his brow and scratched his head. "I will think of what you have said, friend Vadhagh.''

"And what of him?" Corum pointed at Verenak, who was hauling himself from the trough.

"He'll bother us no more. He has many villages to visit with his gloomy news. I doubt if many will even take the trouble to listen to him as we have done.''

Corum nodded. "Very well, but please remember that these minor disputes, these little arguments, these apparently meaningless decisions, like that of the Duke in banishing the priests of Urleh, they are all indications that a greater struggle is to come between Law and Chaos. Verenak senses it just as much as does the Duke. Verenak seeks to gather strength for Chaos while the Duke puts himself in the camp of Law. Neither knows that a threat is coming, but both have sensed something. And I bring news to Lywn-an-Esh that a struggle is about to begin. Take heed of that warning, my friend. Think of what I have said, no matter how you choose to act upon it . . .''

The villager sucked at a tooth. "I will think on it," he agreed at last.

The rest of the villagers were going about their business. Verenak was making for his tethered horse, casting many a glowering glance back at Corum.

"Would you and your company take the hospitality of our village?" the man asked Corum.

Corum shook his head. "I thank you, but what I have seen and heard here confirms that we must make speed to Llarak-an-Fol and release our news. Farewell."

"Farewell, friend." The villager still looked thoughtful.

As they rode back up the hill Jhary was laughing. "As good a comic scene as any I've written for the stage in my time," he said.

"Yet it has tragedy beneath it," Corum told him.

"As does all good comedy."

And now the company galloped where before it had trotted, riding across the Duchy of Bedwilral-nan-Rywm as if the warriors of Lyr-a-Brode were already pursuing them.

And there was tension in the air. In every village they passed through there were apparently meaningless disputes between neighbors as one side supported Urleh and the other Ilah, but both refused to listen to what Corum told them—that the instruments of Chaos would soon be upon their land and they would cease to exist unless they prepared to resist King Lyr and his armies.

And when they came at last to Llarak-an-Fol, they found that there was fighting in the streets.

Very few of the cities of Lywn-an-Esh were walled and Llarak was no exception. She had long, low houses of stone and carved timber, all brightly painted. The house of the Duke of Bedwilral was not immediately evident, for it was little different from the other larger houses in the city, but Rhalina pointed it out. The fighting was quite close to the Duke's residence and near it a building was burning.

The company of Allomglyl began to ride down toward the city, leaving the women in the hills.

"It seems some of those Chaos priests were more persuasive than Verenak," Prince Corum shouted to Rhalina as she prepared her spear.

They galloped into the outskirts of the town. The streets were empty and silent. From the center came a great noise of battle.

"You had best lead us," he said to her, "for you'll know who are the Duke's men and who are not."

She increased her speed without a word and they followed her into the middle of Llarak-an-Fol.

There they were. Men in blue livery with helmets and shields similar to those borne by Rhalina's men were fighting a mixed force of peasants and what were evidently professional soldiers.

"The men in blue are the Duke's," she called. "Those in brown and purple are the city guard. There was always, I gather, a certain rivalry between the two.''

Corum felt reluctance to engage them, not because he was afraid but because he bore no malice toward them.

The peasants, in particular, hardly knew why they fought and doubtless the city guard was barely conscious of the fact that Chaos was working through them to create conflict. They had been filled with a vague sense of unrest and, with the pushing of the priests of Urleh, had resorted to anger and to arms.

But Rhalina was already leading her horsemen through in a lance charge. The spears dipped and the cavalry drove into the mass of men, cutting a wide path through their ranks. Most of the enemy was unmounted and Corum's axe rose up and down as he chopped at the heads of those who, still with astonishment on their faces, sought to stop his advance. His horse reared and whinnied and its hooves flailed and at least a dozen peasants and guards had died before they had joined with the Duke's men and had turned to drive back the way they had come.

Already, to Corum's relief, many of the peasants had dropped their weapons and were running. The few guards fought on and now Corum could see armed priests fighting with them. A small man— almost a dwarf—on a big, yellow charger, a massive broadsword in his left hand, was shouting encouragement to the newcomers. By his dress Corum decided that this must be the Duke himself.

"Lay down your arms!" the small man yelled to the guards. "You will have mercy! You will be spared!"

Corum saw a guard look about him and then drop his sword. Instantly the man was cut down by the Chaos priest nearest to him.

"Fight to the death!" screamed the priest. "If you betray Chaos now your souls will suffer more than your bodies could!"

But the surviving guards had plainly lost heart and one of them turned with resentment on the priest who had slain his comrade. His sword slashed at the man, who went down trying to staunch the blood that suddenly erupted from his severed jugular.

Corum sheathed his war-axe. The pathetic little battle was virtually over. Rhalina's men and the warriors in blue livery closed on the few who still fought and disarmed them.

The small man on the large horse rode up to where Rhalina had joined Corum and Jhary-a-Conel. The little black-and-white cat still clung to Jhary's shoulder and it looked more puzzled than frightened by what it had witnessed.

"I am Duke Gwelhen of Bedwilral," announced the small man. "I thank the mighty for thine aid. But I recognize thee not. Thou art not from Nyvish or Adwyn and, if ye be from farther afield, then ye could not have heard of my plight in time to save me!"

Rhalina removed her helm. She spoke as formally as the Duke. "Dost thou not recognize me, Duke Gwelhen?"

"I fear not. My memory for faces . . ."

She laughed. "It was many years past. I am Rhalina who married your cousin's son . . ."

"Whose responsibility was the Margravate of Allomglyl. But I learned that he died in a shipwreck."

"It is so," she said gravely.

"But I thought Castle Moidel taken by the sea these many years. Where have you been in the meantime, my child?"

"Until recently I ruled at Moidel, but now the barbarians of the East have driven us out and we ride to warn you that what you have experienced today is only a trifle of what Chaos will do if unchecked."

Duke Gwelhen rubbed at his beard. He returned his attention to the prisoners for a moment and issued some orders, then he smiled slowly. "Well, well. And who is this brave fellow with the eye patch—and this one, who has a pretty cat on his shoulder, and . . ."

She laughed. "I will explain, Duke Gwelhen, if we may guest in your hall."

"I would hope that you would! Come. This sad business is done. We'll to the hall now."

In Gwelhen's simple hall they ate a simple meal of cheese and cold meats washed down by the local beer.

"We are not used to fighting these days," Gwelhen said after introductions had been made and they had explained how they came to Llarak. "In some ways today's skirmish was a bloodier business than it might have been. If my men had more experience, they might have contained the thing and taken most of them prisoner, but they panicked. And it's likely that I'd have been dead by now if your company had not arrived. But all you tell me of this war between Law and Chaos makes much sense of various moods I have had of late. You heard how I banished the Temple of Urleh? Its adherents had taken to morbid, unhealthy pursuits. There were some murders—other things . . . I could not explain them. We are content here. None starves nor goes in need of anything. There was no reason for the unrest. So we are victims of powers beyond our control, are we? I like not that—whether it be Law or Chaos. I would prefer to remain neutral . . ."

"Aye," said Jhary-a-Conel. "Any thinking man does in these

conflicts. Yet there are times when sides must be taken lest all that one loves is destroyed. I have never known another answer to the problem, though the taking of an extreme position will always make a man lose something of his humanity."

"My feelings," murmured Gwelhen, motioning with his mug at Jhary.

"And all of ours," Rhalina agreed. "Yet unless we ready for King Lyr's attack, Lywn-an-Esh will be brutally destroyed."

"She is dying, for the sea takes more land every year," said Gwelhen thoughtfully. "Yet she should die at her own speed. We must convince the King, however . . ."

"Who rules now in Halwyg-nan-Vake?" Rhalina asked.

He looked at her in surprise. "The Margravate was indeed remote! Onald-an-Gyss is our king. He is old Onald's nephew—his uncle died without issue . . ."

"And what of his temperament—for these things are decided on temperament—does he favor Law or Chaos?"

"Law, I would think, but I cannot say the same for his captains. Warriors being what they are . . ."

"Perhaps they have already decided," Jhary murmured. "If the whole land is seized by the strife we have witnessed thus far, then a strong man supporting Chaos might have deposed the King, just as an attempt was made to depose you, Duke Gwelhen."

"We must ride at once to Halwyg," Corum said.

The Duke nodded. "Aye—at once. Yet a largish company rides with you. It would be a week at least before you reached the capital."

"The company must follow us," Rhalina decided. "Beldan, will you command it and bring it to Halwyg?"

Beldan grimaced. "Aye, though I wish I could ride with you."

Corum got up from the table. "Then we three will set off for Halwyg tonight. If we may rest an hour or two, Duke Gwelhen, we should be grateful."

Gwelhen's face was grave. "I would advise it. For all we know, you'll have little chance for much rest in the days to come."

The Fourth Chapter

THE WALL BETWEEN THE REALMS

Their riding was swift and it was across a land growing increasingly disturbed, with a people becoming more and more distressed without understanding why these moods descended on them or why they suddenly thought in terms of violence when a short time before they had thought only in terms of love.

And the priests of Chaos, many of them believing themselves to be acting from benevolent motives, continued to encourage strife and uncertainty.

They heard many rumors when they stopped to refresh themselves briefly or to change horses, but none of the rumors came close to the much more terrifying truth and soon they gave up their warnings until they should speak with the King himself so that he might then issue a decree which would carry his authority.

But would they convince the King? What evidence was there that they spoke the truth?

This was the great doubt in their minds as they rode for Halwyg-nan-Vake, across a beautiful landscape of soft hills and quiet farms which might soon be all destroyed.

Halwyg-nan-Vake was an old city of spires and pale stones. From all directions across the plain came white roads, leading to Halwyg. Along these roads traveled merchants and soldiers, peasants and priests, as well as the players and musicians in which Lywn-an-Esh was so rich. Down the Great East Way galloped Corum and Rhalina and Jhary, their armor and their clothes covered in dust, their eyes heavy with weariness.

Halwyg was a walled city, but the walls seemed more decorative than functional, their stonework carved with fanciful motifs, mythical beasts, and complicated scenes of the city's past glories. None of the gates were closed as they came near and there were only a few sleepy guards, who did not bother to hail them when they passed through and found themselves in streets filled with flowers. Every building had a garden surrounding it and every window had boxes in which more plants grew. The city was filled with the rich scents of the flowers and it seemed to Corum, remembering the Plain of Blossoms, that the main business of these people seemed to lie in the nurturing of lovely growing things.

And when they came to the palace of the King, they saw that every tower and battlement, every wall was covered in vines and flowers so that it seemed from a distance to be a castle built entirely of flowers. Even Corum smiled with pleasure when he saw it.

"It is magnificent," he said. "How could anyone wish to destroy all this?"

Jhary looked dubiously at the palace. "But they will," he said. "The barbarians will."

Rhalina addressed herself to a guard at the low wall.

"We come with news for King Onald," she said. "We have traveled far and swiftly and the news is urgent."

The guard, dressed in a handsome, but most unwarlike, fashion, saluted her. "I will see that the King is informed if you will kindly wait here."

And then, at last, they were escorted into the presence of the King.

He sat in a sunlit room which had a view over most of the southern part of the city. There were maps of his country upon a marble table and these had recently been consulted. He was young, with small features and a small frame which made him look almost like a boy. As they entered he rose gracefully to welcome them. He was dressed in a simple robe of pale yellow samite and there was a circlet upon his auburn hair, which was the only indication of his station.

"You are tired," he said when he saw them. He signed to a servant. "Bring comfortable chairs and refreshment." He remained standing until the chairs had been brought and they were all seated near the window with a small table nearby, on which food and wine were placed.

"I am told you come with urgent news," said King Onald. "Have you traveled from our eastern coasts?"

"From the West," said Corum.

"The *West?* Is trouble beginning there, also?"

"Excuse me, King Onald," Rhalina said, removing her helmet and shaking out her long hair, "but we were not aware that there was any strife in the East."

192

"Raiders," he said. "Barbarian pirates. Not long since they took the port of Dowish-an-Wod and razed it, slaying all. Several fleets, as far as we can gather, striking at different points along the coast. In most parts the citizens were unprepared and fell before they could begin to fight, but in one or two small towns the garrisons were able to resist the raiders, and, in one case, took prisoners. One of those prisoners has recently been brought here. He is mad."

"Mad?" Jhary said.

"Aye—he believes himself to be some kind of crusader, destined to destroy the whole land of Lywn-an-Esh. He speaks of supernatural help, of an enormous army which marches against us . . ."

"He is not mad," Corum told him quietly. "At least, not in that respect. That is why we are here—to warn you of a huge invasion. The barbarians of Bro-an-Mabden—doubtless your coastal attackers—and the barbarians of the land you know as Bro-an-Vadhagh have united, have called on the aid of Chaos and those creatures which serve Chaos, and are pledged to destroy all who side, knowingly or unknowingly, with the Lords of Law. For Duke Arioch of Chaos has been but lately banished from this particular domain of the Five Planes and can return only if all who support Law are vanquished. His sister, Queen Xiombarg, cannot give aid directly, but she encourages all her servitors to throw their weight behind the barbarians."

King Onald stroked his lips with a thin finger. "It is graver than I had imagined. I was hard put to think of effective ways of stopping the coastal attacks, but now I can think of nothing which will enable us to resist such a force."

"Your people must be warned of their peril," said Rhalina urgently.

"Of course," replied the King. "We will reopen the arsenals and arm every man that we can. But even then . . ."

"You have forgotten how to fight?" suggested Jhary.

The King nodded. "You have read my thoughts, sir."

"If only Lord Arkyn had consolidated his power over this domain!" Corum said. "He could aid us. But now there is too little time. Lyr's army marches from the East and his allies sail from the North . . ."

"And doubtless this city is their ultimate destination," murmured Onald. "We cannot possibly withstand the might which you say they command."

"And we do not know what supernatural allies they have," Rhalina reminded them. "We could not remain any longer at Moidel to discover that." She explained how they had learned of Lyr's ambitions and Jhary smiled.

"I regret," he said, "that my little cat cannot fly over great stretches of water. The idea distresses him too much."

"Perhaps the priests of Law can help us . . ." Onald said thoughtfully.

"Perhaps," agreed Corum, "but I fear they have little power at this moment."

"And there are no allies we can call upon," Onald sighed. "Well, we must prepare to die."

The three fell silent.

A little later a servant entered and whispered something to the King. He looked surprised and turned to his guests.

"We are all four summoned to the Temple of Law," he said. "Perhaps the powers of the priests are greater than we know, for they seem aware of your presence in the city." To the servant he said, "Have a carriage prepared to take us there please."

While they waited for the carriage, they bathed quickly and cleaned their clothes as best they could, and then the little party left the palace and entered the simple, open carriage which bore them through the streets until it came to a low, pleasant building on the western side of the city. A man stood at the entrance. He looked agitated. He was dressed in a long, white robe on which was embroidered the single straight arrow which was the symbol of Law. He had a short gray beard, long gray hair, and his skin was also almost gray. In all this, his large brown eyes seemed to belong to another.

He bowed as the King approached.

"Greetings, My Lord King. Greetings, Lady Rhalina, Prince Corum, and Sir Jhary-a-Conel. Forgive me for the sudden nature of my summons but—but . . ." He made a vague gesture and then led them into the cool temple, which was almost entirely undecorated.

"I am Aleryon-a-Nyvish," said the priest. "I was awakened early this morning by—by—my master's master. He told me many things, but ended by naming the names of you three travelers and saying that you would soon be at the court of the King. He said I must bring you here . . ."

"Your master's master?" Corum said.

"The Lord Arkyn himself. The Lord Arkyn, Prince Corum. None other."

And then, from the shadows at the far end of the hall a tall man walked. He was a comely man, dressed like a nobleman of Lywn-an-Esh. There was a gentle smile upon his face and his eyes seemed full of a sad wisdom.

The form had changed, but Corum immediately recognized the presence as that of Arkyn of Law.

"My Lord Arkyn," he said.

"Good Corum, how dost thou fare?"

"My mind is full of fear," Corum replied. "For Chaos comes against us all."

"I know, but it will be long before I can rid my domain entirely of Arioch's influence—just as it took him a great long time to rid the domain of mine. There is little material aid I can offer thee as yet, for I am still gathering my strength. However, there are other ways in which I can help. I can tell you that Lyr's allies have now joined him and that they are dreadful things from the nether regions. I can tell you that Lyr has another ally—an unhuman sorcerer who is the personal messenger of Queen Xiombarg and is capable of summoning further aid from her plane, though she would destroy herself if she attempted to come into this realm in person."

"But where might *we* find allies, Lord Arkyn?" Jhary asked reasonably.

"Do you not know, you of many names?" smiled Lord Arkyn. He had recognized Jhary-a-Conel for what he was.

"I know that if there be an answer then it may well be some form of paradox," Jhary replied. "That is one thing I have learned in my profession as Companion to Champions."

Again Arkyn smiled. "Existence is a paradox, friend Jhary. Everything that is Good is also Evil. You know that, I am sure."

"Aye. That is what makes me so insouciant."

"And it is what makes you so concerned?"

"Aye." Jhary laughed. "Then is there an answer, My Lord of Law?"

"That is why I am here, to tell you that unless you find aid for yourselves then Lywn-an-Esh will of a certainty perish and with it the Cause of Law. You know that you have not the strength, ferocity, or experience to withstand Lyr, Glandyth, and the rest—particularly since they may now call upon the power of the Dog and the Bear. There is one people of whom I know who may be willing to ally themselves with your cause. But they do not exist in this plane—or in any of the planes I rule. Save for yourself, Corum, Arioch had succeeded in destroying all with the power to resist Chaos."

"Where do they exist, my lord?" Corum asked.

"In the realm of Queen Xiombarg of Chaos."

"She must be our bitterest enemy!" Rhalina gasped. "If we could enter her realm—and I do not see how that is possible—she would welcome the chance to slay us!"

"I know that she would—once she found you," Lord Arkyn agreed. "But if you went to her realm you would have to hope that her attention would be so focused on the events in this realm that she would not realize you had entered her own."

"And what is there that might help us?" Jhary said. "Surely nothing of Law! Queen Xiombarg was more powerful than her brother Arioch. Chaos must hold full sway in her realm."

"Not quite—and not so much as in her brother Mabelrode's realm. . . . There is a city in her realm which has resisted all she could have brought against it. It is called the City in the Pyramid and the people who dwell in it are of a highly sophisticated civilization. If you can reach the City in the Pyramid, you may find the allies you need."

"But how could we travel to Xiombarg's realm?" Corum said reasonably. "We have no such powers."

"I can make it possible for you to do that."

"And how, in Five Planes, shall we find a single city?" Jhary asked.

"You must ask," said Arkyn simply. "Ask for the City in the Pyramid. The city which has resisted Xiombarg's attacks. Will you go? It is all that I can suggest if you would be saved . . ."

"And if you, too, are to be saved," Jhary pointed out with a smile. "I know you gods and I know that you manipulate mortals only to achieve those things you cannot yourselves achieve, for mortals may scurry where gods may not go. Have you other motives in encouraging this course of action, Lord Arkyn?"

Lord Arkyn looked humorously at Jhary. "You know the ways of gods, as you say. But I can tell you no more save that I gamble with your lives as freely as I gamble with my own destiny. What you risk, I risk. If you do not succeed in all I hope, then I will perish, all that is gentle and good in this realm will perish. And you need not go to Xiombarg's realm . . ."

"If there are potential allies there, then we will go," Corum said firmly.

"Then I will open the Wall Between the Realms," said Arkyn quietly.

He turned and walked back into the shadows.

"Ready yourselves," he said. He was now invisible.

Corum heard a sound in his head—a sound that was—soundless, but which blocked out all other sounds. He looked at the others. They were evidently experiencing the same thing. Something moved in front of his eyes—a dim pattern superimposed on the more solid scene which showed his companions and the simple walls of the temple. Something vibrated.

And then it was there.

A cruciform shape stood in the middle of the temple. They moved around it in wonder, but from whatever angle they regarded it, it retained the same perspective. It was a shimmering silver in the cool darkness of the temple and through it, as through a window, they could see a part of a landscape.

Arkyn's voice came from behind them.

"There is the entrance to Xiombarg's plane."

Strange, black birds flew across the section of sky they could observe through the peculiar window. A distant sound of cackling.

Corum shivered. Rhalina moved closer to him.

Now King Onald's voice. "If you would stay here, I will think no less of you . . ."

"We must go," Corum said almost dreamily. "We must."

But Jhary, with a suggestion of defiant jauntiness, was the first to step through and stand there, looking up at the unpleasant birds, stroking his cat.

"How shall we return?" Corum said.

"If you are successful, then you will find the means to return," said Arkyn. His voice was growing weaker. "Hurry. It takes much from me to hold the gateway open."

Hand in hand with Rhalina, Corum stepped through and looked back.

The cruciform shape of shimmering silver was fading. They saw Onald's concerned face for an instant and then it was gone.

"So this is Xiombarg's realm," said Jhary with a sniff. "It has a brooding air about it."

Black mountains lay on two sides and the sky was bleak. The horrid birds flew into the mountains, still screaming. Ahead, a foul sea washed a rocky shore.

BOOK TWO

*In which Prince Corum and his companions
gain the further enmity of Chaos and experience
a strange, new form of sorcery*

The First Chapter

THE LAKE OF VOICES

"Which way?" Jhary looked about him. "The sea or the mountains? Neither's inviting . . ."

Corum sighed deeply. The morbid landscape had instantly depressed him. Rhalina touched his arm, her eyes full of sympathy.

Though she looked at Corum, she spoke to Jhary, who was now adjusting his ever-present sack on his shoulder. "Inland would be best, surely, since we have no boat."

"And no horses," Jhary reminded her. "It will be a fearfully long walk. And who's to say those mountains are passable when we reach 'em?"

Corum gave Rhalina a quick, sad smile of gratitude. He straightened his shoulders. "Well, we made up our minds to enter this realm, now we must make up our minds which way to go." His hand on the pommel of his sword, he stared toward the mountains. "I have seen something of the power of Chaos when I journeyed to Arioch's court, but it seems to me that that power extends further in this realm. We'll head toward the mountains. There we may discover some inhabitants who may know where lies this City in the Pyramid Lord Arkyn mentioned."

And they set off over the unpleasantly mottled rock.

A while later it became evident that the sun had not moved across the sky. The brooding silence continued, broken only by the ghastly screechings of the black birds, which nested in the peaks of the mountain. It was a land which seemed to radiate despair. For a short time Jhary had attempted to whistle a bright little tune, but the sound had died, as if swallowed by the desolate land.

"I thought Chaos all howling, random creativity," said Corum. "This is worse."

"It is what becomes of a place when Chaos exhausts its invention," Jhary told him. "Ultimately, Chaos brings a more profound stagnation than anything it despises in Law. It must forever seek more and more sensation, more and more empty marvels, until there is nothing left and it has forgotten what true invention is."

And at length weariness overcame them and they lay down on the barren rock and slept. When they awoke it was to observe that only one thing had changed . . .

The great black birds were closer. They were wheeling overhead in the sky.

"What can they live on?" Rhalina wondered. "There is no game here, no vegetation. Where is their food?"

Jhary looked significantly at Corum, who shrugged.

"Come," said the Prince in the Scarlet Robe. "Let us continue. Time may be relative, but I have a feeling that unless we accomplish our mission soon, Lywn-an-Esh will fall."

And the birds circled lower so that they could see their leathery wings and bodies, their tiny, greedy eyes, their long, vicious beaks.

A small, fierce sound escaped from the throat of Jhary's cat. It arched its back slightly as it glared at the birds.

They trudged on until the ground began to rise more sharply and they had reached the nearer slopes of the mountains.

The mountains squatted over them like sleeping monsters that might at any moment awake and devour them. The rocks were glassy, slippery, and they climbed them slowly.

Still the black birds wheeled among the crags and now they were certain that if they allowed themselves to sleep the birds would descend and attack. This knowledge alone kept them climbing.

The frightful screeching grew louder, more insistent, almost gleeful. They heard the flap of obscene wings over their heads, but they refused to look up, as this would have wasted a fraction of the energy they had left.

They were looking now for shelter, for a crack in the rock into which they might crawl and defend themselves against the birds when, finally, they attacked.

They could hear the sound of their own gasping breath, the scrape of their feet on the stone, mingling with the flapping and screechings of the black birds.

Corum spared a glance for Rhalina and saw that there was desperate fear in her eyes and that she was weeping as she climbed. He began to feel that he had been tricked by Arkyn, that they had been sent, cynically, to their doom in this wasteland.

Then the flapping filled his ears and he felt the slap of cold air against his face and a talon grazed his helmet. With a strangled cry he felt for his sword and tried to tug it from the scabbard. He looked up in terror and saw a mass of black, flapping, savage things with glaring eyes and snapping beaks. The sword came free and, wearily, he lunged out at the birds. They cackled sardonically as his sword failed to find flesh. Suddenly his six-fingered jeweled hand reached out instead, moving without his volition, and it clutched one of the birds by its scrawny throat and squeezed that throat as it had squeezed human throats before. The bird gave a single surprised squawk and died. The Hand of Kwll threw the corpse to the glassy rock. The birds flapped a little distance away in consternation and settled in the nearby crags watching Corum warily. It had been so long since the Hand had acted in that way that Corum had almost forgotten its powers. For the first time since it had destroyed the heart of Arioch he was grateful to it. He displayed it to the birds and they made disturbed sounds in their throats, eyeing the corpse of their dead companion.

Rhalina, who had not witnessed the power of the Hand of Kwll before, looked with relieved astonishment at Corum. But Jhary merely pursed his lips and took advantage of the pause to draw his sword and lie propped on his elbows against the hard rock, his cat still on his shoulder.

And thus they sat, the birds and the human beings, regarding each other beneath the silent, brooding sky on the slopes of the bleak mountains until it occurred to Corum that if the Hand of Kwll had saved them from their immediate danger, the Eye of Rhynn might prove even more useful. But he was reluctant to raise the eye patch and look with the eye's full powers into that strange nether region from which he could sometimes summon ghostly allies—the dead men earlier slain at his command. And, particularly, he did not want to summon those last who had been slain at the command of the Hand and the Eye—Queen Ooresé's subjects, the Vadhagh riders, his own race, who had been slain by accident. But something must be done to break this impasse, for none of them had the strength to resist a mass attack by the birds and even if the Hand of Kwll should slay one or two more it would not save Rhalina and Jhary-a-Conel. Reluctantly his hand began to rise toward the jeweled eye patch.

And then the patch was off and the horrid, faceted, alien Eye of the dead god Rhynn glared into a world even more dreadful than the one they now inhabited.

Again Corum saw a cavern in which dim shapes moved hopelessly this way and that. And in the foreground were the beings he had least wished to see. Their dead eyes peered out at him and there was a frightening sadness about the set of their faces. They had wounds in their bodies, but the wounds did not bleed, for these were now the creatures of Limbo, neither dead nor alive. Their mounts were with them, too—creatures with thick, scaly bodies, cloven feet, and nests of horns jutting from their snouts. The last of the Vadhagh folk—a lost part of the race which had once inhabited the Flamelands created by Arioch for his amusement. They were dressed from head to foot in red, tight-fitting garments, with red hoods on their heads. In their hands were their long, barbed lances.

Corum could not bear to look upon them and he made to move the eye patch back into place, but then the Hand of Kwll had reached out, reached into that frightful Limbo, and was gesturing to the dead Vadhagh. Slowly the score of corpses moved forward in answer to the summons. Slowly they mounted their horned beasts. Slowly they rode out of that ghastly cavern in a nameless netherworld and stood, a company of death, upon the slippery slopes of the mountains.

The birds screeched in surprise and anger but for some reason they did not take to the air. They shifted from foot to foot and darted their beaks at the scarlet warriors who now advanced upon them.

The black birds waited until the dead Vadhagh were almost upon them before they began to flap their wings and fly skyward.

Rhalina was staring in horror at the scene. "By all the Great Old Gods, Corum—what new foulness is this?"

"It is a foulness which aids us," said Corum grimly. And he called out, "Strike!"

And the barbed lances were flung by scarlet arms and found the heart of each black bird. There was an agitation in the air and then the creatures had fallen to the slopes.

Rhalina continued to watch wide-eyed as the living-dead riders dismounted and went to collect their prizes. Corum had learned what happened in that netherworld whenever he summoned aid from it. By calling upon his earlier victims he could have their aid if he supplied them with victims of their own—then these victims would replace them and presumably the souls of the first victims would be released to find peace. He hoped that this was so.

The leading Vadhagh picked up two of the birds by their throats and slung them over his back. He turned a face that was half shorn away and looked through eyeless sockets at Corum.

"It is done, Master," droned the dead voice.

"Then you may return," said Corum, half-choking.

"Before I go, I must impart a message to you, Master."

"A message? From whom?"

"From One Who is Closer to You than You Know," said the dead Vadhagh mechanically. "He says that you must seek the Lake of Voices, that if you have the courage to sail across it then you might find help in your quest."

"The Lake of Voices. Where is it? Who is this creature you speak of . . . ?"

"The Lake of Voices lies beyond this mountain range. Now I depart, Master. We thank you for our prizes."

Corum could bear no longer to look at the Vadhagh. He turned away, replacing the jeweled patch over his eye. When he looked back the Vadhagh had gone and so had the birds, all save the one which had been slain by the Hand of Kwll.

Rhalina's face was pale. "These 'allies' of yours are no better than creatures of Chaos. It must corrupt us to use them, Corum . . ."

Jhary got up from the position in which he had been before the arrival of Corum's ghastly warriors. "It is Chaos which corrupts us," he said lightly, "which makes us fight. Chaos brutalizes all—even those who do not serve it. That you must accept, Lady Rhalina. I know it is the truth."

She lowered her eyes. "Let us make our way to this lake," she said. "What was its name?"

"A strange one." Corum looked back at the last dead bird. "The Lake of Voices."

They trudged on through the mountains, resting frequently now that the danger of the birds had been removed, beginning to feel a new threat—that of hunger and thirst, for they had no provisions with them.

Eventually they began to descend, and they saw sparse grass growing on the lower slopes and beyond the grass a lake of blue water—a calm and beautiful lake which they could not believe existed in any realm of Chaos.

"It is lovely!" Rhalina gasped. "And we might find food there —and at least we shall be able to quench our thirst."

"Aye . . ." said Corum, more suspiciously.

And Jhary said, "I think your informant said we should need courage to cross it. I wonder what danger it holds."

• • •

203

They could barely walk by the time they reached the grassy slopes and left the harsh rock behind them. On the grass they rested and they found a stream which sprang from a spring nearby so that they did not have to wait until they reached the lake to quench their thirst. Jhary murmured a word to his cat, which sprang suddenly into the air on its wings and was soon lost from sight.

"Where have you sent the cat, Jhary?" asked Corum.

Jhary winked at him. "Hunting," he said.

Sure enough, in a very short time the cat returned with a small rabbit, almost as big as itself, in its claws. It deposited the rabbit and then left to find another. Jhary busied himself with the building of a fire and soon they had feasted and were sleeping, while one of their number kept watch until he was relieved by another.

Then they continued on their way until they were less than a quarter of a mile from the shores of the lake.

It was then that Corum paused, cocking his head on one side.

"Do you hear them?" he asked.

"I hear nothing," Rhalina said.

But Jhary nodded. "Aye—voices—as of a great throng heard in the distance. Voices . . ."

"That is what I hear," Corum agreed.

And as they neared the lake, walking swiftly over the springy turf, the babble of voices increased until it filled their heads and they covered their ears in horror, for they realized now why it would take courage to cross the Lake of Voices.

The words—the murmurings, the pleadings, the oaths, the shouts, the crying, the laughter—they were all issuing from the blue waters of the apparently peaceful lake.

It was the water that spoke.

It was as if a million people had been drowned in it and continued to talk although their bodies had rotted and been dispersed by the liquid.

Looking desperately about him, his hands still covering his ears, Corum saw that it would be impossible to try to skirt the Lake of Voices, for it was apparent that on both sides of them there stretched marshland which they would be unable to cross.

He forced himself to move closer to the water and the voices of the men and the women and the children were like the voices which must populate hell.

"Please . . ."

"I wish—I wish—I wish . . ."

"Nobody will—"

"This agony . . ."

"There is no peace . . ."

204

"Why . . . ?"

"It was a lie. I was deceived . . ."

"I, too, was deceived. I cannot . . ."

"Aaaaaaa! Aaaaaaa! Aaaaaaa!"

"Help me, I beg thee . . ."

"Help me!"

"Me!"

"The fate which cannot be borne except with . . ."

"Ha!"

"Help . . ."

"Be merciful . . ."

"Save her—save her—save her . . ."

"I suffer so much . . ."

"Ha, ha, ha, ha, ha, ha, ha, ha, ha, ha, ha, ha, ha, ha, ha, ha, ha, ha, ha, ha, ha, ha, ha . . ."

"It seemed so splendid and there were lights all around . . ."

"Beasts, beasts, beasts, beasts, beasts . . ."

"The child. . . . It was the child . . ."

"All morning it wept until the lurching thing entered me . . ."

"Soweth! Tebel art . . ."

"Forlorn in Rendane I composed that strain . . ."

"Peace . . ."

And then Corum saw that a boat was waiting for them on the shore of the Lake of Voices.

And he wondered if he would be sane by the time they reached the other side.

The Second Chapter

THE WHITE RIVER

Corum and Jhary hauled on the boat's long oars while Rhalina lay sobbing in the bow. With every pull upon the oars the water was disturbed further and instead of a splashing sound a new babble of voices broke out. They sensed that the voices did not come from beneath the water but from within it—as if every single drop of water contained a human soul which expressed its pain and the terror of its situation. Corum could not help but wonder if every lake in existence were not like this and if this were the only one they could actually hear. He strove to shut his mind to such fearful speculation.

"Wish that . . ."

"Would that . . ."

"If I . . ."

"Could I . . ."

"Love—love—love . . ."

"Sad soothing songs seeking souls so soft so sensitive seeming smooth silken . . ."

"Stop! Stop!'' begged Rhalina, but the voices went on and Corum and Jhary pulled the harder on their oars, their lips moving in pain.

"I wish—I wish—I wish—I wish . . ."

"Curl awake in kitten time the condemnation of my . . ."

"One—once—once . . ."

"Help us!"

"Release us!"

"Give us peace! Peace!"

"Please, peace, please, peace . . ."

"Opening without resort . . ."

"Cold . . ."

"Cold . . ."

"Cold . . ."

"We cannot help you!" Corum groaned. "There is nothing we can do!"

Rhalina was screaming now.

Only Jhary-a-Conel kept his lips tight shut, his eyes fixed on the middle distance, his body moving rhythmically back and forth as he continued to row.

"Oh, save us!"

"Save me!"

"The child is—the child . . ."

"Bad, mad, sad, glad, bad, sad, mad, glad, mad, bad, glad, sad . . ."

"Be silent! We can do nothing!"

"Corum! Corum! Stop them! Is there no sorcery at your command which will hush their voices?"

"None."

"Aaaah!"

"Oorum canish, oorum canish, oorum canish, sashan faroom alann alann, oorum canish, oorum canish . . ."

"Ha, ha, ha, ha, ha, ha . . ."

"Nobody, nothing, nowhere, needless misery, what purpose doth it serve, which man benefits?"

"Whisper softly, whisper low, whisper, whisper . . ."

"No, no, no, no, no, no, no, no, no, no, no . . ."

Now Corum released one hand from his oar and slapped at his head as if trying to drive the voices out. Rhalina had collapsed completely on the bottom of the boat and he could not distinguish her cries, her pleadings and demands, from the others.

"Stop!"

"Stop, stop, stop, stop . . ."

"Stop . . ."

"Stop . . ."

"Stop . . ."

There were tears flowing down Jhary's face, but he rowed on, not once altering the rhythm of his movements. Only the cat seemed undisturbed. It sat on the seat between him and Corum and it washed its paws. To the cat the water was like any other water and thus to be avoided as much as possible. Once or twice it cast nervous glances over the side of the boat but that was all.

"Save us, save us, save us . . ."

Then a deeper voice, a warm, humorous, pleasant voice, cut through the others and it said,

"Why do you not join them? It would save you this misery. All

you need do is to stop your rowing and leave the boat and enter the water and relax, becoming one with the rest. Why be proud?"

"No! Do not listen! Listen to me!"

"Listen to us!"

"Do not listen to them. They are really happy. It is just that your coming disturbs them. They wish you to join them—to join them— to join them—to join them . . ."

"No, no, no!"

"No!" screamed Corum. He plucked the oar from the oarlocks and he began to beat at the waters of the lake. "Stop! Stop! Stop!"

"Corum!" Jhary spoke for the first time. He clung to the side as the boat rocked badly from side to side. Rhalina looked up in terror.

"Corum! You will make it worse. You will destroy us if we fall into the lake!" Jhary cried.

"Stop! Stop! Stop!"

Keeping one arm on his own oar Jhary reached across and tugged at Corum's scarlet robe. "Corum! Desist!"

Corum sat down suddenly and looked strangely at Jhary as if he were an enemy. Then his expression softened and he put the oar back in its place and began to row. The shore was not too distant now.

"We must get to the shore," Jhary said. "It is the only way in which we'll escape the voices. You must hang on a little longer, that is all."

"Yes," said Corum. "Yes . . ." And he resumed his rowing and avoided looking at Rhalina's tortured features.

"Molten sleeping snakes and old owls and hungry hawks populate my memories of Charatatu . . ."

"Join them and all the splendid memories may be shared. Join them, Prince Corum, Lady Rhalina, Sir Jhary. Join them. Join them. Join them."

"Who are you?" Corum said. "Did you do this to them all?"

"I am the Voice of the Lake of Voices, that is all. I am the true spirit of the Lake. I offer peace and union with all your fellow souls. Do not listen to the minority of discontented ones. They would be discontented wherever they were. There are always such spirits . . ."

"No, no, no, no . . ."

And Corum and Jhary pulled even harder on their sweeps until suddenly the boat scraped up the shore and there was an angry motion in the water and a huge water spout suddenly appeared and began to whine and roar and scream and shout.

"NO! I WILL NOT BE THWARTED! YOU ARE MINE! NONE ESCAPES THE LAKE OF VOICES!"

208

The water spout assumed a form and they could see a fierce, writhing face there—a face full of rage. Hands, too, formed from the water and began to reach out for them.

"*YOU ARE MINE! YOU WILL SING WITH THE REST! YOU WILL BE PART OF MY CHORUS!*"

The three scrambled hastily from the boat and dashed up the shore with the water thing growing larger and larger behind them and its voice roaring louder and louder.

"*YOU ARE MINE! YOU ARE MINE! I WILL NOT ALLOW YOU TO GO!*"

But a thousand tinier voices all babbled:

"*Run—run swiftly—never return—run—run—run . . .*"

"*TRAITORS! STOP!*"

And the voices stopped and there was silence until the rearing creature of water bellowed once more.

"*NO! YOU HAVE MADE ME DISPEL THE VOICES—MY VOICES—MY PETS! I MUST BEGIN AFRESH TO COLLECT MY CHOIR! YOU HAVE MADE ME BANISH THEM! COME BACK! COME BACK!*"

And the creature grew even taller as they ran all the faster, its watery hands reaching out for them.

Then, suddenly, with a scream, it began to tumble back into the lake, no longer able to sustain its shape. They watched it fall, they watched it writhe and gesticulate in anger, and then it was gone and the lake was the peaceful stretch of blue water they had first seen.

But this time there were no voices. The souls were still. By accident the three had made the creature tell its captives to be silent and had evidently broken the spell which it had had over them.

Corum sighed and sat down on the grass. "It is over," he said. "And all those poor spirits are at rest now . . ."

He smiled at the expression of panic on the cat's face and he realized how much more horrifying their last experience had been to the little animal.

Then, when they had rested, they climbed the hill and looked down upon a desert.

It was a brown desert and through it ran a river. But it seemed that the river was not of water. It was white, like pure milk, and it was wide and it wandered lazily through the brown landscape.

Corum sighed. "It seems to go on forever."

"Look," said Rhalina, and she pointed. "Look, a rider!"

Mounting the brow of a hill and coming toward them was a man on a horse. He was slumped in the saddle and plainly had not seen them, but Corum drew his sword nonetheless, and the others drew theirs. The horse moved slowly, plodding on as if it had been walking for days.

They saw that the rider, dressed in patched and battered leather, was asleep in his saddle, a broadsword hanging by a thong from his right wrist, his left hand gripping the reins of the horse. He had a haggard face which gave no indication of his age, a great hooked nose, and untrimmed hair and beard. He seemed a poor man, yet hanging on his saddle pommel was a crown which, though coated with dust, was plainly of gold studded with many precious gems.

"Is he a thief?" Rhalina wondered. "Has he stolen that crown and is he trying to escape those who own it?"

When it was a few feet from them the horse stopped suddenly and looked at them with large, weary eyes. Then it bent and began to crop the grass.

At this the rider stirred. He opened his eyes. He rubbed them. He, too, peered at them and then seemed to ignore them. He mumbled to himself.

"Greetings, sir," said Corum.

The gaunt man screwed up his eyes and looked at Corum again. He reached down behind him for a water bottle, unstopped it, and flung back his head to drink deeply. Then, deliberately, he put the stopper back in to the bottle and replaced the thing behind him.

"Greetings," said Corum again.

The mounted man nodded at him. "Aye," he said.

"From where do you travel, sir?" Jhary asked. "We ourselves are lost and would appreciate some indication of what, for instance, lies beyond that brown waste there . . ."

The man sighed and looked at the waste, at the white, winding river.

"That is the Blood Plain," he said. "The river is called the White River—or by some the Milk River, though it is not milk . . ."

"Why the Blood Plain?" Rhalina asked.

The man stretched and frowned. "Because, madam, it is a plain and it is covered in blood. That brown dust is dried blood—blood spilled an age since in some forgotten battle between Law and Chaos, I understand."

"And what lies beyond it?" Corum said.

"Many things—none that are pleasant. There is nothing that is pleasant in this world since Chaos conquered it."

"You are not on the side of Chaos?"

"Why should I be? Chaos dispossessed me. Chaos exiled me. Chaos would have me dead, but I move all the while and have not been found yet. One day, perhaps . . ."

Jhary introduced his friends and then himself. "We seek a place called the City in the Pyramid," he told the haggard rider.

The rider laughed. "As do I. But I cannot believe it exists! I think Chaos pretends such a place resists it to offer hope to its enemies so that it may give them still more pain. I am called, sir, the King Without a Country. Noreg-Dan was once my name and I ruled a fair land and, I think, I ruled it wisely. But Chaos came and Chaos minions destroyed my nation and my subjects and left me alive to wander the world seeking a mythical city . . ."

"So you have no faith in the City in the Pyramid?"

"I have not found it thus far."

"Could it lie beyond the Blood Plain?" Corum asked.

"It could, but I'm not fool enough to cross it, for it could be endless and you, on foot, would have a smaller chance than would I. I am not without courage," said King Noreg-Dan, "but I still retain a little common sense. If there was wood in these parts, perhaps it would be possible to build a boat and hope to cross the desert by means of the White River, but there is no wood . . ."

"But there is a boat," said Jhary-a-Conel.

"Would it be wise to go back to the Lake of Voices?" Rhalina cautioned.

"The Lake of Voices!" King Noreg-Dan shook his tangled head. "Do not go there—the voices will draw you in . . ."

Corum explained what had happened and the King Without a Country listened intently. Then he smiled and it was a smile of admiration. He dismounted from his horse and came close to Corum, inspecting him. "You're a strange-looking creature, sir, with your hand and your eye patch and your odd armor, but you are a hero and I congratulate you—all of you." He addressed the others. "I'd say it would be worth a foray down to the beach to recover old Freenshak's boat—we could use my horse to haul it up here!"

"Freenshak?" Jhary said.

"One of the names of the creature you encountered. A particularly powerful water sprite which came when Xiombarg began her reign. Shall we try to get the boat?"

"Aye," grinned Corum. "We'll try."

Somewhat nervously they returned to the lake shore, but it seemed that Freenshak was beaten for the moment and they had no difficulty in harnessing the tired horse to the boat and pulling it up the hill and halfway down the other side. In a locker Corum found a sail and saw that a short mast was stowed in lugs along one side of the boat.

As they prepared the boat he said to King Noreg-Dan, "But what of your horse? There'll not be room . . ."

Noreg-Dan drew a deep breath. "It will be a shame, but I will have to abandon him. I think he will be safer alone than with me and, besides, he deserves a rest, for he has served me faithfully since I was forced to flee my land."

Noreg-Dan stripped the horse of its harness and put it in the boat. Then they began the hard task of dragging the vessel down the hill and across the brown, choking dust (all the more unpleasant now that they knew what the dust was) until they reached the nearest shore of the White River. The horse stood watching them from the hillside and then it turned away. Noreg-Dan lowered his head and folded his arms.

And still the sun had not moved across the sky and they had no means of knowing how much time had passed.

The liquid of the river was thicker than water and Noreg-Dan advised them not to touch it.

"It can have a corrosive effect on the skin," he said.

"But what is the stuff?" Rhalina asked as they pushed off and raised the sail. "Will it not rot the boat if it will rot our skin?"

"Aye," said the King Without a Country. "Eventually. We must hope we cross the desert before that happens." He looked back once more to where he had left his horse, but the horse had disappeared. "Some say that while the dust is the dried blood of mortals, the White River is the blood of the Great Old Gods which was spilled in the battle and which will not dry."

Rhalina pointed to the hillside from which the river appeared. "But that cannot be—it comes from somewhere and it goes somewhere . . ."

"Apparently," said Norge-Dan.

"Apparently?"

"This land is ruled by Chaos," he reminded her.

A light breeze was blowing now and Croum raised the sail. The boat began to move more quickly and soon the hills were out of sight and there was nothing to be seen but the Blood Plain stretching to every horizon.

Rhalina slept for a long while and, in turns, the others slept also, there being little else to do. But when Rhalina awoke for the third time and still saw the Blood Plain, she murmured to herself, "So *much* blood spilled. So *much* . . ."

And still the boat sailed on down the milk-white river while Noreg-Dan told them something of what Xiombarg's reign had brought to this domain.

"All creatures not loyal to Chaos were destroyed or else, like me, had jokes played upon them—the Sword Rulers are notorious for their jokes. Every degenerate and vicious impulse in mortals was let loose and horror fell upon this world. My wife, my children were . . ." He broke off. "All of us suffered. But whether this took place a year ago or a hundred, I know not, for it was part of Xiombarg's joke to stop the sun so that we should not know how much time passed . . ."

"If Xiombarg's rule began at the same time as Arioch's," Corum said, "then it was much more than one century, King Noreg-Dan . . ."

"Xiombarg appears to have abolished time on this plane," Jhary put in. "Relatively speaking, of course. What happened here happened at whatever time people agree upon . . ."

"As you say," Corum nodded. "But tell us what you have heard of the City in the Pyramid, King Noreg-Dan."

"It was not originally of this plane at all, I gather—though it existed on one of the Five Planes now ruled by Xiombarg. In its seeking to escape Chaos, it moved from one plane to another, but eventually it was forced to stop and merely be content with protecting itself against Queen Xiombarg's attacks. She has spent, I hear, much of her energy on those attacks. Perhaps that is why I and the few like me are still allowed to exist. I do not know."

"There are others?"

"Aye, other wanderers such as myself. Or, at least, there were. Perhaps Xiombarg has found them now . . ."

"Or perhaps they found the City in the Pyramid."

"Possibly."

"Xiombarg concentrates on watching events in the next realm," Jhary said knowledgeably. "She wants to see the outcome of the battle between the Chaos minions and those who serve Law."

"Just as well for you, Prince Corum," said Noreg-Dan. "For if she knew the destroyer of her brother was actually where she could destroy him herself . . ."

"We'll not speak of that," said Corum.

On and on went the White River and they began to think that perhaps it and the Blood Plain were, indeed, without end, as this world was without time.

"Is there a name for the City in the Pyramid?" Jhary asked.

"You think it might be your Tanelorn?" Rhalina said.

He grinned and shook his head. "No. I know Tanelorn and that description would not, I think, fit it."

"Some say it is built within a huge, featureless pyramid,"

Noreg-Dan told him. "Others say it is merely a pyramid shape, like a great ziggurat. There are many myths, I fear, concerning the city."

"I do not think I have encountered such a city on my travels," Jhardy said.

"It sounds to me," said Corum, "as if it resembles one of the great Sky Cities, such as the one which crashed over the Plain of Broggfythus during the last great battle between the Vadhagh and the Nhadragh. They exist in our legends and I know that one, at least, was real, for the wreckage used to be near Castle Erorn where I was born. Both Vadhagh and Nhadragh had these cities, which were capable of moving through the planes. But when that phase of our history was over, they disappeared and we began to live more contentedly in our castles . . ." He stopped himself from continuing that theme, for it only brought back the bitterness. "It might be such a city," he said rather lamely.

"I think we had better land this craft," said Jhary cheerfully.

"Why?" Corum's back was to the prow.

"Because the White River and the Blood Plain seem to have ended."

Corum looked and was instantly alert. They were heading for a cliff. The plain ended as if sliced off by a gigantic knife and the liquid of the White River was hurtling into the abyss.

The Third Chapter

BEASTS OF THE ABYSS

Now the White River foamed wildly and roared as it rushed over the brink. Corum and Jhary dragged the oars free and used them to steer the rocking boat toward the bank.

"Be ready to jump, Rhalina!" Corum yelled.

She stood upright, holding onto the mast. King Noreg-Dan steadied her.

The boat danced out into midstream again and then, as suddenly, swerved back toward the bank as another current caught it. Corum staggered and almost fell overboard as he manipulated the oar. The sound of the torrent almost drowned their voices. The abyss was much closer and it would not be much longer before they were all hurled over it. Dimly, through the spray, Corum saw the distant wall of the far cliff. It must have been a mile away at least.

Then the boat scraped the bank and Corum yelled, "Jump, Rhalina!"

And she jumped, with Noreg-Dan leaping after her, his arms waving. She landed in the blood-dust and fell, sprawling.

Jhary jumped next. But the boat was turning out into the center of the river again. He landed in the shallows and struggled toward the bank, shouting at Corum.

Corum remembered Noreg-Dan's warning about the properties of the white liquid, but there was nothing for it but to leap in, his mouth tight shut, and flounder for the bank, his armor dragging him down.

But the weight of the armor fought the current and his feet touched the bottom. Shuddering, he climbed to the land, white droplets of liquid oozing down his body.

He lay panting on the bank and watched as the boat reared on the edge of the abyss and then fell from sight.

• • •

They staggered away from the White River, following the edge of the gorge, ankle-deep in the brown dust, and when the roar of the torrent had grown fainter they paused and tried to assess their situation.

The abyss seemed endless. It stretched to both horizons, its edges straight and its sides sheer, so that it was plain that it had not been created naturally. It was as if some gigantic canal had been planned to flow between the cliffs—a mile-wide canal, a mile deep.

They stood on the brink and looked down into the abyss. Corum felt vertigo seize him and he took a step backward. The sides of the cliff were of the same dark obsidian as the mountains they had left earlier, but these sides were utterly smooth. Far, far below a yellowish vapor writhed, obscuring the bottom—if any bottom there were. The four people felt completely dwarfed by the vastness of the scene. They looked backward across the Blood Plain. It was featureless, endless. They tried to make out details of the opposite cliff, but it was too distant.

A faint mist obscured the sun, which still stood at noon above them.

The little figures began to tramp along the edge, through the blood-dust, away from the White River.

Eventually Corum spoke to Noreg-Dan. "Have you heard of this place before, King Noreg-Dan?"

He shook his head. "I never knew what really lay beyond the Blood Plain, but I did not expect this. Perhaps it is new . . ."

"New?" Rhalina looked curiously at him. "What do you mean?"

"Chaos is forever altering the landscape, playing new tricks with it—playing new jokes. Perhaps Queen Xiombarg knows that we are here. Perhaps she is playing a game with us . . ."

Jhary stroked his cat between its ears. "It would be like a queen of Chaos to do such a thing, yet I suspect she would have planned worse than this for the destroyer of her brother."

"This could be just the beginning," Rhalina pointed out. "She could be building up to her true vengeance . . ."

"But I think no," Jhary insisted. "I have fought against Chaos in many worlds and in many guises and one thing that they are is impetuous. I think she would have acknowledged what she was doing by now if she knew who Prince Corum was. No, she still concentrates on the events taking place in the realm we have left. That is not to say we are not in danger," he added with a faint smile.

"In danger of starving again," Corum said. "If nothing else.

This place is the most barren of all—and there is no way down, no way across, no way back . . ."

"We must keep moving until we do find a way down or a way across," Rhalina told him. "Surely the abyss must end somewhere?"

"Possibly," said Noreg-Dan, rubbing at his gaunt face, "but I remind you again that this is a realm completely ruled by Chaos. From what you have told me of Arioch's realm, he never wielded the power which Xiombarg wields—he was the least of the Sword Rulers. It is said that Mabelrode, the King of the Swords, is even more powerful than she—that he has created of his realm a constantly shifting substance which changes shape more swiftly than thought . . ."

"Then I pray we are never forced to visit Mabelrode," Jhary murmured. "This situation is sufficiently terrifying for me. I have witnessed Total Chaos and I like it not at all."

They tramped on beside the unchanging edge of the abyss.

Lost in a daze of weariness and monotony Corum began to realize only gradually that the sky was darkening. He looked up. Was the sun moving?

But the sun seemed to be in the same position. Instead, an eddy of black cloud had risen from somewhere and was streaming across the sky, heading toward the far side of the abyss. He had no means of knowing whether this was some sorcerous manifestation or if it was natural. He stopped. It had grown colder. Now the others noticed the clouds.

Noreg-Dan's eyes held trepidation. He drew his cracked leather coat about him and licked his bearded lips.

Suddenly, from Jhary's shoulder, the little black-and-white cat leapt into the air and sped away on its black, white-tipped wings. It began to circle over the gorge, almost out of their range of vision. Jhary, too, looked perturbed, for the cat was behaving uncharacteristically.

Rhalina drew closer to Corum and put one hand on his arm. He hugged her shoulders and stared skyward at the black streamers of cloud as they dashed from nowhere to nowhere.

"Have you seen such a sight before, King Noreg-Dan?" Corum called through the gloom. "Has it significance for you?"

Noreg-Dan shook his head. "No, I have not seen this before, but it has significance—it is an omen, I fear, of some danger from Chaos. I have seen similar sights."

"We had best be ready for what comes." Corum drew his long, Vadhagh sword and threw back his scarlet robe to expose his silver byrnie. The others drew their own blades and stood there on the edge of that vast pit, waiting for whatever might come to threaten them.

Whiskers, the cat, was flying back. It was meowing shrilly, urgently. It had seen something in the abyss. They stepped to the brink and peered over.

A reddish shadow moved in the yellow mist. Gradually it began to emerge; gradually its shape was defined.

It flew upon billowing crimson wings and its grinning face was that of a shark. It looked like something which should have inhabited the sea rather than the air and this was confirmed by the way in which it flew—with slow, undulating wings as if through liquid. Row upon row of sharp fangs filled its red mouth and its body was the size of a large bull, its wingspan nearly thirty feet.

Out of the frightful pit it came, its jaws opening and closing as if it already anticipated its feast. Its golden eyes burned with hunger and with rage.

"It is the Ghanh," said Noreg-Dan hopelessly. "The Ghanh which led the Chaos pack upon my country. It is one of Queen Xiombarg's favorite creations. It will take us before ever our swords strike a single blow."

"So you call it a Ghanh on this plane?" Jhary said with interest. "I have seen it before and, as I remember, I have seen it destroyed."

"How was it destroyed?" Corum asked him as the Ghanh flew higher and closer.

"That part I forget."

"If we spread out, we shall have a better chance," Corum said, backing away from the gorge's edge. "Quickly."

"If you'll forgive the suggestion, friend Corum," Jhary said as he, too, stepped backward, "I think your netherworld allies would be of use to us here."

"Those allies are now the black birds we fought on the mountain. Could they defeat the Ghanh . . .?"

"I suggest you discover that now."

Corum flung up the eye patch and peered again into the netherworld. There they were—a score of black, brooding birds, each with the mark of the barbed Vadhagh lance in its breast. But they saw Corum now and they recognized him. One of them opened its beak and screeched in a tone so hopeless that Corum felt almost sympathetic to it.

"Can you understand me?" he said.

He heard Rhalina's voice. "It is almost upon us, Corum!"

"We—understand—Master. Have you—a prize—for us?" said one of the birds.

Corum shuddered. "Aye, if you can take it."

The Hand of Kwll reached into that murky cavern and it beckoned to the birds. With a dreadful rustling sound they took to the air.

And they flew into the world in which Corum and his companions stood awaiting the Ghanh.

"There," said Corum. "There is your prize."

The black birds flung their wounded, dead-alive bodies higher into the sky and began to wheel as the Ghanh swam over the edge of the gorge and opened its jaws, giving a piercing scream as it saw the four mortals.

"Run!" Corum shouted.

They took to their heels, scattering, running through the deep drifts of blood-dust as the Ghanh screamed again and hestiated, deciding which human to deal with first.

Corum choked on the stink of the creature as the wind of its breath touched him. He darted a look backward. He remembered how cowardly the birds has been, how they had taken long to make up their minds to attack him before. Would they have the courage—even though it meant their release from Limbo—to attack the Ghanh?

But now the birds were spearing downward again at an incredible speed. The Ghanh had not known they were there and it screamed in surprise as their beaks drove into its soft head. It snapped at them and seized two bodies in its jaws. Yet, though half-eaten by the creature, the beaks continued to peck, for the living-dead could not be slain again.

The Ghanh's wings beat close to the ground and a huge cloud of blood-dust rose all around it. Through this dust Corum and the others could see the fray. The Ghanh leapt and twisted and snapped and screamed, but the black birds' beaks pecked relentlessly at its skull. The Ghanh reared and fell on its back. It twisted in its wings so that it was rolled in them, trying to protect its head, and in this peculiar manner tumbled hither and thither across the dust. The black birds flapped into the air, then descended again, trying to perch on the cocoon as it writhed about, still pecking. Streams of green blood poured from the Ghanh now and the blood-dust stuck to it so that it was all begrimed and tattered.

Then, quite suddenly, it had rolled over the edge of the abyss. The companions ran forward to see what had happened, the disturbed dust stinging their eyes and clogging their lungs. They saw the Ghanh falling. They saw its wings open and slow its descent, but it did not have the power to do more than drift back toward the floor of the pit as the black birds pecked and pecked at its exposed skull. The yellow mist swallowed them all.

Corum waited, but nothing emerged from the mist again.

"Does that mean that you have no more allies in the netherworld, Corum?" Jhary asked. "For the birds did not take their prey with them . . ."

Corum nodded. "I wonder the same." He lifted the eye patch again and saw that the strange, cold cave was bare. "Aye—no allies there."

"So an impasse has been created. The birds have not killed the Ghanh and they have not themselves been destroyed," Jhary-a-Conel said. "Still, at least that danger has been averted. Let's press on."

The black clouds had ceased to stream across the sky but had instead stopped in their tracks and cut out the sunlight. Beneath this dark shroud they stumbled onward.

Corum noticed that Jhary had been brooding deeply since the birds had driven off the Ghanh and at last he said, "What is it that bothers you, Jhary-a-Conel?"

The man adjusted his wide hat on his head and pursed his lips. "It occurred to me that if the Ghanh was not slain but instead returned to its lair—and if the Ghanh is, as King Noreg-Dan says, a favorite pet of Queen Xiombarg's—then fairly soon now (if not already) Queen Xiombarg will become aware of our presence here. Doubtless if she becomes aware of us then she will decide to act to punish us for what we did to her pet . . ."

Corum removed his helmet and ran his gauntleted hand over his hair. He looked at the others, who had stopped to listen to Jhary.

"It is true," said the King Without a Country with a sigh. "We must expect to have Queen Xiombarg upon us very soon—or, at the very least, some more of her minions if she is still not aware that her brother's destroyer is in her realm and thinks only that we are upstart mortals . . ."

Rhalina had been ahead of the rest. She hardly listened to the conversation but instead pointed just in front of her. "Look! Look!" she cried.

They ran toward her and saw that she pointed at a place on the edge of the abyss—a square-cut notch carved from the rock and larger than a man's body. They clustered around it and saw that a stairway led down and down into the distant mist. But the stairway was scarcely more than a foot across and it went straight beside the massive wall of the cliff until it disappeared into the mist a mile below. If one missed one's footing for an instant, then one would be plunged into the abyss.

Corum stood staring at the stairway. Had it just appeared? Was it a trick of Queen Xiombarg's? Would the steps suddenly vanish when they were halfway down—if they ever managed to get halfway down?

But the alternative was to continue the trudge along the edge and perhaps, ultimately, find themselves back at the White River (for Corum was beginning to suspect that the Blood Plain was circular, containing the Lake of Voices and the mountains, and that the abyss extended all around it).

With a sigh Corum gradually lowered himself to the first step and, on weakened legs, his back against the smooth rock, began to descend.

The four little figures inched their way down the slippery steps until the top of the abyss itself was lost in gloom, while the bottom was still shrouded by the yellow mist. There was a frightening silence as they moved. They dared not speak—dared not do anything which would break their concentration as they lowered themselves from step to step with the abyss seeming sometimes to draw them into its depths as their vertigo increased. All were shivering, for the rock chilled them; all were sure that after a few more steps they would lose their footing and plunge down into the yellow mist.

And then they began to hear it. It echoed from the mist. A grunting and a wheezing and a snorting and a cackling which increased as they descended.

Corum stopped and looked back at the others, who lay against the rock and listened with him. Rhalina was closest to him, then Jhary, and finally the King Without a Country.

It was Noreg-Dan who spoke first. "I know the sound," he said. "I have heard it before."

"What is it?" Rhalina whispered.

"It is the noise which Xiombarg's beasts make. I spoke of the Ghanh which led the Chaos pack. Well, those noises are the noises made by the Chaos pack. We should have guessed what lay beyond the yellow mist . . ."

Corum felt a great coldness grip him. He peered downward to where the unseen Beasts of the Abyss awaited their coming.

The Fourth Chapter

THE CHARIOTS OF CHAOS

"What shall we do?" Rhalina whispered. "What *can* we do against them?"

Corum said nothing. Carefully keeping his balance he drew his sword, steadying himself with his six-fingered, jeweled hand.

While the Ghanh lived and fought the black birds, there could be no help from the netherworld.

"Do you hear that now?" Jhary said. "That odd—creaking. . . ?"

Corum nodded. With the creaking was a rumbling sound and it was vaguely familiar. It mingled with the snorts and the grunts and the bellows issuing from the yellow mist.

"There is nought else for it," he said at length. "We must go on and hope that we reach the floor of the abyss soon. At least there we shall be less exposed and able to stand and fight whatever—whatever it is that makes the noise."

They continued their cautious descent, eyes wary for the first signs of the Beasts.

Corum's foot had touched the floor of the abyss before he quite realized it. He had been climbing downward for so long that he had become used to lying flat against the rock and feeling with his foot for each new step. Now there were no more steps and he could see the ground, uneven, covered in boulders, stretching away into the yellow mist, but he could see nothing that lived.

The others joined him as he peered forward. The grunts and the cackles continued and an appalling stink greeted their nostrils, but the source of the sounds and the stink was not yet visible. The creaking and the rumbling also continued.

Corum saw them at last.

"By Elric's Sword!" Jhary groaned. "Those are the Chariots of Chaos. I should have guessed!"

Monstrous lumbering chariots drawn by reptilian beasts were beginning to emerge from the mist. They were filled with a variety of creatures, some even mounted on others' backs. Each beast was a travesty of a human being—each was clad in armor and bore a weapon of some kind. Here were piglike, doglike, cowlike, froglike, horselike things, some more deformed than others—animals warped into parodies of humanity.

"Did Chaos turn these beasts into what they now are?" Corum gasped.

Jhary said, "You are mistaken, Corum."

"What mean you?"

The King Without a Country spoke up. "These beasts," he said, "were once men. Many of them were my subjects who sided with Chaos because they saw that it was more powerful than Law . . ."

"And that transformation was their reward?" Rhalina said in disgust.

"They are probably not aware of the transformation," Jhary told her quietly. "They have degenerated too much to retain much memory of their former existences."

The black chariots creaked closer, bearing their grunting, shrieking, bellowing crews.

There was nothing for it but to turn and run from the chariots, dashing over the uneven ground, swords in hand, coughing on the stink of the Chaos pack and the clinging, yellow mist.

The Chaos pack howled in delight and whipped up their reptilian beasts and the chariots began to move faster. The ghastly, deformed army was enjoying the hunt.

Weakened by their earlier adventures and their lack of food or drink, the four companions could not run swiftly, and at last, behind a large boulder, they were forced to rest. The chariots rumbled on toward them, bringing the cacaphony, the hellish once-human things, the nauseating smells.

Corum hoped that the chariots would pass them by but the Chaos pack could see more easily through the mist and the first chariot turned toward them. Corum began to climb the boulder to get above the chariot. He struck out with his fist as a pig-thing clambered after him. The fist sank into the creature's face and was held there while the thing drew its own brass-studded club and raised its arm to finish Corum. Corum stabbed with his sword and the pig-thing shuddered, fell back. Now the others were under attack. Rhalina defended herself well with her own sword. They stood around the base of the boulder on the opposite side from Corum while he defended their rear. A dog-thing leaped at him. It wore a helmet and a breastplate but its muzzle was full of long teeth which snapped at his arm. He swung the sword and broke that muzzle in a single, smashing blow. Hands which had turned into claws and paws grabbed at him, tore at his cloak, his boots. Swords stabbed and clubs struck the stone at his feet as a whole mass of the creatures began to climb toward him. He stamped on fingers, hacked off limbs, drove his sword through mouths and eyes and hearts and all the time was filled with a sickening panic which only made him fight harder.

The babble of the Chaos pack seemed to grow louder and louder in his ears. Their chariots kept appearing out of the mist until several hundred of the things surrounded the boulder.

Then it became clear to Corum that the pack did not intend, at this stage, to kill them. If they had wished to they could have slain him and his companions by now. Doubtless they planned to torture them in some way—or perhaps turn them into the same kind of creatures that they had become.

Corum remembered the Mabden tortures with horror and he fought all the harder, hoping to drive some member of the Chaos pack to kill him.

But slowly the fearsome tide rolled in until so many corpses pressed about the base of the boulder that Corum's three friends were unable to move their arms and were trapped. Only Corum fought on, hacking at all who sought to take him, and then something clambered over the rocks behind him and seized his legs, dragging him down to where Rhalina, Jhary and the King Without a Country stood, disarmed and bound.

A creature with the lopsided face of a horse swaggered through the ranks of the Chaos pack and curled its lips to reveal huge brown teeth. It gave a whinnying laugh and set its helmet jauntily on its head, its hairy thumbs hooked in the belt around his belly.

"Should we save you for ourselves," he said, "or take you to our mistress? Queen Xiombarg might be interested in you . . ."

"Why should she be interested in four mortal travelers?" Corum asked.

The horse-thing grinned at him. "Perhaps you are more than that? Perhaps you are agents of Law?"

"You know that Law no longer rules here!"

"But Law may *wish* to rule again—you may have been sent here from another realm."

"Do you not recognize me!" cried King Noreg-Dan.

The horse-thing scratched at its forelock and peered stupidly at the King Without a Country. "Why should I recognize you?"

"Because I recognize you. I see the traces of your original features . . ."

"Be silent! I do not know what you mean!" The horse-thing half drew its dagger from its belt. "Be silent!"

"Because you cannot bear to remember!" shouted the King Without a Country. "You were Polib-Bav, Count of Tern! You threw in your lot with Chaos even before my country fell . . ."

A look of fear came into the horse-thing's eyes. It shook its head and snorted. "No!"

"You are Polib-Bav and you were bethrothed to my daughter—the girl whom your Chaos pack—aaagh! I cannot bear to remember that horror!"

"You remember nothing," said Polib-Bav thickly. "I say I am just what I am."

"What is your name?" Noreg-Dan said. "What is your name, if it is not Polib-Bav, Count of Tern?"

The horse-thing struck out at the king's face with its clumsy hand. "What if I am? My loyalty is to Queen Xiombarg, not to you."

"I would not have you serve me," sneered the King as blood welled on his upper lip. "Oh, look what has become of you, Polib-Bav."

The horse-thing turned away. "I live," it said. "I command this legion."

"A legion of pathetic monsters!" Jhary laughed.

A cow-thing kicked at Jhary's groin with its hoof and the Companion to Champions groaned. But he lifted his head and laughed again. "This degeneration is only the beginning. I have seen what mortals who serve Chaos become—foulness, nothingness—shapeless horrors!"

Polib-Bav scratched its head and said more softly, "What of that? The decision was made. It cannot be revoked. Queen Xiombarg promises us eternal life."

"It will be eternal," Jhary said. "But it will not be life. I have traveled to many planes during many ages and I have seen what Chaos comes to—barrenness. That alone is eternal, unless Law can save it."

"Faugh!" said the horse-thing. "Put them in the chariot—in my chariot—and we shall carry them to Queen Xiombarg."

King Norge-Dan tried to appeal again to Polib-Bav. "You were once handsome, Count of Tern. My daughter loved you and you loved her. You were loyal to me in those days."

Polib-Bav turned away. "And now I am loyal to Queen Xiombarg. This is her realm now. Lord Shalod of Law has fled and shall never rule here again. His armies and his allies were destroyed, as you well know, on the Plain of Blood . . ." Polib-Bav pointed upward. He accepted the four swords, which a frog-thing handed him, and tucked them under his arm. "Into the chariot with them. We ride for Queen Xiombarg's palace."

As he was forced to enter Polib-Bav's chariot with the others Corum was in despair. His hands were tied behind his back with strong cords, he could see no way to escape. Once he was taken before Queen Xiombarg she would recognize him. She would destroy him as she would destroy the rest and all hope of saving Lywn-an-Esh would be gone. With King Lyr victorious, the forces of Chaos would begin to gather strength. Another Sword Ruler would be summoned and the Fifteen Planes would be wholly in the control of the Lords of Entropy.

He lay at Polib-Bav's feet now, side by side with his friends, as the Chariots of Chaos began to move along the floor of the abyss, wheels creaking and groaning, bumping over the loose rocks. And soon Corum had lost consciousness.

He awoke blinking in stronger light. The mist was gone. He lifted his head and saw that a great cliff towered behind them. He guessed that they had left the abyss. They seemed to be moving through a sparse forest of sickly, leprous trees which had caught some blight. He moved his bruised head and stared into the face of Rhalina. She had been weeping but now she attempted to smile at him.

"We left the abyss through a tunnel some hours ago," she told him. "It must be a long way to Queen Xiombarg's palace. I wonder why they do not use swifter, more sorcerous means to go there?"

"Chaos is whimsical," said a voice behind her. It was Jhary-a-Conel's. "And in a timeless world there is no need for swiftness in such matters."

"What has become of your little cat?" Corum murmured.

"It was wiser than I: it flew off. I did not see—"

"Silence!" bellowed the voice of the horse-thing driving the chariot. "Your babbling annoys me."

"Perhaps it disturbs you," Jhary ventured. "Perhaps it reminds you that you could once think coherently, speak well . . ."

Polib-Bav kicked him in the face and he spluttered as the blood gushed from his nose.

Corum growled and vainly tried to free himself. Polib-Bav's horse face looked down at him and laughed. "You're grotesque enough, yourself, friend—with that eye and that hand grafted onto you. If I had not known better, I'd have said you served Chaos."

"Perhaps I do," Corum said. "You did not ask. You merely assumed that I served Law."

Polib-Bav frowned, but then his stupid face cleared. "You are trying to trick me. I will do nothing until Queen Xiombarg has seen you . . ." He shook the reins and the reptilian beasts began to move faster. ". . . after all, it is almost certain that it was you and your friends who killed the strongest member of our legion. We saw it attacked and we saw it vanish."

"You speak of the Ghanh!" Corum said, his spirits beginning to lift. "Of the Ghanh!"

And, at that moment, the Hand of Kwll moved once more of its own volition and snapped the cords binding Corum's wrists.

"You see!" Polib-Bav in triumph. "It was I who tricked you. You knew the Ghanh was slain. Therefore it could only have been— What! You are free!" He hauled on the reins. "Stop!" He drew his sword, but Corum had rolled over the floor of the chariot and leaped to the ground. He pushed back his eye patch and at once saw the netherworld cave from which his allies had issued in the past. There, with its head a ruin of congealed blood, lay the Ghanh.

The Hand of Kwll moved into the netherworld as Polib-Bav's creatures advanced on Corum. It beckoned to the Ghanh, which moved its dead head very reluctantly.

"You must do my bidding," Corum said. "And then you will be free. You must take many prizes to pay for your release."

The Ghanh did not speak, but it gave a scream from its fanged jaws as if to acknowledge what it had heard.

"Come!" Corum cried. "Come—take your prizes."

And the Ghanh's crimson wings began to beat as it flapped slowly from the cave, leaving the netherworld behind it and coming back, once again, into the world from which the birds had but lately banished it.

"The Ghanh has come back!" Polib-Bav shouted in triumph. "Oh, lovely Ghanh, thou has returned to us!"

The Chaos pack had seized Corum again, but now he was smiling as, with a tortured screech, the Ghanh's great body engulfed a nearby chariot and its strange wings wrapped themselves around the whole thing and began to crush the occupants to death.

So astonished were the Chaos beasts holding Corum that he was able to tug himself free. They came after him but he turned and the Hand of Kwll smashed into the face of one, cracked another's collarbone. He raced for Polib-Bav's chariot. The leader of the beasts had left his chariot and stood beside it, his huge horse's eyes fixed on what was happening to his companions. Before he had really noticed Corum, the Prince in the Scarlet Robe had grabbed his sword from the floor of the chariot and aimed a blow at Polib-Bav. The horse-thing jumped back, drawing his own sword. But his

227

movements were dazed and clumsy. He parried, tried to stab, missed as Corum dodged aside, and received the Vadhagh metal in his throat. Choking, he died.

Quickly Corum cut the bonds of his friends and they, too, retrieved their swords, ready to fight the Chaos creatures. But the pack, recovering from its initial horror, was fleeing. Its chariots raced hither and yon through the pale, sickly trees as the Ghanh left its first victims and pursued some more. Corum bent and stripped the corpse of Polib-Bav, taking his water bottle and the pouch of coarse bread at his belt. Soon the Chaos pack had disappeared and they were left alone on the road through the forest.

Corum inspected the chariot. The reptiles seemed passive enough.

"Could we drive this, do you think, King Noreg-Dan?" he asked.

The King Without a Country shook his head dubiously. "I am not sure. Perhaps . . ."

"I think I could drive it," Jhary told them. "I've had a little experience of such chariots and the creatures which pull them." His sack bouncing at his belt, the wide brim of his hat waving, he jumped into the chariot, taking up the reins. He turned and grinned at them. "Where would you go? Still to Xiombarg's palace?"

Corum laughed. "Not yet, I think. She'll send for us when she learns what became of her pack. We'll take that direction, I think." He pointed away through the trees. He helped Rhalina into the chariot, then waited while King Noreg-Dan climbed aboard. Finally, he got in himself. Jhary shook the reins and turned the chariot, and soon it had bounced through the leprous forest and was rolling down a hill toward a valley full of what seemed to be upright, slender stones.

The Fifth Chapter

THE FROZEN ARMY

They were not stones.

They were men.

Each man a warrior—each warrior frozen like a statue, his weapons in his hands.

"This," said Noreg-Dan in quiet awe, "is the Frozen Army. The last army to take arms against Chaos . . ."

"Was this its punishment?" Corum asked.

"Aye."

Jhary, gripping the reins, said, "They live? Is that so? They know that we pass through their ranks?"

"Aye. I heard that Queen Xiombarg said that since they supported Law so wholeheartedly they should have a taste of what Law aimed for—they should know the ultimate in tranquility, she said."

Rhalina shivered. "Is this reality what Law comes to?"

"So Chaos would have us believe," Jhary said. "But it matters not, for the Cosmic Balance requires equilibrium—something of Chaos, something of Law—so that each stabilizes the other. The difference is that Law acknowledges the authority of the Balance, while Chaos would deny it. But Chaos cannot deny that authority completely for its adherents know that to disobey some things is to be destroyed. Thus Queen Xiombarg dares not enter the realm of another Great Old God and, as in the case of your realm, must work through others. She, like the rest, must also watch her dealings with mortals, for they cannot be destroyed by her willy-nilly—there are rules . . ."

"But no rules to protect these poor creatures," Rhalina said.

"Some. They have not died. She has not killed them."

Corum remembered the tower where he had found Arioch's heart. There, too, had been frozen men.

"Unless directly attacked," Jhary explained, "Xiombarg cannot kill mortals. But she can use those loyal to her to kill other mortals, do you see, and she can suspend the lives of warriors like these."

"So we are safe from Queen Xiombarg," Corum said.

"If you choose to think so." Jhary smiled. "You are by no means safe from her minions and, as you have seen, she has many of those."

"Aye," said the King Without a Country feelingly. "Aye. Many."

Holding his reins in one hand Jhary dusted at his clothes. They were tattered and bloodstained from the various flesh wounds he had sustained in the battle with the Chaos pack. "I would give much for a new suit," he murmured. "I'd make a bargain with Xiombarg herself . . ."

"We mention that name too often," King Noreg-Dan said nervously as he clung to the side of the jolting chariot. "We shall bring her down on us if we are not more discreet."

Then the sky laughed.

Golden light began to dapple the clouds. A brilliant orange aura sprang up in the distance ahead and cast giant shadows for the frozen warriors.

Jhary jerked the chariot to a halt, his face suddenly pale.

Purple brilliance came from the sky in fragments the size of raindrops.

And the laughter went on and on.

"What is it?" Rhalina's hand went to her sword.

The King Without a Country put his haggard face in his hands and his shoulders slumped. "It is she. I warned you. It is she."

"Xiombarg?" Corum drew his own sword. "Is it Xiombarg, Noreg-Dan?"

"Aye, it is she."

The ground shook with the laughter. Several of the frozen warriors toppled and fell, still in the same positions. Corum looked about for the source of the laughter. Was it in the aura? Or in the golden light? Or in the purple rain?

"Where are you, Queen Xiombarg!" He brandished his sword. His mortal eye flashed his defiance. "Where are you, Creature of Evil?"

"I AM EVERYWHERE!" answered a huge, sweet voice. "I AM THIS REALM AND THIS REALM IS XIOMBARG OF CHAOS!"

"We are surely doomed," stuttered the King Without a Country.

"You said she could not attack us," Corum said to Jhary-a-Conel.

"I said she could not directly attack us. But see . . ."

Corum looked. Over the valley now came hopping things. They hopped on several legs and from their bodies sprouted a dozen or more tentacles. Their huge eyes rolled, their massive fangs clashed.

"The Karmanal of Zert," Jhary said in mild surprise as he dropped the reins and armed himself with sword and poniard. "I have encountered these before."

"How did you escape them?" Rhalina asked.

"I was at that time companion to a champion who had the power to destroy them."

"I, too, have a power," Croum said grimly, raising his hand to his eye. But Jhary shook his head and grimaced.

"I fear not. The Karmanal of Zert are indestructible. Both Law and Chaos have, in their time, taken steps to do away with them—they are fickle creatures who fight for one side or another without apparent reason. They have no souls, no true existence."

"Therefore they should not be able to harm us!"

The laughter ran on.

"I agree that, logically, they should not be able to harm us," Jhary answered equably. "But I am afraid that they can."

About ten of the hopping creatures were nearing their chariot, weaving between the statuelike warriors.

And they were singing.

"The Karmanal of Zert always sing before they feast," Jhary told them. "Always."

Corum wondered if Jhary had gone mad. The tentacled monsters were almost upon them and the Companion to Champions continued to chat without apparent awareness of their danger.

The singing was harmonious and somehow made the creatures even more terrifying while, as a counterpoint, Xiombarg's laughter continued to fill the sky.

When the hopping things were almost upon them Jhary raised his hands, dagger in one, sword in the other, and cried, "Queen Xiombarg! Queen Xiombarg! Who do you think you would destroy!"

The Karmanal of Zert stopped suddenly, as frozen as the army which surrounded them.

"I destroy a few mortals who have set themselves against me, who have caused the deaths of those I loved," said a voice from behind them.

Corum turned to see the most beautiful woman who had ever existed. Her hair was dark gold with streaks of red and black, her face was perfection, and her eyes and lips offered a thousand times more than any woman had offered a man in the whole of history.

Her body was tall and of exquisite shape, clothed in drapes of gold and orange and purple. She smiled tenderly at him.

"Is that what I destroy?" she murmured. "Then what do I destroy, Master Timeras?"

"I am called Jhary-a-Conel now," he said pleasantly. "May I introduce . . . ?"

Corum stepped forward. "Have you betrayed us, Jhary? Are you in league with Chaos?"

"He is not, sadly, in league with Chaos," said Queen Xiombarg. "But I know he rides often with those who serve Law." She looked at him affectionately. "You do not change, Timeras, basically. And I like you best as a man, I think."

"And I like you best as a woman, Xiombarg."

"As a woman I must rule this realm. I know you for a sometime hero's lickspittle, Jhary-Timeras, and assume this handsome Vadhagh with his strange eye and hand is a hero of sorts . . ."

She glared suddenly at Corum.

"Now I know!"

Corum drew himself up.

"NOW I KNOW!"

Her shape began to alter. It began to flow outward and upward. Her face was that of a skull, then that of a bird, then that of a man, until at last it had reverted to that of a beautiful woman. But now Xiombarg stood a hundred feet high and her expression was no longer tender.

"NOW I KNOW!"

Jhary laughed. "May I, as I said, introduce Prince Corum Jhaelen Irsei—he is of the Scarlet Robe?"

"HOW DO YOU DARE ENTER MY REALM—YOU WHO DESTROYED MY BROTHER? EVEN NOW THOSE STILL LOYAL TO ME IN MY BROTHER'S REALM ARE SEEKING FOR YOU. YOU ARE FOOLISH, MORTAL. AH, THE IGNOMINY. I THOUGHT A BRAVE HERO BANISHED MY BROTHER—BUT NOW I KNOW IT WAS A MORON! KARMANAL CREATURES—BEGONE!" The hopping things vanished. "I WILL HAVE A SWEETER VENGEANCE ON YOU, CORUM JHAELEN IRSEI—AND ON ALL WHO TRAVEL WITH YOU!"

The golden light faded, the orange aura disappeared, and the purple rain ceased to fall, but Xiombarg's huge shape still flickered there in the sky. "I SWEAR THIS BY THE COSMIC BALANCE—I WILL RETURN WHEN I HAVE CONSIDERED THE FORM OF MY VENGEANCE. I WILL FOLLOW YOU WHER-

EVER YOU TRY TO ESCAPE. AND I WILL GIVE YOU CAUSE TO WISH THAT YOU HAD NEVER ENCOUNTERED DUKE ARIOCH OF CHAOS AND THUS WON THE ANGER OF HIS SISTER!"

Xiombarg faded and silence returned.

Corum, much shaken, turned to Jhary. "Why did you tell her? Now there is no escape for us! She has promised to pursue us wherever we go—you heard her. Why did you do it?"

"I thought she was about to find out," Jhary said mildly. "Also it was the only way to save us."

"To save us!"

"Aye. Now the Karmanal of Zert no longer threaten us. I assure you that we should have been in their bellies by now if I had not spoken to Queen Xiombarg. I guessed that she could not know very well what you looked like—most of us seem very alike to the Gods—but that she might learn when we fought. Corum—it was the only way to stop the Karmanal."

"But it has done us no good. Now she goes to summon whatever horrors she plans to set upon us. Soon she will return and we shall suffer a worse fate."

"I must admit," said Jhary, "that there was another consideration. Now we have time to see what this is coming yonder."

They looked.

It was something that flew and flashed and droned.

"What is it?" Corum asked.

"It is, I believe, a ship of the air," said Jhary. "I hope it has come to save us."

"Perhaps it has come to harm us?" Corum said reasonably enough. "I still feel you should not have revealed who I was, Jhary . . ."

"It is always best to bring these things out into the open," Jhary said cheerfully.

The Sixth Chapter

THE CITY IN THE PYRAMID

The ship of the air had a hull of blue metal in which were set enamels and ceramics of various rich colors, making a number of complicated designs. It brought a slight smell of almonds with it as it began to descend, and its moan was almost like that of a human voice.

Now Corum could see its brass rails, its steel, silver, and platinum fixtures, its ornate wheelhouse, and he felt that he was reminded of something by it—an image, perhaps, of childhood. He stared curiously at it as it began to land and a small object rose up from it and flew toward them.

It was Jhary's cat.

Suddenly Corum stared at Jhary and laughed. The cat came and settled on the shoulder of the Companion to Heroes and it nuzzled his ear.

"You sent the cat to find help when the Chaos pack set upon us!" Rhalina said before Corum could speak. "That is why you told Xiombarg who Corum was—for you knew that help was coming and thought your plan thwarted at the last moment."

Jhary shrugged. "I did not know the cat would find help, but I guessed."

"From where has that strange flying craft come?" asked the King Without a Country.

"Why, where else but from the City in the Pyramid? It was my instruction to the cat to look for it. I would gather that it found it."

"And how did it communicate with the folk of that city?" Corum asked as they drew nearer to the blue ship of the air.

"In emergencies, as you know, the cat can communicate quite clearly with me. In a very serious emergency it will use more energy and communicate with whom it pleases."

Whiskers purred and licked Jhary's face with its little rough tongue. He murmured something to it and smiled. Then he said to Corum, "We'd best hurry, though, for Xiombarg may begin to wonder why I did reveal your name. It is one of the characteristics of many of the Chaos Lords that they are impetuous and not given overmuch to thinking."

The ship of the air was a good forty feet long and had seats running the whole of its length on both sides. It appeared to be empty, but then a tall, comely man stepped from the wheelhouse and came forward toward them. He was smiling at Corum's complete astonishment.

For the steersman of the ship of the air was quite plainly of no other race but Corum's. He was a Vadhagh. His skull was long, his eyes slanting purple and gold, his ears pointed, and his body slender and delicate but containing a great deal of energy.

"Welcome, Corum in the Scarlet Robe," he said. "I have come to take you to Gwlas-cor-Gwrys, the one bastion this realm has against that Chaos creature you have just met."

Dazed, Corum Jhaelen Irsei entered the ship of the air while the steersman continued to smile at his astonishment.

They took their places near the wheelhouse in the stern and the tall Vadhagh made the ship rise slowly and began to head in the direction it had come. Rhalina looked backward at the forest of frozen warriors they left behind. "Is there nothing we could do to help those poor souls?" she asked Jhary.

"Only help make Law strong in our own realm so that it can one day send aid to this realm, just as Chaos now sends aid to ours," Jhary told her.

They were soon crossing a land of oozing stuff which flung up tendrils at them and sought to drag them down into itself. Sometimes faces appeared in the stuff, sometimes hands raised as if in supplication. "A Chaos sea," King Noreg-Dan told them. "There are several such places in the realm now. Some say that that is what those mortals who serve Chaos finally degenerate to."

"I have seen its like," nodded Jhary.

Strange forests passed below them and valleys filled with perpetually burning fire. They saw rivers of molten metal and beautiful castles made all of jewels. Horrid flying creatures sometimes rushed into the air toward them but turned aside when they recognized the craft, though it was apparently without protection.

"These people must have a powerful sorcery to make boats fly," Rhalina whispered to Corum. And Corum made no reply at first, for he was deep in thought, racking his memory.

At last he spoke. "This is not sorcery, as such," he told her. "It

235

requires no spells and few incantations but is instead mechanical in its nature. Certain forces are harnessed to give power to machines—some of them much more delicate than anything the Mabden could imagine—which propel such vessels through the air and do many other things. Some of the machines could once sunder the fabric of the Walls Between the Realms and pass easily from plane to plane. My ancestors are said to have created such machines but most chose not to use them, preferring a different logic to their living. I dimly remember a legend which says that one Sky City—that was the name they gave to their cities—left our realm altogether, to explore the other worlds of the multiverse. Perhaps there was more than one such city, for I know that one did destroy itself when it went out of control during the Battle of Broggfythus and crashed close to Castle Erorn, as I told you. Perhaps another city was called Gwlas-cor-Cwrys and is now known as the City in the Pyramid.''

Prince Corum was smiling joyfully and speaking excitedly. With his mortal hand he pressed Rhalina's arm. ''Oh, Rhalina, can you understand what I feel at finding that some of my race still live, that Glandyth did not destroy them all?''

She smiled back at him. ''I think so, Corum.''

The air about them began to vibrate and the boat shuddered. The steersman called from the wheelhouse, ''Do not be afraid. We are passing into another plane.''

''Does that mean we are escaping Xiombarg?'' asked the King Without a Country eagerly.

Jhary answered him. ''No. Xiombarg's realm extends for five planes and we are merely going from one of those into a different one. Or so I would think.''

The quality of the light changed and they looked over the side of the ship. A multicolored gas swirled below them.

''The raw stuff of Chaos,'' said Jhary. ''Queen Xiombarg has, as yet, made nothing with it.''

They crossed the great gas and flew over a range of mountains, each more than a thousand feet high, but each one a perfect cube. Beyond the mountains was a dark jungle and beyond that a crystal-line desert. The crystals of the desert moved constantly, their motion creating a tinkling music which was not pleasant. Among these crystals moved ocher beasts of enormous proportions but of primitive development. They were feeding off the crystals.

Then the crystal desert gave way to a flat, black plain and they saw ahead of them the City in the Pyramid.

The city was, in fact, a many-sided ziggurat. On each terrace were a large number of houses. Flowers, shrubs, and trees grew along the terraces and the streets teemed with people. Over the whole city a greenish light flickered and the light took the form of a pyramid, enclosing the ziggurat. As the ship of the air flew toward it, a darker oval of green appeared in the flickering light and through this the ship passed. It circled the top-most building—a many-towered castle built all of metal—and then began to descend until it landed on a raised platform on the castle's battlements. Corum shouted with pleasure as he saw the gathering which welcomed them.

"They are my people!" he exclaimed to his companions. "They are all my people!"

The steersman left the wheelhouse and put his hand on Corum's shoulder. He signed to the men and women below and suddenly they were no longer on the ship of the air but were standing with the group, beneath the platform, looking up at the faces of Rhalina, Jhary, and the King Without a Country as they peered over the rail of the ship in astonishment.

Corum was equally astonished to see the three suddenly vanish and appear beside him. One of the group then stepped forward. He was a thin, ancient man with a straight bearing, dressed in a thick robe and holding a staff.

"Greetings," he said. "Welcome to Law's last bastion."

Later they sat around a table of beautifully fashioned ruby-metal and listened to the old man, who had introduced himself as Prince Yurette Hasdun Nury, Commander of Gwlas-cor-Gwrys, the City in the Pyramid. He had explained how Corum's speculations were substantially correct.

As they had eaten he had explained how Corum's people had chosen to remain in their castles after the Battle of Broggfythus and devote themselves to learning while his people had decided to take their Sky City and try to fly it beyond the Five Planes, through the Wall Between the Realms. They had succeeded, but had failed to return due to some power loss which they could not then restore. Since then they had managed only to explore these Five Planes and then, when the struggle between Law and Chaos had begun to build, they had remained neutral.

"We were fools to do so. We thought we were above such disputes. And slowly we saw Law conquered and Chaos emerge in all its grisly triumph to create its travesties of beauty. But by that time, though we did take our city against Xiombarg's creatures, we were too late. Chaos had gained all power and we could not fight it. Xiombarg sent—and still sends—armies against us. These we resisted, not without danger. And now it is stalemate. Every so often Xiombarg will send another army—some frightful, monstrous army—and we are forced to fight it. But we can do no more than that. I fear we are all that is left of Law, save you."

"Law has regained its power in our Five Planes," Corum told him. He described his adventures, his battle with Arioch, and the final result, which was to restore Lord Arkyn to his realm. "But that, too, is threatened, for Law has still only a slender hold on the realm and all the forces of Chaos are being brought to bear on it."

"But Law has some power!" Prince Yurette said. "We did not know that. We learned that the Sword Rulers controlled all the realms. If only we could return—take our city back through the Wall Between the Realms—and give you our aid. But we cannot. We have tried too often. The materials are not available on these planes for building up the massive power it needs."

"And if you had those materials?" Corum asked. "How long would it be before you could return to our realm?"

"Not long. But we are weakening already. A few more of Xiombarg's attacks—perhaps just one massive one—and we shall be destroyed."

Corum stared bitterly at the table. Was he to find Vadhagh folk still living only to see them die—crushed, as his family was crushed, by the forces of Chaos?

"We had hoped to take you back with us, to relieve Lywn-an-Esh," he said. "But now we learn that is impossible and, it seems, we, too, are stranded in this realm, unable to go to the aid of our friends."

"If we had those rare minerals . . ." Prince Yurette paused. "But you could get them for us."

"We cannot return," Jhary-a-Conel pointed out. "We cannot get back to our realm. If it were possible, of course we could find the materials you need—or at least try to do so—but even then we could not be sure of being able to return here . . ."

Prince Yurette frowned. "It would be possible for us to send just one sky ship through the Wall Between the Realms. We have the power to do that, though it would dangerously weaken our defenses here. Yet it is worth the risk, I think."

Corum's spirits lifted. "Aye, Prince Yurette—anything is worth the risk if the cause of Law is to be saved."

While Prince Yurette conferred with his scientists, the four companions wandered through the marvelous city of Gwlas-cor-Gwrys. It was all made of metal—but metals so magnificent, so strange in texture, and so rich in color that even Corum could not guess at how they had been manufactured. Towers, domes, trellises, arches, and pathways were of these metals, as were the ramps

238

and stairways between the terraces. Everything in the city functioned independently of the outside world. Even the air was created within the confines of the shimmering pyramid of green light which cast its glow on all the outer flanks of Gwlas-cor-Gwrys.

And everywhere did the folk of the City in the Pyramid go about their day-to-day business. Some tended gardens and others saw to the distribution of food. There were many artists at work, performing musical compositions or displaying the pictures they had made—pictures on velvet and marble and glass very similar in technique to those produced by Corum's own Vadhagh folk, but often with different styles and subjects, some of which Corum could not find it in him to like, perhaps because they were so strange.

They were shown the huge, beautiful machines which kept the city alive. They were shown its armaments, which protected it from the attacks of Chaos, the bays where its ships of the air were kept. They saw its schools and its hostelries and its theatres, its museums and its art galleries. And here was everything which Corum thought destroyed forever by Glandyth-a-Krae and his barbarians. But now all this, too, was threatened with destruction—and destruction from the same source, ultimately.

They slept, they ate, and their tattered, battered clothes were copied by the tailors and arms smiths of Gwlas-cor-Gwrys so that when they awoke they found themselves with fresh raiment identical to that which they had worn upon starting out on their quest for the city.

Jhary-a-Conel was particularly pleased by this example of the city's hospitality and when, at last, they were invited to attend upon Prince Yurette, he expressed that gratitude roundly.

"The sky ship is ready," said Prince Yurette gravely. "You must go quickly now, for Queen Xiombarg, I learn, mounts a great attack upon us."

"Will you be able to withstand it with your power weakened?" Jhary asked.

"I hope so."

The King Without a Country stepped forward. "Forgive me, Prince Yurette, but I would stay here with you. If Law is to battle Chaos in my own realm, then I would battle with it."

Yurette inclined his head. "It shall be as you wish. But now hurry, Prince Corum. The sky ship awaits you on the roof. Stand on that mosaic circle there and you will be transported to the ship. Farewell."

They stood within the mosaic circle on the prince's floor and, a heartbeat later, were once again upon the deck of the ornate flying craft.

The steersman was the same who had first greeted them.

"I am Bwydyth-a-Horn," he said. "Please sit where you sat before and cling tightly to the rail."

"Look!" Corum pointed beyond the green pyramid, out across the black plain. The huge shape of Queen Xiombarg could be seen again, her face alive with fury. And beneath her there marched a vast army, a foul army of fiends.

Then the sky ship had entered the air and sailed through the dark green oval into a world which rang with the voices of the fiends.

And over all these voices sounded the hideous, vengeful laughter of Queen Xiombarg of Chaos.

"BEFORE I MERELY TOYED WITH THEM BECAUSE I ENJOYED THE GAME! BUT NOW THAT THEY HARBOR THE DESTROYER OF MY BROTHER, THEY WILL PERISH IN BLACK AGONY!"

The air began to vibrate, a green globe of light now encircled the ship. The City in the Pyramid, the army of hell, Queen Xiombarg, all faded. The ship rocked crazily up and down, the moaning increased in pitch until it became a painful whine.

And then they had left the realm of Queen Xiombarg and come again to the realm of Arkyn of Law.

They sailed over the land of Lywn-an-Esh and it was not very different from the world they had just left. Chaos, here too, was on the march.

BOOK THREE

*In which Prince Corum and his companions wage
war, win a victory, and wonder
at the ways of Law*

The First Chapter

THE HORDE FROM HELL

Thick smoke coiled from blazing villages, towns, and cities. They were to the southeast of the River Ogyn in the Duchy of Kernow-a-Laun and it was plain that one of King Lyr-a-Brode's armies had landed on the coast, well south of Moidel's Mount.

"I wonder if Glandyth has yet discovered our leaving," Corum said as he stared miserably from the sky ship at the burning land. Crops had been destroyed, corpses lay rotting in the summer sun, even animals had been needlessly slaughtered. Rhalina was sickened by what had happened to her country and she could not look at it for long.

"Doubtless he has," she said quietly. "Their army has plainly been on the march for some time."

From time to time they saw small parties of barbarians in chariots or riding shaggy ponies, looting what was left of the settlements, though there was none left for them to slay or torture. Sometimes, too, they saw the refugees streaming southward toward the mountains, where doubtless they hoped to find a hiding place.

When, finally, they came to the River Ogyn itself it was clogged with death. Corpses of whole families rotted in the river, along with cattle, dogs, and horses. The barbarians were ranging widely, following the main army, making sure that nothing lived where it had passed. And now Rhalina was weeping openly and Corum and

241

Jhary were grim-faced as they strove to keep the stink of death from their nostrils and fretted that the sky ship, moving faster than any horse could, did not move more swiftly.

And then they saw the farmhouse.

Children were running inside the house, shepherded by their father, who was armed with an old, rusty broadsword. The mother was putting up crude barricades.

Corum saw the source of their fear. A party of barbarians, about a dozen strong, were riding down the valley toward the farm. They had brands in their hands and were riding rapidly, whooping and roaring.

Corum had seen Mabden like these. He had been captured by them, tortured by them. They were no different from Glandyth-a-Krae's Denledhyssi, save that they rode ponies instead of chariots. They wore filthy furs and bore captured bracelets and necklaces all over them, their braids laced with ribbons of jewels.

He got up and went into the wheelhouse. "We must go down," he said harshly to Bwydyth-a-Horn. "There is a family—it is about to be attacked . . ."

Bwydyth looked at him sadly. "But there is so little time, Prince Corum." He tapped his jerkin. "We have to get this list of substances to Halwyg-nan-Vake if we are to rescue the city and, in turn, save Lywn-an-Esh . . ."

"Go down," Corum ordered.

Bwydyth said softly, "Very well." And he made adjustments to the controls, looking through a viewer which showed him the country below. "That farm?"

"Aye—that farm."

The sky ship began to descend. Corum went out on deck to watch. The barbarians had seen the ship and were pointing upward in consternation, reining in their ponies. The ship began to circle toward the farmyard, where there was barely space for it to land. Chickens ran squawking as its shadow fell on them. A pig scampered into its sty.

The ship's moaning dropped in pitch as it descended.

"Have your sword ready, Master Jhary," Corum said.

Jhary's sword was already in his hand. "There are ten or more of them," he cautioned. "Two of us. Will you use your—powers?"

"I hope not. I am disgusted by all that is of Chaos."

"But, two against ten . . ."

"There is the steersman. And the farmer."

Jhary pursed his lips but said no more. The ship bumped to the ground. The steersman emerged holding a long pole-axe.

242

"Who are you?" came a nervous voice from within the low wooden house.

"Friends," Corum called. He said to the steersman, "Get the women and children on board the craft." He vaulted over the rail. "We'll try to hold them off while you do that."

Jhary followed him and stood unsteadily on the ground. He was not used to a surface which did not move beneath him.

The barbarians were approaching cautiously. The leader laughed when he saw how many there were to deal with. He gave a blood-thirsty yell, cast aside his brand, drew a huge mace from his belt, and spurred his pony forward, leaping the wicker barricade the farmer had erected. Corum danced aside as the mace whizzed past his helmet. He lunged. The sword caught the man in the knee and he shouted in rage. Jhary jumped through the barricade and ran to pick up the discarded brand, the other horsemen on his heels. He dashed back into the farmyard and fired the wicker work. It began to splutter as another rider leaped his horse over it. Jhary flung his poniard and it went true to the barbarian's eye. The man screamed and fell backward off his pony. Jhary grabbed the reins and mounted the unruly creature, yanking savagely at the bit to turn it. Meanwhile the barricade was beginning to burn and Corum dodged the mace, which was studded with the fangs of animals. He saw an opening, lunged again and caught the barbarian in the side. The man went forward over his pony's neck, clutching at his wound, and was borne away across the farmyard. Corum saw others trying to force their horses to brave the smoky blaze.

Now Bwydyth was helping the farmer's young wife carry a cot to the sky ship. Two boys and an older girl came with them. The farmer, still a little dazed by what was happening, came last, holding the rusty broadsword in both hands.

Three riders leaped suddenly through the barricade and bore down on the group.

But Jhary was there. He had recovered his poniard and he flung it again. Again it went straight into the eye of the nearest rider, again the rider fell backward, his feet easily coming free from the leather loops he used as stirrups. Corum dashed for the pony and leaped into the saddle, flinging up his sword to protect himself from a heavy war-axe aimed at him. He slid his sword down the haft of the axe and forced the man to shorten his grip on it so that it was hard to bring back. While the man struggled to raise the axe Jhary took him from the rear, stabbing him through the heart so that his saber point appeared on the other side of the barbarian's body. There were more barbarians now. The farmer had hacked the legs of a pony from

243

under one and before the warrior could disentangle himself had split him from shoulder to breastbone, using the sword rather like a woodman would use an axe.

The children and the woman were on board the ship. Corum took another barbarian in the throat and leaned down to pull at the farmer, who was hacking blindly at the corpse. He pointed at the ship. The farmer did not seem to understand at first, but then dropped his bloody broadsword and ran to the ship. Corum slashed at his last opponent and Jhary dismounted to recover his poniard. Corum turned the horse, extended an arm to Jhary, who sheathed his weapons and took the arm, riding in the stirrup until they reached the sky ship. They both hauled themselves aboard. The ship was already rising through the smoky air. Two riders were left staring up at the disappearing ship. They did not look happy, for they had expected an easy slaying and now most of their number were dead and their prey was escaping.

"My stock," said the farmer, looking down.

"You are alive," Jhary pointed out.

Rhalina was comforting the woman. The Margravine had drawn her sword, ready to join the men if they were too hard-pressed. It lay on the seat nearby. Now she held the smallest boy in her arms and stroked his hair.

Jhary's cat peered out from a locker under the seat, was assured that the danger was over, and fluttered up to settle again on its master's shoulder.

"Do you know anything of their main army?" Corum asked the farmer. The Prince in the Scarlet Robe dabbed at a minor wound he had received on his mortal hand.

"I have heard—heard things. I have heard that it is not a human army at all."

"That may be true," Corum agreed, "but do you know its whereabouts?"

"It is almost upon Halwyg—if not there already. Pray, sir, where do you take us?"

"I fear it is to Halwyg," Corum told him.

The sky ship sailed on over the desolated land. And now they could see that the bands of outriders were larger—plainly part of the main army. Many noticed the ship's passage over their heads and a few cast their lances at it or shot an arrow or two before returning to their burning, their raping, and their murder.

It was not these that Corum feared but the sorcery which Lyr-a-Brode might now command.

The farmer was peering earthward. "Is it all like this?" he asked grimly.

"As far as we know. Two forces march on Halwyg—one from the East and one from the Southwest. I doubt if the barbarians of Bro-an-Mabden are any more merciful than their comrades." Corum turned away from the rail.

"I wonder how Llarak-an-Fol fared," said Rhalina as she cradled a sleeping child. "And did Beldan stay there or was he able to continue with our men to Halwyg? And what of the Duke?"

"We shall know all this soon, I hope." Jhary allowed a little dark-haired boy to stroke his cat. The cat bore the assault with gravity.

Corum moved nervously about the deck, peering ahead to seek Halwyg's beflowered towers.

Then: "There they are," said Jhary softly. "There's your host from hell."

Corum looked down and saw the tide of flesh and steel that swept across the land. Mabden horsemen in their thousands. Mabden charioteers. Madben infantry. And things which were not Mabden —things summoned by sorcery and recruited from the Realm of Chaos. There was the Army of the Dog—huge, loping beasts the size of horses, more vulpine than canine. There was the Army of the Bear—each massive bear walking upright and carrying a shield and a club. And there was the Army of Chaos itself—misshapen warriors like those they had met earlier in the yellow abyss, led by a tall horseman in dazzling plate armor which clothed him from head to foot—doubtless the messenger of Queen Xiombarg of whom they had heard.

And just ahead of the host's leaders were the walls of Halwyg-nan-Vake, looking from this distance like a huge, complicated floral model.

Drums sounded from the ranks of the host of hell. Harsh trumpets cried out the Mabden bloodlust. Horrid laughter rose toward the sky ship and howls escaped the throats of the Army of the Dog— mocking howls that anticipated victory.

Corum spat down on the horde, the stench of Chaos now strong again in his nostrils. His mortal eye changed to burning black with an iris of flaming gold as his anger seized him and he spat a second time upon the flowing vileness below. He made a noise in his throat and his hand went to the hilt of his sword as he remembered all his hatred of the Mabden, who had slain his family and maimed him. He saw the banner of King Lyr-a-Brode—a crude, tattered thing bearing the Sign of the Dog and the Sign of the Bear. He sought to find his great enemy, Earl Glandyth-a-Krae amongst the ranks.

Rhalina called, "Corum—do not waste your strength now. Calm yourself and save your energy for the fight which must yet come!"

He sank down upon the seat, his mortal eye slowly fading back to its original color. He panted like one of the dogs that marched below and the jewels covering his faceted, alien eye seemed to shift and glitter with a different rage from his own . . .

Rhalina shivered when she saw him thus, with hardly any trace of the mortal about him. He was like some possessed demigod of the darkest legends of her people and her love of him turned to terror.

Corum buried his ruined head in his grafted, six-fingered hand and whimpered until the mood was driven out of him and he could look up and seem sane again. His rage and his fight to vanquish it had exhausted him. Pale and limp, he lay back in the seat, one hand on the brass rail of the sky ship as it began to circle down over Halwyg.

"Not much more than a mile away," Jhary murmured. "They'll have surrounded the walls by the morning, if not stopped."

"What army of ours could stop them?" Rhalina asked him hopelessly. "Lord Arkyn's reign is to be short-lived I fear."

The drums continued to rattle out their jubilation. The trumpets continued to blare their triumph. The howls of the Army of the Dog, the grunts of the Army of the Bear, the cacklings and shriekings of the Army of Chaos, the ground-shaking thunder of the ponies' hooves, the rumble of the iron-bound chariot wheels, the clatter of the war gear, the creak of harness, the bellowing laughter of the barbarians, all seemed to come closer with each heartbeat as the horde of hell swept inevitably toward the City of the Flowers.

The Second Chapter

THE SIEGE BEGINS

The sky ship circled lower and lower over the tense and silent city as the sun began to set and the towers echoed the sounds of the satanic horde still marching relentlessly toward it.

The streets and parts of Halwyg were packed with weary soldiers, camped wherever they could find an open space. Flowers had been trampled underfoot and edible shrubs had been stripped to feed the red-eyed warriors who had been driven back to Halwyg by the barbarian force. They were so tired that only a few looked up when the sky ship passed over their heads on its way to the roof of King Onald's palace. It landed on deserted battlements but almost immediately guards, in the murex helms and the mother-of-pearl breastplates, bearing the round shell shields of Lywn-an-Esh, with spears and swords, rushed up to apprehend them, doubtless thinking they were enemies. But when they saw Rhalina and Corum they lowered their weapons in relief. Several of them were wounded from previous encounters with the barbarian host and all looked as if they would be improved by more than a night's sleep.

"Prince Corum," said the leader. "I will tell the King that you are here."

"I thank you. In the meantime, I hope some of your men will help these people here, whom we saved from Lyr's men a short time back."

"It will be done, though food is scarce."

Corum had considered this. "The sky ship here can forage for you, though it must not be endangered. It may find a little food."

The steersman took a scroll from inside his jerkin and handed it to Corum. "Here, Prince Corum, are the rare substances our city needs if it is to attempt to crash once again through the Wall Between the Realms."

"If Arkyn can be summoned," Corum told him, "I will give him this list, for he is a God and therefore more knowledgeable about such things than any of us."

In Onald's simple room, still covered with maps of his land, they found the grim-faced King.

"How fares your nation, King Onald?" Jhary-a-Conel asked him as they entered.

"It is scarcely a nation any longer. We have been forced further and further back until barely all that's left of us is gathered here in Halwyg." He pointed at a large map of Lywn-an-Esh and he spoke in a hollow voice. "The County of Arluth-a-Cal—taken by the sea raiders from Bro-an-Mabden—the County of Pengarde and its ancient capital Enyn-an-Aldarn—burned—it flames all the way to Lake Calenyk by all reports. I have heard that the Duchy of Orynnan-Calywn still resists them in its most southern mountains, as does the Duchy of Haun-a-Gwyragh—but Bedwilral-nan-Rywm is completely taken, as is the County of Gal-a-Gorow. Of the Duchy of Palantyrn-an-Kenak, I do not know . . ."

"Fallen," said Corum.

"Ah—fallen . . ."

"They close in now from all quarters it seems," Jhary said, looking carefully at the map. "They landed along each of your coasts and then systematically began to tighten their circle—the whole horde converging on Halwyg-nan-Vake. I would not have thought barbarians capable of such sophisticated tactics—or of keeping to them even if they thought of them . . ."

"You forget Xiombarg's messenger," Corum said. "He doubtless helped them make this plan and trained them in its manipulation."

"You speak of the creature all in brilliant armor that rides at the head of his deformed army?" King Onald said.

"Aye. What news have you of him?"

"None that can help us. He is invulnerable, by all accounts, but, as you say, has much to do with the organizing of the barbarian army. He rides often at King Lyr's side. His name, I have heard, is Gaynor—Prince Gaynor the Damned . . ."

Jhary nodded. "He figures often in such conflicts. He is doomed to serve Chaos through all eternity. So now he is Queen Xiombarg's lackey, is he? It is a better position than some he has attained to in the past—or the future—whichever it is . . ."

King Onald looked oddly at Jhary and then continued. "Even without the aid of Chaos they would outnumber us ten to one. With our better weapons and superior tactics we might have resisted them for years—at least kept them on our coasts—but this Prince Gaynor advises them on every move. And his advice is good.''

"He had had plenty of experience," said Jhary, rubbing at his chin.

"How long can you withstand a siege?" Rhalina asked the king.

He shrugged and stared miserably out of the window at his crowded city. "I know not. The warriors are all weary, our walls are not particularly high, and Chaos fights on Lyr's side . . .''

"We had best hasten to the temple," Corum said, "and see if Lord Arkyn can be summoned.''

Through the packed streets they rode, seeing hopeless faces on all sides. Carts cluttered the broad avenues and campfires burned on the lawns. Half the army seemed to bear wounds of one description or another and others were inadequately armed and armored. It hardly seemed that Halwyg could stand Lyr's first assault. The siege would not be long, thought Corum as he tried to make faster headway through the throng.

At last they reached the Temple. The grounds of this were packed with sleeping, wounded soldiers and Aleryon-a-Nyvish, the priest, was standing in the entrance to the Temple as if he had known they were coming.

He welcomed them eagerly. "Did you find aid?"

"Perhaps," answered Corum. "But we must speak with Lord Arkyn. Can he be summoned?"

"He awaits you. He came not a few moments since.''

They strode rapidly into the cool darkness. Pallets filled it but they were at this time unoccupied. They awaited the wounded and the dying.

The handsome shape which Lord Arkyn had chosen to assume stepped from the shadows. "How fared you in Xiombarg's realm?"

Corum told him what had transpired and Arkyn looked disturbed by what he heard. He stretched out his hand. "Give me the scroll. I will seek the substances needed by the City in the Pyramid. But it will take even me some time to locate them.''

"And in the meanwhile the fate of two besieged cities is in doubt," Rhalina said. "Gwlas-cor-Gwrys in Xiombarg's realm and Halwyg-nan-Vake here. The destiny of one depends upon the other.''

"Such mirrorings are common enough in the struggle between Law and Chaos," murmured Jhary.

"Aye—they are," agreed Lord Arkyn. "But you must try to hold Halwyg until I return. Even then we cannot be sure that

Gwlas-cor-Gwrys will still be standing. Our one advantage is that Queen Xiombarg now concentrates upon two battles—the one in my realm and the one in her own."

"Yet her messenger Prince Gaynor the Damned is here and seems to represent her adequately," Corum pointed out.

"If Gaynor were destroyed," Arkyn said, "much of the barbarian advantage would go. They are not natural tacticians and without him there will be some confusion."

"But their numbers alone represent a mighty advantage," Jhary said. "And then there are the Army of the Dog and the Army of the Bear . . ."

"Agreed, Master Jhary. Still, I say, your most important enemy is Gaynor the Damned."

"But he is indestructible."

"He can be destroyed by one as strong and fate-heavy as himself." Arkyn looked significantly at Corum. "But it would take much courage and could mean that both would be destroyed . . ."

Corum inclined his head. "I will consider what you have said, Lord Arkyn."

"And now I go."

The handsome figure vanished and they were left alone in the Temple.

Corum looked at Rhalina and then he looked at Jhary. Neither met his gaze. They both knew what Lord Arkyn had asked of him—of the responsibility which had been put upon his shoulders.

He frowned, fingering the jeweled patch on his eye, flexing the fingers of the six-fingered alien hand extending from his left wrist.

"With the Eye of Rhynn and the Hand of Kwll," he said. "With Shool's obscene gifts which were grafted to my soul almost as wholly as they were grafted to my body, I will attempt to rid this realm of Prince Gaynor the Damned."

The Third Chapter

PRINCE GAYNOR THE DAMNED

"He was once a hero," said Jhary as they stood on the walls that night, peering out at the thousand campfires of the Chaos army surrounding the city. "This Prince Gaynor. He, too, fought on the side of Law. But then he fell in love with something—perhaps it was a woman—and became a renegade, throwing in his lot with Chaos. He was punished—punished, some say, by the Power of the Balance. Now he must serve Chaos eternally, just as you, eternally, serve Law . . ."

"Eternally?" Corum said, disturbed.

"I'll speak no more of that," Jhary said. "But you sometimes know peace. Prince Gaynor only remembers peace and can never, throughout all the ages, expect to find it again."

"Not even in death?"

"He is doomed never to die, for death there is peace, even if that death lasts only an instant before another rebirth."

"Then I cannot slay him?"

"You can slay him no more than you can slay one of the Great Old Gods. But you can banish him. You must know how to do that, however . . ."

"Do you know, Jhary?"

"I think so." Jhary lowered his head in concentration as he paced the walls beside Corum. "I remember tales that Gaynor can be defeated only if his visor is opened and his face looked upon by one who serves Law. But his visor can be opened only by a greater force than any mortal wields. Such is the familiar condition of a sorcerous fate. It is all I know."

"It's precious little," Corum said gracelessly.

"Aye."

"It must be tonight. They will expect no attack from us—especially on the first night of their siege. We must go against the

Chaos host, strike swiftly, and attempt to slay—or banish, whatever it is—Prince Gaynor the Damned. He controls the malformed army and they will be drawn back to their own realm if he is no longer present."

"A simple plan," said Jhary sardonically. "Who rides with us? Beldan is here. I have seen him."

"I'll not risk any of the defenders. They'll be needed if the plan fails."

"We'll ride alone," Corum said.

Jhary shrugged and sighed. "You'd best stay here, little friend," he told his cat.

Through the night they slipped, leading their horses, whose hooves were bound in thick rags to muffle their sound, toward the camp of Chaos where the Mabden reveled and kept poor guard.

The smell was sufficient to tell them where Prince Gaynor's hellish band was camped. The half-men shambled about in strange, ritual dances, resembling the movements of mating beasts rather than those of human folk. The stupid beast faces were slack-mouthed, dull-eyed, and they drank much sour wine to make them forget what once they had been before they had pledged themselves to the corruption that was Chaos.

Prince Gaynor sat in the middle of this, near the leaping fire, all encased from head to foot in his flashing armor. It was sometimes silver, sometimes gold, sometimes bluish steel. A dark yellow plume nodded on the helm and on the breastplate was engraved the Arms of Chaos—eight arrows radiating from a central hub, representing, according to Chaos, all the rich possibilities inherent in its philosophy. Prince Gaynor did not carouse. He did not eat and he did not drink. He merely stared at his warriors, his metal-gloved hands upon the pommel of his big sword, which was also sometimes silver, sometimes gold, sometimes bluish steel. He was all of a piece, Prince Gaynor the Damned.

They had to skirt several snoring barbarian guards before they could creep into Gaynor's camp, which was set some distance from the rest of the camp, just as the Army of the Dog and the Army of the Bear were camped the other side. Some of Lyr's men staggered past them, but, because Corum and Jhary were swathed in cowled cloaks, hardly gave them a second glance. None suspected that the warriors of Lywn-an-Esh would come in couples to their camp.

When they reached the edge of the firelight and were close to the leaping throng of beast-men, they mounted their horses and waited for a long moment while they regarded the mysterious figure of Prince Gaynor the Damned.

He had not moved once since they had first observed him. Seated on an ornate, high saddle of ebony and ivory, his hands on the pommel of his great broadsword, he continued to stare without interest at the caperings of his obscene followers.

Then they rode into the circle of fiery light and Prince Corum Jhaelen Irsei, Servant of Law, faced Prince Gaynor the Damned, Servant of Chaos.

Corum wore all his Vadhagh gear—his delicate, silver mail, his conical helm, his scarlet robe. His tall spear was in his right hand and his great round war-board was upon his left arm.

Prince Gaynor rose from where he was seated and he lifted an arm to stop the revels. The legion of hell turned to regard Corum and they began to snarl and gibber when they recognized him.

"Be silent!" Prince Gaynor the Damned commanded, stepping forward in his flickering armor and sheathing his sword. "Saddle my charger, one of you, for I think Prince Corum and his friend come to do battle with me." His voice was vibrant and, on the surface, amused. But there was a bleak quality underlying it, a tragic sadness.

"Will you fight me alone, Prince Gaynor?" Corum asked.

The Prince of Chaos laughed. "Why should I? It is long since I subscribed to your ideas of chivalry, Prince Corum. And I have a pledge to my mistress, Queen Xiombarg, that I must use any means to destroy you. I have never known her to hate—but she hates you, Sir Vadhagh. How she hates you!"

"It could be because she fears me," Corum suggested.

"Aye. It could be."

"Then you will set your whole host upon us?"

"Why should I not? If you are foolish enough to enter my power . . ."

"You have no pride?"

"None, I think."

"No honor?"

"None."

"No courage?"

"I have no absolute qualities at all, I fear—save that, perhaps—save fear, itself."

"You are honest, however."

A deep laugh issued from the closed visor. "If you would believe it. Why have you come to my camp, Prince Corum?"

253

"You know why, do you not?"

"You hope to slay me, because I am the brain which controls all this barbarian brawn? A good idea. But I cannot be slain. Would that I could—I have prayed for death, often enough. You hope that if you defeat me you will buy time for building up your defenses. Perhaps you would do so, but I regret that I will slay you and thus rob Halwyg-nan-Vake of its chief supply of brain and resourcefulness."

"If you cannot be slain, why not fight me personally?"

"Because I would not waste time. Warriors!"

The misshapen beast-men arrayed themselves behind their master, who mounted his white charger, on which had been placed the high saddle of ebony and ivory. He settled his own spear in its rest and drew his own shield onto his arm.

Corum lifted his jeweled eye patch and looked beyond Prince Gaynor and his men, into the netherworld cavern where his last victims were. Here were the Chaos pack, all the more distorted since the Ghanh had taken them into the folds of its crushing wings. There was Polib-Bav, the pack's horse-faced leader. Into the netherworld reached the Hand of Kwll and summoned the Chaos pack to Corum's aid.

"Now Chaos shall war once more with Chaos!" Corum cried. "Take your prizes, Polib-Bav, and be released from Limbo!"

And foulness met foulness and horror clashed with horror as the Chaos pack rushed into Gaynor's camp and began to set upon their brother beasts. Dog-thing fought cow-thing, horse-thing fought frog-thing, and their bludgeons and their carvers and their axes rose and fell in a frightful massing. Screams, grunts, bellows, groans, oaths, squeals, cackles rose from the heap of embattled creatures and Prince Gaynor the Damned looked at it and then turned his horse so that it faced Corum.

"I congratulate you, Prince in the Scarlet Robe. I see you did not rely upon my chivalry. Now, will both of you fight me?"

"Not that," Corum said, preparing his spear and lifting himself in his stirrups so that he was now seated on the high part of his saddle, almost standing upright. "My friend is here to report the outcome of this fight should I perish. He will fight only to protect himself."

"A fair tourney, eh?" Prince Gaynor laughed again. "Very well!" And he, too, put himself into the fighting position in his saddle.

Then he charged.

Corum spurred his own war-horse toward his foe, spear raised to strike, shield up to protect his face, for he lacked Gaynor's visor.

Prince Gaynor's flashing armor half-blinded him as he galloped on, then flung back his arm and hurled the great spear with all his might at Gaynor's head. It struck full against the helm but did not pierce, did not appear to dent it. However, Gaynor reeled in his saddle and did not immediately retaliate with his own spear, giving Corum time to stretch out his hand and catch the haft of his weapon as it bounced back. Gaynor laughed when he saw this and jabbed at Corum's face, but the Prince in the Scarlet Robe brought up his war-board to block the blow.

Elsewhere the grisly fight between the two parties of beast-men went on. The Chaos pack was smaller than Gaynor's force, but it had the advantage that it had already been slain once and therefore could not be slain again.

Now both horses reared at once, hooves tangling, almost throwing their riders off. Corum flung his spear as he clung to the reins. Again it struck the Prince of the Damned who was hurled backward from his saddle and lay in the filthy mud of his camp. He sprang up at once, his spear still in his hand and returned Corum's cast. The spear pierced the war-board and its point came a fraction of an inch to entering Corum's jewled eye. The spear hanging in his shield, he drew his sword and charged down upon Prince Gaynor. Gaynor's helm rang with a bitter glee and now his broadsword was in his right hand, his shield raised to take Corum's first blow. Gaynor's stroke was not at Corum but at the horse. He hacked off one of its feet and it collapsed to the ground, throwing Corum sprawling.

Swiftly, in spite of his heavy plate armor, Prince Gaynor raised his sword and ran at Corum as he desperately tried to regain his footing in the mud. The sword whistled down and was met by the shield. The blade bit through the layers of leather and metal and wood which was still protruding from Corum's war-board. Corum swiped at Gaynor's feet, but the Prince of the Damned leaped high and escaped the blow while Corum rolled back and at last managed to climb to a standing position, his shield all split and near useless.

Gaynor still laughed, his voice echoing in the helm that was never opened.

"You fight well, Corum, but you are mortal—and I no longer am!"

The sounds of battle had alerted the rest of the camp, but the barbarians were unsure of what was hapening. They were used to obeying Lyr, who had come to rely upon Gaynor's commands and now Gaynor had no time to tell Lyr what to do.

The two champions began to circle each other while to one side of them the beast-men of Chaos continued to fight to the death.

In the shadows beyond the firelight, the faces of superstitious,

255

wide-eyed barbarians watched the fray, not understanding how this thing had come about.

Corum abandoned his shield and unslung his war-axe from his back, holding it in the six-fingered Hand of Kwll. He increased the distance between himself and his enemy, adjusting his grip on the axe. It was a perfectly balanced throwing axe, normally used by Vadhagh infantry in the old days when they had battled the Nhadragh. Corum hoped that Prince Gaynor would not realize what he intended to do.

Swiftly he raised his arm and flung the axe. It flashed through the air toward the Prince of the Damned—and was caught upon the shield.

But Gaynor staggered back under the force of the blow, his shield completely split in twain. He threw aside the pieces, took his broadsword in both hands and closed with Corum.

Corum blocked the first blow and the second and the third, being forced back by the ferocity of Gaynor's attack. He jumped to one side and aimed a darting thrust designed to pierce one of the joins in Gaynor's armor. Gaynor shifted his sword into his right hand and turned the thrust aside, taking two steps backward. He was panting now. Corum heard his breath hissing in his helm.

"Immortal you may be, Prince Gaynor the Damned—but tireless you are not."

"You cannot slay me! Do you not think I would welcome death?"

"Then surrender to me." Corum was panting himself. His heart beat rapidly, his chest heaved. "Surrender to me and see if I cannot kill you!"

"To surrender would be to betray my pledge to Queen Xiombarg."

"So you do know honor?"

"Honor!" Gaynor laughed. "Not honor—fear, as I told you. If I betray her, Xiombarg will punish me. I do not think you could comprehend what that means, Prince in the Scarlet Robe." And again Prince Gaynor rushed upon Corum, the broadsword shrieking around his head.

Corum ducked under the whirling broadsword and came in with a swipe to Gaynor's legs so powerful that one knee buckled for an instant before the Prince of the Damned hopped backward, darting a glance over his shoulder to see how his minions fared.

The Chaos pack was finishing them. One by one the creatures Corum had summoned from the netherworld were gathering in their prizes and vanishing to whence they had come.

With a cry Gaynor threw himself once more on Corum. Corum

summoned all his strength to turn the lunge and thrust back. Then Gaynor closed in, grabbing Corum's sword arm and raising his broadsword to bring it down on Corum's head. Corum wrestled himself free and the blade struck his shoulder, cut through the first layer of mail and was stopped by the second.

And he was defenseless. Prince Gaynor had clung to his sword and now held it triumphantly in his left gauntlet.

"Yield to me, Prince Corum. Yield to me and I will spare your life."

"So that you can take me back to your mistress Xiombarg."

"It is what I must do."

"Then I will not yield!"

"So I must kill you, then?" Gaynor panted as he dropped Corum's sword to the mud, took a grip with both hands on the hilt of his own broadsword, and stumbled forward to finish his foe.

The Fourth Chapter

THE BARBARIAN ATTACK

Instinctively Corum flung up his hands to ward off Gaynor's blow and then something happened to the Hand of Kwll.

More than once the Hand had saved his life—often in anticipation of the threat—and now it acted of its own volition again to reach out and grasp Gaynor's blade, wrenching it from the hands of the Damned Prince and bringing it rapidly up, then down to dash the pommel against the top of Gaynor's head.

Prince Gaynor staggered, groaning, and slowly fell to his knees.

Now Corum jumped forward and with one arm encircled Gaynor's neck. "Do you yield, Prince?"

"I cannot yield," Gaynor replied in a strangled voice. "I have nothing *to* yield."

But he no longer struggled as the sinister Hand of Kwll grasped the lip of his visor and tugged.

"NO!" Prince Gaynor cried as he realized what Corum planned. "You cannot. No mortal may see my face!" He began to writhe, but Corum held him firmly and the Hand of Kwll tugged again at the visor.

"PLEASE!"

The visor shifted slightly.

"I BEG THEE, PRINCE IN THE SCARLET ROBE! LET ME GO AND I WILL OFFER THEE NO FURTHER HARM!"

"You have not the right to swear such an oath," Corum reminded him fiercely. "You are Xiombarg's thing and are without honor or will."

The pleading voice echoed strangely. "Have mercy, Prince Corum."

"And I have not the right to grant you that mercy, for I serve Arkyn," Corum told him.

The Hand of Kwll wrenched for a third time at the visor and it came away.

Corum stared at a youthful face which writhed as if composed of a million white worms. Dead, red eyes peered from the face and all the horrors Corum had ever witnessed could not compare with the simple, tragic horror of that visage. He screamed and his scream blended with that of Prince Gaynor the Damned as the flesh of the face began to putrefy and change into a score of foul colors which gave off a more pungent stench than anything which had issued from the Chaos pack itself. And as Corum watched the face changed its features. Sometimes it was the face of a middle-aged man, sometimes the face of a woman, sometimes that of a boy—and once, fleetingly, he recognized his own face. How many guises had Prince Gaynor known through all the eternity of his damnation? Corum saw a million years of despair recorded there. And still the face writhed, still the red eyes blazed in terror and agony, still the features changed and changed and changed and changed . . .

More than a million years. Aeons of misery. The price of Gaynor's nameless crime, his betrayal of his oath to Law. A fate imposed upon him not by Law but by the Power of the Balance. What crime could it have been if the neutral Cosmic Balance had been required to act? Some suggestion of it appeared and disappeared in the various features that flashed within the helm. And now Corum did not grip Gaynor's neck, but instead cradled the tormented head in his arms and wept for the Prince of the Damned, who had paid a price—was paying a price—which no being should ever have to pay.

Here, Corum felt as he wept, was the ultimate in justice—or the ultimate in injustice. Both seemed at that moment to be the same.

And even now Prince Gaynor was not dying. He was merely undergoing a transition from one existence to another. Soon, in some other distant realm, far from the Fifteen Planes and the realms of the Sword Rulers, he would be doomed to continue his servitude to Chaos.

At last the face disappeared and the flashing armor was empty. Prince Gaynor the Damned was gone.

Corum lifted his head dazedly and heard Jhary-a-Conel's voice in his ears. "Quickly, Corum, take Gaynor's horse. The barbarians are gathering their courage. Our work is done here!"

The Companion to Champions was shaking him. Corum got up, found his sword where Gaynor had dropped it in the mud, let Jhary help him into the ebony and ivory saddle . . .

. . . Then they were galloping toward the walls of Halwyg-nan-Vake with the Mabden warriors howling behind them.

The gates opened for them and closed instantly. Barbarian fists beat uselessly on the iron-shod timbers as they dismounted to find that King Onald and Rhalina were waiting for them.

"Prince Gaynor?" said King Onald eagerly. "Does he still live?"

"Aye," Corum answered hollowly. "He still lives."

"Then you failed!"

"No." Corum walked away from them, leading his foe's horse, walking into the darkness, unwilling to speak to anyone, not even Rhalina.

King Onald followed him and then paused, looking up at Jhary who was lowering himself from his saddle. "He did not fail?"

"Prince Gaynor's power is gone," Jhary said tiredly. "Corum defeated him. Now the barbarians have no brain—they have only their numbers, their brutality, their Dogs and their Bears." He laughed without humor. "That is all, King Onald."

They all stared after Corum, who, with bowed back and dragging feet, passed into the shadows.

"I will prepare us for their attack," Onald said. "They will come at us in the morning, I think."

"It is likely," Rhalina agreed. She had an impulse to go to Corum then, but she restrained it.

And at dawn the barbarian army of King Lyr-a-Brode joined with the army of Bro-an-Mabden and, still with the strength of the Army of the Dog and the Army of the Bear, began to close in on Halwyg-nan-Vake.

Warriors were packed on all Halwyg's low walls. The barbarians had no siege engines with them, since they had relied on Prince Gaynor's strategy and his host of Chaos in their taking of all other cities. But there were many of them—so many that it was almost impossible to see the last ranks of their legions. They rode on horses and in chariots or they marched.

Corum had rested for a few hours but had not able to sleep. He could not rid himself of the vision of Prince Gaynor's face. He tried to remember his hatred of Glandyth-a-Krae and sought the Earl amongst the barbarian horde, but Glandyth was apparently nowhere present. Perhaps he searched for Corum still in the region of Moidel's Mount?

King Lyr sat a big horse and clutched his own crude battle banner. Beside him was the hump-backed shape of King Cronekyn-a-Drok, ruler of the tribes of Bro-an-Mabden. Half-idiot was King Cronekyn and well was he nick-named the Little Toad.

The barbarians marched raggedly, without much order, and it

260

seemed that the sunken-featured King looked about him nervously as if he were not sure he could control such a force now that Prince Gaynor was gone.

King Lyr-a-Brode lifted his great iron sword and a sheet of flaming arrows suddenly leapt from behind his horsemen and whistled over the walls of Halwyg, setting light to shrubs which had dried from lack of watering. But King Onald had prepared for this and for some days the citizens had been preserving their urine to throw upon the flames. King Onald had heard of the fate of other besieged cities in his kingdom and he had learned what was necessary.

Several of the defenders staggered about on the walls beating at the flaming arrows which stuck in them. One man ran by Corum with his face burning but Corum hardly noticed him.

With a huge roar the barbarians rode right up to the walls and began to scale them.

The attack on Halwyg had begun in earnest.

But Corum watched for the Army of the Dog and the Army of the Bear, wondering when they would be brought against them. They seemed to be holding them in reserve and he could not quite see why.

Now his attention was forced back to the immediate threat as a gasping barbarian, brand in one hand, sword in his teeth, hauled himself over the battlements. He gave a yell of surprise as Corum cut him down. But others were coming now.

All through that morning Corum fought mechanically, though he fought well. Elsewhere on the walls Rhalina, Jhary, and Beldan were commanding detachments of defenders. A thousand barbarians died, but a thousand more replaced them, for Lyr had had the sense at least to rest his men and bring them up in waves. There was no chance of such strategy amongst those who manned the walls. Every warrior who could carry a sword was being used.

Corum's ears rang with the roar and the clash of battle. He must have taken a score of lives, yet he was hardly aware of it. His mail was torn in a dozen places, he was bleeding from several minor wounds, but he did not notice that, either.

More flame arrows crossed the walls and the women and children came with buckets to douse the fires that started.

Behind the defenders was a thin haze of smoke. Before them was a mass of stinking barbarian warriors. And everywhere was the hysteria of battle. Blood splashed all surfaces. Human guts smeared the walls. Broken weapons littered the ground and corpses were piled several deep on the battlements in a vain attempt to raise the walls and stem the attack.

Below them, at the gates, barbarians used tree trunks to try to split the iron-shod wood, but so far it had held.

Corum, only distantly aware of the noise and the sights of the battle, knew that his fight with Prince Gaynor had been worthwhile. There was no doubt that Gaynor's hell creatures and Gaynor's tactics would have taken the city by now.

But how much time was there? When would Arkyn return with the substances needed by Prince Yurette? And did the City in the Pyramid still stand?

Corum smiled grimly then. Xiombarg would know by now that he had slain her servant, Prince Gaynor. Her anger would be that much greater, her sense of impotence the stronger. Perhaps this would lessen the fury of her attack upon Gwlas-cor-Gwrys?

Or perhaps it would strengthen it?

Corum strove to banish the speculations from his mind. There was no use in them. He picked up a spear, hurled by a barbarian, and flung it back so that it pierced the stomach of a Mabden attacker, who clutched the shaft and swayed on the wall for a moment before toppling head over heels to join the other corpses on the ground below.

Then, soon after noon, the barbarians began to retreat, dragging their dead with them.

Corum saw King Lyr and King Cronekyn conferring. Perhaps they were wondering whether to bring up the Army of the Dog and the Army of the Bear. Were they considering new strategy which would not waste so many of their men? Perhaps they did not care about the men they wasted?

A boy found Corum on the wall. "Prince Corum, a message. Will you join Aleryon there?"

On aching legs Corum left the battlements and got into a chariot, driving it slowly through the streets to the Temple.

And now the Temple was packed with wounded both within and without. Corum met Aleryon at the entrance.

"Is Arkyn returned?"

"He is, Prince."

Corum strode in, looking questioningly at the prone bodies on the floor.

"They are dying," said Aleryon quietly. "They are hardly aware of anything. There is no need for discretion with these poor lads."

Arkyn stepped again from the shadows. For all he was a God and the form he assumed was not his true form, he looked tired. "Here," he said, handing Corum a small box of plain, dull metal.

262

"Do not open it, for the substances are very powerful and their radiance can kill you. Take it to the messenger from Gwlas-cor-Gwrys and tell him to go back through the Wall Between the Realms in his sky ship . . ."

"But he has not the power to return?" Corum argued.

"I will manufacture an opening for him—or at least I hope I will, for I am close to exhaustion. Xiombarg is working against me in subtle ways. I am not sure I will be able to find an opening near to his city, but I will try. If it is far from his city he may be in danger, trying to get back there, but it will be the best I can do."

Corum nodded and took the box. "Let us pray that Gwlas-cor-Gwrys still stands."

Arkyn gave a sardonic smile. "Do not pray to me, then," he said. "For I know no better than you."

Corum hurried from the Temple with the box under his arm. It was heavy and it throbbed. He climbed into his chariot, whipped up the horses, and raced through the miserable avenues until he came to the roof where the sky ship awaited him. He handed the box to the steersman and told him what Lord Arkyn had said. The steersman looked dubious but took the box and placed it carefully in a locker in the wheelhouse.

"Farewell, Bwydyth-a-Horn," Corum said earnestly. "May you find your City in the Pyramid and may you bring it back to this realm in time."

Bwydyth saluted him as he took the ship into the air.

Suddenly a ragged gap appeared in the sky. It was unstable. It quivered and it sparked. Beyond it a vivid golden sky could be seen, scarred with purple and orange light which shouted.

Through the gap went the sky ship. It was swallowed suddenly and the gap shrank behind it until there was no gap there at all.

Corum stood watching the sky for a moment before he heard a great roar suddenly go up from the walls.

A new attack must be beginning.

He ran down the steps, back through the palace, out into the street. And then he saw the women. They were on their knees. They were weeping. A board was being borne on the shoulders of four tall warriors. On the board was something covered by a cloak.

"What is it?" Corum asked one of the warriors. "Who is dead?"

"They have slain our King Onald," said the warrior sorrowfully. "And they have sent the Armies of the Dog and the Horned Bear against us. Destruction comes to Halwyg, Prince Corum. Now nothing can stop it!"

The Fifth Chapter

THE FURY OF QUEEN XIOMBARG

Savagely Corum whipped the horses back through the streets to the wall. A silence had fallen upon the citizens of Halwyg-nan-Vake and now, it seemed, they waited passively for the death which the victorious barbarians would bring them. Already two women had committed suicide as he passed, hurling themselves from the roofs of their houses. Perhaps they were wise, he thought.

He jumped from the chariot and ran up the steps to the wall where Rhalina and Jhary-a-Conel stood together. He did not need to listen to what they told him, for he could see what was coming.

The great Dogs, eyes glaring, tongues lolling, were loping swiftly toward the city, towering over the barbarians who ran beside them. And behind the Dogs came the gigantic Bears with their clubs and their shields and with black horns curling from their heads, lumbering on their hind legs.

Corum knew that the Dogs could leap the walls and that the Bears would batter down the gates with their clubs and he reached a decision.

"To the palace!" he shouted. "All warriors to the palace. All civilians find what cover they can!"

"You are abandoning the citizens?" Rhalina asked him, shivering when she saw that his single eye burned black and gold.

"I am doing what I can for them, hoping that our retreat will bring us a little time. From the palace we shall be able to defend ourselves better. Hurry!" he shouted. "Hurry!"

Some of the warriors moved swiftly, in relief, but others were reluctant.

Corum stayed on the walls, watching as the soldiers straggled back toward the distant palace, herding the citizens with them, carrying the wounded.

Soon only he, Rhalina, and Jhary remained on the walls, watching the Dogs lope nearer, watching the Bears come closer.

Then the three companions descended to the streets and began to run through the ruined, deserted avenues, past burned bushes and crushed flowers and corpses, until they arrived at the palace and supervised the barricading of windows and doors.

The howls of the Dogs and the Bears, the yells of the triumphant barbarians could now be heard in the distance.

A kind of peace fell over the waiting palace as the three companions climbed to the roof and stood watching.

"How long?" Rhalina whispered. "How long, Corum, before they come?"

"The beasts? Some minutes before they reach the walls."

"And then?"

"A few more minutes while they nose about for a trap."

"And then?"

"A minute or two before they attack the palace. And then—I do not know. We cannot stand for long against such powerful foes."

"Have you no other plan?"

"I have one more plan. But against so many . . ." His voice trailed off. "I am not sure. I simply do not know the power . . ."

The howling and the grunting grew louder, then stopped.

"They are at the walls," said Jhary.

Corum arranged his torn, scarlet robe about his shoulders. He kissed Rhalina. "Farewell, my margravine," he said.

"Farewell? What—?"

"Farewell, Jhary—Companion to Champions. I think you may have to find another hero to befriend."

Jhary tried to smile. "Do you want me with you?"

"No."

The first of the huge Dogs leaped the wall and stood panting in the street, sniffing this way and that. They saw it in the distance.

Corum left them as they watched, going back down the steps within the palace, squeezing through the barricade at the entrance and walking out down the broad path, past the gates of the palace, until he stood in the main avenue looking toward the walls.

Some bushes were burning nearby. Gardens and lawns were littered with the dead and the near dead. A small winged cat circled over Corum's head and then flew back toward the battlements.

More Dogs had leaped the walls and, heads down, tongues panting, eyes wary, came slowly along the avenue to where the single small figure of Corum waited for them.

Behind the Dogs the main gates of the city suddenly splintered, cracked, and were forced down. The first of the Horned Bears waddled through, nostrils dilating, club ready.

Corum was seen to raise his hand to his jeweled eye then. He was seen to blanch and stagger slightly, he was seen to stretch out his sorcerous Hand of Kwll, and it vanished so that it seemed he had only a stump on his wrist.

And, then, all around him, frightful things suddenly appeared. Ghastly, ruined, misshapen things—the things which had been the followers of Prince Gaynor the Damned and were now loyal to Corum only because he promised them release if they would find new victims to imprison in the Cavern of Limbo.

Corum pointed with the Hand of Kwll, which had now reappeared.

Rhalina turned her horrified gaze to Jhary-a-Conel, who viewed the scene with a certain equanimity. "How can such—such maimed things hope to beat those Dogs and those Bears and the thousands of barbarians who follow behind them?"

Jhary said, "I do not know. I think Corum is testing their power. If they are beaten completely, then it means that the Hand of Kwll and the Eye of Rhynn are all but useless to him and will not be able to save us if we try to escape."

"And that is what he knew and did not speak of," said Rhalina, nodding her beautiful head.

The creatures of Chaos began to race up the avenue toward the gigantic Dogs and Bears. The animals were puzzled, growling a little, but not sure whether these were friends or foes.

Scampering, malformed things they were, many with limbs missing, many with huge gaping wounds, some with no head, some with no legs at all, so that they clung to their fellows or, where they could, propelled themselves on their hands. A wretched mob with but one advantage—and that was that they were already dead.

Down the long, desolate avenue they poured and the Dogs barked, their voices reverberating among the roofs of ruined Halwyg, warning the creatures to go back.

But the creatures came on. They could not stop. To slay the Army of the Dog and the Army of the Bear was to assure their release from terrifying Limbo—to assure that their souls might die completely—and true death was all they sought now.

Corum remained where he was at the end of the avenue and he could not believe that such wounded creatures could possibly overcome the fierce and agile beasts. He saw that all the Bears had entered the gates and that the barbarians were crowding in behind them, led by King Lyr and King Cronekyn. He hoped that even if the Chaos things were not successful that a part of an hour might be granted Halwyg before the attack on the palace began.

He looked back, behind the palace, to where the roof of the Temple of Law could just be seen. Was Arkyn there? Was Arkyn waiting to see what would happen?

The Dogs began to snap at the first of the Chaos creatures to reach them. One of the huge beasts flung its head back with an armless, struggling living-dead thing in its jaws. It shook it and flung it aside, but it began to crawl toward the Dog again, the moment it had fallen. The Dog flattened its ears and its tail dropped when it saw this.

Large as they were, thought Corum, fierce as they were, they were still Dogs. It was one of the things he had counted upon.

The Bears moved forward, red mouths glistening with white fangs, clubs and shields raised, striking about them with their bludgeons so that Chaos creatures were flung in all directions. But they did not die. They picked themselves up and they attacked again.

Chaos creatures clung to the fur of the Dogs and the Bears. One Dog went down at last, threshing on its back as Corum's maimed corpses tore out its throat. Corum smiled an unpleasant smile.

But now he saw that what he feared might happen was happening. Lyr-a-Brode was leading his riders around the fighting beasts. They moved warily, but they were beginning to fill the approach to the long avenue.

Corum turned and ran back toward the palace.

Before he had reached the roof the barbarians were pouring down the avenue toward the palace, while behind them the Army of the Dog and the Army of the Bear still struggled with the living-dead Chaos creatures.

Arrows whirred from the windows of the palace and Corum saw that King Cronekyn was one of the first to fall with an arrow in each eye. King Lyr-a-Brode was better armored than his brother monarch and the arrows merely bounced off his helmet and breastplate. He waved his sword in mockery of the archers and flung his barbarians against the palace. They began to batter down the barricades.

A captain of the Royal Guard came running to the roof. "We can hold the lower floors a few moments longer, Prince Corum, but that is all."

Corum nodded. "Retreat as slowly as you can. We'll join you soon."

Rhalina said, "What did you think would happen to you down there, Corum?"

"I have a feeling that Xiombarg is exerting great pressures on this realm since I destroyed Prince Gaynor. I thought she might have the power to turn those things upon me."

"But she cannot personally come to this realm," Rhalina said. "We were told that. It would be to sin against the Rule of the Balance and even the Great Old Gods will not defy the Cosmic Balance so openly."

"Perhaps," said Corum. "But I am beginning to suspect that Xiombarg's fury is so great she may attempt to break through into this realm."

"That will mean the end of us without doubt," she murmured. "What is Arkyn doing?"

"Engaging himself with what he can. He cannot interfere directly in our aid—and I suspect that he, too, prepares himself for Xiombarg. Come, we had best join the defenders."

They were two flights down when they saw the retreating warriors vainly trying to force back the roaring barbarians who pressed blindly upward, careless of the threat of death. The captain who had earlier addressed Corum spread his hands hopelessly. "There are more detachments elsewhere in the palace, but I fear they're as hard-pressed as we."

Corum looked at the steps, which were crowded with the invaders. The wall of guards was thin and would soon break. "Then we must go to the roof," he said. "At least we will be able to hold them there a little longer. We must conserve our forces as best we can."

"But we are defeated, are we not, Prince Corum?" said the captain calmly.

"I fear so, Captain. I fear so."

And then, from somewhere, they heard a scream. It was not a human scream and yet it was plainly a scream of pure anger.

Rhalina covered her face with her hands. "Xiombarg?" she whispered. "It is Xiombarg's voice, Corum."

Corum's mouth was dry. He could not answer her. He licked his lips.

The scream came again. But there was another sound with it—a humming which rose higher and higher in pitch until it hurt their ears.

"The roof!" Corum cried. "Quickly."

Gasping for breath they reached the roof and flung up their arms to protect their eyes against the powerful lights which swam in the sky and obscured the sun.

Corum saw it first. Xiombarg's face, contorted with insensate fury, huge upon the horizon, her auburn hair flowing as clouds might flow across the sky, a mighty sword in her hand, large enough to slice the whole world in twain.

"It is she," groaned Rhalina. "The Queen of the Swords. She has defied the Balance and she has come to destroy us."

"Look there!" Jhary-a-Conel cried. "That is why she is here. She has followed them to our realm! They have escaped her. All her plans were thwarted and she defied the Balance in her impotence and her rage!"

It was the City in the Pyramid. It hovered in the sky over battered Halwyg-nan-Vake, its green light flickering and threatening to fade and then bursting into increased brilliance. From the City in the Pyramid came the whining sound they had heard.

Something left the city and flew down toward the palace. Corum turned away from the image of Xiombarg's raging face and her waving sword and he watched the sky ship descend. In it was the King Without a Country. He held something in his arms.

The sky ship settled on the roof and the King Without a Country smiled at Corum. "A gift," he said. "In return for your help to Gwlas-cor-Gwrys . . ."

"I thank you," Corum said, "but this is no time—"

"The gift has powers. It is a weapon. Take it."

Corum took the thing. It was a cylinder covered in peculiar designs and with a spade grip at one end. The other end tapered.

"It is a weapon," repeated Noreg-Dan. "It will destroy those at whom you point it."

Corum looked at the vision of Xiombarg, heard her screaming begin again, saw her raise the sword. He pointed it at her.

"No," said the King Without a Country. "Not Xiombarg, for she is a Great Old God—a Sword Ruler. Your mortal enemies."

Corum rushed to the stairs and descended. The barbarians, King Lyr now leading them, had reached the last flight.

"Point it and press the handle," called Noreg-Dan.

Corum pointed it at King Lyr-a-Brode. The tall king was striding up the stairs, his braided beard fluttering, his bearing triumphant, and all his huge Grim Guard behind him. He saw Corum and he laughed.

"Do you wish to surrender, Last of the Vadhagh?"

And Corum laughed back at him. "I am not the last of the Vadhagh, King Lyr-a-Brode, as this shows you." He pressed the grip and suddenly the King clutched at his chest, choked, and fell backward into the arms of his Guard, his tongue protruding from his lips, his gray braids falling over his eyes.

"He is dead!" shrieked the leader of the Grim Guard. "Our king! Vengeance!"

Waving his sword he rushed at Corum. But again Corum depressed the grip and he, too, died in the manner of his king. Corum pointed the weapon several times. Each time a Grim Guard fell until there were no more Grim Guards living.

He looked back at the King Without a Country. Noreg-Dan was smiling. "We used such things against Xiombarg's minions. That is one of the reasons why she expresses such rage. It will take her time to create new mortal things to do her work."

"But she has defied the Balance in one thing," Corum said. "She may defy it in another."

The monstrous, beautiful, furious face of the Queen of the Swords rose higher over the horizon and now her shoulders could be seen, her breasts, her waist.

"AH! CORUM! DREADFUL ASSASSIN OF ALL I LOVE!"

The voice was so loud that it made Corum's ears throb with pain. He staggered backward against the battlements, watching, transfixed, as the great sword filled the sky and Xiombarg's eyes blazed like two mighty suns. She was engulfing the world with her presence. The sword began to fall and Corum readied himself for death. Rhalina rushed to his arms and they hugged one another.

Then: "YOU HAVE MOCKED THE RULING OF THE COSMIC BALANCE, SISTER XIOMBARG!"

Against the far horizon stood Arkyn, as gigantic as the Queen of the Swords. Lord Arkyn of Law in all his godly finery, with a sword in his hand as large as Xiombarg's. And the city and its inhabitants were more insignificant than a tiny ants' nest and its occupants would be to two humans confronting each other in a meadow.

"YOU HAVE MOCKED THE BALANCE, QUEEN OF THE SWORDS."

"I AM NOT THE FIRST!"

"THERE IS ONLY ONE WHO HAS SURVIVED AND HE IS THE NAMELESS FORCE! YOU HAVE RELINQUISHED YOUR RIGHT TO RULE YOUR REALM!"

"NO! THE BALANCE HAS NO POWER OVER ME!"

"BUT IT HAS . . ."

And the Cosmic Balance, that Corum had seen once before in a vision after he had banished Arioch of Chaos, appeared in the sky between Lord Arkyn and Queen Xiombarg and it was so great that it dwarfed them.

"IT HAS."

said a voice that was not the voice of Xiombarg or Arkyn.

And the Balance began to tip toward Arkyn.

"IT HAS."

Queen Xiombarg screamed in fear and it was a scream that shook the whole world and threatened to send it spinning from its course about the sun.

"IT HAS."

The sword that was the symbol of her power was wrenched effortlessly from her hand and appeared for an instant in the bowl of the Balance, which tilted toward Lord Arkyn.

"NO!" begged Queen Xiombarg. "IT WAS A TRICK—ARKYN PLANNED THIS. HE LURED ME HERE. HE KNEW . . ." Her voice was fading. *He knew. . . . He knew . . .*"

And the substance of Queen Xiombarg began to disperse. It drifted away like wisps of cloud and then was gone.

For a moment the Cosmic Balance remained framed in the sky, then that, too, disappeared.

Only Lord Arkyn remained now, all clothed in white radiance, his white sword in his hand.

"IT IS DONE!" said his voice and it seemed that warmth flooded through all the world.

"IT IS DONE!"

Corum cried, "Lord Arkyn! Did you know that Xiombarg's fury would be so great that she would risk the wrath of the Balance and enter this realm."

"I HOPED IT. I MERELY HOPED IT."

"Then much of what you have asked me to do was with this in mind?"

"AYE."

Corum thought of all the bitterness he had experienced, all the strife. He thought of Prince Gaynor's thousands of faces flickering before him . . .

"I could come to hate all Gods," he said.

"IT WOULD BE YOUR RIGHT. WE MUST USE MORTALS FOR ENDS WE CANNOT OURSELVES ACHIEVE."

And then Lord Arkyn had vanished also and all that was left were the circling sky ships of Gwlas-cor-Gwrys sending down invisible death to the shrieking, terrified barbarians, who were scattering now all over the churned lawns, avenues, and gardens of Halwyg-nan-Vake.

Beyond the walls a few barbarians were fleeing, but the sky ships found them. The sky ships found them all.

Corum noted that the Army of the Dog and the Army of the Bear had gone, as had the creatures of Chaos he had summoned to his aid. Had they been recalled by their masters—the Dog and the Horned Bear—or were they now occupying the Cavern of Limbo? He put a finger to his jeweled eye patch but then dropped it. He could not bear, for a long time, to look upon that netherworld.

The King Without a Country came forward. "You see how useful the gift was, Prince Corum."

"Aye."

"And now Xiombarg is banished from her realm only one more realm has a Sword Ruler. Mabelrode must fear us now."

"I am sure that he does," said Corum without joy.

"And I am no longer a king without a country. I can begin to rebuild my kingdom once I have returned to my own plane."

"That is good," said Corum tonelessly.

He went to the battlements and he looked down at the corpse-strewn city. A few of the citizens were beginning to emerge from their houses. The power of the Mabden barbarians was ended forever. Peace had come to Arkyn's realm and peace, no doubt, would come to the realm now to be ruled by his brother Lord of Law.

"Shall we return to Moidel in the sea?" Rhalina asked him softly, stroking his haggard face.

He shrugged. "I doubt if it exists. Glandyth would have razed it."

"And what of Earl Glandyth?" Jhary-a-Conel stroked the chin of his purring, winged cat, which sat again upon his shoulder. "Where is he? What became of him?"

"I do not think he is dead," said Corum. "I think I shall encounter him again. I have served Law and performed all the deeds Arkyn asked of me. But I have still to take my vengeance."

A sky ship came toward them. In its prow stood the old, handsome Vadhagh Prince Yurette. He was smiling as the ship of the air settled on the roof. "Corum. Will you guest with us at Gwlas-cor-Gwrys? I wish to speak of matters concerning the restoration of Vadhagh lands, of Vadhagh castles—so that your land may once again be called Bro-an-Vadhagh. We will send the remaining Mabden back to their original kingdom of Bro-an-Mabden and the pleasant forests and fields will bloom again."

And at last Corum's gaunt face softened and he smiled.

"I thank you, Prince Yurette. We should be honored to guest with you."

"Now that we have returned to our own realm, I think we shall cease our venturings for a while," said Prince Yurette.

"And," Corum added feelingly, "I hope that I, too, may cease my own venturings. A little tranquility would be welcome."

Far out across the plain the City in the Pyramid was beginning to descend to Earth.

EPILOGUE

Glandyth-a-Krae was weary, as were his men, the charioteers who massed behind him. From the cover of the hill he had witnessed the confrontation between Queen Xiombarg and Lord Arkyn and he had seen his folk destroyed by the Vadhagh Shefanhow in their sorcerous flying craft.

For many months he had sought Corum Jhaelen Irsei and that *gast* of a renegade, the Margravine Rhalina. And at last he had turned from his search to join the main army in its attack upon Halwyg-nan-Vake, only to witness the sudden defeat of the Mabden horde and its allies.

Earl Glandyth glowered. It was he who was the outlaw now—he who must hide and scheme and know fear—for the Vadhagh had returned and Law ruled all.

At last, as night fell, and the world was illuminated by the strange green glow from the monstrous, sorcerous city, Glandyth ordered his men to go back along the road they had traveled, back to the sea and into the dark forests of the Northeast. And he vowed that he would yet find an ally strong enough to destroy Corum and all that Corum loved.

And he believed he knew whom to summon.

He believe he knew.

*This ends the Second Book
of Corum*

THE BOOKS OF CORUM

*Being a History in Three Volumes
Concerning the Quests and Adventures
of Corum Jhaelen Irsei of the Vadhagh
Folk, Who Is Also Called the Prince in
the Scarlet Robe*

Volume the Third

THE KING OF THE SWORDS

This book is for Renata

INTRODUCTION

In those days there were oceans of light and cities in the skies and wild flying beasts of bronze. There were herds of crimson cattle that roared and were taller than castles. There were shrill, viridian things that haunted bleak rivers. It was a time of gods, manifesting themselves upon our world in all her aspects; a time of giants who walked on water; of mindless sprites and misshapen creatures who could be summoned by an ill-considered thought but driven away only on pain of some fearful sacrifice; of magics, phantasms, unstable nature, impossible events, insane paradoxes, dreams come true, dreams gone awry, of nightmares assuming reality.

It was a rich time and a dark time. The time of the Sword Rulers. The time when the Vadhagh and the Nhadragh, age-old enemies, were dying. The time when Man, the slave of fear, was emerging, unaware that much of the terror he experienced was the result of nothing else but the fact that he, himself, had come into existence. It was one of many ironies connected with Man (who, in those days, called his race Mabden).

The Mabden lived brief lives and bred prodigiously. Within a few centuries they rose to dominate the westerly continent on which they had evolved. Superstition stopped them from sending many of their ships toward Vadhagh and Nhadragh lands for another century or two, but gradually they gained courage when no resistance was offered. They began to feel jealous of the older races; they began to feel malicious.

The Vadhagh and the Nhadragh were not aware of this. They had dwelt a million or more years upon the planet, which now, at last, seemed at rest. They knew of the Mabden but considered them not greatly different from other beasts. Though continuing to indulge their traditional hatreds of one another, the Vadhagh and the

277

Nhadragh spent their long hours in considering abstractions, in the creation of works of art and the like. Rational, sophisticated, at one with themselves, these older races were unable to believe in the changes that had come. Thus, as it almost always is, they ignored the signs.

There was no exchange of knowledge between the two ancient enemies, even though they had fought their last battle many centuries before.

The Vadhagh lived in family groups occupying isolated castles scattered across a continent called by them Bro-an-Vadhagh. There was scarcely any communication between these families, for the Vadhagh had long since lost the impulse to travel. The Nhadragh lived in their cities built on the islands in the seas to the northwest of Bro-an-Vadhagh. They, also, had little contact, even with their closest kin. Both races reckoned themselves invulnerable. Both were wrong.

Upstart Man was beginning to breed and spread like a pestilence across the world. This pestilence struck down the old races wherever it touched them. And it was not only death that Man brought, but terror, too. Willfully, he made of the older world nothing but ruins and bones. Unwittingly, he brought psychic and supernatural disruption of a magnitude which even the Great Old Gods failed to comprehend.

And the Great Old Gods began to know Fear.

And Man, slave of fear, arrogant in his ignorance, continued his stumbling progress. He was blind to the huge disruptions aroused by his apparently petty ambitions. As well, Man was deficient in sensitivity, had no awareness of the multitude of dimensions that filled the universe, each plane intersecting with several others. Not so the Vadhagh or the Nhadragh, who had known what it was to move at will between the dimensions they termed the Five Planes. They had glimpsed and understood the nature of the many planes, other than the five, through which the Earth moved.

Therefore it seemed a dreadful injustice that these wise races should perish at the hands of creatures who were still little more than animals. It was as if vultures feasted on and squabbled over the paralyzed body of the youthful poet who could only stare at them with puzzled eyes as they slowly robbed him of an exquisite existence they would never appreciate, never know they were taking.

"If they valued what they stole, if they knew what they were destroying," says the old Vadhagh in the story, "The Only Autumn Flower," "then I would be consoled."

It was unjust.

By creating Man, the universe had betrayed the old races.

But it was a perpetual and familiar injustice. The sentient may perceive and love the universe, but the universe cannot perceive and love the sentient. The universe sees no distinction between the multitude of creatures and elements which comprise it. All are equal. None is favored. The universe, equipped with nothing but the materials and the power of creation, continues to create: something of this, something of that. It cannot control what it creates and it cannot, it seems, be controlled by its creations (though a few might deceive themselves otherwise). Those who curse the workings of the universe curse that which is deaf. Those who strike out at those workings fight that which is inviolate. Those who shake their fists, shake their fists at blind stars.

But this does not mean that there are some who will not try to do battle with and destroy the invulnerable.

There will always be such beings, sometimes beings of great wisdom, who cannot bear to believe in an insouciant universe.

Prince Corum Jhaelen Irsei was one of these. Perhaps the last of the Vadhagh race, he was sometimes known as the Prince in the Scarlet Robe.

This chronicle concerns him.

We have already learned how the Mabden followers of Earl Glandyth-a-Krae (who called themselves the Denledhyssi—or Murderers) killed Prince Corum's relatives and his nearest kin and thus taught the Prince in the Scarlet Robe how to hate, how to kill, and how to desire vengeance. We have heard how Glandyth tortured Corum and took away a hand and an eye and how Corum was rescued by the Giant of Laahr and taken to the castle of the Margravine Rhalina—a castle set upon a mount surrounded by the sea. Though Rhalina was a Mabden woman (of the gentler folk of Lywm-an-Esh), Corum and she fell in love. When Glandyth roused the Pony Tribes, the forest barbarians, to attack the Margravine's castle, she and Corum sought supernatural aid and thus fell into the hands of the sorcerer Shool, whose domain was the island called Svi-an-Fanla-Brool—Home of the Gorged God. And now Corum had direct experience of the morbid, unfamiliar powers at work in the world. Shool spoke of dreams and realities. ("I see you are beginning to argue in Mabden terms," he told Corum. "It is just as well for you, if you wish to survive in this Mabden dream."—"It is a dream . . . ?" said Corum.—"Of sorts. Real enough. It is what you might call the dream of a God. There again you might say that it is a dream that a God has allowed to become reality. I refer of course to the Knight of the Swords, who rules the Five Planes.")

With Rhalina his prisoner Shool could make a bargain with Corum. He gave him two gifts—the Hand of Kwll and the Eye of

Rhynn—to replace his own missing organs. These jeweled and alien things were once the property of two brother gods known as the Lost Gods since they mysteriously vanished.

Now Shool told Corum what he must do if he wished to see Rhalina saved. Corum must go to the realm of the Knight of the Swords—Lord Arioch of Chaos, who ruled the Five Planes since he had wrested them from the control of Lord Arkyn of Law. There Corum must find the heart of the Knight of the Swords—a thing which was kept in a tower of his castle and which enabled him to take material shape on Earth and thus wield power (without a material shape—or a number of them—the Lords of Chaos could not rule mortals).

With little hope Corum set off in a boat for the domain of Arioch but on his way was wrecked when a huge giant passed by him, merely fishing. In the land of the strange Ragha-da-Kheta he discovered that the Eye could summon dreadful beings from those worlds to aid him—also the Hand seemed to sense danger before it came and was ruthless in slaying even when Corum did not desire to slay. Then he realized that, by accepting Shool's gifts, he had accepted the logic of Shool's world and could not escape from it now.

During these adventures Corum learned of the eternal struggle between Law and Chaos. A cheerful traveler from Lywm-an-Esh enlightened him. It was, he said, "the Chaos Lords' will that rules you. Arioch is one of them. Long since there was a war between the forces of Order and the forces of Chaos. The forces of Chaos won and came to dominate the Fifteen Planes and, as I understand it, much that lies beyond them. Some say that Order was defeated completely and all her Gods vanished. They say the Cosmic Balance tipped too far in one direction and that is why there are so many arbitrary events taking place in the world. They say that once the world was round instead of dish-shaped . . . ."—"Some Vadhagh legends say it was once round," Corum informed him.— "Aye. Well, the Vadhagh began their rise before Order was banished. That is why the Sword Rulers hate the old races so much. They are not their creation at all. But the Great Gods are not allowed to interfere too directly in mortal affairs, so they have worked through the Mabden, chiefly . . ."—Corum said, "Is this the truth?"—Hanafax shrugged. "It is a truth."

Later, in the Flamelands where the Blind Queen Ooresé lived, Corum saw a mysterious figure who almost immediately vanished after he had slain poor Hanafax with the Hand of Kwll (which knew Hanafax would betray him). He learned that Arioch was the Knight of the Swords and that Xiombarg was the Queen of the Swords ruling the next group of Five Planes, while the most powerful Sword Ruler of all ruled the last of the Five Planes—Mabelrode, King of the Swords. Corum learned that all the hearts of the Sword Rulers were hidden where even they could not touch them. But after further adventures in Arioch's castle, he at last succeeded in finding the heart of the Knight of the Swords and, to save his life, destroyed it, thus banishing Arioch to limbo and allowing Arkyn of Law to return to occupy his old castle. But Corum had earned the Bane of the Sword Rulers and by destroying Arioch's heart had set a pattern of destiny for himself. A voice told him, "Neither Law nor Chaos must dominate the destinies of the mortal planes. There must be equilibrium." But it seemed to Corum that there was no equilibrium, that Chaos ruled all. "The balance sometimes tips," replied the voice. "It must be righted. And that is the power of mortals, to adjust the balance. You have begun the work already. Now you must continue until it is finished. You may perish before it is complete, but some other will follow you."

Corum shouted, "I do not want this. I cannot bear such a burden."

The voice replied, "YOU MUST!"

And then Corum returned to find Shool's power gone and Rhalina free.

They returned to the lovely castle on Moidel's Mount, knowing that they were no longer in any sense in control of their own fates.

Soon the Wading God was seen again, fishing the seas near Moidel's Mount, forever discarding his catch and casting for a new one. An omen, they knew. And that night there was a knocking on the door of Moidel's Castle and a young stranger presented himself to them—a dandy who had as a pet a little winged cat. This was Jhary-a-Conel, who announced his profession as a "Companion to Champions" and seemed to know a great deal of Corum's destiny, not to mention his own. With the help of the little cat they learned of the great Mabden massing at Kalenwyr, of the intention of the Mabden to march against Lywm-an-Esh and destroy that land because it had adopted Vadhagh ways. The people of the castle knew that they would be swept away by such a mighty advance and they abandoned Moidel's Mount, going by ship to Lywm-an-Esh to discover that the invasion was already taking place on some coasts and that the followers of Law and of Chaos were divided, fighting. In the capital, Halwyg-nan-Vake, they saw the king and learned that Arkyn would speak with them at his Temple. Here Arkyn told them to enter Xiombarg's plane and seek out the City in the Pyramid, that this city would aid them. On Xiombarg's plane they encountered many strange marvels, horrible examples of the power

281

of Chaos—the Lake of Voices, the White River, and many other things—until they found the City in the Pyramid. This strange city of metal was peopled by Vadhagh and Corum learned that they had left their own plane centuries before but had been unable to return. Xiombarg began to attack the City and Corum and his companions fled through the planes to Halwyg to find it under dire siege. At last the means to bring the City in the Pyramid back to its own plane was found and they broke through, bringing destruction to the Mabden and forever wiping out the threat. Angered, Xiombarg followed— breaking the paramount rule of the Cosmic Balance—and was thus destroyed. It seemed that a wonderful new era of peace had been granted to them all. But Earl Glandyth-a-Krae, who hated Corum most fiercely, had escaped the destruction of his folk. And he planned revenge.

—The Book of Corum

BOOK ONE

In which Prince Corum sees serenity transformed into strife

The First Chapter

THE SHAPE ON THE HILL

Not long since men had died here and others had expected to die. But now King Onold's palace was repaired, repainted, and covered once more in flowers, and the battlements had once again become balconies and bowers. But King Onold of Lywn-an-Esh would not see his ruined Halwyg-nan-Vake reborn, for he, too, had been slain in the siege and his mother ruled as regent till his son should come of age. Scaffolding lingered in some parts of the Floral City, for King Lyr-a-Brode and his barbarians had done much damage. New sculptures were being erected, fresh fountains made, and it was now plain that Halwyg's quiet magnificence would be yet finer than before. So it was across all the land of Lywm-an-Esh.

And so it was beyond the sea, in Bro-an-Vadhagh. The Mabden had been driven back to the land from which they had first come, Bro-an-Mabden, grim continent to the northeast. And their fear of the power of the Vadhagh was strong again.

In the sweet land of gentle hills and deep, comforting forests and placid rivers and soft valleys which was Bro-an-Vadhagh only the ruins of gloomy Kalenwyr remained—ruins avoided but remembered.

And off the coast, on the Nhadragh Isles, the few who had survived the Mabden killings—frightened, degenerate creatures— were allowed to live out their lives. Perhaps these wretched Nhadragh would breed prouder children and their race would flourish again, as it had in its centuries of glory, before too many years passed.

The world returned to peace. The people who had come back to this place in the magical Gwlas-cor-Gwrys, the City in the Pyramid, set to work to restore the ravaged Vadhagh castles and lands. They abandoned their strange city of metal in favor of the traditional homes of their Vadhagh ancestors. Presently Gwlas-cor-Gwrys was all but deserted, standing amongst the pines of a remote forest, not far from one of the broken Mabden fortresses.

It seemed that a wonderful new age of peace had dawned both for the Mabden of Lywm-an-Esh and for the Vadhagh who had been that land's saviors. The threat of Chaos was forgotten. Now two out of three realms—ten out of fifteen planes—were ruled by Law. Surely, therefore, Law was stronger?

Most thought so. Queen Crief, the Regent of Lywm-an-Esh thought so and told her grandson, King Analt, that it was so, and the little king told his subjects that it was so. Prince Yurette Hasdun Nury, ex-Commander of Gwlas-cor-Gwrys, believed it pretty much. The rest of the Vadhagh believed it, too.

There was one Vadhagh, however, who was not sure. He was unlike others of his race, though he had the same tall beauty of form, the tapering head, the gold-flecked rose-pink skin, fair hair, and almond-shaped yellow-and-purple eyes. But instead of a right eye he had an object like the jeweled eye of a fly and instead of a left hand he had what appeared to be a six-fingered gauntlet of similar design, encrusted with dark jewels. Upon his back he wore a scarlet robe and he was Corum Jhaelen Irsei, who had slain gods and been instrumental in banishing others, who desired nothing but peace but could not trust the peace he had, who hated his alien eye and his alien hand, though they had saved his life many times and thus had saved both Lywm-an-Esh and Bro-an-Vadhagh and furthered the cause of Law.

Yet even Corum, burdened by his destiny, knew joy as he saw his old home reborn, for they were building Castle Erorn again on the headland where she had stood for centuries before Glandyth-a-Krae had razed her. Corum remembered every detail of his ancient family home and his pleasure grew as the castle grew. Slender, tinted towers stood again against the sky and overlooked the sea, which was all boisterous white and green and leaped about the rocks below and in and out of the great sea caves as if it danced with delight at Erorn's return to the eminence.

And inside, the ingenuity and skills of the craftsmen of Gwlas-cor-Gwrys had wrought the sensitive walls which would change shape and color with every change in the elements, the musical instruments of crystal and water which would play tunes according to the manner in which they were arranged. But they could not replace the paintings and the sculpture and the manuscripts which Corum and Corum's ancestors had created in more innocent times, for Glandyth-a-Krae had destroyed them when he had destroyed Corum's father, Prince Khlonskey, and his mother, Colatalarna, his twin sisters, his uncle, his cousin, and their retainers.

When he thought of all that was lost Corum felt a return of his old hatred of the Mabden earl. Glandyth's body had not been found amongst those who had died at Halwyg, neither had they found the bodies of his charioteers, his Denledhyssi. Glandyth had vanished—or perhaps he and his men had died in some remote battle. It required all Corum's self-discipline not to let his mind dwell on Glandyth and what Glandyth had done. He preferred to think of ways of making Castle Erorn still more beautiful so that his wife and his love, Rhalina, Margravine of Allomglyl, would be even more enraptured and would forget that when they had found her castle it had been torn down by Glandyth so thoroughly that only a few stones of it could be seen in the shallows at the bottom of Moidel's Mount.

Jhary-a-Conel, who rarely admitted such a thing, was impressed by Castle Erorn. It inspired him, he said, and he took to writing sonnets, which, somewhat insistently, he would often read to them. And he painted passable portraits of Corum in his scarlet robe and of Rhalina in her gown of blue brocade and he painted a fair quantity of self-portraits, which they would come across in more than one chamber of Castle Erorn. And Jhary would also pass his time designing splendid clothes for himself, sometimes making whole wardrobes, even trying new hats (though he was much attached to his old one and always returned to it). His little black-and-white cat with the black-and-white wings would fly through the rooms sometimes, but most often it would be discovered sleeping somewhere where it was most inconvenient for it to sleep.

And so they passed their days.

The coastline on which Castle Erorn was built was well known for the softness of its summers and the mildness of its winters. Two, sometimes three, crops could be grown the year round in normal times and there was usually little frost and one snowfall in the coldest month. Often it did not snow at all. But the winter after Erorn was completed the snow began to fall early and did not stop until the oaks and the pines and the birches bent beneath huge burdens of glittering whiteness or were hidden altogether. The snow was so deep that a mounted man could not see above it in some places, and although the sun shone clear and red through the day it did not melt the snow much and that which did melt was soon replaced by another fall.

To Corum there was a hint of something ominous in this unexpected weather. They were snug enough in their castle and had no lack of provisions and sometimes a sky ship would bring a visitor from one of the other newly rebuilt castles. The recently settled Vadhagh had not given up their ships of the air when they had left Gwlas-cor-Gwrys. Thus there was no danger of losing contact with the outside world. But still Corum fretted and Jhary watched him with a certain amusement, while Rhalina took his state of mind more seriously and was careful to soothe him whenever possible, for she thought he brooded on Glandyth again.

One day Corum and Jhary stood on the balcony of a tall tower and looked inland at the wide expanse of whiteness.

"Why should I be troubled by the weather?" Corum asked Jhary. "I suspect the hand of gods in everything, these days. Why should gods bother to make it snow?"

Jhary shrugged. "You'll remember that under Law the world was said to be round. Perhaps it is round now, again, and the result of this roundness is a change in the weather you may expect in these parts."

Corum shook his head in puzzlement, hardly hearing Jhary's words. He leaned on a snowy parapet, blinking in the snow's glare. Far away there was a line of hills, as white as everything else in that landscape. He looked toward the hills. "When Bwydyth-a-Horn came visiting last week he said that it was the same over the whole land of Bro-an-Vadhagh. One cannot help but seek significance in so strange an event." He sniffed the cold, clean air. "Yet why should Chaos send a little snow, since it inconveniences no one."

"It might inconvenience the farmers of Lywm-an-Esh," Jhary said.

"True—but Lywm-an-Esh has not had this especially heavy snowfall. It was as if something sought to—to freeze us—to paralyze us . . ."

"Chaos would choose more spectacular displays than a heavy fall of snow," Jhary pointed out.

"Unless it was the best they could do, now that Law rules two of the realms."

"I am unconvinced. I think that, if anything, this is Law's doing. The result of a few minor geographical changes involved in ridding our Five Planes of the last effects of Chaos."

"I agree that that is the most logical explanation," Corum nodded.

"If an explanation is needed at all."

"Aye. I'm oversuspicious. You are probably right." He began to turn back to the entrance of the tower but then felt Jhary's hand on his arm. "Look at the hills."

"The hills?" Corum peered into the distance. And a shock went through him. Something moved there. At first he thought it must be a forest animal—a fox, perhaps, hunting for food? But it was too large. It was too large to be a man—even a large man mounted on a horse. The shape was familiar, yet he could not remember where he had seen it before. It flickered, as if only partly in this plane and partly in another. It began to move away from them, toward the north. It paused and perhaps it turned, for Corum felt that something peered at him. Involuntarily his jeweled hand went to his jeweled eye, fingering the jeweled patch which covered it and stopped him from seeing into that terrible netherworld from which he had, in the past, summoned supernatural allies. With an effort he lowered his hand. Did he associate that shape with something he had seen in the netherworld? Or perhaps it was some creature of Chaos, returned to make war on Erorn?

"I cannot make anything of it," Jhary said. "Is it a beast or a man?"

Corum found difficulty in replying. "Neither, I think," he said at last.

The shape resumed its original direction, crossing over the brow of the hill and vanishing.

"We still have that sky ship below," Jhary said. "Shall we follow the thing?"

Corum's throat was dry. "No," he said.

"Did you know what it was, Corum? Did you recognize it?"

"I have seen it before. But I do not remember where or in what circumstances. Did it—did it look at me, Jhary, or did I imagine that?"

"I understand you. A peculiar sensation—the sort of sensation one has when one meets another's eyes by accident."

"Aye—something of the sort."

"I wonder what it could want with us or if it is connected with this snowfall in any way."

"I do not associate it with snow. I think rather of—fire! I remember! I remember where I saw it—or something like it—in the Flamelands, after I had strangled—after this hand of mine had strangled—Hanafax. I told you of that!"

287

Shuddering, he remembered the scene. The Hand of Kwll squeezing the life from the struggling, shrieking Hanafax, who had done Corum no harm at all. The roaring flames. The corpse. The Blind Queen Ooresé with her impassive face. The hill. The smoke. A figure standing on the hill watching him. A figure obscured by a sudden drift of smoke.

"Perhaps it is only madness," he murmured. "My conscience reminding me of the innocent soul I took when I slew Hanafax. Perhaps I am remembering my guilt and see that guilt as an accusing figure on a hillside."

"A pretty theory," said Jhary almost grimly. "But I had nothing to do with the slaying of Hanafax and neither do I suffer from this guilt you people always speak of. I saw the figure first, Corum."

"So you did. So you did." His head bowed, Corum stumbled through the door of the tower. From his mortal eye streamed tears.

As Jhary closed the door behind them, Corum turned on the stairs and stared up at his friend.

"Then what was it, Jhary?"

"I know not, Corum."

"But you know so much."

"And I forget much. I am not a hero. I am a companion to heroes I admire. I marvel. I offer sage advice which is rarely taken. I sympathize. I save lives. I express the fears heroes cannot express. I council caution . . ."

"Enough, Jhary. Do you jest?"

"I suppose I jest. I, too, am tired, my friend. I am tired of the company of gloomy heroes, of those who are doomed to terrible destinies—not to mention a lack of humor. I would have the company of ordinary men for a while. I would drink in taverns. Tell obscene stories. Fart. Lose my head to a doxie . . ."

"Jhary? You do not jest! Why are you saying these things?"

"Because I am weary of . . ." Jhary frowned. "Why, indeed Prince Corum? It is not like me, at all. That carping voice—was mine!"

"Aye. It was." Corum's frown matched Jhary's. "And I liked it not at all. Why, if you sought to provoke me, Jhary, then . . ."

"Wait!" Jhary raised his hand to his head. "Wait, Corum. I feel as if something seeks possession of my mind, seeks to turn me against my friends. Concentrate. Do you not feel the same thing?"

Corum glared at Jhary for a moment and then his face lost its anger and became puzzled. "Aye. You are right. A kind of nagging shadow at the back of my head. It hints at hatred, contention. Is it the influence of the thing we saw on the hill?"

Jhary shook his head. "Who knows? I apologize for my outburst. I do not believe that it was myself speaking to you."

"I, too, apologize. Let us hope the shadow disappears."

In thoughtful silence they descended to the main part of the castle. The walls were silvery, shimmering. It meant that the snow had begun to fall outside once more.

Rhalina met them in one of the galleries where fountains and crystals sang softly a work by Corum's father, a love song to Corum's mother. It was soothing and Corum managed to smile at her.

"Corum," she said. "A few moments ago I was seized with a strange fury. I cannot explain it. I was tempted to hit one of the retainers. I . . ."

He took her in his arms. He kissed her brow. "I know. Jhary and I experienced the same thing. I fear that Chaos works subtly in us, turning us against each other. We must resist such impulses. We must try to find their cause. Something wishes us to destroy one another, I think."

There was horror in her eyes. "Oh, Corum . . ."

"We must resist," he said again.

Jhary scratched his nose, himself once more. He raised an eyebrow. "I wonder if we are the only folk who suffer this—this possession. What if it has seized the whole land, Corum?"

The Second Chapter

THE SICKNESS SPREADS

It was in the night that the worst thoughts came to Corum as he lay in bed beside Rhalina. Sometimes his visions were of his hated enemy Glandyth-a-Krae, but sometimes they were of Lord Arkyn of Law, whom he was now beginning to blame for all his hardships and miseries, and sometimes they were of Jhary-a-Conel, whose easy irony was now seen as facetious malice, and sometimes they were of Rhalina, whom he decided had snared him, directed him away from his true destiny. And these latter visions were the worst and he fought against them more fiercely even than the others. He would feel his face twist with hatred, his fingers clench, his lips snarl, his body shake with rage and a wish to destroy. All through the nights he would fight these terrible impulses and he knew that as he fought so did Rhalina—fighting the fury welling up inside her own head. Irrational fury—rage which had no purpose and yet which would focus on anything and seek to vent itself.

Bloody visions. Visions of torturing and maiming worse than Glandyth had ever performed on him. And *he* was the torturer and those he tortured were those he loved most.

Many a night he would awake shrieking. Crying aloud the single word, "No! No! No!" he would leap from his bed and glare down at Rhalina.

And Rhalina would glare back.

Rhalina's lips would curl away from her white teeth. Rhalina's nostrils would flare like those of a beast. And strange sounds would come from her throat.

Then he would fight off the impulses and cry to her, remind her of what was happening to them. And they would lie in each other's arms, drained of emotion.

● ● ●

The snow had begun to melt. It was as if, having brought the sickness of rage and malice, it could now leave. Corum rushed about in it one day, slashing at it with his naked sword and cursing it, blaming it for their ills.

But Jhary was sure now that the snow had merely been a natural occurrence, a coincidence. He ran out to try to pacify his friend. He succeeded in making Corum lower his sword and sheath it. They stood shivering in the morning light, both half-clad.

"And what of the shape on the hill?" Corum panted. "Was that coincidence, my friend?"

"It could have been. I have a feeling that all these things happened at the same time because, perhaps, something else happened. These are hints. Do you understand me?"

Corum shrugged and wrenched his arm away from Jhary's grasp. "A larger event? Is that what you mean?"

"Aye. A larger event."

"Is not what is happening to us already sufficiently unpleasant?"

"Aye. It is."

Corum saw that his friend was humoring him. He tired to smile. A sense of exhaustion filled him. All his energy was going to battle his own terrible desires. He wiped his brow with the back of his right hand.

"There must be something which can help us. I fear—I fear . . ."

"We all fear, Prince Corum."

"I fear I'll slay Rhalina one night. I do, Jhary."

"We had best take to living apart, locking ourselves in our rooms. The retainers also are suffering as badly as we."

"I have noticed."

"They, too, must be separated. Shall I tell them?"

Corum fingered the pommel of his sword and his red-rimmed left eye had a wide, staring look. "Aye," he said absently. "Tell them."

"And you will do the same, Corum? I am even now trying to concoct a potion—something which will calm us and make sure we do not harm each other. Doubtless it will make us less alert, but that is better than killing ourselves."

"Killing? Aye." Corum stared at Jhary. The dandy's silk jerkin offended him, though not long since he had thought he admired it. And the man's face had an expression on it. What was it? Mocking? Why was Jhary mocking him?

"Why do you—?" He broke off, realizing that he was once again possessed. "We must leave Castle Erorn," he said. "Perhaps some—some ghost inhabits it now. Some evil force left behind by Glandyth. That is possible, Jhary, for I have heard of such things."

Jhary looked skeptical.

"It is a possibility!" Corum yelled. Why was Jhary so stupid sometimes?

"A possibility." Jhary rubbed at his forehead and pinched the bridge of his nose. His eyes, too, were rimmed red and had a tendency to stare wildly this way and that. "A possibility, aye. But we must leave here. You are right. We must see if only Castle Erorn is affected. We must see if anywhere else suffers what we suffer. If we can get the sky ship from the courtyard. . . . The snow has melted from it now. . . . We must go to . . . I must . . ." He stopped himself. "I'm babbling now. It's the weariness. But we must seek out a friend—Prince Yurette, perhaps—ask him if he has felt the same impulses."

"You proposed that yesterday," Corum reminded him.

"And we agreed, did we not?"

"Aye." Corum began to stumble back toward the castle gate. "We agreed. And we agreed the day before yesterday, also."

"We must make preparations. Will Rhalina stay here or come with us?"

"Why do you ask? It is impertinent . . ." Again Corum controlled himself. "Forgive me, Jhary."

"I do."

"What force is it that could possess us so? Turn old friends against each other? Make me desire, sometimes, to slay the woman I love most in the world?"

"We shall never discover that if we remain here," Jhary told him rather sharply.

"Very well, then," Corum said. "We'll take the air boat. We'll seek Prince Yurette. Do you feel strong enough to fly the craft?"

"I'll find the strength."

The world turned gray as the snow continued to melt. All the trees seemed gray and the hills seemed gray and the grass seemed gray. Even Castle Erorn's marvelously tinted towers took on a gray appearance and the walls within were also gray.

In the late afternoon, before sunset, Rhalina called for Corum and for Jhary. "Come," she shouted. "Sky ships approach us. They are behaving strangely"

They gathered at one of the windows facing the sea.

In the distance two of the beautiful metallic sky ships were wheeling and diving as if in a complicated dance, skimming close to the gray ocean and then hurling themselves upward at great speed. It seemed that each was attempting to get behind the other.

Something glittered.

Rhalina gasped.

"They are using those weapons—those fearful weapons with which they destroyed King Lyr and his army! They are fighting, Corum!"

"Aye," he said grimly. "They are fighting."

One of the ships suddenly staggered in the air and seemed to come to a complete stop. Then it turned over and they saw tiny figures falling from it. It righted itself. It drove upward at the other craft, trying to ram it, but the craft managed to dodge just in time and the damaged craft continued on its course, rising higher and higher into the gray sky until it was only a shadow among the clouds.

It came back, diving at its enemy, which, this time, was struck in its stern and began to spiral down toward the sea. The other ship plunged straight into the ocean and disappeared. There was a little foam on the sea where it had entered.

The remaining sky ship corrected its own fall and began to limp through the sky toward the land, making for the cliff across the bay from Castle Erorn, changing course in a jerky movement and heading straight for the castle.

"Does he mean to strike us?" Jhary asked.

Corum shrugged. He had come to see Castle Erorn as a haunted prison rather than as his ancient home. If the sky ship smashed into Erorn's towers it would almost be as if it smashed into his own skull, driving the terrifying fury from his brain.

But the craft turned aside at the last minute and began to circle to land on the gray sward just beyond the gates.

It landed badly and Corum saw a wisp of smoke rise from its stern and curl sluggishly in the air. Men began to clamber from the ship. They were undoubtably Vadhagh, tall men with flowing cloaks and mail byrnies of gold or silver, conical helms on their heads, slender swords in their hands. They marched through the slush toward the castle.

Corum was the first to recognize the man who led them. "It is Bwydyth! Bwydyth-a-Horn! He must need our help. Come, let us greet him."

Jhary was more reluctant, but he said nothing as he followed Corum and Rhalina to the gates.

Bwydyth and his men were already ascending the path up the hill toward the gates when Corum opened them himself and stepped out, calling their friend's name.

"Greetings, Bwydyth! You are welcome here to Castle Erorn."

Bwydyth-a-Horn made no answer, but continued to march up the hill.

All at once Corum Jhaelen Irsei felt suspicion well in him. He dismissed it. The effect of the shadow lurking in his brain. He smiled and spread his arms wide.

"Bwydyth! It is I—Corum."

Jhary muttered, "Best ready yourself to draw your sword. Rhalina—you had best go inside."

She gave him a startled look. "Why? It is Bwydyth. Not an enemy."

He merely stared at her for a moment. She lowered her eyes and did as he suggested.

Corum fought against the anger within him. He breathed hard. "If Bwydyth means to fight, then he will find . . ."

"Corum!" Jhary said urgently. "Keep your head clear. It is possible that we can reason with Bwydyth, for I suspect he suffers from what we have been suffering from." He called out. "Bwydyth, old friend. We are not your enemies. Come, enjoy the peace of Castle Erorn. There's no need for strifing here. We have all known these sudden furies and we must gather to discuss their nature and their cause, decide how best to discover their source."

But Bwydyth marched on up the hill toward them, and his men, grim-faced and pale, marched on behind him. Their cloaks curled in the thin breeze which had begun to blow, the steel of their swords did not shine but was as gray as the landscape.

"Bwydyth!" It was Rhalina crying from behind them. "Do not give in to that which has seized your mind. Do not fight with Corum. He is your friend. Corum found the means to bring you back to your homeland."

Bwydyth stopped. His men stopped. Bwydyth glared up at them. "Is that another thing I must hate you for, Corum?"

"Another thing? What else do you hate me for, Bwydyth?"

"Why for—for your dreadful deformities. You are unsightly. For your alliance with demons. For your choice of women and your choice of friends. For your cowardice."

"Cowardice, eh?" Jhary growled and reached for his own sword.

Corum stopped him. "Bwydyth, we know that a sickness of the mind has come upon us. It makes us hate those we love, seek to kill those whom we most desire to live. Plainly this sickness is on you and it is on us, but if we give in to it, we give in to whatever it is which wants us to destroy each other. This suggests a common enemy—something we must seek out and slay."

Bwydyth frowned, lowering his sword. "Aye. I have thought the same. Sometimes I have wondered why the fighting has started everywhere. Perhaps you are right, Corum. Aye, we will talk." He began to turn to address his company. "Men, we will . . ."

One of the nearest swordsmen lunged forward with a snarl of hatred. "Fool! I knew you for a fool! You are proven a fool! You die for your foolishness." The sword passed through the byrnie and buried itself in Bwydyth's body. He cried out, groaned, tried to stagger toward his friends, and then fell face down in the melting snow.

"So the poison is acting swiftly," said Jhary.

Already another man had fallen on the swordsman who had struck Bwydyth down. Two more were slain in almost as many heartbeats. Cries of rage and hatred burst from the lips of the rest. Blood spurted in the gray evening light.

The civilized folk of Gwlas-cor-Gyrys were butchering each other without reason. They were fighting amongst themselves like so many carrion dogs over a carcass.

The Third Chapter

CHAOS RETURNED

Soon the winding path to the castle was strewn with corpses. Four men were left on their feet when something seemed to seize their heads and turn them to glare with blazing eyes at Corum and Jhary, who still stood by the gates. The four began to move up the hill again. Corum and Jhary readied their swords.

Corum felt the anger rising in his own head, shaking his body with its intensity. It was a relief to be able to vent it at last. With a chilling yell he rushed down the hill toward the attackers, his bright sword raised, Jhary behind him.

One of the swordsmen went down before Corum's first thrust. These men were gaunt-faced and exhausted. It looked as if they had not slept for many days. Normally Corum would have known pity for them, would have tried to disarm them or merely wound them. But his own rage made him strike to kill.

And soon they were all dead.

And Corum Jhaelen Irsei stood over their corpses and panted like a mad wolf, the blood dripping from his blade onto the gray ground. He stood thus for some moments until a small sound reached his ears. He turned. Jhary-a-Conel was already kneeling beside the man who had made the sound. It was Bwydyth-a-Horn and he was not quite dead.

"Corum . . ." Jhary looked up at his friend. "He is calling your name, Corum."

His fury abated for the moment, Corum went to Bwydyth's side. "Aye, friend," he murmured gently.

"I tried, Corum, to fight what was inside my skull. I tried for many days, but eventually it defeated me. I am sorry, Corum . . ."

"We have all suffered the sickness."

"When rational I decided to come to you in the hope that you

296

would know of a cure. At least, I thought, I could warn you . . ."

"And that is why your ship came to be in these parts, eh?"

"Aye. But we were followed. There was a battle and it brought back all my rage again. The whole Vadhagh race is at war, Corum—and Lywm-an-Esh is no better. . . . Strife governs all . . ." Bwydyth's voice grew fainter.

"Do you know why, Bwydyth?"

"No . . . Prince Yurette hoped to discover. . . . He, too, was overcome by the berserk fury. . . . He—died. . . . Reason is banished. . . . We are in the grip of demons. . . . Chaos is returned. . . . We should have remained in our city . . ."

Corum nodded. "It is Chaos's work, without doubt. We became complacent too quickly, we ceased to be wary—and Chaos struck. But it cannot be Mabelrode, for if he came to our plane he would be destroyed as Xiombarg was destroyed. He must be working through an agency. But who?"

"Glandyth?" whispered Jhary. "Could it be the Earl of Krae? All Chaos needs is one willing to serve it. If the will exists, the power is given."

Bwydyth-a-Horn began to cough. "Ah, Corum, forgive me for this . . ."

"There is nought to forgive, since we are equally possessed by something which is beyond our power to fight."

"Find what it is, Corum . . ." Bwydyth's eyes burned near-black as he raised himself on one elbow. "Destroy it if you can. . . . Revenge me . . . revenge us all . . ."

And Bwydyth died.

Corum was trembling with emotion. "Jhary—have you manufactured the potion of which you spoke?"

"It is almost ready, though I make no claims for it yet. It might not counter the madness."

"Be quick."

Corum rose to his feet and walked back to the castle, sheathing his sword.

As he entered the gates he heard a scream and went running through the gray galleries until he entered a room of bright fountains. There was Rhalina beating off the attack of two of the female retainers. The women were shrieking like beasts and striking at her with their nails. Corum drew his sword again, reversed it, struck the nearest woman on the base of the skull. She went down and the other whirled, foaming at the mouth. Corum leaped foward and with his jeweled hand struck her on the jaw. She, too, fell.

Corum felt his rage rising in him again. He glared at the weeping Rhalina. "What did you do to offend them?"

She looked at him in astonishment. "I? Nothing, Corum. Corum! I did nothing!"

"Then why—?" He realized his voice was harsh, shrill. Deliberately he took control of himself. "I am sorry, Rhalina. I understand. Ready yourself for a journey. We leave in our sky ship as soon as possible. Jhary may have a medicine which will calm us. We must go to Lywm-an-Esh to see if there is any hope there. We must try to contact Lord Arkyn and hope the Lord of Law will help us."

"Why is he not already helping us?" she asked bitterly. "We aided him to regain his realm and now, it seems, he abandons us to Chaos."

"If Chaos is active here, then it is active elsewhere. It could be that there are worse dangers in his realm, or in the realm of his brother Lord of Law. You know that none of the gods may interfere directly in mortal affairs."

"But Chaos tries more frequently," she said.

"That is the nature of Chaos and that is why mortals are best served by Law, for Law believes in the freedom of mortals and Chaos sees us merely as playthings to be molded and used according to its whims. Quickly, now, prepare to leave."

"But it is hopeless, Corum. Chaos must be so much more powerful than Law. We have done all we can to fight it. Why not admit that we are doomed?"

"Chaos only seems more powerful because it is aggressive and willing to use any means to gain its end. Law endures. Make no mistake, I do not like the role in which Fate has cast me—I would that someone else had my burden—but the power of Law must be preserved if possible. Now go—hurry."

She went away reluctantly while Corum made sure that the retainers were not badly hurt. He did not like to leave them, for he was sure that they would turn upon each other soon. He decided that he would leave them some of the potion Jhary was preparing and hope that it would last them.

He frowned. Could Glandyth really be the cause of this? But Glandyth was no sorcerer—he was a brute, a bloody-handed warrior, a good tactician, and, in his own terms, had many virtues, but he had little subtlety or even desire to use sorcery, for he feared it.

Yet there were no others left in this realm who would willingly make themselves servants of Chaos—and one had to be willing or Chaos could not gain entry to the realm at all . . .

Corum decided to wait until he discovered more before continuing to speculate. If he could reach Halwyg-nan-Vake and the

Temple of Law, he might be able to contact Lord Arkyn and seek his advice.

He went to the room where he kept his arms and armor and he drew on his silver byrnie, his silver greaves, and his conical silver helm with the three characters set into it over the peak—characters which stood for his full name. And over all this he put his scarlet robe. Then he selected weapons—a bow, arrows, a lance, and a war-axe of exquisite workmanship—and he buckled on his long, strong sword. Once again he garbed himself for war and he made both a magnificent and a terrible figure, with his glittering six-fingered hand and the jeweled patch which covered the jeweled Eye of Rhynn. He had prayed that he would never have to dress himself thus again, that he would never have to use the alien hand grafted to his left wrist or peer through the eye into the fearsome netherworld to summon the living dead to his aid. Yet in his heart he had known that the power of Chaos had not been vanquished, that the worst was still to come.

He felt weary, however, for his battle with the madness in his skull was as exhausting as any physical fight.

Jhary came in and he, too, was dressed for traveling, though he disdained armor, wearing a quilted leather jerkin, stamped with designs in gold and platinum, in lieu of a breastplate—his only concession. His wide-brimmed hat was placed at a jaunty angle on his head, his long hair was brushed so that it shone and fell over his shoulders. He wore flamboyant silks and satins, elaborately decorated boots trimmed with red and white lace, and was the very picture of effete dandyism. Only the soldier's sword at his belt denied the impression. On his shoulder was the small black-and-white winged cat, which was his constant companion. In his hand he held a bottle with a thin neck. A brownish liquid swirled inside.

"It is made." He spoke slowly, as if in a trance. "And it has the desired effect, I think. It has driven away my fury, though I feel drowsy. Some of the drowsiness should wear off. I hope it does."

Corum looked at him suspiciously. "It might counter the fury—but we shall be slow to defend ourselves if attacked. It slows the wits, Jhary?"

"It offers a different perspective, I grant you." Jhary smiled a dreamy smile. "But it's our only chance, Corum. And, speaking for myself, I would rather die in peace than in mental anguish."

"I'll grant you that." Corum accepted the bottle. "How much shall I take?"

"It is strong. Just a little on the tip of the forefinger."

Corum tilted the bottle and got a small amount of the potion on his finger. Cautiously, he licked it. He gave Jhary back the bottle. "I

299

feel no different. Perhaps it does not work on the Vadhagh metabolism."

"Perhaps. Now you must give some to Rhalina . . ."

"And the servants."

"Aye—fair enough—the servants . . ."

They stood in the courtyard brushing the last of the snow off the canopy covering the sky ship, peeling back the cloth to reveal the rich blues, greens, and yellows of the metallic hull. Jhary clambered slowly in and began to pass his hands over the variously colored crystals on the panel in the prow. This was not as large a sky ship as the first they had encountered. This one was open to the elements when not utilizing the protective power of its invisible energy screen. A whisper of sound came from the ship and it lifted an inch off the ground. Corum helped Rhalina in and then he, too, was aboard, lying on one of the couches and watching Jhary as he prepared the craft for flight.

Jhary moved slowly, a slight smile on his face. Corum, full of a sense of well-being, watched him. He looked over to the couch where Rhalina had placed herself and he saw that she was almost asleep. The potion was working well in that the sense of fury had disappeared. But part of Corum still knew that his present euphoria might be as dangerous as his earlier rage. He knew that he had exchanged one madness for another, in some senses.

He hoped that another sky ship would not attack them, as Bwydyth's had been attacked, for, apart from their present disability, they were all unfamiliar with the art of aerial warfare. It was the best Jhary could do to pilot the sky ship in the desired direction.

At last the craft lifted gently into the cold, gray air, turning west and moving along the coast toward Lywm-an-Esh.

And as the ship drifted on its way Corum looked down at the world, all bleak and frozen, and wondered if spring would ever come again to Bro-an-Vadhagh.

He opened his lips to speak to Jhary, but the dandy was absorbed with the controls. He watched as, suddenly, the little black-and-white cat sprang from Jhary's shoulder, clung for a moment to the side of the sky ship, and then flew off over the land, to disappear behind a line of hills.

For a moment Corum wondered why the cat had deserted them, but then he forgot about it as he once again became interested in the sea and the landscape below.

The Fourth Chapter

A NEW ALLY FOR EARL GLANDYTH

The little cat flew steadily through the day, changing its direction constantly as if it followed an invisible and winding path through the sky. Soon it had ceased to fly inland, hesitated, then headed out over the cliffs and over the sea, which it hated. Islands came in sight.

They were the Nhadragh Isles where lived the remainder of the folk who had become groveling slaves of the Mabden in order to preserve their lives. Though presently released from that slavery, they had become so degenerate that their race might still die from apathy, for most could not even hate the Vadhagh now.

The cat was searching for something, following a psychic rather than a physical scent; a scent which only he could distinguish.

Once before had the little winged cat followed a similar scent, when he had gone to Kalenwyr to witness the great massing of Mabden and the summoning of their now banished gods the Dog and the Horned Bear. This time, however, the cat was acting upon its own impulses: it had not been sent to the Nhadragh Isles by Jhary-a-Conel, its master.

In what was almost the exact center of the group of green islands was the largest of them, called Maliful by the Nhadragh. Like all the islands it contained many ruins—ruins of towns, ruins of castles, ruins of villages. Some were ruins thanks to the passage of time, but others were ruins thanks to the passage of Mabden armies when they had attacked the Nhadragh Isles at the height of King Lyr-a-Brode's power. It had been Earl Glandyth and his Denledhyssi chariot warriors who had led these expeditions, just as, later, he had led expeditions to the Vadhagh castles and destroyed what was left of the Vadhagh race, save Corum—or so he had thought. The destruction of the two elder races—the Shefanhow as Glandyth called them—had taken a matter of a few years. They had been completely unprepared for Mabden attack, had not been able to believe in the power of creatures scarcely more intelligent or cultured than other beasts. So they had died.

And only a few Nhadragh had been spared—used like dogs to hunt down their fellows, to search for their ancient Vadhagh enemies, to see into other dimensions and tell their masters what they perceived. These had been the least brave of their race—those who preferred degenerate slavery to death.

The little cat saw some of their camps amongst the ruins of the towns. They had been returned here after the Battle of Halwyg, when their Mabden masters had been defeated. They had made no attempt to rebuild their castles or cities, but lived like primitives, many of them unaware that the ruins had once been buildings created by their own kind. They were dressed in iron and fur, after the manner of the Nhadragh. They had dark, flat features and the hair of their heads grew down to meet bushy eyebrows sprouting above deep sockets. They were thickset people, heavily muscled and strong. Once they had been as powerful and as civilized as the Vadhagh but the Vadhagh decline had not come so swiftly as theirs.

Now the broken towers of Os, once the capital of Maliful and the whole of the Nhadragh lands, came in sight. Os the Beautiful, the city had been called by its inhabitants, but it was beautiful no longer. Broken walls were festooned with weeds, towers were stretched upon the ground, houses gave shelter to rats and weasels and other vermin, but not to Nhadragh.

The cat continued to follow the psychic scent. It circled over a squat building which was still intact. Upon the flat roof of the building a dome had been built. The dome was transparent and it glowed. Within two figures could be seen, black against the yellow light. One figure was burly, armored, and the other was shorter, dressed in furs, but wider than its companion. Muffled voices came from within the dome. The cat landed on the roof, stalked toward the dome, flattened its little head against the transparent material and, its eyes wide, watched and listened.

Glandyth-a-Krae frowned as he peered over Ertil's shoulder into the billowing smoke and the boiling liquid below. "Does the spell continue to work, Ertil?"

The Nhadragh nodded his head. "They still battle amongst themselves. Never has my sorcery worked so well."

"That is because the powers of Chaos aid you, fool! Or aid me, I should say, for it is I who am pledged, body and soul, to the Lords of Chaos." He glanced around the littered dome. It was full of dead animals, bunches of herbs, bottles of dust and liquids. Some rats and monkeys sat apathetically in cages along one wall, a shelf of scrolls below them. Once Ertil's father had been a wise scholar and he had taught Ertil much. But Ertil was devolving as the other Nhadragh devolved. He translated the wisdom into sorcery, superstition. But the wisdom itself was still powerful, as Earl Glandyth-a-Krae, picking now at his yellow fangs, had discovered.

Earl Glandyth's red, acned face was half hidden by his huge beard, which had been braided and laced with ribbons, just as his long, black hair was braided. His gray eyes hinted at an inner disease, just as his fat, red lips suggested corrupted offal. Earl Glandyth snarled. "What of Prince Corum? And the others who befriended him? What of all the Shefanhow who came from the magic city?"

"I cannot see what befalls individuals, my lord," whined the sorcerer. "I only know the spell is working."

"I hope you speak truly, sorcerer."

"I do, my lord. Was it not a spell given us by the powers of Chaos? The Cloud of Contention spreads, invisible upon the wind, turning each man against his companion, against his children, his wife." A tremulous grin appeared on the Nhadragh's dark face. "The Vadhagh fall upon each other. They die. They all die."

"Aye—but does Corum die? That is what I must know. That the others perish is well and good, but not so important. With Corum gone and disruption in the land, I can rally supporters in Lywm-an-Esh and, with my Denledhyssi, reconquer the lands King Lyr lost. Can you not concoct a special spell for Corum, sorcerer?"

Ertil trembled. "Corum is mortal—he must suffer as the others suffer."

"He is cunning—he has powerful help—he might escape. We sail for Lywm-an-Esh tomorrow. Is there no way of telling for certain that Corum is dead or seized by the madness which seizes the others?"

"No way that I know, master."

Glandyth scratched at his pitted face with his broken fingernails. "Are you sure you do not deceive me, Shefanhow?"

"I would not, master. I would not!"

Glandyth grinned into the terrified eyes of the Nhadragh sorcerer. "I believe you, Ertil." He laughed. "Still, a little more aid from Chaos would not go amiss. Summon that demon again—the one from Mabelrode's plane."

Ertil whimpered. "It takes a year off my life every time I perform such a summoning."

Glandyth drew his long knife. He placed the tip on Ertil's flat nose. "Summon it, Ertil!"

"I will summon it."

Ertil shuffled to the other side of the dome and took one of the monkeys from its cage. The creature whimpered in echo of Ertil's own whimperings. Although it looked at the Nhadragh in fear, it clung to him as if for safety, finding security nowhere else in the room. Next Ertil took an X-shaped frame from a corner and he stood this in a specially made indentation in the scarred surface of the table. All the while he shuddered. All the while he moaned. And Glandyth paced impatiently, refusing to see or hear the signs of the Nhadragh sorcerer's distress.

Now Ertil gave the monkey something to sniff and the beast became quiescent. Ertil positioned it against the frame and took nails and a hammer from his pouch.

Methodically, he began to crucify the monkey while it gibbered and squawked and blood ran out of the holes in its little hands and feet.

Ertil was pale and he looked as if he might vomit.

The cat's eyes widened further as it watched this barbaric ritual and it became just a trifle nervous, the hairs stiffening on the back of its neck and its tail jerking back and forth, but it continued to observe the scene in the dome.

"Hurry, you Shefanhow filth!" Glandyth growled. "Hurry, lest I seek another sorcerer!"

"You know there are no others left who would aid you or Chaos," Ertil mumbled.

"Be silent! Continue with your damned business."

Glandyth scowled. It was plain that Ertil spoke the truth. None feared the Mabden now—none save the Nhadragh, who had developed the habit of fearing them.

The monkey's teeth were chattering. Its eyes rolled. Ertil heated an iron in the brazier. While the iron got hot, he traced a complicated figure around the crucified beast. Then he placed bowls in each of the ten corners and he lit what was in the bowls. He took a scroll in one hand and the white-hot iron in the other. The dome began to fill with green and yellow smoke. Glandyth coughed and took a kerchief from inside his iron-studded jerkin. He looked nervous and backed into a corner.

"Yrkoon, Yrkoon, Esel Asan. Yrkoon, Yrkoon, Nasha Fasal . . ." The chant went on and on and with every verse Ertil plunged the hot iron into the writhing body of the monkey. The monkey did not die, for the iron missed its vitals, but it was plainly in dreadful agony. "Yrkoon, Yrkoon, Meshel Feran. Yrkoon, Yrkoon, Palaps Oli."

The smoke thickened and the cat could see only shadow in the room.

"Yrkoon, Yrkoon, Cenil Pordit . . ."

A distant noise. It mingled with the shrieks of the tortured monkey.

A wind blowing.

The smoke cleared suddenly. The scene in the dome was as sharp as before. No longer was the monkey crucified upon the frame. Something else hung there. It had a human form but was no larger than the monkey. Its features were closer to those of the Vadhagh than the Mabden, though there was evil and malice in the tiny face.

"You summoned me again, Ertil." The voice was of the pitch and loudness of an ordinary voice. It seemed strange that it issued from such a small mouth.

"Aye—I summoned you, Yrkoon. We need help from your master Mabelrode . . ."

"More help?" The voice was bantering. Yrkoon smiled. "More?"

"You know that we work for him. Without us you would have no means of reaching this realm at all."

"What of it? Why should my master Lord Mabelrode be interested in your realm?"

"You know why! He wants both the old Sword Realms back for Chaos—and he wants vengeance on Corum, who was instrumental in destroying the power of his brother Arioch and his sister Xiombarg, the Knight and the Queen of the Swords!"

Hanging comfortably on the frame the demon shrugged. "And so? What is it you want?"

Glandyth stepped forward, bunching his fist.

"It is what I want, not what this sorcerer wants! I want power, demon! I want the means of destroying Corum—of destroying the power of Law on this plane! Give me that power, demon!"

"I have given you much power already," the demon said reasonably. "I gave you the means of creating the Cloud of Contention. Your enemies fight each other to the death. And you are still not satisfied!"

"Tell me if Corum lives!"

"I can tell you nothing. We have no means of reaching this plane unless you summon us, and, as you well know, we cannot remain here for long—we can only take the place of another creature for a short while. Thus is the Balance deceived—or, if not deceived, mollified."

"Give me more power, Sir Demon!"

305

"I cannot *give* you power. I can only tell you how to acquire it. And know this, Glandyth-a-Krae, and be warned—if you take more of the gifts of Chaos, then you will assume the attributes of all those who accept those gifts. Are you ready to become what you most profess to loathe?"

"What's that?"

Yrkoon chuckled. "A Shefanhow. A demon. I was human once . . ."

Glandyth's mouth twisted and he clenched his fists. "I'll make any bargain to have my revenge on Corum and his kind!"

"And thus we shall be mutually served. Very well. Power you shall have."

"And power for my men—power for the Denledhyssi!"

"Very well. Power for them, too."

"Great, fierce power!" Glandyth's eyes were afire. "Massive power! Invincible power!"

"There is no such thing while the Balance rules. You shall have what you can carry."

"Good. I can carry much. I shall sail for the mainland, take their cities and their castles once again, while they fight amongst themselves. I will rule this whole world. Lyr and the rest were weak. But I shall be strong, with the Power of Chaos at my command!"

"Lyr, too, had aid from Chaos," Yrkoon reminded him sardonically.

"But he knew not how to use it. I begged him to give me more men to destroy Corum, but he would not give me enough. If Corum were dead, Lyr would be alive today. That is my proof."

"It must give you satisfaction," said the demon. "Now listen. I will tell you what you must do."

The Fifth Chapter

THE DESERTED CITY

The sky ship flew over the hill in the sea where Castle Moidel had once stood. There was no castle there now. Corum looked down on it with a sense of regret which was quickly gone, for the euphoria of the potion was still upon him. And soon they had reached the coast of Lywm-an-Esh. At first the land seemed normal, but after a while they saw small groups of riders, rarely more than three or four, rushing wildly through fields and forests, attacking any other group they came upon. Women fought women and children fought children. There were many corpses.

Corum's apathy slowly changed to horror and he was glad that Rhalina slept, that Jhary had time to look down only occasionally.

"Make haste for Halwyg-nan-Vake," Corum told his friend when Jhary glanced questioningly at him. "There is nothing we can do for them until we discover what causes their madness."

Jhary took the bottle from his pouch and held it up, but Corum shook his head. "No. There is not enough. Besides, how could we persuade them to take it? If we are to save any lives at all, we must attack that which attacks us."

Jhary sighed. "How do you attack a madness, Corum?"

"That we must discover. I pray that the Temple of Law still stands and that Arkyn will come to it if we attempt to summon him."

Jhary jerked his thumb downward. "This is like the madness which touched them before."

"Only it is stronger. Before it merely nibbled at their brains. Now it eats them entirely."

"They destroy all that they rebuilt. Is there any point in—?"

"They can rebuild again. There is a point."

Jhary shrugged. "I wonder where my cat has gone," he said.

When the sky ship circled over Halwyg-nan-Vake and began to land near the Temple of Law Rhalina woke up. She smiled at Corum as if she had forgotten all that had recently passed. But then she frowned as if remembering a nightmare. "Corum?"

"It is true," he said softly. "And we are at Halwyg now. The Floral City seems deserted. I do not know the explanation."

He had half expected to see the beaitful city in flames. Instead, save for one or two damaged buildings and gardens, it was intact. Yet none walked its streets or patrolled its walls. The palace was unoccupied as far as he could tell.

Jhary brought the sky ship down as he had learned to do when, in gentler times, Bwydyth-a-Horn had taught him its secrets.

They landed in a wide, white street. Nearby stood the Temple of Law, of but one story and without ostentatious decoration. A simple building with a sign over its portal—a single straight arrow—the Arrow of Law.

They climbed down the sky ship on trembling legs. The combination of the flight and the potion had weakened them somewhat. They began, unsteadily, to advance up the path toward the temple.

It was then that a figure appeared in the doorway. His clothes were torn and bloody and one eye had been gouged from his old face. He was sobbing, but his hands clawed out at them like the talons of a wounded, ferocious animal.

"It is Aleryon!" Rhalina gasped. "The priest—Aleryon-a-Nyvish! The sickness is upon him, too!"

The old man was weak and he could not resist when Corum and Jhary stepped swiftly forward and grasped him, pinning his arms to his sides while Jhary removed the stopper of his bottle with his teeth, dabbed a little of his potion on his finger and let Corum force the old man's jaw open. Jhary smeared the stuff on Aleryon's tongue. The priest tried to spit it out, his eyes rolling, his nostrils dilating like those of a horse in fever. But almost immediately he was quiet. His body went limp and he began to slide to the ground.

"Let us take him into the Temple," Corum said.

When they lifted him he offered no resistance. They carried him into the coolness of the interior and laid him on the floor.

"Corum?" croaked the priest, opening his eyes. "The Chaos fury leaves me. I am myself again—or almost so."

"What has happened to the folk of Halwyg?" Jhary asked him. "Are they all destroyed? Where have they gone?"

"They are mad. Not one was sane by yesterday. I fought the sickness as long as I could . . ."

"But where are they, Aleryon?"

"Gone. They are off in the hills, on the plains, in the forests. They are hiding from each other—attacking each other from time to time. Not one man trusted another and so they left the city, you see . . ."

"Has Lord Arkyn visited your Temple?" Corum asked the old priest. "Has he spoken to you?"

"Once—early on. He told me to send for you, but I could not. No one would go and I knew of no other way of reaching you, Prince Corum. And when the rage came, then I was in no state to—to receive Lord Arkyn. I could not summon him, as, traditionally, I summoned him every day."

Corum helped Aleryon to his feet. "Summon him now. The whole world is possessed by Chaos. Summon him now, Aleryon!"

"I am not sure."

"You must."

"I will try." Aleryon's wounded face grew grim, for now he fought against the euphoria of Jhary's potion. "I will try."

And he tried. He tried for all the rest of that afternoon, his voice growing hoarse as he chanted the ritual prayer to Law. For many years that prayer had gone unanswered, while Law was banished and Arioch ruled in the name of Chaos. But recently the prayer had sometimes summoned the great Lord of Law.

Now there was no answer.

Aleryon paused at last. "He does not hear. Or, if he hears, he cannot come. Is Chaos returned in all her power, Corum?"

Corum Jhaelen Irsei looked at the floor and slowly shook his head. "Perhaps."

"Look!" said Rhalina, pushing her long black hair away from her face. "Jhary, it is your cat."

The little black-and-white cat flew through the door and settled on Jhary's shoulder. It nuzzled his ear, a series of low sounds coming from its throat. Jhary looked surprised and then became intent, listening closely to the cat.

"It speaks to him!" Aleryon murmured in astonishment. "The creature speaks!"

"It communicates," Jhary told him, "yes."

At length the cat became quiet and, balancing on Jhary's shoulder still, began to wash itself.

"What did it tell you?" Corum asked.

"It told me of Glandyth-a-Krae."

"So—he does live!"

"Not only does he live but he appears to have made a pact with

King Mabelrode of Chaos—through the medium of a treacherous Nhadragh sorcerer. And Chaos told him of the spell which is now upon us. And Chaos has promised him yet greater power.''

"Where is Glandyth?"

"On Maliful—in Os."

"We must go there, find Glandyth, destroy him."

"No point. Glandyth is coming to us."

"By sea? There is still time."

"Across the sea. He and his men have some Chaos beasts at their command—things which the cat could not describe. Even now Glandyth flies for Lywm-an-Esh—and he is seeking us, Corum."

"We shall be here and we shall fight him at long last."

Jhary looked skeptical. "The two of us—drugged so that our reactions are slow and our sense of survival low?"

"We will find others—administer your potion . . ." Corum stopped. He knew that it was impossible—that even under normal conditions he would be hard put to fight the Denledhyssi, even with the aid. . . . His face cleared and then grew dark again. "Perhaps it can be done, Jhary, if I make use of the Hand of Kwll and the Eye of Rhynn once more."

Jhary-a-Conel shrugged. "We must hope so, for there is naught else we can do. If only we could find Tanelorn, as I wanted to do before. I am sure we should find help there. But I have no clue as to its current whereabouts."

"You speak of the mythical city of tranquillity—Eternal Tanelorn?" said Aleryon. "You know it exists?"

Jhary smiled. "If I have a home—then that home is Tanelorn. It exists in every age, at every time, on every plane—but it is sometimes hard to find."

"Can we not search the planes in the sky ship?" Rhalina said. "For the sky ship can travel between the realms as we know."

"My knowledge does not extend to guiding it through those strange dimensions," Jhary told them. "Bwydyth told me something of how to make it travel through the walls between the realms, but I know nothing of steering it. No, we must hope to find Tanelorn on this plane, if we are to find it at all. But in the meantime we must think more of Glandyth and escaping him."

"Or doing battle with him," Corum said. "We might have the means of defeating him."

"We might, aye."

"You must go to watch for him," Aleryon said. "I will stay here with the Lady Rhalina. Together we shall continue to try summoning Lord Arkyn."

Corum nodded his agreement. "You are a brave old man, priest. I thank you."

Outside in the silent streets Corum and Jhary walked listlessly toward the center of the city. Time upon time Corum would raise his alien left hand and inspect it. Time upon time he would lower it and then touch his jeweled eye patch with his right hand. Then he would glance up into the sky through his one mortal eye, his silver helm glinting in the sunlight, for the clouds had cleared and it was a calm winter's day.

Neither man could express his thoughts. They were thoughts both profound and desperate. It seemed that the end had come when they had least expected it. Somehow Law had been vanquished, Chaos had regained all its old strength—perhaps was stronger. And they had not, until a short time before, had any hint of it. They felt confused, betrayed, doomed, impotent.

The dead city seemed to symbolize the emptiness in their own souls. They hoped that they would see an inhabitant—just one human, even if he attacked them.

The flowers blew gently in the breeze, but instead of signifying peace, they signified an ominous calm.

Glandyth was coming from the sky, his strength reinforced by the power of Chaos.

It was with hardly any emotion at all that Corum eventually noticed them. Black shadows flying from the east—a score of them. He indicated them to Jhary.

"We had best return to the Temple and warn Aleryon and Rhalina."

"Would not they be safest in the Temple of Law?"

"I think not—not now, Jhary."

Black shadows flying from the east. Flying low. Flying purposefully. Huge wings beating, strange cries sounding in the evening air, cries which were fierce and yet full of melancholy, the cries of damned souls. Yet these were beasts. Long-necked beasts, whose heads writhed at the end of their stalks, staring this way and that, scanning the ground as hawks might scan for prey. Long, thin heads with long, thin fangs projecting from their red mouths. Blank, miserable eyes. Despairing voices, cawing as if pleading for release. And on their black, broad backs were strapped the wheelless chariots of the Denledhyssi, and in these hastily fashioned howdahs were the Mabden murderers themselves, and in the leading one stood a figure in a horned helm with a great iron sword in his hand. And they thought they could hear his laughter, though it must be another sound, perhaps a sound from the monstrous black flying things.

"It is Glandyth of course," said Corum. A crooked smile was on his face. "Well, we must try to fight him. If I can summon aid, it can engage Glandyth and his things while we run to warn Rhalina."

He raised his good right hand to his bad right eye, to pull back the patch and let himself see into the netherworld, where walked those whom he had slain with the power of the Hand of Kwll and the Eye of Rhynn, who were now his prisoners, waiting to be released to take other foes who might replace them and so free them from that netherworld for good. But the patch would not move, it was as if it was glued to the eye beneath. He pulled with all his strength. He raised the Hand of Kwll with its supernatural strength to pull back the patch, but the Hand of Kwll refused to approach the patch. Those things which had aided him now plainly refused to aid him.

Was the power of Chaos so great that it could control even these?

With a sob Corum turned and began to run through the streets, back toward the Temple of Law.

The Sixth Chapter

THE WEARY GOD

And when Corum and Jhary came to the Temple of Law with horror in their hearts, they saw that Rhalina was waiting for them and she was smiling.

"He is here! He has come!" she cried. "It is Lord Arkyn . . ."

"And Glandyth comes from the east," panted Jhary. "We must flee in the sky ship. It is all we can do. Corum's power is gone—neither the Hand nor the Eye will obey him."

Corum strode into the Temple. He was resentful and wished to express his resentment to Arkyn of Law, whom he had helped and who was not now helping him.

There was something hovering at the far end of the Temple, close to where a pale Aleryon sat with his back against the wall. A face? A body? Corum peered hard, but his peering seemed to make it fainter.

"Lord Arkyn?"

A far away voice: *"Aye . . ."*

"What is the matter? Why are the forces of Law so weak?"

"They are stretched so thinly through the two realms which we control. Mabelrode sends all his forces to aid those who serve Chaos here. . . . We fight on ten planes, Corum . . . ten planes . . . and we are so recently established . . . our power is still weak . . ."

Corum held up his useless, alien hand. "Why do I no longer control the Eye of Rhynn and the Hand of Kwll? It was our one hope of defeating Glandyth, who even now comes against us!"

"I know that. . . . You must escape . . . take your sky ship through the dimensions . . . seek Eternal Tanelorn . . . there is a correspondence between your powerlessness and your need to find Tanelorn . . ."

"A correspondence? What correspondence?"

"I can only sense it . . . I am weakened by this struggle, Corum . . . I am weary. . . . My powers are thin now. . . . Find Tanelorn . . ."

"How can I? Jhary cannot steer the sky ship through the dimensions."

"He must try to do so . . ."

"Lord Arkyn—you must give me clearer instructions. Even now Glandyth comes to Halwyg. He intends to seize this whole plane and rule it. He intends to destroy all of us who remain. How can we defend those who suffer the Chaos madness?"

"Tanelorn. . . . Seek Tanelorn. . . . It is the only way you can hope to save them. . . . I can tell you no more. . . . It is all I see . . . all I see . . ."

"You are a feeble god, Lord Arkyn. Perhaps I should have pledged my loyalty to Chaos, for if horror and death are to rule the world, one might as well become that horror and that death . . ."

"Do not be bitter, Corum. . . . There is still some hope that you may succeed in banishing Chaos from all the Fifteen Planes . . ."

"It is strength I need now—not hope."

"Hope to find the strength you need in Tanelorn. Farewell . . ."

And the vague shape vanished. Outside Corum heard the cries of the black flying things. He went to where Aleryon lay. The old man had exhausted himself trying to call Arkyn. "Come, old man. We will take you to the sky ship with us— if there is time."

But Aleryon did not reply for, while Corum had conversed with the weary god, he had died.

Rhalina and Jhary-a-Conel were already standing by the sky ship, staring upward as the great black beasts began to descend on Halwyg.

"I spoke to Arkyn," Corum told them. "He was of little help. He said we must escape through the dimensions and seek Tanelorn. I told him that you could not guide the craft beyond this plane. He said that we must."

Jhary shrugged and helped Rhalina aboard. "Then we must. Or, at least, we must try."

"If only we could rally defenders from the City in the Pyramid. Their weapons would destroy even Glandyth's Chaos allies."

"But they destroy each other with them. This is what Glandyth knew."

They stood all three in the sky ship as Jhary passed his hands over the crystals and brought them to life. The craft began to rise. Jhary pointed its prow toward the west, away from Glandyth.

But Glandyth had seen them now. The black wings beat louder and the cries increased in volume. The Denledhyssi began to sweep down toward the only three mortals in the world who were aware of what had happened to them.

Jhary bit his lip as he studied the crystals. "It is a question of making accurate passes over these things," he said. "I am striving to remember what Bwydyth taught me."

The sky ship was moving swiftly now, but their pursuers kept pace with them. The long necks of the flying beasts were poised like snakes about to strike. Red mouths stretched wide. Fangs flashed.

Something foul streamed from those mouths like oily black smoke. Like the tongues of lizards they shot toward the sky ship. Desperately Jhary turned the craft this way and that, attempting to avoid the tendrils. One curled around the stern and the ship stopped moving for a moment before it broke free. Rhalina clung to Corum. Uselessly, he had drawn his sword.

The little black-and-white cat clung with all its claws to Jhary's shoulder. It had recognized Glandyth and its eyes had widened in something akin to fear.

Now Corum heard a yell and he knew that Glandyth realized who it was trying to escape from Halwyg. Although the barbarian was a good distance away, Corum thought he felt Glandyth's eyes glaring into his own. He stared back with his one human eye, the sword raised to protect himself and Rhalina, and he saw that Glandyth, too, brandished his great iron broadsword, almost as if challenging him to single combat. The flying serpents hissed and cackled and sent from their throats more of the smoky tendrils.

Four of the things coiled around the ship. Jhary attempted to increase the speed.

"We can go no faster! We are trapped!"

"Then you must try to move through the planes. We might escape them that way."

"Those are Chaos creatures. It is likely they too can cross the walls between the realms!"

Hopelessly Corum hacked at the tendrils with his blade, but it was as if he cut through smoke. Inexorably they were being pulled back to where the Denledhyssi hovered, triumphantly waiting for them to be drawn close enough so that they could board the sky ship and slay its occupants.

Then the black wings grew hazy and Corum saw that the city below was beginning to fade. Lightning seemed to flicker through sudden darkness. Globes of purple light appeared. The boat shuddered like a frightened deer and Corum felt a familiar nausea seize him. Furiously the black wings beat as they became clearer. He had guessed rightly, had Jhary. The creatures were able to follow them through the dimensions.

Jhary made more passes over the instruments. The boat rocked and threatened to turn over. Again came the peculiar sensations, the vibrations, the lightnings and globes of golden flame in a rushing, turbulent cloud of red and orange.

The tongues of smoke which restrained them disappeared. The black creatures still flew on, sighted through the zigzags of utter darkness and blinding brightness. Their voices could still be heard, as also could be heard the roaring rage of Glandyth-a-Krae.

And then there was silence.

Corum could not see Rhalina. He could not see Jhary. He could only feel the boat still beneath his feet.

They were drifting in total blackness and absolute silence, in neither one dimensions nor another.

BOOK TWO

*In which Prince Corum and his companions
learn the full import of what Chaos
is and what it intends to become and
discover something more concerning
the nature of time and identity*

The First Chapter

CHAOS UNBOUNDED

"Corum."

It was Rhalina's voice.

"Corum?"

"I am here."

He stretched out his right hand and tried to touch her. At last he felt her hair beneath his fingers. He encircled her shoulders with his arm.

"Jhary?" he said. "Are you there?"

"I am here. I am trying different configurations, but the crystals do not respond. Is this Limbo, Corum?"

"I assume so. If it were not that we can breathe and it is relatively warm, I would think the sky ship adrift in the cosmos, beyond the sky."

Silence.

And then a thin line of golden light could be seen, cutting across the blackness as if dividing it in two, rather like a horizon, or the crack of light from beneath a gigantic door. And while they remained in the blackness the area of blackness above the golden line began, it seemed, to move upward, like a curtain in a vast theater.

And now, though they could still not see each other, they saw the wide area of gold, saw it begin to change.

"What is it, Corum?"

"I know not, Rhalina. Jhary?"

"This Limbo might be the domain of the Cosmic Balance—a neutral territory, as it were, where no gods or mortals come in ordinary circumstances."

"Have we drifted into it by accident?"

"I do not know."

This is what they saw then:

All was huge, but in proportion. A rider spurring his horse across a desert beneath a white and purple sky. The rider had milk-white hair and it streamed behind him. His eyes were red and full of wild bitterness, his skin was bone white. Physically he somewhat resembled the Vadhagh, for he had the same unhuman face. He was an albino, clothed all in black, baroque armor, every part of it covered in fine, detailed metal-work, a huge helm upon his head, a black sword at his side.

And now the rider was no longer upon a horse. He rode a beast that somewhat resembled those which had pursued them—a flying beast—a dragon. The black sword was in his hand and it gave off a strange, black radiance. The rider rode the dragon as if it were a horse, seated in a saddle, his feet in stirrups, but he was strapped to the saddle to save him from falling. He was crying out.

And below him there were other dragons, evidently brothers to the one he rode. They were engaged in aerial battles with misshapen things with the jaws of whales. A green mist drifted across the scene and obscured it.

Now they saw the asymmetrical outlines of a gigantic castle, flowing upward to form its shape even as they watched. Battlements, turrets, towers all appeared. The dragon-rider ordered his beasts toward it and they released flaming venom from their mouths, directing it at the castle. A few others who followed the rider also sat upon the backs of the dragons.

They passed the blazing castle and came now to an undulating plain. Upon this plain stood all the demons and corrupt, warped things of Chaos, arranged as if for battle. And here, too, were gods—Dukes of Hell every one—Malohin, Xiombarg, Zhortra and more—Chardros the Reaper, with monstrous, hairless head and sweeping scythe—and the oldest of the gods, Slortar the Old, slender and lovely as a youth of sixteen.

And it was this massed might that the dragon-riders attacked. Surely they must perish.

Fiery venom splashed across the scene and again there was only golden light.

"What did we see?" Corum whispered. "Do you know, Jhary?"

"Aye, I know. I have been there—or will be there. We see another age, another plane. The mightiest battle between Law and Chaos, Gods and Mortals, that I have ever witnessed. The white-faced one I served in a different guise. He is called Elric of Melniboné."

"You mentioned him once, when we first met."

"He is, like you, a champion chosen by destiny to fight so that the equilibrium of the Cosmic Balance might be preserved." Jhary's voice sounded sad. "I remember his friend Moonglum, but his friend Moonglum does not remember me . . ."

The remark seemed inconsequential to Corum.

"What does it mean to us, Jhary?"

"I do not know. Look—something else comes upon the stage."

There was a city upon a plain. Corum felt that he knew it, but then realized that he had never seen it before, for it was not like any city in Bro-an-Vadhagh or Lywm-an-Esh. Of white marble and black granite, it was simple and it was magnificent. It was under siege. Silver-snouted weapons were upon its walls, directed at the attackers—a great horde of cavalry and infantry which had pitched its tents below. The attackers were clad in massive armor, but the defenders wore light protection and they, too, like the one Jhary had called Elric, were more like the Vadhagh than like other mortals. Corum began to wonder if the Vadhagh occupied many plains.

A horseman in bulky armor rode from the camp toward the black-and-white walls of the city. He carried a banner and seemed to have come to parley. He called up at the walls and eventually a gate opened to admit him. The watchers could not see his face.

The scene changed again.

Now, strangely, the one who had been attacking the city was defending it.

Sudden glimpses of terrible massacres. The humans were being destroyed by weapons even more powerful than those possessed by the folk of Gwlas-cor-Gwrys and it was one of their own kind who directed their murder . . .

It was gone. Golden, pure light returned.

"Erekosë," Murmured Jhary. "I think I see significance in these scenes. I think it is the Balance and it is hinting at something. But

319

the implications are so profound that my poor head cannot contain them.''

"Speak of them, please!" Corum begged into the darkness, his eyes still upon the golden stage.

"There are no words. I have told you already that I am a Companion to Champions—that there is only one Champion and only one Companion, but that we do not always know each other, or even know of our fate. Circumstances change from time to time, but the basic destiny does not. It was Erekosë's burden that he should be aware of this—aware of all his previous incarnations, his incarnations to come. You, at least, are spared that, Corum.''

Corum shuddered. "Say no more.''

Rhalina said, "And what of this hero's lovers? You have spoken of his friend . . .''

And a new scene came upon the golden stage before she could continue.

The face of a man, wracked with pain, covered in sweat, a dark, throbbing jewel imbedded in his forehead. He drew down over this face a helm of such highly polished metal that it became a perfect mirror. In the mirror could be seen a group of riders who at first appeared to be men with the heads of beasts. Then it became plain that these heads were in fact helmets, fashioned to resemble pigs, goats, bulls, and dogs.

There was a pitched battle. There were several riders in the same polished helms. They were greatly outnumbered by their enemies in the beast masks.

One of those in the mirror helmets—perhaps the man they had first seen—held something aloft—a short staff from which pulsed many-colored rays. This staff struck fear into the beast riders and many had to be driven on by their leaders.

The fight continued.

The scene vanished, to be replaced, once more, by nothing but the pure, golden light.

"Hawkmoon," murmured Jhary. "The Runestaff. What can all this mean? You have witnessed yourself, Corum, in three other incarnations. I have never experienced such a thing before.''

Corum was trembling. He could not bear to consider Jhary's words. They suggested that it was his fate to experience an eternity of battle, of death, of misery.

"What can it mean?" Jhary said again. "Is it a warning? A prediction of something about to take place? Or has it no special significance?''

Slowly the blackness descended on the golden light until there was only a faint line of gold, and then that, too, vanished.

They hung once more in Limbo.

Jhary's voice came to Corum. The tone was distant, as if the dandy spoke to himself. "I think it means we must find Tanelorn. There, all destinies meet—there, all things are constant. Neither Law nor Chaos can effect Tanelorn's existence, though her occupants can sometimes be threatened. But even I do not know where Tanelorn lies in this age, in these dimensions. If I could only discover some sign which would give me my bearings . . ."

"Perhaps it is not Tanelorn we should seek," Rhalina said. "Perhaps these events we have been shown indicate some different quest?"

"It is all bound up together," Jhary mused, seeming to answer a question he had put to himself. "It is all bound up together. Elric, Erekosë, Hawkmoon, Corum. Four aspects of the same thing, as I am another aspect of it, as Rhalina is a sixth aspect. Some disruption has occurred in the universe, perhaps. Or some new cycle is about to take place. I do not know . . ."

The sky ship lurched. It moved as if along a crazily undulating track. Massive teardrops of green and blue light began to fall all around them. There was the sound of a raging wind, but no wind touched them. An almost human voice, echoing on and on and on.

And then they were flying through swiftly moving shadows—the shadows of things and people all rushing in the same direction.

Below, Corum saw a thousand volcanoes, each one spewing red cinders and smoke, but somehow the cinders and smoke did not touch the sky ship. There was a stink of burning and it was suddenly replaced by the smell of flowers. The volcanoes had become so many huge blossoms, like anemones opening red petals.

Singing came from somewhere. A joyful, martial tune like the song of a victorious army. It died away. There was a laugh, cut off short.

The bulk of enormous beasts rose from seas of excrement and the beasts raised their square snouts to the skies and groaned before sinking again beneath the surface.

A mottled, pink-white plain, apparently of stones. It was not stones. The plain was comprised entirely of corpses, each one neatly laid beside the other, each one face down.

"Where are we, Jhary, do you know?" Corum called, peering through disturbed air at his friend.

"This place is ruled by Chaos, that is all I know at present, Corum. What you see is Chaos unbounded. Law has no power here at all. I believe we must be in Mabelrode's Realm and I am attempting to take the sky ship out of it, but it will not respond.''

"We are moving through the dimensions, however," Rhalina said. "The scenes change so rapidly. That must be the case."

Jhary offered her a desperate grin as he turned to look at her over his shoulder. "We are not moving through the dimensions. This is Chaos, Lady Rhalina. Pure, unchained Chaos."

The Second Chapter

THE CASTLE BUILT OF BLOOD

"It is surely Mabelrode's Realm," Jhary said, "unless Chaos has conquered suddenly and all fifteen Planes are once again under its domination."

Foul shapes flew about the sky ship for a moment and then were gone.

"My brain reels," Rhalina gasped. "It is as if I am mad. I can hardly believe I do not dream."

"Someone dreams," Jhary told her. "Someone dreams, lady. A god."

Corum could not speak. His head was aching. Peculiar memories threatened to come to him, but they remained elusive.

Sometimes he would listen hard, believing that he heard voices. He would peer over the rail of the craft to see if they came from beneath the ship. He would stare into the sky. "Do you hear them, Rhalina?"

"I hear nothing, Corum."

"I cannot make out the words. Perhaps they are not words."

"Forget them," Jhary said sharply. "Pay no attention to anything of that sort. We are in Chaos lands and our senses will deceive us in every way. Remember that we three are the only realities—and be careful to inspect anything which looks like me or Rhalina very carefully before you trust it."

"You mean demons will try to make me think that they are those I love?"

"That is what they will do, call them what you will."

A huge wave advanced toward them. It took the form of a human hand. It clenched itself into a fist. It threatened to smash the boat. It disappeared. Jhary flew on. He was sweating.

A spring day dawned. They flew over the morning fields as the

323

dew sparkled. Flowers grew in the grass and there were little bright pools of water, tiny rivers. In the shade of oak trees stood horses and cows. A little way ahead was a low, white farmhouse with smoke curling from its chimney. Birds sang. Pigs rooted in the farmyard.

"I cannot believe it is not real," Corum said to Jhary.

"It is real," Jhary told him. "But it is short-lived. Chaos delights in creation but swiftly becomes bored with what it creates, for it seeks not order or justice or constancy but sensation, entertainment. Sometimes it suits it to create something which you and I would value or find pleasure in. But it is an accident."

The fields remained. The farmhouse remained. The sense of peace grew.

Jhary frowned. "Perhaps, after all, we have left the Realm of Chaos and . . ."

The fields gradually began to swirl, like stagnant water stirred by a stick. The farmhouse spread to become scum on top of the water. The flowers were now festering growths on the surface.

"It becomes so easy to believe what one wishes to believe," Jhary said wearily. "So easy."

"We must escape from here," said Corum.

"Escape? I cannot control the sky ship. I have not controlled it since we entered Limbo."

"Then some other force controls us?"

"Aye—but it may not be sentient." Jhary's voice was strained, his face was pale. Even the little cat was nestling hard against his neck as if seeking comfort.

Stretching to every horizon now was seething stuff, grayish-green with what looked like pieces of rotting vegetation floating in it. The vegetation seemed to assume the shapes of crustaceans—crabs and lobsters scuttling across its surface, only slightly different in shade.

"An island," Rhalina said.

Out of all this rose an island of dark blue rock. Upon the rock was a building, a great castle all colored scarlet. And the scarlet rippled as if water had somehow been molded into a permanent shape. A familiar, salty smell came from the scarlet castle. Jhary turned the ship to avoid it, but then the castle was ahead of them again. Again he turned. Again it was ahead of them. For several moments he altered the course of the sky ship and each time the castle reappeared before them.

"It seeks to stop us." Jhary tried again to avoid it.

"What is it?" Rhalina asked.

Jhary shook his head. "I know not, but it is unlike the other things we have seen. We are being drawn toward it now. That stench! It clogs my nostrils!"

Closer came the sky ship, until it hovered directly above the scarlet turrets of the castle. And then it had landed.

Corum peered over the side. The substance of the castle still rippled like liquid. It did not look solid, yet it held the sky ship. He drew his sword and looked toward a black gap in the nearby tower. An entrance. And a figure was emerging from it.

The figure was fat, about twice as broad as an ordinary man. It had a head which was essentially human but from which boarlike tusks sprouted. It moved over the rippling scarlet surface on bowed, thick legs, naked but for a tabard embroidered with a design not immediately recognizeable. It was grinning at them. "I have been short of guests," it grunted. "Are you mine?"

Corum said, "Your guests?"

"No, no, no. Did I make you or did you come from elsewhere? Are you inventions of one of my brother dukes?"

"I do not understand—" Corum began.

Jhary interrupted him. "I know you. You are Duke Teer."

"Of course I am Duke Teer. What of it? Why, I do not believe you are inventions at all—not of this realm at all. How satisfying. Welcome, mortals, to my castle. How remarkable! Welcome, welcome, welcome. How exquisite! Welcome!"

"You are Duke Teer of Chaos and your liege lord is Mabelrode the Faceless. I was right, then. This is King Mabelrode's Realm."

"How intelligent! How marvelous!" The boar face split in an ugly grin and rotting teeth were displayed. "Do you bring me some message, perhaps?"

"We, too, serve King Mabelrode," Jhary said swiftly. "We fight in Arkyn's Realm to restore the rule of Chaos there."

"How excellent! But do not say you come for aid, mortals, for all my aid already goes to that other realm where Law attempts to hold sway. Every Duke of Hell sends his resources to the fight. The time might yet arise when we can go personally to do battle with Law, but that is not yet. We lend our powers, our servants, everything but ourselves—for doubtless you have learned what became of Xiombarg when he—or she, I should say, of course—attempted to cross into Arkyn's Realm. How unpleasant!"

"We had hoped for aid," Corum said, falling in with Jhary's attempted deception. "Law has thwarted us too often."

"I, as you know, am only a minor Lord of Chaos. My powers have never been great. Most of my efforts have gone—and peers may laugh—into the creation of my beautiful castle. I love it so much."

325

"What is it made of?" Rhalina asked him nervously. She plainly did not think they could remain undetected for long.

"You have not heard of Teer's Castle? How strange! Why, my pretty mortal, it is built of blood—it is built all of blood. Many thousands have died to make my castle. I must slay many thousands more before it is properly completed. Blood, my dear—blood and blood and blood! Can you not sniff its delicious tang? What you sniff is blood. What you see—it is all blood. Mortal blood—immortal blood—it all mingles. All blood is equal when it goes to build Teer's Castle, eh? Why, you have blood enough for part of a small wall of a tower. I could make a room from all three of you. You would be astonished to learn how far blood can be made to stretch as a building material. And it is tasty, eh?" He shrugged and waved a thick hand. "Or perhaps not to you. I know mortals and their fads. But for me—ah, it is delightful!"

"It was an honor to see the famous Castle Built of Blood," Jhary said as smoothly as he could, "but now the business of the moment presses and we must go to seek help in our fight against Law. Will you allow us to leave now, Duke Teer?"

"Leave?" The small eyes glinted. A fat, rough tongue licked the coarse lips. Teer fingered one of his tusks.

"We are, after all, upon King Mabelrode's service," said Corum.

"So you are! How superb!"

"It is urgent, our quest."

"It is rare for mortals to come directly to King Mabelrode's Realm," Duke Teer said.

"These are rare times, with two of our realms in the hands of Law," Jhary pointed out.

"How true! What is that running from the lips of the female?" Rhalina was vomiting. She had done all she could to contain her nausea, but the stink had become too much for her.

Duke Teer's eyes narrowed. "I know mortals. I know them. She is distressed. By what? By what?"

"By the thought of Law's return," said Jhary weakly.

"She is destressed by me, eh? She is not wholly given up to serving Chaos, eh? Not a very good specimen for King Mabelrode to pick to serve him, eh?"

"He picked us," Corum said. "She merely accompanies us."

"Then she is of little use to King Mabelrode—or to you. Here, then, is what I want in return for my allowing you to see the splendor of my Castle Built of Blood . . ."

"No," said Corum, guessing what he meant. "We cannot do

that. Let us go now, I beg you, Duke Teer. You know we must make haste! King Mabelrode will not be pleased if you delay us."

"He will not be pleased with you if you delay. Simply give me the female. Keep the flesh and bones, if you desire. All I require is the blood."

"No!" screamed Rhalina in terror.

"How stupid!"

"Let us go, Duke Teer!"

"Let me have the female first!"

"No!" said Jhary and Corum in unison. And they drew their swords, whereupon Duke Teer burst into grunting laughter that was at once mocking and incredulous.

The Third Chapter

THE RIDER ON THE YELLOW HORSE

The Duke of Hell stretched as a man might stretch when awakening from a luxurious sleep. His arms grew longer, his body wider, and, within a space of seconds, he had doubled his size. He looked down on them, still laughing. "How badly you lie!"

"We do not lie!" cried Corum. "We beg you—let us be on our way."

Duke Teer frowned. "I have no wish to earn King Mabelrode's displeasure. Yet if you truly served Chaos you would not show such silly emotions—you would give the female to me. She is useless to you, but she can be of great use to me. I exist only to build my castle, make it more elaborate, more beautiful." He began to stretch out one great hand. "Here, I will take her and then you may go your way and I'll—"

"See," called Jhary suddenly. "Our enemies! They have followed us to this plane. How stupid of them—to cross into the realm of their enemy King Mabelrode."

"What?" Duke Teer looked up. He saw the score of black flying things with their long necks and their red jaws, the men upon their backs. "Who are they?"

"Their leader is called Corum Jhaelen Irsei," said Corum. "They are sworn enemies of Chaos and desire our deaths. Destroy them, Duke Teer, and Mabelrode will be mightily pleased with you."

Duke Teer glared upward. "Is this truth?"

"It is!" Jhary shouted.

"I believe I have heard of this mortal, Corum. Was it not he who destroyed Arioch's heart? Is he the one who lured Xiombarg to her doom?"

"He is the same!" Rhalina cried.

"My nets," muttered Duke Teer, reducing his size and hurrying back into his tower. "I will help you."

"There is enough blood in them to build a whole new hall!" Jhary yelled. He leaped for the controls and hastily passed his hands over them. They came to life and the sky ship sprang into the air.

Glandyth and his flying pack had seen them. The black beasts turned, wings sounding like thunder, and sped toward the sky ship.

But they were free of the Castle Built of Blood now and Duke Teer was engaged with his nets. He had one in each hand and he grew larger and larger, casting toward the disconcerted Earl of Krae.

Jhary's face was set. "I am going to try everything I can to hurl the sky ship from this foul dimension," he said. "It will be better to die than remain here. Duke Teer will learn soon enough that Glandyth serves Chaos and not Law. And Glandyth will tell him who we are. All the Dukes of Hell will seek us out." He removed a transparent cover and began to rearrange the crystals. "I know not what this will accomplish, but I am determined to try to find out!"

The sky ship began to oscillate throughout its length. Clinging to the rail Corum felt his entire body vibrate until he was sure he would shake to pieces. He clung to Rhalina. The ship began to dive toward a sea of violet and orange. They were flung forward, upon Jhary. The ship struck something. They passed into a liquid which stifled them. Another mighty wrench and Corum lost his grasp on Rhalina. Through the darkness he tried to find her, but she had gone. He felt his feet leave the deck of the ship.

He began to drift.

He tried to call her name, but the stuff blocked his mouth. He tried to peer through it, but it stuck to his eyes.

He drifted languidly, sinking deeper and deeper. His heart began to bang against his chest. No air entered his lungs. He knew he was dying.

And he knew Rhalina and Jhary were dying, somewhere nearby in the viscous stuff.

He was almost relieved that his quest had ended so, that his responsibility to the Cause of Law was over. He grieved for Rhalina and he grieved for Jhary, but he could not grieve for himself.

Suddenly he was falling. He saw a piece of the sky ship—a twisted rail—fall with him. He was falling through clear air but the speed of his descent still made it impossible for him to breathe.

He began to glide. He looked about him. There was blue sky on all sides—below him, above him. He spread his arms. The piece of twisted rail was still gliding with him. He looked for Rhalina. He looked for Jhary. They were nowhere in sight in all the blue vastness. There was just the piece of rail.

He called out, "Rhalina?"

There was no reply.

He was alone in a universe of blue light.

He began to feel drowsy. His eyes closed. He fought to open them but he could not. It was as if his brain refused any longer to experience further terrors.

When he awoke he was lying on something soft and very comfortable. He felt warm and he realized he was naked. He opened his eyes and saw the beams of a roof above him. He turned his head. He was in a room. Sunlight came through a window.

Was this a further illusion? The room was plainly at the top of a house, for its walls sloped. It was simply furnished. The home of a well-to-do peasant farmer, Corum thought. He looked at the varnished door with its simple metal latch. He heard a voice singing behind it.

How had he come here? It was possible that it was a trick. Jhary had warned him to beware of such visions. He drew his hands from beneath the bedsheets. On his left wrist there still remained the Hand of Kwll, six-fingered and bejeweled. He touched his face. The Eye of Rhynn, useless though it now was, still filled the socket of his right eye. On a chest in one corner all his clothes had been laid and his weapons were stacked nearby.

Had he somehow returned to his own plane and had sanity been restored to it. Could Duke Teer have slain Glandyth and thus lifted Glandyth's spell from the land?

The room was not familiar, neither were the designs on the chest and the bedposts. This was not, he was sure, Lywm-an-Esh and it was most certainly not Bro-an-Vadhagh.

The door opened and a fat man entered. He looked amused and said something which Corum could not understand.

"Do you speak the language of Vadhagh or Mabden?" Corum asked him politely.

The fat man—not a farmer by his embroidered shirt and silk breeks—shook his head and spread his hands, speaking again in the strange language.

"Where is this place?" Corum asked him.

The fat man pointed out of the window, pointed to the floor, spoke at some length, laughed, and indicated with further gestures that Corum might like to eat. Corum nodded. He was very hungry.

Before the man left, he said, "Rhalina? Jhary?" hoping that he would recognize the names and know where the two were. The man shook his head, laughed again and closed the door behind him.

Corum got up. He felt weak but not totally weary. He pulled on his clothes, picked up the byrnie, and then laid it down again with the helm and the greaves. He went to the door and peered out. He saw a landing, varnished with the same brown varnish, a staircase leading downward. He stepped onto the landing and tried to peer below, but saw only another landing. He heard voices—a woman's voice, the laughter of the fat man. He went back into the room and looked out of the window.

The house lay on the outskirts of a town. But it was not a town like any he had seen before. All the houses had red, sloping roofs and were built of a mixture of timber and gray brick. The streets were cobbled and carts passed this way and that along them. Most of the people wore drabber clothes than those he had seen on the fat man, but they looked cheerful enough, often calling out greetings to each other, stopping to pass the time of day.

The town seemed quite large and in the distance Corum could see a wall, the spires of taller buildings plainly more expensively built than the ordinary houses. Sometimes carriages passed by, or well-dressed men on horseback made their way through the throng—nobles or possibly merchants.

Corum rubbed his head and went to sit on the edge of the bed. He tried to think clearly. The evidence was that he was on another plane. And there seemed to be no battle between Law or Chaos here. Everyone was, as far as he could tell, leading ordinary, sedate lives. Yet he had it both from Lord Arkyn and from Duke Teer that every one of the Fifteen Planes was in conflict as Law fought Chaos. Was this some plane ruled by Arkyn or his brother which had not yet succumbed? It was unlikely. And he could not speak the language while they could not understand him. That had never happened to him before. Jhary's rearrangement of the crystals before the sky ship had been destroyed had evidently produced a drastic result. He was cut off from anything he knew. He might never learn where he was. And all this suggested that Rhalina and Jhary, if they lived, were similarly abandoned on some unfamiliar plane.

The fat man opened the door and an equally fat woman in voluminous white skirts entered the room with a tray on which was arranged meat, vegetables, fruit, and a steaming bowl of soup. She smiled at him and offered him the tray rather as if she were offering food to a caged wild animal. He bowed and smiled and took the tray. She was careful to avoid touching his six-fingered hand.

"You are kind," said Corum, knowing she would not understand, but wishing her to know that he was grateful. While they watched, he began to eat. The food was not particularly well-cooked or flavored, but he was hungry. He ate it all as gracefully as he could and eventually, with another bow, returned the tray to the silent pair.

He had eaten too much too swiftly and his stomach felt heavy. He had never been much attracted to Mabden food at any time and this was coarser than most. But he made a great pretense of being satisfied, for he had become unusued to kindness of late.

Now the fat man asked another question. It sounded like a single word. "Fenk?"

"Fenk?" said Corum and shook his head.

"Fenk?"

Again Corum shook his head.

"Pannis?"

Another shake of the head. There were several more questions of the same sort—just a single word—and each time Corum indicated that he did not understand. Now it was his turn. He tried several words in the Mabden dialect, a language derived from Badhagh. The man did not understand. He pointed at Corum's six-fingered hand, frowning, pulling at one of his own hands, chopping at it, until Corum realized that he was asking if the hand had been lost in battle and this was an artificial one. Corum nodded rapidly and smiled, tapping at his eye also. The man seemed satisfied but extremely curious. He inspected the hand, marveling. Doubtless he believed it to be mortal work and Corum could not explain that it had been grafted to him by means of sorcery. The man indicated that Corum should come with him through the door. Corum willingly consented and was led down the stairs and into what was plainly a workshop.

And now he understood. The man was a maker of artificial limbs. He was plainly experimenting with many different kinds. There were wooden, bone, and metal legs, some of them of very complicated manufacture. There were hands carved from ivory or made of jointed steel. There were arms, feet, even something which seemed to be a steel rib cage. There were also many anatomical drawings in a peculiar, alien style and Corum was fascinated by them. He saw a pile of scrolls bound into single sheets between leather covers and he opened one. It seemed to be a book concerning medicine. Although cruder in design and although the strange, angular letters were not at all beautiful in themselves, the book seemed as sophisticated as many which the Vadhagh had created before the coming of the Mabden. He tapped the book and made an approving noise.

"It is good," he said.

The man smiled and tapped again at Corum's hand. Corum wondered what the doctor would say if he could explain how he came by it. The poor man would probably be horrified or, perhaps more likely, convinced that Corum was mad, as Corum would have been before he began to encounter sorcery.

Corum let the doctor inspect the eyepatch and the peculiar eye beneath it.

This puzzled the fat man even more. He shook his head, frowning. Corum lowered the patch back over the eye. He half wished that he could demonstrate to the doctor exactly what the eye and the hand were used for.

Corum began to guess how he had come here. Evidently some citizens had found him unconscious and sent for the doctor, or brought Corum to the doctor. The doctor, obsessed with his study of artificial limbs, had been only too pleased to take Corum in, though what he had made of Corum's arms and armor the Prince in the Scarlet Robe did not know.

But now Corum became filled with a sense of urgency, with fears for Rhalina and Jhary. If they were in this world he must find them. It was even possible that Jhary, who had traveled so often between the planes, could speak the language. He took up a piece of blank parchment and a quill, dipped the quill in ink (it was little different to the pens used by the Mabden) and drew a picture of a man and a woman. He held up two fingers and pointed outside, frowning and gesturing to show that he did not know where they were. The fat doctor nodded vigorously, understanding. But then he showed, almost comically, that he did not know where Jhary and Rhalina were, that he had not seen them, that Corum had been found alone.

"I must look for them," Corum said urgently, pointing to himself and then pointing out of the house. The doctor understood and nodded. He thought for a moment and then signed for Corum to stay there. He left and returned wearing a jerkin. He gave Corum a plain cloak to wrap around his clothes, which were, for the place, outlandish. Together they left the house.

Many glanced at Corum as he and the doctor walked through the streets. Obviously the news of the stranger had gone everywhere. The doctor led Corum through the crowds and beneath an arch through the wall. A white, dusty road led through fields. There were one or two farmhouses in the distance.

They came eventually to a small wood and here the doctor stopped, showing Corum where he had been found. Corum looked about him and at last discovered the thing he sought. It was the twisted rail of the sky ship. He showed it to the doctor, who had certainly seen nothing like it, for he gasped in astonishment, turning it this way and that in his hands.

333

It was proof to Corum that he had not gone mad, that he had but recently left the realm of Chaos.

He looked around him at the peaceful scenery. Were there really such places where the eternal struggle was unknown? He began to feel jealous of the inhabitants of this plane. Doubtless they had their own sorrows and discomforts. Evidently there was war and pain, for why else would the doctor be so interested in making artificial limbs? And yet there was a sense of order here and he was sure that no gods—either of Law or of Chaos—existed here. But he knew that it would be stupid to entertain the idea of remaining here, for he was not like them, he hardly resembled them physically, even. He wondered what speculations the doctor had made to explain his coming here.

He began to walk amongst the trees, calling out the names of Rhalina and Jhary.

He heard a cry later and whirled round, hoping it was the woman he loved. But it was not. It was a tall, grim-faced man in a black gown, striding across the fields toward them, his gray hair blowing in the breeze. The doctor approached him and they began to converse, looking often at Corum, who stood watching them. There was a dispute between them and both became angrier. The newcomer pointed a long, accusing finger at Corum and waved his other hand.

Corum felt trepidation, wishing he had brought his sword with him.

Suddenly the man in the robe turned and marched back toward the town leaving the doctor frowning and rubbing at his jowl.

Corum became nervous, sensing that something was wrong, that the man in the robe objected to his presence in the town, was suspicious of his peculiar physical appearance. And the man in the robe also seemed to have more authority than the doctor. And far less sympathy for Corum.

Head bowed, the doctor moved toward Corum. He raised his head, his lips pursed. He murmured something in his own language, speaking to Corum as a man might speak to a pet for which he had great affection—a pet which was about to be killed or sent away.

Corum decided that he must have his armor and weapons at once. He pointed toward the town and began to walk back. The doctor followed, still deep in worried thought.

Back in the doctor's house Corum donned his silver byrnie, his silver greaves, and his silver helm. He buckled on his long strong sword and looped his bow, his arrows, and his lance upon his back.

He realized that he looked more incongruous than ever, but he also felt more secure. He looked out of the window at the street. Night was falling. Only a few people walked in the town now. He left the room and went down the stairs to the main door of the house. The doctor shouted at him and tired to stop him from leaving, but Corum gently brushed him aside, opened the latch, and went out.

The doctor called to him—a warning cry. But Corum ignored it, both because he did not need to be warned of potential danger and also because he did not see why the kindly man should share his danger. He strode into the night.

Few saw him. None stopped him or even tried to do so, though they peered curiously at him and laughed among themselves, evidently taking him for an idiot. It was better that they laughed at him than feared him, or else the danger would have been much increased, thought Corum.

He strode through the streets for some time until he came to a partially ruined house which had been deserted. He decided that he would make this his resting place for the night, hiding here until he could think of his next action.

He stumbled through the broken door and rats fled as he entered. He climbed the swaying staircase until he came to a room with a window through which he could observe the street. He was hardly aware of his own reasons for leaving the doctor's house, save that he did not wish to become involved with the man in the robe. If they were seriously trying to find him, then, of course, they would discover him soon enough. But if they had a little superstition, they might think he had vanished as mysteriously as he had arrived.

He settled down to sleep, ignoring the sound the rats made.

He woke at dawn and peered down into the street. This seemed to be the main street of the city and it was already alive with tradesmen and others, some with donkeys or horses, others with handcars, calling out greetings to each other.

He smelled fresh bread and began to feel hungry, but curbed his impulse, when a baker's cart stopped immediately beneath him, to sneak out and steal a loaf. He dozed again. When it was night, he would try to find a horse and leave the city behind him, seek other towns where there might be news of Rhalina or Jhary.

Toward midday he heard a great deal of cheering in the street and he edged his way to the window.

There were flags waving and a band of some sort was playing raucous music. A procession was marching through the streets—a martial procession by the look of it, for many of the riders were undoubtably warriors in their steel breastplates and with their swords and lances.

In the middle of the procession, hardly acknowledging the crowd's cheers, was the man who was the object of their celebration. He rode a big yellow horse and he wore a high-collared red cloak which at first hid his face from Corum. There was a hat on his head, a sword at his side. He was frowning a little.

Then Corum saw with mild surprise that the man's left hand was missing. He cluthced his reins in a specially made hook device. The warrior turned his head and Corum was this time completely astonished. He gasped, for the man on the yellow horse had an eye patch over his right eye. And, though his face was of the Mabden cast, he bore a strong resemblance to Corum.

Corum stood up, about to cry out to the man who was almost his double. But then he felt a hand close over his mouth and strong arms bear him down to the floor.

He wrenched his head about to see who attacked him. His eyes widened.

"Jhary!" he said. "So you are on this plane! And Rhalina? Have you seen her?"

The dandy, who was dressed in the clothes of the local inhabitants, shook his head. "I have not. I had hoped that you and she stayed together. You have made yourself conspicuous here, I gather."

"Do you know this plane?"

"I know it vaguely. I can speak one or two of their languages."

"And the man on the yellow horse—who is he?"

"He is the reason why you should leave here as soon as possible. He is yourself, Corum. He is your incarnation on this plane in this age. And it goes against all the laws of the cosmos that you and he should occupy the same plane at the same time. We are in great danger, Corum, but these folk could also be in danger if we continue—however unwittingly—to disrupt the order, the very balance of the multiverse."

The Fourth Chapter

THE MANOR IN THE FOREST

"You know this world, Jhary?"

The dandy put a finger to his lips and drew Corum into the shadows as the parade went by. "I know most worlds," he murmured, "but this less well then many. The sky ship's destruction flung us through time as well as through the dimensions and we are marooned in a world whose logic is in most cases essentially different. Secondly, our 'selves' exist here and we therefore threaten to upset the fine balance of this age and, doubtless, others, too. To create paradoxes in a world not used to them would be dangerous, you see . . ."

"Then let us leave this world with all speed! Let us find Rhalina and go!"

Jhary smiled. "We cannot leave an age and a plane as we would leave a room, as you well know. Besides, I do not believe Rhalina to be here if she has not been seen. But that can be discovered. There used to be a lady not far from here who was something of a seeress. I am hoping that she will help us. The folk of this age have an uncommon respect for people like ourselves—though often that respect turns to hatred and they hound us. You know you are sought by a priest who wants to burn you at the stake?"

"I knew a man disliked me."

Jhary laughed. "Aye—disliked you enough to want to torture you to death. He is a dignitary of their religion. He has great power and has already called out warriors to search for you. We must get horses as soon as possible."

Jhary paced the rickety floor, stroking his chin. "We must return to the Fifteen Planes with all speed. We have no right to be here . . ."

"And no wish to be," Corum reminded him.

Outside the sound of pipes and drums faded and the crowd began to disperse.

"I remember her name now!" Jhary muttered. He snapped his fingers. "It is the Lady Jane Pentallyon and she dwells in a house close to a village called Warleggon."

"These are strange names, Jhary-a-Conel!"

"No stranger than ours are to them. We must make speed for Warleggon as soon as possible and we must pray that Lady Jane Pentallyon is in residence and has not, herself, been burned by now."

Corum stepped closer to the window and glanced down. "The priest comes," he said, "with his men."

"I thought it likely you would be seen entering here. They have waited until after the parade lest you escaped in the confusion. I like not the thought of killing them, when we have no business in their age at all . . ."

"And I like not the thought of being killed," Corum pointed out. He drew his long, strong sword and made for the stairs.

He was halfway down when the first of them burst in, the priest in the gown at their head. He called out to them and made a sign at Corum—doubtless some superstitious Mabden charm. Corum sprang forward and stabbed him in the throat, his single eye blazing fiercely. The warriors gasped at this. Evidently they had not expected their leader to die so soon. They hesitated in the doorway.

Jhary said softly from behind Corum, "That was foolish. They take it ill when their holy men are slain. Now the whole town will be against us and our leavetaking will be the harder."

Corum shrugged and began to advance toward the three warriors crowded in the doorway. "These men have horses. Let us take them and have done with it, Jhary. I am weary of hesitation. Defend yourselves, Mabden!"

The Mabden parried his thrusts but, in so doing, became entangled with each other. Corum took one in the heart and wounded another in the hand. The pair fled into the street yelling.

Corum and Jhary followed, though Jhary's face was set and disapproving. He preferred subtler plans than this. But his own sword whisked out to take the life of a mounted man who tried to ride him down and he pushed the body from the saddle, leaping upon the back of the horse. It reared and arched its neck but Jhary got it under control and defended himself against two more who came at him from the end of the street.

Corum was still on his feet. He used his jeweled hand as a club, forcing his way through to where several horses stood without riders. The Mabden were terrified, it seemed, of the touch of his six-fingered, alien hand and dodged to avoid it. Two more died before Corum reached the horses and sprang into the saddle. He called out, "Which way, Jhary?"

"This way!" Without looking behind him, Jhary galloped the horse down the street.

Striking aside one who tried to grab at his reins, Corum followed the dandy. A great hubbub began to spread through the city as they raced toward the west wall. Tradesmen and peasants tried to block their path, they were forced to leap over carts and force a path through cattle or sheep. More warriors were coming, too, from two sides.

And then they had ducked under the archway and were through the low wall and riding swiftly down the white, dusty road away from the city, a pack of warriors at their backs.

Arrows began to whistle past their heads as archers came to the walls and shot at them. Corum was astonished at the range of the bowmen. "Are these sorcerous arrows, Jhary?"

"No! It is a kind of bow unknown in your age. These people are masters of it. We are lucky, however, that it is too bulky a bow to be shot from a horse. There, see, the arrows are beginning to fall short. But the horsemen stay with us. Into yonder wood, Corum. Swiftly!"

They plunged off the road and into a deep, sweet-smelling forest, leaping a small stream, the horses' hooves slipping for a moment in damp moss.

"How will the doctor fare?" Corum called. "The one who took me in."

"He will die unless he is clever and denounces you," Jhary told him.

"But he was a man of great intelligence and humanity. A man of science, too—of learning."

"All the more reason for killing him, if their priesthood has its way. Superstition, not learning, is respected here."

"Yet it is such a pleasant land. The people seem well-meaning and kind!"

"You can say that, with those warriors at our backs?" Jhary laughed as he slapped his horse's rump to make it gallop faster. "You have seen too much of Glandyth and his kind, of Chaos and the like, if this seems paradise to you!"

"Compared with what we have left behind, it is paradise, Jhary."

"Aye, perhaps you speak truth."

By much backtracking and hiding they had managed to throw off their pursuers before sunset and they now walked along a narrow track, leading their tired horses.

"It is a good many miles to Warleggon yet," Jhary said. "I would that I had a map, Prince Corum, to guide us, for it was in another body with different eyes that I last saw this land."

"What is the land itself called?" asked the Prince in the Scarlet Robe.

"It is, like Lywm-an-Esh, divided into a number of lands under the dominion of one monarch. This one is called Kernow—or Cornwall, depending whether you speak the language of the region or the language of the realm as a whole. It's a superstition-ridden land, though its traditions go back further than most other parts of the country of which it is part, and you will find much of it like your own Bro-an-Vadhagh. Its memories stretch back longer than do the memories of the rest of the realm. The memories have darkened, but they still have partial legends of a people like yourself who once lived here."

"You mean this Kernow lies in my future?"

"In one future, probably not yours. The future of a corresponding plane, perhaps. There are doubtless other futures where the Badhagh have proliferated and the Mabden died out. The multiverse contains, after all, an infinity of possibilities."

"Your knowledge is great, Jhary-a-Conel."

The dandy reached into his shirt and drew out his little black-and-white cat. It had been there all the time they had been fighting and escaping. It began to purr, stretching its limbs and its wings. It settled on Jhary's shoulder.

"My knowledge is partial," said Jhary wearily. "It consists generally of half-memories."

"But why do you know so much of this plane?"

"Because I dwell here even now. There is really no such thing as time, you see. I remember what to you is the 'future.' I remember one of my many incarnations. If you had watched the parade longer you would have seen not only yourself but myself. I am called by some grand title here, but I serve the one you saw on the yellow horse. He was born in that city we have left and he is reckoned a great soldier by these people, though, like you, I think he would prefer peace to war. That is the fate of the Champion Eternal."

"I'll hear no more of that," Corum said quickly. "It disturbs me too much."

"I cannot blame you."

They stopped at last to water their horses and take turns to sleep. Sometimes in the distance groups of horsemen would ride by, their brands flaring in the night, but they never came close enough to be a great threat.

In the morning they reached the edges of a wide expanse of heather. A light rain fell but it did not discomfort them, rather it refreshed them. Their surefooted horses began to canter over the moor and brought them soon to a valley and a forest.

"We have skirted Warleggon now," said Jhary. "I thought it wise. But there is the forest I sought. See the smoke rising deep within. That, I hope, is the manor of the Lady Jane."

Along a winding path protected on each side by high banks of rich-scented moss and wild flowers they rode and there at last were two posts of brown stone which were topped by two carvings of spread-winged hawks, mellowed by the weather. The gates of bent iron were open and they walked their horses along a gravel path until they turned a corner and saw the house. It was a large house of three stories, made of the same light brown stone, with a gray slate roof and five chimneys of a reddish tint. Lattice windows were set into the house and there was a low doorway in the center. Two old men came round the side of the house at the sound of their horses' hooves on the gravel. The men had dark features, heavy brows, and long, gray hair. They were dressed in leather and skins and, if they wore any expression at all, their eyes seemed to hold a look of grim satisfaction as they looked at Corum in his high helm and his silver byrnie.

Jhary spoke to them in their own language—a language which was not that Corum had heard in the city but a language which seemed to hold faint echoes of the Vadhagh speech.

One of the men took their horses to be stabled. The other entered the house by the main door. Corum and Jhary waited without.

And then she came to the door.

She was an old, beautiful woman, her long hair pure white and braided, a mantle upon her brow. She wore a flowing gown of light blue silk, with wide sleeves and gold embroidery at neck and hem.

Jhary spoke to her in her own tongue, but she smiled then.

She spoke in the pure, rippling speech of the Vadhagh.

"I know who you are," she said. "We have been waiting for you here at the Manor in the Forest."

The Fifth Chapter

THE LADY JANE PENTALLYON

The old, beautiful lady led them into the cool room. Meats and wines and fruits were upon the table of polished oak. Jars of flowers everywhere made the air sweet. She looked at Corum more often than she looked at Jhary. And at Corum she looked almost fondly.

Corum removed his helm with a bow. "We thank you, lady, for this gracious hospitality. I find much kindness in your land, as well as hatred."

She smiled, nodding. "Some are kind," she said, "but not many. The elf folk as a race are kinder."

He said politely: "The elf folk, lady?"

"Your folk."

Jhary removed a crumpled hat from within his jerkin. It was the hat he always wore. He looked at it sorrowfully.

"It will take much to straighten that to its proper shape. These adventures are hardest of all on hats, I fear. The Lady Jane Pentallyon speaks of the Vadhagh race, Prince Corum, or their kin, the Eldren, who are not greatly different, save for the eyes, just as the Melniboneans and the Nilanrians are offshoots of the same race. In this land they are known sometimes as elves—sometimes as devils, djins, even gods, depending upon the region."

"I am sorry," said the Lady Jane Pentallyon gently. "I had forgotten that your people prefers to use its own names for its race. And yet the name 'elf' is sweet to my ears, just as it is sweet to speak your language again after so many years."

"Call me what you will, lady," Corum said gallantly, "for almost certainly I owe you my life and, perhaps, my peace of mind. How came you to learn our tongue?"

"Eat," she said. "I have made the food as tender as I could,

342

knowing that the elf folk have more delicate palates than we. I will tell you my story while you banish your hunger.''

And Corum began to eat, discovering that this was the finest Mabden food he had ever eaten. Compared with the food he had had in the town it was light as air and delicately flavored. The Lady Jane Pentallyon began to speak, her voice distant and nostalgic.

"I was a girl," she said, "of seventeen years, and I was already mistress of this manor, for my father had died crusading and my mother had contracted the plague while on a visit to her sister. So, too, had my little brother died, for she had taken him with her. I was distressed, of course, but not old enough to know then that the best way of dealing with sorrow is to face it, not try to escape it. I affected not to care that all my family were dead. I took to reading romances and to dreaming of myself as a Guinevere or an Isolde. These servants you have seen were with me then and they seemed little younger in those days. They respected my moods and there was none to check me as a kind of quiet madness came over me and I dwelt more and more in my own dreams and less and less thought of the world, which, anyway, was far away and sent no news. And then one day there came an Egyptian tribe past the manor and they begged permission to set up their camp in a glade in the woods not far from here. I had never seen such strange, dark faces and glittering black eyes and I was fascinated by them and believed them to be the guardians of magic wisdom such as Merlin had known. I know now that most of them knew nothing at all. But there was one girl of my own age who had been orphaned like me and with whom I identified myself. She was dark and I was fair, but we were of a height and shape and, doubtless because narcissism had become one of my faults, I invited her to live in the house with me after the rest of the tribe had moved on—taking, I need not say, much of our livestock with them. But I did not care, for Aireda's tales— learned from her parents, I understood—were far wilder than any I had read in my books or imagined for myself. She spoke of dark old ones who could still be summoned to carry young girls off to lands of magic delight, to worlds where great demigods with magic swords disrupted the very stuff of nature if their moods willed it. I think now that Aireda was inventing much of what she told me— elaborating stories she had heard from her mother and father—but the essence of what she told me was, of course, true. Aireda had learned spells which, she said, would summon these beings, but she was afraid to use them. I begged her to conjure each of us a god from another world to be our lovers, but she became afraid and would not. A year passed and our deep, dark games went on, our minds became more and more full of the idea of magic and demons and gods, and Aireda, at my constant behest, slowly weakened in her resolve not to speak the spells and perform the rituals she knew . . ."

The Lady Jane Pentallyon took up a dish of sliced fruit and offered it to Corum. He accepted it. "Please continue, lady."

"Well, I learned from her the patterns to carve upon the stones of the floor, the herbs to brew, the arrangements of precious stones and particular kinds of rocks, or candles, and the like. I got from her every piece of knowledge save the incantations and the signs which must be traced in the air with a witch knife of glowing crystal. So I carved the patterns in the stones, I gathered the herbs, I collected the stones and the rocks, and I sent to the city for the candles. And I presented them all to Aireda one day, telling her that she must call for the old ones who ruled this land before the druids, who, themselves, came before the Christians. And she agreed to do it, for by this time she had become as mad as I. We chose All Hallows Eve for the ritual, though I do not believe now that it has any special significance. We arranged the stones and the rocks and we traced the designs in the air with the crystal witch knife and we burned the candles and we brewed the herbs and we drank what we brewed and we were successful . . ."

Jhary sat back in his chair, his eyes fixed on the Lady Jane Pentallyon. He was eating an apple. "You were successful, lady," he said, "in conjuring up a demon?"

"A demon? I think not, though he looked to us like a demon with his slanting eyes and his pointed ears—a face not unlike your own, Prince Corum—and we were at first afraid, for he stood in the center of our magic ring and he was furious, shouting, threatening in a language which I could not, in those days, understand. Well, the tale grows long and I will not bore you, save to say that this poor 'demon' was of course a man of your race, dragged from his own world by our incantations and our diagrams and our crystals, and most anxious to return there."

"And did he return, lady?" Corum asked gently, for he saw that her eyes had a suggestion of tears in them. She shook her head.

"He could not, for we had no means of returning him. After the astonishment—for truly we had not really believed in our game!—we made him as comfortable here as we could, for we instantly felt sorry for what we had done when we realized that he was helpless. He learned something of our language and we learned something of his. We thought him very wise, though he insisted he was only a minor member of a large and not very important family of moderate nobility, that he was a soldier and not a scholar or a sorcerer. We understood his modesty but continued to admire him very much. I think he enjoyed that, although he continued to beg us to try to return him to his own age and his own plane.''

Corum smiled. ''I know how I should feel if two young girls had been responsible for tearing me suddenly away from all I knew and cared for and had then told me that they had only been playing a game and could not send me back!''

And the Lady Jane smiled in reply. ''Aye. Well, by and by Gerane—that was one of his names—became reconciled to some degree and he and I fell in love and were happy for a short while. Sadly, I had not accounted for the fact that Aireda was also in love with Gerane.'' She sighed. ''I had dreamed of being Guinevere, of Isolde, of other heroines of romance, but I had forgotten that all these women were the victims of tragedy in the end. Our tragedy began to play itself out and at first I was not aware of it. Jealousy took power over Aireda and she grew to hate first me and then Gerane. She would plan revenges on us of varying sorts, but they were never completely satisfying to her. She had heard that Gerane's people had enemies—another race with bleaker souls— and she had guessed that one of her mother's rituals had to do with summoning members of this race—other demons, her mother had thought. Her first attempts were unsuccessful, but she absorbed herself in remembering every detail of those old spells.''

''She conjured up Gerane's enemies?''

''Aye. Three of them came one night into the house. She was their first victim, for they hate humans as much as they hate elves—your folk. Shambling, awkward, poorly fashioned creatures they were, completely unlike your folk, Prince Corum. We should call them trolls or some such name.''

''And what did they do after they had slain Aireda?''

''She was not slain, but badly wounded, for it was in conversation with her later that I learned what she had done . . .''

''And Gerane?''

''He had no sword. He had come with none. He had needed none in the Manor in the Forest.''

''He was killed?''

''He heard the noise in the hall and came down to see what caused it. They butchered him there, by the door.'' She pointed. The tears shone on her cheeks now. ''They cut him into sections, my elfin love . . .'' She lowered her head.

Corum got up and went to comfort the old, beautiful Lady Jane Pentallyon. She gripped his mortal hand just once and had once again contained her grief. She straightened her back. ''The— trolls—did not remain in the house. Doubtless they were confused

345

by what had happened to them. They ran off into the night.''

"Do you know what became of them?"Jhary asked.

"I heard several years later that beasts resembling men had begun to terrorize the folk of Exmoor and had eventually been taken and had stakes driven through their hearts, for they were thought to be the Devil's spawn. But the story spoke of only two, so perhaps one still lives in some lonely spot, still unaware of what had happened to him or where he is. I feel a certain sympathy for him . . .''

"Do not grieve yourself, lady, by any further telling of this tale,'' said Corum gently.

"Since then,'' she went on, "I have concerned myself with the study of old wisdom. I learned something from Gerane and I have since spoken with various men and women who reckon themselves versed in the mystic arts. It was my hope, once, to seek the plane of Gerane's people, but it is evident now that our planes are no longer in conjunction, for I have learned enough to know that the planes circle as some say the planets circle about each other. I have learned a little of the art of seeing into the future and the past, into other planes, as Gerane's folk could . . .''

"My folk also possess something of that art,'' said Corum in confirmation of her questioning glance, "but we have been losing it of late and can do nothing now beyond see into the five planes which comprise our realm.''

"Aye.'' She nodded. "I cannot explain why these powers wax and wane as they do.''

"It is something to do with the gods,'' said Jhary. "Or our belief in them, perhaps.''

"Your second sight gave you a glimpse into the future and that is how you knew we were seeking your help,'' Corum said.

Again she nodded.

"So you know that we are trying to return to our own age,where urgent deeds are necessary?''

"Aye.''

"Can you help us?''

"I know of one who can put you on the road which leads to the achievement of that desire, but he can do no more.''

"A sorcerer?''

"Of sorts. He, like you, is not of this age. Like you, he seeks constantly to return to his own world. He can move easily through the few centuries bordering this time, but he seeks to travel many millenia and that he cannot do.''

"Is his name Bolorhiag?'' asked Jhary suddenly. "An old man with a withered leg?''

"You describe the man, but to us he is known merely as the Friar, for he is inclined to wear clerical garb since this offers him the greatest protection in the periods of history he visits.''

"It is Bolorhiag,'' said Jhary. "Another lost one. There are a few such souls who are whisked about the multiverse in this manner. Sometimes they are not at fault at all, but have been plucked, willy nilly, by whatever winds they are which blow through the dimensions. Others, like Bolorhiag, are experimenters—sorcerers, scientists, scholars, call them what you will—who have understood something of the nature of time and space but not enough to protect themselves. They, too, find themselves blown by those winds. There are also, as you know, ones like me who appear to be natural dwellers in the whole multiverse—or there are heroes, like yourself, Corum, who are doomed to move from age to age and plane to plane, from identity to identity, fighting for the cause of Law. And there are women of a certain sort, like yourself, Lady Jane, who love these heroes. And there are malicious ones who hate them. What object there is to this myriad of existences I know not and it is probably better that we know nothing of them . . .''

Lady Jane nodded gravely. "I think you are right, Sir Jhary, for the more one discovers, the less point there seems in life at all. However, we are concerned not with philosophy but with immediate problems. I have sent out a summoning for the Friar and hope that he hears it and comes—it is not always the case. Meanwhile I have a gift for you, Prince Corum, for I feel that it may be useful to you. It appears that there is a mighty conjunction about to take place in the multiverse, when for a moment in time all ages and all planes will meet. I have never heard of such a thing before. That is part of my gift, the information. The other part is this . . .'' From a thong around her neck she now drew out a slender object which though of a milky white color also sparkled with every color in the spectrum. It was a knife carved of a crystal which Corum had never seen before.

"Is it . . . ?'' he began.

She inclined her head to remove the thong. "It is the witch knife which brought Gerane to me. It will, I think, bring aid to you when you need it greatly. It will call your brother to you . . .''

"My brother? I have no—''

"I was told this,'' she said. "And I can add nothing to it. But here is the witch knife. Please take it.''

Corum accepted it and placed the thong around his own neck. "Thank you, lady.''

"Another will tell you when and how to use it,'' she said. "And now, gentlemen, will you rest here at the Manor in the Forest, until such time as the Friar may present himself to us?''

"We should be honored," said Corum. "But tell me, lady, if you know anything of the woman I love, for we are separated. I speak of the Lady Rhalina of Allomglyl and I fear much for her safety."

The Lady Jane frowned. "There was something concerning a woman which came momentarily into my head. I have the feeling that if you succeed in your present quest, then you will succeed in being reunited with her. If you fail, then you shall never see her again."

Corum's smile was grim.

"Then I must not fail," he said.

The Sixth Chapter

SAILING ON THE SEAS OF TIME

Three days went by and in normal circumstances Corum would have grown frustrated, impatient. But the old, beautiful lady calmed him, telling him something of the world she lived in but hardly ever saw. Some aspects of it were strange to him, but he began to understand why strange folk such as himself were, in the main, treated with suspicion, for what the Mabden of this world desired more than anything was equilibrium, stability not threatened by the doings of gods and demons and heroes, and he came to sympathize with them, though he felt that an understanding of what they feared would give them less to fear. They had invented for themselves a remote god whom they called simply the God and they had placed him far away from them. Some half-remembered fragments of the knowledge concerning the Cosmic Balance were theirs, and they had legends which might relate to the struggle between Law and Chaos. As he told the Lady Jane, all the Balance stood for was equilibrium—but stability could be achieved only by an understanding of the forces which were at work in the world, not a rejection of them.

On the third day one of the old retainers came running along the path up to the house, where Jhary-y-Conel, Corum, and the Lady Jane stood conversing. Speaking in his own language the man pointed into the forest.

"They still search for you, it seems," she told them. "Your horses were released a day's ride away in order to put them off the scent and make them think you hid near Liskeard, but doubtless they come here because I am suspected a witch." She smiled. "I deserve their suspicion far more than do the poor souls they sometimes catch and burn."

"Will they find us?"

349

"There is a place for you to hide. Others have been hidden there in the past. Old Kyn will take you there." She spoke to the old man and he nodded, grinning as if he enjoyed the excitement.

They were led into the attic of the house and there Old Kyn unlocked a false wall. Inside it was smoky and cramped but there was room to stretch and sleep if they wished to. They climbed into the darkness and Old Kyn replaced the false wall.

Sometime later they heard voices, booted feet on the stairs. They pressed their backs against the false wall so that if it were thumped it would sound more solid. It was thumped, but it passed the inspection of the searchers, whose coarse voices were grumbling and tired as if they had been at work ever since Corum and Jhary had escaped from the city.

The footsteps went away. Faintly they heard the jingle of harness, more voices, the sound of hooves on the gravel, and then silence.

A little later Old Kyn removed the false wall and leered into their hiding place. He winked. Corum grinned at him and climbed out, dusting down his garments. Jhary blew plaster from his cat's coat and began to stroke the little beast. He said something in Old Kyn's language which made the man wheeze with laughter.

Downstairs Lady Jane's face was serious. "I think they will return," she said. "They noticed that our chapel has not been used for a good while."

"Your chapel?"

"Where we are meant to pray if we do not go to church. There are laws governing such things."

Corum shook his head in astonishment. "Laws?" He rubbed at his face. "This world is indeed hard to fathom."

"If the Friar does not come soon, you may have to leave here and seek fresh sanctuary," she said. "I have already sent for a friend who is a priest. Next time those soldiers come they shall find a very devout Lady Jane, I hope."

"Lady, I hope that you will not suffer for us," said Corum seriously.

"Worry not. There's little they can prove. When this fear dies down they will forget me again for a while."

"I pray it is true."

Corum went to bed that night, for he felt unnaturally weary. The main fear was for Lady Jane and he could not help but feel she had made too little of the incident. At last he slept, but was awakened shortly after midnight.

It was Jhary and he was dressed, with his hat upon his head and his cat upon his shoulder. "The time has come," he said, "to come to time."

Corum rubbed at his eyes, not understanding the dandy's remark.

"Bolorhiag is here."

Corum swung himself from the bed. "I will dress and come down directly."

When he descended the stairs he saw that Lady Jane, wrapped in a dark cloak, her white hair unbound, stood there with Jhary-a-Conel and a small, wizened man who walked with the aid of a staff. The man's head was disproportionately large for his frail body, which even the folds of his priest's gown could not hide. He was speaking in a high, querulous voice.

"I know you, Timeras. You are a rogue."

"I am not Timeras in this identity, Bolorhiag. I am Jhary-a-Conel . . ."

"But still a rogue. I resent even speaking the same tongue as you and only do so for the sake of the lovely Lady Jane."

"You are both rogues!" laughed the old, beautiful woman. "And you know that you cannot help but like each other."

"I only help him because you have asked me to do so," insisted the wizened man, "and because he may one day admit that he can help me."

"I have told you before, Bolorhiag, that I have much knowledge and hardly any skills. I would help you if I could, but my mind is a patchwork of memories—fragments of a thousand lives are in my skull. You should have sympathy for a wretch such as I."

"Bah!" Bolorhiag turned his twisted back and looked at Corum with his bright blue eyes. "And this is the other rogue, eh?"

Corum bowed.

"The Lady Jane requests me to ship you out of this age and into another where you will be less bothersome to her," Bolorhiag went on. "I will do it willingly, of course, for her heart is too kind for her own good. But I do no favors for you, young man, you understand."

"I understand, sir."

"Then let us get about it. The winds blow through and may be gone again before we can set our course. My carriage is outside."

Corum approached Lady Jane Pentallyon and took her hand, kissing it gently. "I thank you for this, my lady. I thank you for your hospitality, your confidence, your gifts, and I pray that you will know happiness one day."

"Perhaps in another life," she said. "Thank you for such thoughts, and let me kiss you now." She bent and touched his forehead with her lips. "Farewell, my elfin prince . . ."

351

He turned away so that she would not see that he had noticed the tears in her eyes. He followed the wizened man as he hopped toward the door.

It was a small vessel he saw on the gravel outside the house. It was hardly large enough for three and had plainly been designed to take one in comfort. It had a high, curved prow of a substance neither wood nor metal but much pitted and scored as if it had weathered many storms. A mast rose from the center, though there was no sail furled on the yard.

"Sit there," said Bolorhiag impatiently, indicating the bench to his right. "I will sit between you and steer the craft."

After Corum had squeezed himself into place, Bolorhiag sat next to him and Jhary sat on the other side of the old man. A globe on a pivot seemed the only controls of the quaintly shaped craft, and now Bolorhiag raised his hand to salute the Lady Jane, who stood in the shadows of the doorway, then took the globe between both palms.

Again Corum and Jhary bowed toward the door, but now the Lady Jane had disappeared altogether. Corum felt a tear form in his own good eye and he thought he knew why she did not watch them leave.

Suddenly something shimmered around the mast and Corum saw that it was a faint area of light shaped like a triangular sail. It grew stronger and stronger until it resembled an ordinary sail of cloth, bulging in a wind, though no wind blew.

Bolorhiag muttered to himself and the little craft seemed to move and yet did not move.

Corum glanced at the Manor in the Forest. It seemed framed in dancing brightness.

Daylight suddenly surrounded them. They saw figures outside the house, all around them, but the figures did not appear to see them. Horsemen—the soldiers who had searched the house the day before. They vanished. It was dark again and then light and then the house was gone and the boat rocked, turned, bounced.

"What is happening?" Corum cried out.

"What you wanted to happen, I gather," snapped Bolorhiag. "You are enjoying a short voyage upon the seas of time."

Everywhere now was what appeared to be clouds of dark gray. The sail continued to strain at the mast. The unfelt wind continued to blow. The boat moved on, with its inventor in his black robe muttering over his globe, steering it this way and that.

Sometimes the gray clouds would change color, become green or blue or deep brown, and Corum would feel peculiar pressures upon him, find it difficult to breathe for a few moments, but the experience would quickly pass. Bolorhiag seemed completely oblivious of these sensations and even Jhary gave them no special attention. Once or twice the cat would give a faint cry and cling closer to its master, but that was the only sign that others felt the discomforts that Corum felt.

And then the ship's sail went limp and began to fade. Bolorhiag cursed in a harsh language of many consonants and spun the globe so that the ship whirled at a dizzying speed and Corum felt his stomach turn over.

Then the old man grunted in satisfaction as the sail reappeared and filled out again. "I thought we had lost the wind for good," he said. "There is nothing more aggravating than being becalmed on the time seas. Hardly anything more dangerous, either, if one is passing through some solid substance!" He laughed richly at this, nudging Jhary in the ribs. "You look ill, Timeras, you rogue."

"How long will this voyage last, Bolorhiag?" said Jhary in a strained voice.

"How long?" Bolorhiag stroked the globe, seeing something within it that they could not see. "What meaningless remark is that? You should know better, Timeras!"

"I should have known better than to begin on this voyage. I suspect you of becoming senile, old man."

"After several thousand years I am bound to begin to feel my years." The old man grinned wickedly at Jhary's consternation.

The speed of the ship seemed to increase.

"Stand by to turn about!" shouted Bolorhiag, apparently quite mad, almost hysterical. "Ready to drop anchor, lads! Date ahoy!"

The ship swung as if caught by a powerful current. The peculiar sail sagged and vanished. The gray light began to grow brighter.

The ship stood upon an expanse of dark rock overlooking a green valley far, far below.

Bolorhiag began to chuckle as he saw their expressions. "I have few pleasures," he said, "but my favorite is to terrify my passengers. It is, in part, what I regard as my just payment. I am not mad, I think, gentlemen. I am merely desperate."

The Seventh Chapter

THE LAND OF TALL STONES

Bolorhiag allowed them to disembark from his tiny craft. Corum looked around him at the rather bleak landscape. Everywhere he looked he saw in the distance tall columns of stone, sometimes standing singly, sometimes in groups. The stone varied in color but had plainly been put there by some intelligence.

"What are they?" he asked.

Bolorhiag shrugged. "Stones. The inhabitants of these parts raise them."

"For what purpose?"

"For the same purpose that makes them dig deep holes in the ground—you will discover those as well—to pass the time. They cannot explain it any other way. I understand that it is their art. No better or worse than much of the art one sees."

"I suppose so," said Corum doubtfully. "And now perhaps you will explain, Master Bolorhiag, why we have been brought here."

"This age corresponds roughly with the age of your own Fifteen Planes. The conjunction comes soon and you are better here than elsewhere. There is a building which is occasionally seen here and which has the name in some parts of the Vanishing Tower. It comes and goes through the planes. Timeras here knows the story, I am sure."

Jhary nodded. "I know it. But this is dangerous, Bolorhiag. We could enter the Vanishing Tower and never return. You are aware that—?"

"I am aware of most things about the tower, but you have little choice. It is your only means of getting back to your own age and your own plane, believe me. I know of no other method. You must risk the dangers."

Jhary shrugged. "As you say. We will risk them."

"Here." Bolorhiag offered him a rolled sheet of parchment. "It is a map of how to get there from here. A rather rough map, I am afraid. Geography was never my strong point."

"We are most grateful to you, Master Bolorhiag," Corum said gracefully.

"I want no gratitude, but I do want information. I am some ten thousand years away from my own age and wonder what barrier it is which allows me to cross it one way but not the other. If you should ever discover a clue to the answer to this question and if you, Timeras, ever pass through this age and plane again, I should want to hear of it."

"I will make a point of it, Bolorhiag."

"Then farewell, both of you."

The old man hunched himself once more over his steering crystal. Once more the peculiar sail appeared and filled with the unfelt wind. And then the little ship and its occupant had faded.

Corum stared thoughtfully at the huge, mysterious stones.

Jhary had unrolled the map. "We must climb down this cliff until we reach the valley," he said. "Come, Prince Corum, we had best start now."

They found the least steep part of the cliff and began to inch their way down it.

They had not gone very far when they heard a shout above them and looked up. It was the little wizened man and he was hopping up and down on his stick. "Corum! Timeras or whatever pseudonym you're using! Wait!"

"What is it, Master Bolorhiag?"

"I forgot to tell you, Prince Corum, that if you find yourself in extreme danger or distress within the next day—and only the next day—go to a point where you see a storm which is isolated. Do you hear?"

"I hear. But what—?"

"I cannot repeat myself, the time tide changes. Enter the storm and take out the witch knife given you by the Lady Jane. Hold it so that it traps the lightning. Then call upon the name of Elric of Melnibone and say that he must come to make the Three Who Are One—the Three Who Are One. Remember that. You are part of the same thing. It will be all you need to do for the Third—the Many-Named Hero—will be drawn to the Two."

"Who told you all this, Master Bolorhiag?" Jhary called, clinging to the rock of the cliff and not looking down.

"Oh, a creature. It does not matter who told me. But you must remember that, Prince Corum. The storm—the knife—the incantation. Remember it!"

Corum called, half to humor the old man, "I will remember."

"Farewell, again." And Bolorhiag stepped back from the cliff top and was gone.

They climbed down in silence, too intent on finding holds in the rock face to discuss Bolorhiag's peculiar message.

And when, eventually, they reached the floor of the valley, they were too exhausted to speak, but lay still, looking up at the great sky.

Later Corum said, "Did you understand the old man's words, Jhary?"

Jhary shook his head. "The Three Who Are One. It sounds ominous. I wonder if it has any connection with what we saw in Limbo?"

"Why should it?"

"I know not. Just a thought which popped into my brain because it was empty. We had best forget that for a while and hope to discover the Vanishing Tower. Bolorhiag was right. The map *is* crude."

"And what is the Vanishing Tower?"

"It once existed in your own realm, Corum, I believe—in one of the Five Planes, but not yours. On the edge of a place called Balwya Moor in a valley much like this one which was called Darkvale. Chaos was fighting Law and winning in those days. It came against Darkvale and its keep—a small castle, rather than a tower. The knight of the keep sought the aid of the Lords of Law and they granted that aid, enabling him to move his tower into another dimension. But Chaos had gained great power then and cursed the tower, decreeing that it should shift for all time, never staying more than a few hours on any one plane. And so it shifts to this day. The original knight—who was protecting a fugitive from Chaos—was soon insane, as was the fugitive. Then came Voilodion Ghagnasdiak to the Vanishing Tower and there he remains."

"Who is he?"

"An unpleasant creature. Trapped in the tower now and fearing to step outside, he uses the tower to lure the unsuspecting to him. He keeps them there until they bore him and then he slays them."

"And that is whom we must fight when we enter the Vanishing Tower?"

"Exactly."

"Well, there are two of us and we are armed."

"Voilodion Ghagnasdiak is very powerful—a sorcerer of no mean skill."

356

"Then we cannot conquer him! My hand and eye no longer come to my assistance."

Jhary shrugged. He stroked his cat's chin. "Aye. I said it was dangerous, but as Bolorhiag pointed out, we have little choice, have we? After all, we are still on our way to find Tanelorn. I am beginning to feel that my sense of direction returns. We are nearer Tanelorn now than we have been before."

"How do you know?"

"I know. I know, that is all."

Corum sighed. "I am weary of mysteries, of sorceries, of tragedies. I am a simple . . ."

"No time for self-pity, Prince Corum. Come, this is the way we want to go."

They followed a roaring river upstream for two miles. The river rushed through a steep valley and they climbed along the sloping sides, using the trees to stop them from falling down into the white rapids. Then they came to a place where the river forked and Jhary pointed to a place where it was shallow, running over pebbles. "A ford. We need yonder island. That is where the Vanishing Tower will appear, when it appears."

"Will we wait long?"

"I do not know. Still the island looks as if it has game on it and the river has fish in it. We shall not starve while we wait."

"I think of Rhalina, Jhary—not to mention the fate of Bro-an-Vadhagh and Lywm-an-Esh. I grow impatient."

"Our only means of getting back to the Fifteen Planes is to enter the Vanishing Tower. Thus, we must await the pleasure of the tower."

Corum shrugged and began to wade through the ice-cold stream toward the island.

Suddenly Jhary shouted and pushed past Corum. "It is there! It is there already! Quickly, Corum!"

He ran to where a stone keep stood above the trees. It seemed an ordinary sort of tower. Corum could hardly believe that this was their goal.

"Soon we shall see Tanelorn!" cried Jhary jubilantly. He reached the other side of the island, with Corum running some distance behind him, and began to crash through the undergrowth.

There was a doorway at the base of the keep and it was open.

"Come, Corum!"

Jhary was almost inside the door now. Corum went more warily, remembering what he had heard of Voilodion Ghagnasdiak, the dweller in the tower. But Jhary, his cat as ever upon his shoulder, had gone through the door.

Corum broke into a run, his hand on his sword hilt. He reached the tower.

The door closed suddenly. He heard Jhary's yell of horror from within. He clung to the wood of the door, he beat on it.

Inside Jhary was calling, "Find the Three Who Are One whatever it is. It is our only hope now, Corum! Find the Three Who Are One!" There came a chuckle which was not Jhary's.

"Open!" roared Corum. "Open your damned door!"

But the door would not budge.

The chuckle was fat and warm. It grew louder and Corum could no longer hear Jhary's voice at all. The fat, warm voice said, "Welcome to the home of Voilodion Ghagnasdiak, friend. You are an honored guest."

Corum felt something happen to the tower. He looked back. The forest was disappearing. He clung to the handle, kept his feet on the step for a moment. His body was racked by painful spasms, one following closely upon the other. Every tooth in his head ached, every bone in his body throbbed.

And then he had lost his grip upon the tower and saw it vanish away. He fell.

He fell and landed on wet, marshy ground. It was night. Somewhere a dark bird hooted.

The Eighth Chapter

INTO THE SMALL STORM

Daybreak found Corum walking. His feet were weary and he was lost, but still he walked. He could think of nothing else to do and he felt bound to do something. Marshland stretched everywhere. Marsh birds rose in flocks into the red morning sky. Marsh animals slithered or hopped across the wet ground in search of food.

Corum selected another clump of reeds and made it his goal.

When he reached the clump of reeds he paused for a moment and then fixed his eye on another clump and began to make for that.

And so he progressed.

He was desolate. He had lost Rhalina. Now he had lost Jhary and thus his hope of finding either Rhalina or Tanelorn. And so he had lost Bro-an-Vadhagh and Lywm-an-Esh and he had lost them to conquering Chaos, to Glandyth-a-Krae.

All lost.

"All lost," he murmured through his numbed lips.

"All lost."

The marsh birds cackled and screeched. The marsh animals scuttled through the reeds, unseen as they ran on hasty errands.

Was this whole world a marsh? It seemed so. Marsh upon marsh.

He reached the next clump of reeds and he sat down on the damp ground, looking at the wide sky, the red clouds, the emerging sun. It was getting hot.

Steam began to rise over the marsh.

Corum took off his helmet. His silver greaves were grimed with mud, his hands were filthy—even the six-fingered Hand of Kwll was coated in mire.

Steam moved slowly over the marsh as if seeking something. He wet his face and lips with the brackish water, tempted to remove his scarlet robe and his silver byrnie and yet, for the moment, preferring

359

their security should he be attacked by a larger marsh dweller than any he had so far seen.

Steam was everywhere. In places the mud bubbled and spat. The hot, damp air began to pain his throat and lungs and his eyelids became heavy as a great weariness came over him.

And it seemed to him that he saw a figure moving through the steam. A tall figure wading slowly through the boiling mud. A giant who dragged something heavy behind it. His head dropped to his chest and he raised it with difficulty. He no longer saw the figure. He realized that some marsh gas was making him drowsy, making him hallucinate.

He rubbed at his eyes but only succeeded in making his mortal eye fill with mud.

And then he felt a presence behind him.

He turned.

Something loomed there, as white and intangible as the steam. Something fell upon him, entangling his arms and legs. He tried to draw his sword but he could not free himself. He was carried upward and other creatures struggled nearby, snapping and shouting. The heat began to disperse and then it was terribly cold, so cold that all the other creatures were suddenly silent. Then it was dark.

And then it was wet. He spat salt water from his mouth and cursed. He was free again and he felt soft sand beneath his feet and he waded waist-deep through the water, the silver helm still clutched in his hand, and fell upon a dark yellow beach, gasping.

Corum thought he knew what had happened to him, but he found it hard to believe. For the third time he had seen the mysterious Wading God and for the third time the gigantic fisherman had influenced his destiny—first by hurling him upon the coast of the Ragha-da-Kheta, second by bringing Jhary-a-Conel to Moidel's Mount, and third by saving him from the marsh world—a world, it now appeared, which must be on one of the Fifteen Planes—as this new world must be.

If it were a new world, of course, and not merely part of the same one.

Whichever it was, it was an improvement. He began to pick himself up.

And he saw the old woman standing there. She was a dumpy little woman and her red face was at once frightened and prim. She was soaking wet and wringing out her bonnet with her hands.

"Who are you?" Corum said.

"Who are you, young man? I was walking along the beach minding my own business when this terrible wave suddenly appeared and completely drenched me! It is none of your doing, is it?"

"I hope not, ma'am."

"Are you some mariner, then, who has been shipwrecked?"

"That is the truth of it," Corum agreed. "Tell me, ma'am, where is this land?"

"You are near the fishing town of Chynezh Port, young sir. Up there," she pointed up the cliffs, "lies the great Balwyn Moor and then . . ."

"Balwyn Moor. Beyond it lies Darkvale, eh?"

The old woman pursed her lips. "Aye. Darkvale. None visits it these days, however."

"But that is the place of the Vanishing Tower?"

"So 'tis said."

"Is it possible to purchase a horse in Chynezh Port?"

"I suppose so. The horse breeders of Balwyn Moor are famous and they bring some of their best to Chynezh for the foreign trade—or did before the fighting."

"There is a war taking place?"

"Call it that. Things came out of the sea and attacked our boats. We have heard that folk have suffered much worse elsewhere and that we are relatively safe from the most dreadful of these monsters. But we lost half our menfolk and now none dares fish and, of course, no foreign ships put into our harbor to buy horses."

"So Chaos returns here, too," mused Corum. He sighed.

"You must aid me, old woman," he told her. "For I may in turn aid you and make these seas safe again. Now—the horse."

She led him along the beach and round a cliff and he saw a pleasant fishing town with a good, strong harbor and in the harbor were all their boats, their sails tightly furled.

"You see," she said. "Unless the boats go out again soon we of Chynezh Port shall starve, for fish is our livelihood."

"Aye." Corum put his mortal hand upon her shoulder. "Now, take me to where I can purchase a steed."

She led him to a stable on the outskirts of the town, near the road which wound up the cliff toward the moor. Here a peasant sold him a pair of horses, one white and one black, almost twins, with all the necessary gear. Corum had taken it into his head that he would need two horses, though he hardly knew why.

Riding the white horse and leading the black one, he began to ascend the winding road, making for Darkvale under the puzzled gaze of the old woman and the peasant. He reached the top and saw that the road went on along the cliff until it disappeared into a wooded dale. The day was warm and pleasant and it was hard to believe that this world was threatened by Chaos too. It was very much like his own land of Bro-an-Vadhagh and parts of the coastline even seemed half familiar.

He became filled with a sense of anticipation as he entered the wood and listened to the birdsong in the trees. It was very peaceful and yet something seemed strange. He slowed his horses to a walk, proceeding almost hesitantly.

And then he saw it ahead.

A black cloud on the road through the trees. A cloud which began to grumble with thunder and flash with lightning.

Corum reined in his horses and dismounted. From the neck of his byrnie he pulled out the crystal witch knife which the Lady Jane had given him. He strove to remember Bolorhiag's shouted words. *Go to the point where you see a storm which is isolated. Take out the witch knife given you by the Lady Jane. Hold it so that it traps the lightning. Then call upon the name of Elric of Melnibone and say that he must come to make the Three Who Are One . . . You are part of the same thing . . . The Third—the Many-Named Hero— will be drawn to the Two . . .*

"Well," he said to himself, "there is nothing else for it. In truth I'll need allies to go against Voilodion Ghagnasdiak in his Vanishing Tower. And if these allies are powerful, then so much the better."

With the crystal witch knife held aloft he stepped into the roaring cloud.

Lightning struck the witch knife and filled him with shivering energy. All about him was disturbance and noise. He opened his mouth and cried.

"Elric of Melnibone! You must come to make the Three Who Are One! Elric of Melnibone! You must come to make the Three Who Are One! Elric of Melnibone!"

And then a fierce bolt of lightning came down and shattered the witch knife, flung Corum down to the ground. Voices seemed to wail across the world, winds swept in all directions. He staggered upright wondering suddenly if he had been betrayed. He could see nothing but the lightning, hear nothing but the thunder.

He fell and struck his head. He began to raise himself to his feet.

And then mellow light filled the forest once more and the birds sang.

"The storm. It has gone." He looked about him and then he saw the man who lay on the grass. He recognized him. It was the man he had seen fighting on dragonback when he hung in Limbo. "And you? Are you called Elric of Melnibone?"

The albino got to his feet. His crimson eyes were full of a permanent sorrow. He answered politely enough.

"I am Elric of Melnibone. Are you to thank for rescuing me from those creatures Theleb K'aarna summoned?"

Corum shook his head. Elric was dressed in a travel-stained shirt and breeks of black silk. There were black boots on his feet and a black belt around his waist, which supported a black scabbard in which the albino sheathed a huge black broadsword carved from hilt to tip with peculiar runes. Over all this black was drawn a voluminous cloak of white silk with a large hood attached to it. Elric's milk-white hair seemed to flow over the cloak and blend with it.

" 'Twas I that summoned you," Corum admitted, "but I know of no Theleb K'aarna. I was told that I had only one opportunity to receive your aid and that I must take it in this particular place at this particular time. I am called Corum Jhaelen Irsei—the Prince in the Scarlet Robe—and I ride upon a quest of grave import."

Elric was frowning and looking about him. "Where is this forest?"

"It is nowhere on your plane or in your time, Prince Elric. I summoned you to aid me in my battle against the Lords of Chaos. Already I have been instrumental in destroying two of the Sword Rulers—Arioch and Xiombarg—but the third, the most powerful remains . . ."

"Arioch of Chaos—and Xiombarg?" The albino looked unconvinced. "You have destroyed two of the most powerful members of the company of Chaos? Yet but a month since I spoke with Arioch. He is my patron . . ."

Corum realized that Elric was not as familiar as he with the structure of the multiverse. "There are many planes of existence," he said as gently as he could. "In some the Lords of Chaos are strong. In some they are weak. In some, I have heard, they do not exist at all. You must accept that here Arioch and Xiombarg have been banished so that effectively they no longer exist in my world. It is the third of the Sword Rulers who threatens us now—the strongest, King Mabelrode."

The albino was frowning and Corum feared that the willful prince would choose not to aid him after all. "In my—plane—Mabelrode is no stronger than Arioch and Xiombarg. This makes a travesty of all my understanding . . ."

Corum drew a deep breath. "I will explain," he said, "as much as I can. For some reason Fate has selected me to be the hero who

363

must banish the domination of Chaos from the Fifteen Planes of Earth. I am at present traveling on my way to seek a city which we call Tanelorn, where I hope to find aid. But my guide is a prisoner in a castle close to here and before I can continue I must rescue him. I was told how I might summon aid to—help me effect this rescue. . . . And I used the spell to bring you to me. I—'' Corum hesitated a fraction of a second, for he knew that Bolorhiag had not told him this and yet he knew it was the truth he spoke—''was to tell you that if you aided me, then you would aid yourself—that if I was successful then you would receive something which would make your task easier . . .''

"Who told you this?"

"A wise man."

Corum watched the puzzled albino go and sit down upon a treetrunk and place his head in his hands. "I have been drawn away at an unfortunate time," said Elric. "I pray that you speak the truth to me, Prince Corum." Suddenly he looked up and fixed Corum with those strange, crimson eyes. "It is a marvel that you speak at all—or at least that I understand you. How can this be?"

"I was—informed that we should be able to communicate easily—because 'we are part of the same thing.' Do not ask me to explain more, Prince Elric, for I know no more."

"Well this may be an illusion. I may have killed myself or become digested by that machine of Theleb K'aarna's, but plainly I have no choice but to agree to aid you in the hope that I am, in turn, aided." The albino glanced hard at Corum.

Corum went to get the horses where he had left them further up the road. He returned with them as the albino stood up, his hands on his hips, staring around him. He knew what it was to be plunged suddenly into a new world and he sympathized with the Melnibonean. He handed the black horse's reins to Elric and the albino climbed into the saddle and stood upright in the stirrups for a moment as he got the feel of the trappings, for he was plainly not used to the particular kind of saddle and stirrup.

They began to ride.

"You spoke of Tanelorn," said Elric. "It is for the sake of Tanelorn that I find myself in this dreamworld of yours."

Corum was astonished at Elric's casual mention of Tanelorn. "You know where Tanelorn lies?"

"In my own world, aye—but why should it lie in this one?"

"Tanelorn lies in all planes, though in different guises. There is one Tanelorn and it is eternal with many forms."

The two men continued to make their way through the forest as they spoke. Corum could hardly believe that Elric was real—just as

364

Elric could hardly believe, it seemed, that this world was real. The albino rubbed his face several times and peered hard at Corum.

"Where go we now?" asked Elric finally. "To the castle?"

Corum spoke hesitantly, remembering Bolorhiag's words. "First we must have the Third Hero—the Many-Named Hero."

"And you will summon him with sorcery, too?"

Corum shook his head. "I was told not. I was told that he would meet us—drawn from whichever age he exists in by the necessity to complete the Three Who Are One."

"What mean these phrases? What is the Three Who Are One?"

"I know little more than you, friend Elric, save that it will need all three of us to defeat him who holds my guide prisoner."

Now they came to Balwyn Moor, leaving the forest behind them. On one side were the cliffs and the sea and the world was silent and at rest so that any threat from Chaos seemed very distant.

"Your gauntlet is of curious manufacture," Elric said.

Corum laughed. "So thought a doctor I lately encountered. He believed it was a man-made limb. But it is said to have belonged to a god—one of the Lost Gods, who mysteriously left the world millenia ago. Once it had special properties, just as this eye did. It could see into a netherworld—a terrible place from which I could sometimes draw aid."

"All you tell me makes the complicated sorceries and cosmologies of my world seem simple in comparison."

"It only seems complicated because it is strange," Corum answered. "Your world would doubtless seem incomprehensible to me if I were suddenly flung into it." Corum broke into laughter again. "Besides, this particular plane is not my world, either, though it resembles it more than do many. We have one thing in common, Elric, and that is that we are both doomed to play a role in the constant struggle between the Lords of the Higher Worlds—and we shall never understand why that struggle takes place, why it is eternal. We fight, we suffer agonies of mind and soul, but we are never sure that our suffering is worthwhile."

Elric plainly agreed completely. "You are right. We have much in common, you and I, Corum."

Corum looked down the road and there was a mounted man sitting stock still in his saddle. The warrior seemed to be waiting for them.

"Perhaps this is the Third of whom Bolorhiag spoke," said Corum as they slowed their pace and began, cautiously, to approach the warrior.

He was jet black with a huge, heavy, handsome head covered by

365

the snarling mask of a snarling bear, its pelt going down his back. The mask could be used for a visor, Corum thought, but was now pushed off the face to reveal the melancholy eyes. He wore featureless plate armor, which was also black and, like Elric, he had a great black-hilted sword in a black scabbard. The pair of them made Corum feel almost gaudy in comparison. The black warrior's horse was not black—it was a strong, tall roan, a war horse. Hanging from his saddle was a great round shield.

The man did not seem pleased to see them. Rather he was horrified.

"I know you! I know you both!" he gasped.

Corum had never seen the man before and yet he, too, felt recognition.

"How came you here to Balwyn Moor, friend?" he asked.

The black warrior licked his lips, his eyes almost glazed. "Balwyn Moor? This is Balwyn Moor? I have been here but a few moments. Before that I was—I was. . . . Ah! The memory starts to fade again." He pressed one massive black hand to his brow. "A name—another name! No more! Elric! Corum! But I—I am now . . ."

"How do you know our names?" cried Elric, aghast.

The man replied in a whisper. "Because—don't you see?—I am Elric—I am Corum—oh, this is the worst agony. . . . Or, at least, I have been or am to be Elric and Corum . . ."

Corum was sympathetic. He remembered what Jhary had told him of the Champion Eternal. "Your name, sir?"

"A thousand names are mine. A thousand heroes I have been. Ah! I am—I am—John Daker—Erekosë—Urlik—many, many, many more. . . . The memories, the dreams, the existences." He stared at them suddenly through his pain-filled eyes. "Do you not understand? I am he who has been called the Champion Eternal—I am the hero who has existed forever—and, yes, I am Elric of Melniboné—Prince Corum Jhaelen Irsei—I am you, also. We three are the same creature and a myriad of other creatures besides. We three are one thing—doomed to struggle forever and never understand why. Oh! My head pounds. Who tortures me so? Who?"

From beside Corum Elric spoke. "You say you are another incarnation of myself?"

"If you would phrase it so! You are both other incarnations of *myself*!"

"So," Corum said, "that is what Bolorhiag meant by the Three Who Are One. We are all aspects of the same man, yet we have tripled our strength because we have been drawn from three different ages. It is the only power which might successfully go against Voilodion Ghagnasdiak of the Vanishing Tower."

Elric spoke quietly. "Is that the castle wherein your guide is imprisoned?"

"Aye." Corum took a stronger grip on the reins. "The Vanishing Tower flickers from one plane to another, from one age to another, and exists in a single location only for a few moments at a time. But because we are three separate incarnations of a single hero it is possible that we form a sorcery of some kind which will enable us to follow the tower and attack it. Then, if we free my guide, we can continue on to Tanelorn . . ."

The black warrior raised his head, hope beginning to replace despair. "Tanelorn! I, too, seek Tanelorn. Only there may I discover some remedy to my dreadful fate—which is to know all previous incarnations and be hurled at random from one existence to another! Tanelorn—I must find her!"

"I, too, must discover Tanelorn." The albino seemed half amused, as if beginning to enjoy the strange situation. "For on my own plane her inhabitants are in great danger."

"So we have a common purpose as well as a common identity," said Corum. Perhaps now there was some chance of saving Jhary and finding Rhalina. "Therefore we shall fight in concert, I pray. First we must free my guide, then go on to Tanelorn."

The black giant growled, "I'll aid you willingly."

Corum bowed his head in thanks. "And what shall we call you—you who are ourselves?"

"Call me Erekosë—though another name suggests itself to me—for it was as Erekosë that I came closest to knowing forgetfulness and the fulfillment of love."

The black giant shook his reins and fell in beside Corum. He gave Elric a sideways stare and his mouth was crooked. "You have no inkling of what it is I must forget." He turned to the Prince in the Scarlet Robe. "Now Corum—which way to the Vanishing Tower?"

"This road leads to it. We ride down now to Darkvale, I believe."

With a man who was a shadow of himself on either side of him, with a sense of doom filling his mind when it should have begun to feel hope, Corum guided his horse down toward Darkvale.

BOOK THREE

In which Prince Corum discovers far more than Tanelorn

The First Chapter

VOILODION GHAGNASDIAK

Now the road narrowed and became much steeper. Corum saw it disappear into the black shadows between two high cliffs and he knew that he had come to Darkvale.

He felt ill at ease still, with the two men who were himself, and he fought not to brood upon the implications of what all this meant. He pointed down the hill and spoke as lightly as possible.

"Darkvale." He looked at the albino face on one side of him, the jet black face on the other. Both were grim and set. "I am told there was a village here once. An uninviting spot, eh—brothers . . ."

"I have seen worse." Erekosë clapped his legs hard against his horse's sides. "Come, let's get all this done with . . ." He spurred the roan ahead and galloped wildly down toward the gap in the cliffs.

Corum followed him more slowly and Elric was the slowest of all. As he rode into the darkness, Corum looked up. The cliffs came so close together at the top that they met, cutting off all but a little light. And at the foot of the cliffs were ruins—what was left of the town of Darkvale after Chaos came against it. The ruins were all twisted and warped as if they had become liquid and then turned solid again. Corum searched for the most likely spot where he would find the Vanishing Tower and at last he came to a pit which seemed freshly dug. He inspected it closely. It was of a size with the Vanishing Tower. "Here is where we must wait," he said.

Elric joined him. "What must we wait for, friend Corum?"

"For the tower. I would guess that this is where it appears when it is in this plane."

"And when will it appear?"

"At no particular time. We must wait. And then, as soon as we see it we must rush it and attempt to enter before it vanishes again, moving on to the next plane."

Corum looked for Erekosë. The black giant was sitting on the ground with his back against a slab of the twisted rock. Elric approached him.

"You seem more patient than I, Erekosë."

"I have learned patience, for I have lived since time began and will live on at the end of time."

Elric loosened his horse's girth strap, calling out to Corum. "Who told you that the Tower would appear here?"

"A sorcerer who doubtless serves Law as I do, for I am a mortal doomed to battle Chaos."

"As am I," said Erekosë.

"As am I," said the albino, "though I'm sworn to serve it." He shrugged and looked strangely at the other two. Corum guessed what he was thinking. "And why do you seek Tanelorn, Erekosë?"

Erekosë stared up at the crack of light where the cliffs met. "I have been told that I may find peace there—and wisdom—a means of returning to the world of the Eldren where dwells the woman I love, for it has been said that since Talenorn exists in all planes at all times it is easier for a man who dwells there to pass between the planes, discover the particular one he seeks. What interest have you in Talenorn, Lord Elric?"

"I know Talenorn and I know that you are right to seek it. My mission seems to be the defense of that city upon my own plane—but even now my friends may be destroyed by that which has been brought against them. I pray Corum is right and that in the Vanishing Tower I shall find a means to defeat Theleb K'aarna's beasts and their masters . . ."

Corum raised his jeweled hand to his jeweled eye. "I seek Tanelorn for I have heard the city can aid me in my struggle against Chaos." He said no more of Arkyn's whispered instructions so long ago in the Temple of Law.

"But Tanelorn," Elric told him, "will fight neither Law nor Chaos. That is why she exists for eternity."

Corum had heard as much from Jhary. "Aye," he said. "Like Erekosë I do not seek swords, but wisdom."

When night came the three took turns to stand watch, occasionally conversing, but more often than not merely sitting or standing and staring at the place where the Vanishing Tower might appear.

Corum found his two companions rather heavy company after Jhary and he felt a certain dislike for them, perhaps because they were so much like himself.

But then at dawn, while Erekosë nodded and Elric slept soundly, the air shuddered and Corum saw the familiar outlines of Voilodion Ghagnasdiak's tower begin to grow solid.

"It is here!" he shouted. Erekosë sprang up at once but Elric was only just stirring. "Hasten Elric!"

Now Elric joined them and he, like Erekosë, had his black sword in his hand. The swords were almost brothers—both black, both terrible in aspect, both carved with runes.

Corum was ahead of the others, determined not to be shut out this time. He ran into the dark doorway and was at first blinded, shouting for his friends to join him. "Hasten! Hasten!"

Corum ran into a small antechamber and saw that reddish light illuminated the room, spilling from a great oil lamp which hung in chains from the ceiling. But then the door closed suddenly behind them and Corum knew they were trapped, prayed that they three would be powerful enough to resist the sorcerer. His eyes caught a movement at the slit window in the wall. Darkvale had gone and there was nothing but blue sea where it had been. The tower was already moving. He pointed it out silently to his companions.

Then he raised his head and yelled, "Jhary! Jhary-a-Conel!"

Was the dandy dead? He prayed that he was not.

He listened carefully and heard a tiny noise which might have been a reply.

"Jhary!"

Corum motioned with his long, strong sword. "Voilodion Ghagnasdiak? Am I to be thwarted? Have you left this place?"

"I have not left it. What do you want with me?"

Corum looked toward the next room, beneath a pointed arch. He led the way forward.

Brightness like the golden brightness he had seen in Limbo flickered and framed the humped shape of Voilodion Ghagnasdiak—a dwarf, overdressed in silks, ermine, and satin, a miniature sword clutched in his coarse hand, a handsome head upon his tiny shoulders, bright eyes beneath thick black brows, which met in the middle, a grin of welcome like the grin of a wolf. "At last someone new to relieve my ennui. But lay down your swords, gentlemen, I beg you, for you are to be my guests."

371

"I know what fate your guests may expect," Corum said. "Know this, Voilodion Ghagnasdiak, we have come to release Jhary-a-Conel, whom you hold prisoner. Give him up to us and we will not harm you."

The dwarf's handsome features grinned impishly back at Corum. "But I am very powerful. You cannot defeat me." He opened his arms. "Watch."

Waving his sword he made more lightning flash here and there in the room and forced Elric to half-raise his sword as if it attacked him. Plainly this made him feel foolish and he stepped toward the dwarf. "Know this, Voilodion Ghagnasdiak, I am Elric of Melnibone and I have much power. I bear the Black Sword and it thirsts to drink your soul unless you release Prince Corum's friend!"

The dwarf's mirth was not abated. "Swords? What power have they?"

Erekosë growled, "Our swords are not ordinary blades. And we have been brought here by forces you could not comprehend—wrenched from our own ages by the power of the gods themselves—specifically to demand that this Jhary-a-Conel be given up to us."

"You are deceived," said Voilodion Ghagnasdiak, addressing all three. "Or you seek to deceive me. This Jhary is a witty fellow, I'd agree, but what interest could gods have in him?"

The albino impulsively raised his great black sword and Corum heard a sound like a moan of bloodlust come from it. He thought the sword an unhealthy weapon to bear.

But then Elric was hurtling backward, his sword flying from his grip. Voilodion Ghagdasdiak had merely bounced a yellow ball off his forehead—but it had been powerful.

Corum let Erekosë go to Elric's aid and while he kept his attention on the sorcerer, but as soon as Elric was on his feet Voilodion hurled another ball and this time the black sword deflected it so that it bounced harmelssly toward the far wall and then exploded. The heat seared their faces and the blast knocked the wind from them. Corum saw a blackness begin to writhe from the fire left behind by the explosion.

Voilodion Ghagnasdiak spoke equably enough. "It is dangerous to destroy the globes," he said, "for now what is in them will destroy you."

The black thing increased its size and the flame disappeared. "I am free."

The voice came from the writhing shadow.

Voilodion Ghagnasdiak chuckled. "Aye. Free to kill these fools who reject my hospitality!"

"Free to be slain!" Elric cried impetuously.

Corum stared in terrified fascination as the thing began to grow like flowing, sentient hair, which then slowly compressed and became a creature with a tiger's head, a gorilla's body, and a hide as coarse as that of a rhinoceros. Black wings sprouted on its back and these flapped rapidly as if shifted its grip on its weapon—a long, scythelike thing which lashed out at the nearest man, the albino.

Corum moved to help Elric, remembering that Elric might be relying on him to use the power of the hand and the eye. He shouted, "My eye—it will not see into the netherworld. I cannot summon help."

But then Corum sat one of the yellow balls coming at him and another being flung at Erekosë. Both managed to deflect them so that they landed on the ground and burst. More winged monsters emerged and soon Corum had no time to think of aiding Elric, for he was concerned with fighting for his own life, ducking the whistling scythe as it sought to decapitate him.

Several times Corum managed to get under the monster's guard, but even when he did the thick skin turned his thrusts. And the beast moved quickly—far faster than it would seem it could. Sometimes it would leap into the air, hovering on its wings before sweeping down on Corum again.

The Prince in the Scarlet Robe began to think that he had been deceived by Chaos into coming here, for the other two were as helpless against the monsters as was he.

He cursed himself for overconfidence and wished that they had formed a more coherent plan before rushing into the Vanishing Tower.

And over the sound of battle came the screeches of Voilodion Ghagnasdiak as he threw more of the yellow spheres into the room and they burst and more tiger-headed monsters formed in the air and pressed into the fray. The three men found themselves pushed back to the far wall.

"I fear I have summoned you two to your destruction." Corum was panting and his sword arm was weary. "I had no warning that our powers would be so limited here. The tower must shift so fast that even the ordinary laws of sorcery do not apply within its walls."

Elric defended himself as two scythes swung at him at the same time. "They seem to work well enough for the dwarf! If I could slay but a single . . ."

One of the scythes drew blood and another ripped the albino's cloak. Yet another slashed his arm. Corum tried to help him, but a blade ripped his silver byrnie and another nicked his ear. He saw

Elric stab a tiger-monster in the throat without seeming to harm the beast at all. He heard Elric's sword howl as if in fury at being thwarted of its prey.

Then Corum saw Elric grab a scythe from the hands of the tiger-thing and reverse it. The albino stabbed the monster in the chest and then blood spurted in earnest and the thing screamed as it was mortally wounded.

"I was right!" called the Prince of Melnibone. "Only their own weapons can harm them!" His runesword in one hand and the scythe in the other he charged at another flapping beast, then moved toward Voilodion Ghagnasdiak, who screeched and ran toward a small doorway.

The tiger-creatures had bunched near the ceiling. Now they flew down again. Corum made every effort to wrest one of the scythes from the beast who attacked him. Then his chance came when Elric took one in the back and sliced off his head. Corum picked up the dead thing's scythe and slashed at a third tiger-man, who fell with his throat ripped out. Corum kicked the fallen scythe in Erekosë's direction.

The air was full of a sickening stench and black feathers stuck to the sweat and the blood on Corum's face and hands. He led the others back to the door through which they had entered the room and there they were able to defend themselves the better, for only so many of the creatures could come through at a time.

Corum felt mightily tired and he knew that he and his companions were bound to lose this struggle for, from his cover, Voilodion Ghagnasdiak was still throwing more globes into the room. Then he saw something fluttering behind the dwarf but, before he could make out what it was, a tiger-man blocked his view and he was forced to swing his body aside to avoid the blow of a scythe.

Then Corum heard a voice and when he next looked Voilodion Ghagnasdiak was struggling with something which clung to his face and Jhary-a-Conel stood there signaling to an astonished Elric, who had just noticed him.

"Jhary!" shouted Corum.

"The one you came to save?" Elric slashed open the belly of yet another tiger beast.

"Aye."

Elric was closest to Jhary and he prepared himself to cross the room. Jhary shouted back, "No! No! Stay there!"

There was no need for the remark for Elric was once again engaged with two of the tiger monsters, who attacked him from both sides.

Jhary called out desperately. "You misunderstood what Bolorhiag told you."

Now Elric could see Jhary again, as could Erekosë. The black giant had, up to that time, been absorbed in the killing, seeming to take more pleasure in it than the others.

"Link arms! Corum in the center!" Jhary called. "And you two draw your swords!"

Corum knew enough to guess that Jhary understood more than he had mentioned earlier. And now Elric was wounded in the leg.

"Hurry!" Jhary-a-Conel stood over the swarf who strove to rip the thing from his face. "It is your only chance—and mine!"

Elric seemed uncertain.

"He is wise, my friend," Corum told the albino. "He knows many things which we do not. Here, I will stand in the center."

Erekosë seemed to awaken from a trance. He looked at Corum over his bloody scythe, shook his great black head, and then placed his right arm in Corum's, his sword in his left hand. Elric linked his left arm in Corum's right arm and drew his own strange sword.

And then Corum felt a power flow into his weary flesh and he almost laughed with delight at the sense of pleasure which filled him. Elric, himself, was laughing and even Erekosë smiled. They had combined. They had become the Three Who Are One and they moved as one, laughed as one, fought as one.

Although Corum did not fight, he felt as if he fought. He felt that he had a sword in each hand and that he guided those hands.

The tiger-beasts fell back before the shrieking runeswords. They sought to escape this strange new power. They flapped wildly about the room.

Corum laughed in triumph. "Let us finish them!" And he knew they cried the same thing. No longer were their swords useless against the winged tiger-men. Instead they were invincible. Blood poured down as wounded beasts sought to escape, but none did escape.

As if weakened by the power released within it, the Vanishing Tower began to tremble. The floor tilted. Voilodion Ghagnasdiak's voice screamed from somewhere, "The tower! The tower! This will destroy the tower!"

Corum could hardly keep his balance on the blood-slippery floor.

And then Jhary-a-Conel had entered the room, an expression of faint disgust on his face as he regarded the slaughter. "It is true. The sorcery we have worked today must have its effect. Whiskers—to me!"

And then Corum realized that the creature which had clung to

Voilodion Ghagnasdiak's face was the little black-and-white cat. Once again it had been the cause of their salvation. It flew to Jhary's shoulder and settled there, staring about with wide, green eyes.

Elric broke away from the other two and dashed into the other room to peer through the window slit. Corum heard him cry, "We are in Limbo!"

Slowly Corum broke his own link with Erekosë. He did not have the energy to see what Elric meant, but he guessed that the tower was in that timeless, spaceless place where once he had been in the sky ship. And it was swaying even more crazily now. He looked at the crumpled figure of the dwarf, who had his hands to his face. Through the fingers welled fountains of blood.

Jhary went past Corum into the other room and spoke to Elric. As he returned Corum heard him say, "Come, friend Elric, help me seek my hat."

"At such a time you look for a—hat?"

"Aye." Jhary winked at Corum and stroked his cat. "Prince Corum—Lord Erekosë—will you come with me, too?"

They went past the weeping dwarf, down the narrow tunnel, until they came to a flight of stairs. The stairs led toward a cellar. The tower quaked. With a lighted brand held aloft Jhary led them down the steps.

When a slab of masonry dislodged itself from the roof and fell at Elric's feet he said quietly, "I would prefer to seek a means of escape from the tower. If it falls now we shall be buried."

"Trust me, Prince Elric."

They came at length to a circular room with a huge metal door set in it.

"Voilodion's vault. Here you will find all the things you seek," said Jhary. "And I, I hope, will find my hat. The hat was specially made and is the only one which properly matches my other clothes . . ."

"How do we open a door like that?" Erekosë sheathed his sword in an angry gesture. Then he drew it out again and put the point to the door. "It is made of steel, surely."

Jhary's voice was almost amused again. "If you linked arms again, my friends."

Corum offered Jhary an amused glance in spite of the danger.

"I will show you how the door may be opened," said Jhary.

And so they linked arms again and again the vast, exquisite sense of strength flowed through them and again they laughed to each other, feeling true fulfillment now that they were combined.

Perhaps this was their destiny. Perhaps when they ceased to be individual heroes they would become the one thing again and then they would experience happiness. It offered them hope, this thought.

Jhary said quietly, "And now, Prince Corum, if you would strike with your foot once upon the door . . ."

Corum swung his foot and kicked at the solid steel and watched as the door fell down without resistance. He did not like to break the link with his fellow heroes. He could see how they could live as a single entity and know satisfaction. But he was forced to in order to enter the vault.

The tower shook and seemed to fall sideways and the four of them tumbled into Voilodion's vault to land amongst treasure.

Corum picked himself up. Elric was inspecting a golden throne. Erekosë had picked up a battle-axe too big for even him to wield.

Here were the things Voilodion had stolen from all his victims as his tower had traveled through the planes.

Corum wondered if ever such a museum had existed before. He went from object to object inspecting them and marveling. Meanwhile Jhary handed something to Elric and spoke with him. Corum heard Elric say to Jhary, "How can you know all this?"

Jhary made some vague reply and then bent with a cry of pleasure. He picked up his hat and began to slap at the dust which covered it. Then he saw another thing and picked that up. A goblet. "Take it," he told Corum. "It will prove useful, I think."

Jhary walked over to a corner and removed a small sack, placing it on his shoulder. There was a jewel chest nearby and he delved through this until he discovered a ring. This he handed to Erekosë. "This is your reward, Erekosë, for helping to free me from my captor." He spoke grandly but self-mockingly.

Even Erekosë smiled then. "I have the feeling you need no help, young man."

"You are mistaken, friend Erekosë. I doubt if I have ever been in greater peril." He took a lingering look around the room and then lost his footing as the floor tilted once more.

"We should take steps to leave," said Elric, the bundle of metal under his arm.

"Exactly." Jhary moved rapidly across the vault. "The last thing. In his pride Voilodion showed me his possessions, but he did not know the value of all of them."

Corum frowned. "What do you mean?"

"He killed the traveler who brought this with him. The traveler was right in assuming he had the means to stop the tower from

377

vanishing, but he did not have time to use it before Voilodion slew him.'' Jhary displayed the object. It was a small baton of a dull ocher color. It hardly seemed valuable. ''Here it is. The Runestaff. Hawkmoon had this with him when I traveled with him to the Dark Empire.''

The Second Chapter

TO TANELORN

"What is the Runestaff?" Corum asked.

"I remember one description—but I am poor at naming and explaining things . . ."

Elric almost smiled. "That has not escaped my attention."

Corum looked closely at the staff, unable to believe it had any special significance.

"It is an object," said Jhary, "which can exist only under a certain set of special and physical laws. In order to continue to exist, it must exert a field in which it can contain itself. That field must accord with those laws—the same laws under which we best survive."

Large slabs of masonry fell from the roof.

Erekosë growled. "The tower is breaking up!"

Corum saw that Jhary was passing his hand in a stroking motion over the dull ocher staff, tracing out a pattern. "Please gather near me, my friends."

As the three closed in, the roof of the tower fell. Corum saw great blocks of stone descend to crush him and then he was staring at a blue sky breathing cool air and the ground was firm beneath his feet. Yet from only a few inches on all sides of them there was blackness—the total blackness of Limbo. "Do not step outside this small area," Jhary said, "or you will be doomed." He frowned. "Let the Runestaff seek what we seek."

Corum knew his friend's voice and he knew that it was not as confident as usual.

The ground changed color, the air was hot and then freezingly cold and Corum realized that they were moving rapidly through the planes as the Vanishing Tower had traveled, but they were not moving at random, he was sure of that.

Now there was sand beneath Corum's feet and a hot wind blowing in his face and Jhary was shouting, "Now!"

Running with the others into the blackness, Corum burst into sunlight and saw a glowing metallic sky.

"A desert," Erekosë said softly. "A vast desert . . ."

On all sides rolled yellow dunes and the wind was sad as it whispered across them.

Jhary was plainly pleased with himself. "Do you recognize it, friend Elric?"

Elric was relieved. "Is it the Sighing Desert?"

"Listen."

Elric listened to the sad wind but he looked at something else. Corum turned his head and saw that Jhary had dropped the Runestaff, that it was fading.

"Are you all to come with me to the defense of Tanelorn?" Elric asked Jhary, doubtless expecting him to assent.

But Jhary shook his head. "No. We go the other way. We go to seek the device Theleb K'aarna activated with the help of the Lords of Chaos. Where lies it?"

Elric searched the dunes with his eyes. He frowned and then pointed hesitantly. "That way, I think."

"Then let us go to it now."

"But I must try to help Tanelorn!" Elric protested.

"You must destroy the device after we have used it, friend Elric, lest Theleb K'aarna or his like try to activate it again."

"But Tanelorn . . ."

Corum listened with curiosity to the conversation. Why did Jhary know so much of Elric's world and its needs?

"I do not believe," said Jhary calmly, "that Theleb K'aarna and his beasts have yet reached the city."

"Not reached it! But so much time has passed!"

"Less than a day," said Jhary.

Corum wondered if that applied to them all or just to Elric's world. He sympathized with the albino as he rubbed his hand over his face and wondered whether to trust Jhary. Then he said, "Very well. I will take you to the machine."

"But if Tanelorn lies so near," Corum said to Jhary, "why seek it elsewhere?"

"Because this is not the Tanelorn we wish to find," Jhary told him.

"It will suit me," Erekosë said almost humbly. "I will remain with Elric. Then, perhaps . . ." There was longing in his eyes.

But Jhary was horrified. "My friend," he said sadly, "already much of time and space is threatened with destruction. Eternal barriers could soon fall—the fabric of the multiverse could decay. You do not understand. Such a thing as has happened in the Vanishing Tower can happen only once in an eternity and even then it is dangerous to all concerned. You must do as I say. I promise that you will have just as good a chance of finding Tanelorn where I take you.''

Erekosë bowed his head. ''Very well.''

''Come.'' Elric was impatient, already walking away from them. ''For all your talk of time, there is precious little left for me.''

''For all of us,'' said Jhary feelingly.

They stumbled through the desert and the mourning wind found an echo of sadness in their own souls, but at last they came to a place of rocks, a natural amphitheater which had in its center a deserted camp. Tent flaps slapped as the wind blew them, but it was not the tent which drew their attention, it was the great bowl in the center of the amphitheater—a bowl which contained something far stranger than anything Corum had seen in Gwlas-an-Gwrys or in the world of Lady Jane Pentallyon. It had many planes and curves and angles of many colors and it dizzied him to look upon it too long.

''What is it?'' he murmured.

''A machine,'' Jhary told him, ''used by the ancients. It is what I have been seeking to take us to Tanelorn.''

''But why not go with Elric to *his* Tanelorn?''

''We have the geography but we still need the time and the dimension,'' Jhary said. ''Bear with me, Corum, for, unless we are stopped, we shall soon see the Tanelorn we seek.''

''And we shall find aid against Glandyth?''

''That I cannot tell you.''

Jhary went up to the machine in the bowl and he walked around it as if familiar with it. He seemed satisfied. He began to trace patterns on the bowl and these brought responses in the machine. Something deep within it began to pulse like a heart. The planes and curves and angles began to shift subtly and change color. A sense of urgency came about Jhary's movements then. He made Corum and Erekosë stand with their backs pressed against the bowl and he took a small vial from his jerkin, handing it to Elric.

''When we have departed,'' said Jhary, ''hurl this through the top of the bowl, take your horse, which I still see yonder and ride as fast as you can for Tanelorn. Follow these instructions perfectly and you will serve us all.''

Gingerly, Elric took the vial. ''Very well.''

Jhary smiled a secret smile as he stood beside the other two. ''And please give my compliments to my brother Moonglum.''

Elric's crimson eyes widened. ''You know him? What—?''

381

"Farewell, Elric. We shall doubtless meet many times in the future, though we may not recognize each other."

Elric stood there, his white face stained by the light from the bowl.

"And that will be for the best, I suppose," Jhary added under his breath, looking at the albino with some sympathy.

But Elric was gone, as was the desert, as was the machine in the bowl.

Then something like an invisible hand threw them backward.

Jhary sighed with satisfaction. "The machine is destroyed. That is good."

"But how may we return to our own plane?" Corum asked. They were surrounded by tall, waving grass—grass so high that it grew over their heads. "Where is Erekosë?"

"Gone on. Gone down his own road to Tanelorn," Jhary said. He looked at the sun. He took a bunch of the thick grass and wiped his face with it. There was dew on the grass and it refreshed him. "As we must now go down ours."

"Tanelorn is close?" Excitement suffused Corum. "Is it close, Jhary?"

"It is close. I feel its closeness."

"This is your city? You know its inhabitants?"

"This is my city. Tanelorn is ever my city. But this Tanelorn I do not know. I think I know of it, however—I hope I do or all my poor scheming will be for nothing."

"What are those schemes, Jhary? You must tell me more."

"I can tell you little. I knew of Elric's plight because I once rode with Elric—still do as far as he is concerned. Also I knew how to aid Erekosë, because I was once—or shall be—his friend, too. But it is not wisdom which guides me, Prince Corum. It is instinct. Come."

And he led the way through the tall, waving grass as if he followed a well-marked road.

The Third Chapter

THE CONJUNCTION OF THE MILLION SPHERES

And there was Tanelorn.

It was a blue city and it gave off a strong blue aura which merged with the expanse of the blue sky which framed it, but its buildings were of such a variety of shades of blue as to make them seem many-colored. These tall spires and domes clustered together and intersected and adjoined each other and rose in wild spirals and curves, seeming to fling themselves joyfully at the heavens as if silently delighting in their own blue beauty, in all their colors from near-black to pale violet, in all their shapes of shining metal.

"It is not a mortal settlement," whispered Corum Jhaelen Irsei as he emerged with Jhary-a-Conel from the tall grass and drew his scarlet robe about him, feeling insignificant beneath the splendor of the city.

"I'll grant you that," said Jhary almost grimly. "It is not a Tanelorn which I have seen before. Why this is almost sinister, Corum . . ."

"What mean you?"

"It is beautiful and it is wondrous, but it might almost be some false Talenorn or some counter-Tanelorn, or some Tanelorn existing in an utterly different logic . . ."

"I hardly follow you. You spoke of peace. Well, this Tanelorn is peaceful. You said that there were many Talenorns and that they have existed before the beginning of time and will exist when time is ended. And if this Tanelorn is stranger than some you know, what of that?"

Jhary drew a heavy breath. "I believe I have some inkling of the truth now. If Tanelorn exists upon the only area in the multiverse not subject to flux, then it might have other purposes than to act as a resting place for weary heroes and the like . . ."

383

"You think we are in danger there?"

"Danger? It depends what you regard as dangerous. Some wisdom may be dangerous to one man and not to another. Danger is contained in safety, as you have discovered, and safety in danger. The nearest we ever come to knowing truth is when we are witnesses to a paradox and therefore—I should have considered this before—Tanelorn must be a paradox, too. We had best enter the city, Corum, and learn why we have been drawn here."

Corum hesitated. "Mabelrode threatens to vanquish Law. Glandyth-a-Krae aims to conquer my plane. Rhalina is lost. We have much to sacrifice if we have made a mistake, Jhary."

"Aye. All."

"Then should we not first make certain that we are not victims of some cosmic deceit."

Jhary turned and laughed aloud. "And how may we decide that, Corum Jhaelen Irsei?"

Corum glared at Jhary and then lowered his eyes. "You are right. We will enter this Tanelorn."

They crossed a lawn made blue by the light from the city and they stood at the beginning of a wide avenue lined with blue plants and breathed air which was not quite like the air of any of the planes they had visited.

And Corum becan to weep at the sight of so much marvelous beauty, falling to his knees as if in worship, feeling that he would give his life to it willingly. And Jhary, standing beside his friend and placing a hand on his bowed shoulder, murmured, "Ah, this is still truly Tanelorn."

Corum's very body seemed lighter as he and Jhary wandered down the avenue and looked for the inhabitants of Tanelorn. Corum began to feel sure that there would be help here, that Mabelrode could, after all, be defeated, that his folk and the folk of Lywm-an-Esh could be stopped from slaying one another. And yet, though they wandered long, no citizens of Tanelorn emerged to greet them. All there was was silence.

At the end of the avenue Corum now made out a shape standing framed against a complicated fountain of blue water. The shape seemed to be that of a statue, the first representation of its kind Corum had seen in the city. And there was a slight suggestion of familiarity about it which made him begin to hope, for, in the back of his mind, he equated this statue with salvation, though he did not know why.

He began to walk more swiftly until Jhary held him back, a restraining hand on his arm. "Rush not, Corum, in Tanelorn."

The statue's detail became clearer as they advanced.

It was more barbaric in appearance than the rest of the city and it was predominantly green rather than blue. It did not seem to be of the same manufacture as the spires and the domes. It stood upon four legs arranged at each corner of its torso. It had four arms, two folded and two at its side. It had a large, human head but no nose. Instead, its nostrils were set directly into the head. The mouth was much wider than a human mouth and it was molded so that it grinned. The eyes glittered and they too were completely unlike human eyes but rather resembled clusters of jewels.

"The eyes . . ." Corum murmured, drawing still closer.

"Aye." Jhary knew what he meant.

The statue was not much taller than Corum and its whole body was encrusted with the dark, glowing jewels. He reached out to touch it but then stopped, for he had seen one of the folded arms and realization was beginning to freeze his bones. On the right arm was a six-fingered hand. But on the left arm was no hand at all. The mate of the right hand was attached to Corum's wrist. He tried to retreat, his heart beating and his head pounding so that he could hear nothing else.

Slowly the grin on the statue's alien face widened still further. Slowly the hands at the sides came up toward Corum.

Then came the voice.

Never had Corum heard such a mixture of sound. Intelligent, savage, humorous, barbaric, cold, warm, soft, and harsh, there were a thousand qualities in it as it said, "The key may still not be mine until it is offered willingly."

The faceted eyes, twins of the one in Corum's skull, gleamed and shifted, while still the other two arms remained folded and the four legs remained as if paralyzed.

In his shock, Corum could not speak. He was as petrified as the being seemed to be. Jhary stepped up beside him.

Quietly the dandy said, "You are Kwll."

"I am Kwll."

"And Tanelorn is your prison?"

"It has been my prison . . ."

". . . for only Timeless Tanelorn may hold a being of your power. I understand."

"But even Tanelorn cannot hold me unless I am incomplete."

Jhary lifted Corum's limp left arm. He touched the six-fingered hand which was grafted there. "And this will make you complete."

"It is the key to my release. But the key may still not be mine until it is offered willingly."

"And you have worked for this, have you not, through the power

385

of your brain, which is not held by Tanelorn. It was not the Balance which allowed Elric and Erekosë to join this part of them called Corum. It was you, for only you or your brother is strong enough, though you be prisoners, to defy the essential laws—the Law of the Balance."

"Only Kwll and Rhynn are so strong, for only one law rules them."

"And you broke it. Eternities ago, you broke it. You fought each other and Rhynn struck off your hand while, Kwll, you took out Rhynn's eye. You forgot your vows to each other—the sole vows you would ever consider obeying—and Rhynn, he—"

"He brought me here to Tanelorn and here I have remained, through all those cycles, those many cycles."

"And Rhynn, your brother? What punishment did you decree he suffer?"

"That he search, without rest, for his missing eye, but that he must find the eye alone, not with the hand."

"And the eye and hand have always been together."

"As they are now."

"And so Rhynn has never succeeded."

"It is as you say, mortal. You know much."

"It is because," answered Jhary, seeming to speak to himself, "because I am one of those mortals doomed to immortality."

"The key must be offered willingly," said Kwll again.

"Was it your shadow I saw in the Flamelands?" Corum asked suddenly, moving back from the being on trembling legs. "Was it you I saw on the hill from Castle Erorn?"

"You saw my shadow, aye. But you did not, could not see me. And I saved your life in the Flamelands and elsewhere. I used my hand and I killed your enemies."

"They were not enemies," Corum clutched the six-fingered hand to him, looking at it with loathing. "And you gave the hand the power to summon the dead to my aid?"

"The hand has that power. It is nothing. A trick."

"And you did this merely with your brain—your thoughts?"

"I have done more than that. The key must be offered willingly. I cannot force you, mortal, to give me back my hand."

"And if I keep it?"

"Then I shall have to wait through the Cycle of Cycles once again until the Million Spheres are again in conjunction. Have you not understood that?"

"I have come to understand it," Jhary said gravely. "How else could so many planes be open to mortals? How else could so many

386

discover fragments of wisdom usually denied them? How else could three aspects of the same entity exist upon the same plane? How else could I remember other existences? It is the Conjunction of the Million Spheres. A conjunction which takes place so rarely that a being could think he lived for eternity and still not witness it. And when that conjunction takes place, I have heard, old laws are broken and new ones established—the very nature of space and time and reality are altered."

"Would that mean the end of Tanelorn?" Corum asked.

"Perhaps even the end of Tanelorn," said Kwll, "but of that alone I am not sure. The key must be offered willingly."

"And what do I release if I offer the key?" Corum said to Jhary.

Jhary-a-Conel shook his head and took his little black-and-white cat partly from within his jerkin and stroked its head, deep in thought.

"You release Kwll," said Kwll. "You release Rhynn. Both has paid his price."

"What shall I do, Jhary?"

"I do not . . ."

"Shall I strike a bargain? Shall I say that he may have his hand if he will help us against the King of the Swords, help us restore peace to my land, help us find Rhalina?"

Jhary shrugged.

"What shall I do, Jhary?"

But Jhary refused to reply, so Corum looked directly into the face of Kwll. "I will give you back your hand on condition that you will use your great powers to destroy the rule of Chaos on the Fifteen Planes, that you will slay Mabelrode, the King of the Swords, that you will help me discover where my love, the Lady Rhalina, lies, that you will help me bring peace to my own world so that it may dwell under the rule of Law. Say you will do this."

"I will do it."

"Then willingly I offer you the key. Take your hand, Lost God, for it has brought me little but pain!"

"You fool!" It was Jhary shouting. "I told you that . . ."

But his voice was faint and growing yet fainter. Corum relived the torment he had suffered in the forest, when Glandyth had struck off his hand. He screamed as the pain came to his wrist once more and then there was fire in his face and he knew that Kwll had plucked his brother's jeweled eye from his skull, now that his powers were restored. Red darkness swam in his brain. Red fire drained his energy. Red pain consumed his flesh.

". . . they obey only one law—the law of loyalty to each other!" Jhary shouted. "I prayed your decision would not be this."

"I am . . ." Corum spoke thickly, looking at the stump where the hand had been, touching the smooth flesh where his eye had been. "I am a cripple once again."

"And I am whole." Kwll's strange voice had not changed in tone, but his jeweled body glowed the brighter and he stretched his four legs and all his four arms and he sighed with pleasure. "Whole."

In one of his hands the Lost God held his brother's eye and he held it so that it shone in the blue light from the city. "And free," he said. "Soon, brother, we shall range again the Million Spheres as we always ranged before our fight—in joy and in delight at all the variety of things. We two are the only beings who really know pleasure! I must find you brother!"

"The bargain," said Corum insistently, ignoring Jhary. "You told me you would help me, Kwll."

"Mortal, I make no bargains, I obey no laws save the one of which you have already learned. I care not for Law nor for Chaos nor for the Cosmic Balance. Kwll and Rhynn exist for the love of existence and nothing else and we do not concern ourselves with the illusory struggles of petty mortals and their pettier gods. Do you not know that you *dream* of these gods—that you are stronger than they—that when you are fearful, why then you bring fearsome gods upon yourselves? Is this not evident to you?"

"I do not understand your words. I say that you must keep your bargain."

"I go now to seek my brother, Rhynn, and toss this eye somewhere where he may easily find it and so be free like me."

"Kwll! You owe me much!"

"Owe? I acknowledge no debts save my debt to myself to follow my own desires and those of my brother. Owe? What do I owe?"

"Without me, you would not now be free."

"Without my previous aid you would not now be alive. Be grateful."

"I have been ill-used by gods, Kwll. I weary of it. A pawn of Chaos and then Law and now Kwll. At least Law acknowledges that power must have responsibility. You are no better than the Lords of Chaos!"

"Untrue! We harm no one, Rhynn and I. What pleasure is there in playing these silly games of Law and Chaos, of manipulating the fate of mortals and demigods? You mortals are used because you wish to be used, because *you* can then place the responsibility of your actions upon these gods of yours. Forget all gods—forget me. You'll be happier."

"Yet you did use me, Kwll. That you must admit."

Kwll turned his back on Corum, tossing a dark, many-barbed spear into the air and making it vanish. "I use many things—I use my weapons—but I do not feel indebted to them once they are no longer of use."

"You are unjust, Kwll!"

"Justice?" Kwll shook with laughter. "What is that?"

Corum poised himself to spring at the Lost God, but Jhary held him back. The dandy said, "If you train a dog to fetch your quarry for you, Kwll, you reward it, do you not? Then, if you need it, it will fetch for you again."

Kwll spun round on his four legs, his faceted eyes glittering. "But if it will not, then one trains a new dog."

"I am immortal," Jhary said. "And I will make it my business to warn all the other dogs that there is nought to be gained from running the Lost Gods' errands . . ."

"I have no further need of dogs."

"Have you not? Even you cannot anticipate what will come about after the Conjunction of the Million Spheres."

"I could destroy you, mortal who is immortal."

"You would be as petty as those you despise."

"Then I will help you." Kwll flung back his jeweled head and laughed so that even Tanelorn seemed to shake with his mirth. "It will save me time, I think."

"You will keep your bargain?" Corum demanded.

"I admit no bargain. But I will help you." Kwll leaped forward suddenly and seized Corum under one arm and Jhary under another. "First, to the Realm of the King of the Swords."

And blue Tanelorn was gone and all around them rose the unstable stuff of Chaos, dancing like lava in an erupting volcano, and through it Corum saw Rhalina.

But Rhalina was five thousand feet high.

The Fourth Chapter

THE KING OF THE SWORDS

Kwll set them down and stared at the gigantic woman. "It is not flesh," he said. "It is a castle."

It was a castle fashioned to resemble Rhalina. But what had built it and for what purpose? And where was Rhalina herself?

"We'll visit the castle," Kwll said, stepping through the leaping Chaos matter as another might pass through smoke. "Stay closely with me."

They walked on until they came to a flight of white stone steps which led up and up into the distance and ended finally at a doorway set in the navel of the towering statue. His four legs moving surprisingly clumsily, Kwll began to climb the steps. He was singing to himself.

At last they reached the top and entered the circular doorway to find themselves in a great hall illuminated by light which poured downward from the distant head.

And in the center of the light stood a great group of creatures, all armed as if ready for battle. These creatures were both uniformed and beautiful and they wore a variety of kinds of armor and bore a variety of weapons. Some had heads which resembled those of beasts, while some looked like beautiful women. They were all smiling at the three who entered the chamber. And Corum knew them for the gathered Dukes of Hell—those who served Mabelrode, the King of the Swords.

Kwll, Corum, and Jhary paused at the doorway. Kwll bowed and smiled back and they seemed a little astonished to see him but plainly did not recognize what he was. Their ranks parted and there stood two more figures.

One of them was tall and naked but for a light robe. His white skin was smooth and without hair and his body was perfectly proportioned. Long, fair hair flowed to his shoulders, but he had no face. Completely featureless skin covered the head where the eyes and the nose and the mouth would have been.

Corum knew this must be Mabelrode, who was called the Faceless.

The other figure was Rhalina.

"I hoped you would come," said the King of Swords, though he had no lips to form the words. "That is why I built my castle—to act as a lure to you when you returned to seek your lady. Mortals are so loyal!"

"Aye, we are that," agreed Corum. "Are you safe, Rhalina?"

"I am safe—and my fury keeps me sane," she said. "I thought you dead, Corum, when the sky ship was wrecked. But this creature told me it was unlikely. Have you found help? It seems not. You have lost your hand and your eye again, I see." She spoke flatly.

Tears came into Corum's eye. "Mabelrode will pay for having discomforted you," he told her.

The faceless god laughed and his dukes laughed with him. It was as if beasts had learned the power of laughter. Mabelrode reached behind Rhalina and drew out a great golden sword, which dazzled them with its light. "I swore that I would avenge both Arioch and Xiombarg," said Mabelrode the Faceless. "I swore I would not risk my life or my position until you, Corum, were in my power. And when Duke Teer was tricked by you" (Duke Teer lowered his porcine head at this) "into fighting our servant Glandyth, whom I also allowed to play a part in preparing my trap, then you almost fled into my snare. But something happened. Only the girl was caught and you and the other thing vanished. So I used the girl, this time, as bait. And I waited. And you came. And now I may administer your punishment. My first intention is to mold your flesh a little, mixing it with that of your companions until you become more foul to look upon than anything of mine you affect to loathe. As this I will let you linger a year or two—or however long your little brain can endure it—and than I will restore you to your original forms and make you hate each other and lust for each other at the same time—you are already experienced, I think, of something I can do in that direction. Then . . ."

"What mundane imaginations these Lords of Chaos have," said Kwll in his many-toned voice. "What modest ambitions they entertain! What petty dreams they dream." He laughed. "They are hardly men, let alone gods."

The Dukes of Hell fell silent and turned their heads to watch their king.

Mabelrode held his golden sword in his two hands and from it burst a thousand shadows, all twisting and dancing in the air, all suggesting shapes to Corum, but shapes which he could not name.

"My power is not mundane, creature! What are you that you can mock the most powerful of the Sword Rulers, Mabelrode the Faceless?"

"I do not mock," said Kwll. "I am Kwll." He reached into the air and took a several-bladed sword from it. "I state that which is evident."

"Kwll is dead," said Mabelrode, "as Rhynn is dead. Dead. You are a charlatan. Your conjuring is not entertaining."

"I am Kwll."

"Kwll is dead."

"I am Kwll."

Three of the Dukes of Hell rushed at the being then, their swords raised.

"Slay him," said Mabelrode, "so that I may begin to have the pleasure of my vengeance."

Kwll plucked two more many-bladed swords from the air. He let the swords of the Dukes of Hell fall upon his jeweled body before casually skewering each one of them and tossing them away so that they vanished.

"Kwll," he said. "The power of the multiverse is mine."

"No single being can have such power!" Mabelrode shouted. "The Cosmic Balance denies it."

"I do not obey the Cosmic Balance, however," said Kwll reasonably. He turned to Corum and Jhary and he handed Corum the Eye of Rhynn. "I will dispense with these. Take my brother's eye to your own plane and cast it into the sea. There'll be no need for you to do else."

"And Glandyth?"

"Surely you can deal with a fellow mortal without my aid. You grow lazy, mortal."

"But—Rhalina . . ."

"Ah."

Kwll's hand seemed to extend through the gathered ranks of the Dukes of Hell, past King Mabelrode the Faceless, and pluck Rhalina from the Sword Ruler's side.

"There."

Rhalina sobbed in Corum's arms.

Corum heard Mabelrode cry, "Summon all my strength! Summon all the creatures of all the planes who are pledged to me. Ready yourselves, my Dukes of Hell! Chaos must be defended!''

Jhary shouted back at him, ''Do you fear one being, King of the Swords? Just one?''

Mabelrode's golden sword flickered in his hand. His back seemed bowed, his voice was low. ''I fear Kwll,'' he said.

''You are wise to do so,'' said Kwll. He waved one of his hands. ''Now, let us dismiss all these silly trappings and concern ourselves with the fight.''

The castle shaped like Rhalina began to melt around them. The Dukes of Hell cried out in terror, their shapes changing as they sought to find the one which would serve them best. Mabelrode the Faceless began to increase in size until his huge, faceless head loomed over them.

Fierce colors slashed the skies. Pools of darkness appeared. Screams were heard and grunts and sucking sounds. From all points came things which hopped and things which slithered and things which galloped and things which flew and things which walked— all things of Chaos come to aid King Mabelrode.

Kwll tapped Jhary on the shoulder and the dandy disappeared.

Corum gasped. ''Even you cannot go against the entire strength of Chaos! I regret my bargain. I release you from it!''

''I made no bargain.'' Two hands came out and tapped Corum and Rhalina. Corum felt himself being drawn away from the realm of Chaos.

''They will destroy you, Kwll!''

''I admit I have not fought for some time, but doubtless I will remember my old skills.''

Corum glimpsed the roaring terror that was Chaos hurling itself upon the Lost God. ''No . . .''

He struggled to draw his own sword, but he was falling now. Falling as he had fallen once before when the sky ship had been wrecked. But this time he held tightly to Rhalina.

Even as his senses clouded he kept his grip upon her arm until he heard her calling his name.

''Corum! Corum! You pain me!''

His eyes were closed. He opened them. She and he were standing on blackened stone and the sea was all around them. He did not recognize the place at first, for the castle was no longer there. And then he remembered that Glandyth had burned it.

They stood on Moidel's Mount.

The tide was beginning to go out and they glimpsed the causeway as it was slowly uncovered.

"Look," said Rhalina, pointing toward the forest.

He looked and he saw several corpses.

"So the strife continues," he said. He was about to help her to climb down when he looked at the thing he had clutched even as he had clutched Rhalina with his single hand. It was the Eye of Rhynn.

He drew back his arm and flung it far out into the sea. It flashed in the air and then disappeared beneath the waves.

"I am not sorry to see that dismissed at last," he said.

The Fifth Chapter

THE LAST OF GLANDYTH

When they had crossed the causeway and reached the mainland, they could better distinguish the corpses sprawled near the edge of the forest. They were of their old enemies, the Pony Tribesmen. They had fought each other savagely and for some time, by all the signs. They lay in their furs and their necklets and bracelets of copper and bronze with their crude swords and axes in their hands, each man bearing at least a dozen wounds. They had plainly been gripped by the Cloud of Contention, which the Nhadragh's sorcery had brought to the land. Corum bent down and inspected the nearest corpse.

"Not dead long," he said. "It means the sickness is still strong. And yet it does not touch us. Perhaps it takes time to enter our brains. Ah, the poor folk of Lywm-an-Esh—my poor Vad-hagh . . ."

A movement in the trees.

Corum drew his sword, feeling for the first time the lack of his left hand and right eye. He felt off-balance. Then he grinned in relief.

It was Jhary-a-Conel leading three of the dead Tribesmen's ponies by their bridle ropes.

"Not the most comfortable beasts to ride, but better than walking. Where do you head for, Corum? For Halwyg?"

Corum shook his head. "I have been thinking of the only positive deed we can try to perform. There's little to be done in Halwyg. I doubt if Glandyth has yet set up his court there, for, doubtless, he still hunts for us on other planes. We'll go to Erorn, I think. There is a boat there we can use and it will take us to the Nhadragh Isles."

"Where the sorcerer dwells who has put this spell upon the world."

"Just so."

Jhary-a-Conel stroked his cat under its chin. "Your idea is sound, Corum Jhaelen Irsei. Let us make speed."

Soon they were mounted on the shaggy ponies and were driving them as hard as they could go through the woods of Bro-an-Vadhagh. Twice they were forced to hide while small groups of Vadhagh hunted each other. Once they witnessed a massacre, but there was nothing they could do to save the victims.

Corum was relieved to sight the towers of Castle Erorn at long last, for he had wondered if Glandyth or some other had destroyed it again. The castle was as they had left it. The snow had all melted and a mild spring was beginning to touch the trees and shrubs. Gratefully they entered the castle.

But they had forgotten the retainers.

The retainers had not resisted the sickness long. They found two corpses just inside the doorway, horribly butchered. Others were elsewhere in the castle and all had been murdered save one—the last survivor, his aggression had turned to self-hatred and he had hanged himself in one of the rooms of music. His presence caused the fountains and the crystals to make a sour, dreadful sound which almost drove Corum, Rhalina, and Jhary back out of the castle.

The work of disposing of the corpses done, Corum took the passage down to the large sea-cave below the castle. Here was the little boat in which he and Rhalina had sailed for pleasure in the short-lived days of peace. It was ready for immediate use.

Rhalina and Jhary brought down the provisions while Corum checked the rigging and the sail. They waited for the tide to turn and then sailed beneath the great, rugged arch of the sea cave and out into open water. It would be two days before they sighted the first of the Nhadragh Isles.

With only the sea surrounding him, Corum thought about his adventures upon the different planes. He had entered so many worlds he had lost count of them. Were there really a million spheres, each sphere containing a number of planes? It was hard to conceive of so many worlds. And on each world a struggle was taking place.

"Are there no worlds which know permanent peace?" he asked Jhary as he took over the rudder of the boat while the dandy adjusted the sail. "Are there none, Jhary?"

The dandy shrugged. "Perhaps there are, though I have never seen one. Perhaps it is not my fate to see one. But it is basic to Nature to know struggle of some kind, surely?"

"Some creatures live in peace all their lives."

"Aye, some do. There is a legend that once there was only one world—one planet like ours—which was tranquil and perfect. But something evil invaded it and it learned strife and in learning strife created other examples of itself where strife could flourish the better. But there are many legends which say the past was perfect or that the future will be perfect. I have seen many pasts and many futures. None of them were perfect, my friend."

Corum felt the boat rock and he tightened his grip on the rudder. The waves became larger and the sea was choppy.

Rhalina pointed into the distance. "The Wading God—see! He goes toward our coast, still fishing."

"Perhaps the Wading God knows peace," said Corum when the sea settled and the giant had gone.

Jhary stroked the head of his cat. The little creature looked nervously at the water. "I think not," said Jhary quietly.

Another day went by before they saw the outer islands of the group. They were predominantly dark green and brown and as they sailed by them they saw the black ruins of the towns and the castles which the Mabden had fired when they had come reaving to the Nhadragh Isles. Once or twice a shambling figure would wave to them from a beach but they ignored him, for doubtless the Cloud of Contention had touched those who were left of the Nhadragh.

"There," said Corum. "That large island. It is Maliful, where lies the city of Os and the Nhadragh sorcerer Ertil. I think I feel the Cloud of Contention begin to gnaw again at my brain . . . ."

"Then we had best hurry and do our work, if we can," Jhary said.

They landed the small boat on a stony, deserted beach quite close to Os, whose walls they could already see.

"Go, Whiskers," murmured Jhary to his cat, "show us the way to the sorcerer's keep."

The cat spread its wings and flew high into the air, hovering to keep pace with them as they moved cautiously toward the city. Then, as they climbed over the rubble of what had once been a gateway and began to make their way through piles of weed-grown masonry, the cat flew to the squat building with the yellow dome upon its roof. It flew twice around the dome and then came back to settle on Jhary's shoulder.

Corum felt a twinge of annoyance at the cat. It was reasonless anger and he knew what caused it. He began to run toward the squat building.

There was only one entrance and it was filled with a hard, wooden door.

"To break that," whispered Jhary, "would be to make our presence known. Look, here—steps lead up the side."

A flight of stone steps led to the roof and up these the three went, Rhalina following in the wake of the men.

Together they crept up to the dome and peered inside. At first it was hard to make out what was in there. They saw the clutter of parchments and animal cages and cauldrons. But there was a form moving about in one corner. It could only be the sorcerer.

"I'm tired of this caution!" Corum shouted. "Let's end it now!" With a yell he reversed his sword hilt and struck heavily at the dome. It groaned and a crack appeared. He struck again and the stuff shattered, falling into the room.

But Corum had released a stink which drove them back for a few yards until it had dispersed it the cleaner outer air. Corum, feeling the unreasoning fury rising in him again, dashed to the edge of the broken dome and leaped through the hole he had made, landing with a crash upon the scored table below.

Sword ready, he glared around him.

And what he saw drove the fury from his head. It was the Nhadragh, Ertil.

The corrupt sorcerer had plainly succumbed to his own spell. There was foam on his lips. His dark eyes rolled.

"I killed them," he said, "as I will kill you. They would not obey me—so I killed them."

With his one remaining arm he held up his severed leg. Another leg and an arm bled nearby.

"I killed them!"

Corum turned away, kicking out at the bubbling cauldron, the vials of herbs and chemicals, scattering them about the room.

"I killed them!" babbled the sorcerer. His voice rose to a shriek and then subsided. The blood was pouring from his body. He would only live a few seconds more.

"How made you the Cloud of Contention?" Corum asked him.

Weakly Ertil grinned and gestured with the severed leg. "There —the censer. Only a little censer—but it has destroyed you all!"

"Not all." Corum grabbed the censer by its chains and immersed it in one of the cauldrons. Green steam boiled from its sides and evil faces flickered in that steam for a moment before fading away.

"I have destroyed that which destroyed so many of my folk, sorcerer," Corum said.

Ertil looked up at him through glazed eyes. "Then destroy me, too, Vadhagh. I deserve it."

Corum shook his head. "I'll let you continue to die in the manner you chose."

From above came Jhary's voice.

"Corum!"

The Prince in the Scarlet Robe looked up and saw Jhary's face framed in the hole of the dome. Jhary looked daunted.

"What is it, Jhary?"

"Glandyth must have sensed the decline in the sorcerer's sanity."

"What mean you?"

"He comes, Corum. His beasts still bear him."

Corum sheather his sword and jumped from the table. "I'll join you below. I can't get back that way."

He stepped over what was left of Ertil the Nhadragh and he pulled open the door. As he went down the stairs he heard the voices of the caged animals chattering and crying, begging him to release them.

Outside Jhary was already waiting for him with Rhalina. Corum took Rhalina and made her enter the building.

"Stay there, Rhalina. It is a foul place but it offers greater safety. Please stay there."

Black wings beat in the sky. Glandyth was near.

Corum and Jhary ran out until they stood in what had once been a square. Now piles of rubble filled it.

The Denledhyssi were fewer in number. Doubtless some had died in the encounter with Duke Teer. But there were still a dozen black monsters in the air above Os.

A blood-curdling yell of triumph suddenly sounded from the sky and it echoed through the ruined city.

"Corum!"

It was Glandyth-a-Krae and he had seen his enemy.

"Where are your sorcerous hand and eye, Shefanhow? Gone back to the netherworld you conjured them from, eh?"

Glandyth began to laugh.

"So, after all, we are to die at the hands of the Mabden," Corum said quietly as he watched the black beasts land on the far side of the square. "Prepare to perish, Jhary."

They waited with their swords ready as Glandyth dismounted from his Chaos monster and began to tramp across the ruins, his Denledhyssi at his back.

Thinking that he might save Jhary and Rhalina, Corum called to the huge man, "Will you fight me fairly, Earl Glandyth? Will you tell your men to stand back while we battle?"

Glandyth-a-Krae adjusted his bulky furs on his back and he tilted his helm further over his red face. Laughter exploded from his thick lips. "If you think it is fair for me to fight a wretch with but one hand

and one eye, yes. I'll fight you, Corum.'' He winked at his men.
"Stand back as he says. I'll let you have his other hand and his other
eye in a little while.''

The barbarians yelled with mirth at their leader's jest.

The Mabden earl came closer until only a few yards separated
them. He glowered at the Vadhagh.

"You have caused me much discomfort of late, Shefanhow. But
now my pleasure makes me forget it all. I am most glad to see you.''
He drew his great war-axe from his belt and slid his sword from its
scabbard. "We shall complete what was begun in the woods at
Castle Erorn.''

He took a step forward but then a frightened yell from his men
made him stop and glance back.

The black beasts were rising into the air and flying eastward. And
as they flew they vanished.

"Going back to Chaos,'' Corum told Glandyth. "Their master
needs them, for he is hard pressed. If I kill you, Glandyth, will your
men set me free?''

Glandyth grinned his wolf grin. "They love me greatly, do my
Denledhyssi.''

"So I have little to gain,'' Corum said. "One moment.'' He
murmured to Jhary. "Take Rhalina now. Get to the boat. Even if I
am killed the Denledhyssi have no transportation now and will not
be able to follow you. It is the wisest thing, Jhary, do not deny
that.''

Jhary sighed. "I do not deny it. I will do as you say. I go.''

"You will let him leave Os, will you not?'' Corum said.

Glandyth shrugged. "Very well. If we become bored we can
always hunt him down later. And do not think that I miss the loss of
a few Chaos beasts. I have my own sorcerer to conjure up something
new if I need it.''

"Ertil?''

Glandyth's unhealthy eyes narrowed. "What of Ertil?''

"He has killed himself. The Cloud of Contention reached even
him.''

"No matter. I will—haaiii!'' The Earl of Krae flung himself
suddenly at Corum, the battle-axe and the sword slashing from two
sides.

Corum jumped back, caught his foot, fell as the axe whistled over
his head. He rolled as the sword clashed down on the block of
masonry where he had lain. He supported himself on the stump
of his left hand and got to his feet, blocking a wild blow from the
axe.

The barbarian was as strong and as swift as ever, for all his girth.

400

His presence alone made Corum feel as weak as a child in comparison. He strove to take the offensive, but Glandyth allowed him no respite, forcing him further and further back over the rubble. Corum's only hope was that Jhary had managed to get Rhalina to the boat and that, by the time Glandyth slew him, they would be sailing back for Castle Erorn.

Both axe and sword came down on Corum's upraised blade and his arm went numb beneath the force of the blow. He slid his sword down the haft of the axe, trying to cut Glandyth's fingers, but the Earl of Krae withdrew the axe and aimed it at Corum's head.

Corum dodged and the axe sheared off the links of the byrnie on his left shoulder but only grazed the flesh.

Glandyth grinned. His foul breath was in Corum's face, his mad eyes were full of death-lust. He stabbed with his sword and Corum felt the steel slide into his thigh. He backed off and saw that there was blood running down the silver mail.

Panting, Glandyth paused, readying himself for the kill.

And Corum dashed in, struck with his blade at Glandyth's face and gashed his cheek before the barbarian's sword came up and pushed away his weapon.

Blood continued to pour from the wound in his thigh. Corum hobbled backward over the ruins, trying to put a little distance between himself and his enemy. Glandyth did not follow but stood there, relishing Corum's pain.

"I think I can still have the pleasure of making your death a slow one. Would you care to run a little way, Prince Corum, to purchase a few extra seconds of life?"

Corum straightened his back. He was almost fainting. He could say nothing. He stared at Glandyth through his single eye and then he took a step forward.

Glandyth chuckled. "I slew all your race, save you. Now, after much patient waiting, I can slay the last of your filthy kind."

Corum took another step forward.

Glandyth readied his weapons. "You want to die, eh?"

Corum swayed. He could hardly see the Earl of Krae. He raised his sword with difficulty and tried to take a further step.

"Come," said Glandyth, "come."

A shadow passed over the ruins. At first Corum thought he imagined it. He shook his head to try to clear it.

Glandyth had seen the shadow, too. His red mouth fell open in astonishment, his bloodshot eyes widened.

And while he stared up at the thing which cast the shadow, Corum fell forward behind his sword and plunged the steel into Glandyth's throat.

Glandyth made a hollow, gurgling sound and blood welled from his mouth.

"For my family," said Corum.

The shadow moved on. It was a giant who cast it. A giant with a great net, which he cast down over the terrified men of the Denledhyssi and dragged them upward and hurled their bodies far out over the city. It was a giant with two glittering, jeweled eyes.

Corum fell down beside the corpse of Glandyth-a-Krae, looking up at the giant. "The Wading God," he said.

Jhary appeared beside him, staunching the blood from his thigh. "The Wading God," he said to Corum. "But he no longer fishes the seas of the world for he found what he sought."

"His soul?"

"His eye. The Wading God is Rhynn."

Corum's vision was even more blurred. But through a pink mist he saw Kwll come, a grin upon his jeweled face.

"Your Chaos gods are gone," said Kwll. "With my brother's help I slew them all and all their minions."

"I thank you," Corum said thickly. "And Lord Arkyn will thank you, too."

Kwll chuckled. "I think not."

"Why—why so?"

"For good measure we slew the Lords of Law as well. Now you mortals are free of gods on these planes."

"But Arkyn—Arkyn was good . . ."

"Find the same good in yourselves if that is what you respect. It is the time of the Conjunction of the Million Spheres and that means change—profound alterations in the nature of existence. Perhaps that was our function—to rid the Fifteen Planes of its silly gods and their silly schemes."

"But the Balance . . . ?"

"Let it swing up and down with a will. It has nothing to weigh now. You are on your own, mortal—you and your kind. Farewell."

Corum tried to speak again, but the pain in his thigh swamped all thought. At last he fainted.

Once more Kwll's many-toned voice sounded in his skull before his senses were engulfed completely.

"Now you can make your own destiny."

EPILOGUE

Again the land had healed and again mortals went about their business, repairing what had been destroyed. A new king was found for Lywm-an-Esh, and the Vadhagh who had escaped death returned to their castles.

At Castle Erorn by the sea Corum Jhaelen Irsei, the Prince in the Scarlet Robe, recovered his health, thanks to the potions of Jhary-a-Conel and the nursing of the Lady Rhalina and he found a new hobby for himself, remembering what he had seen at the doctor's house when trapped upon the plane of Lady Jane Pentallyon, which was the manufacture of artificial hands. He had yet to make one that satisfied him.

One day came Jhary-a-Conel in his hat with his bag on his back and his cat on his shoulder and he said good-bye to them with some reluctance. They begged him to stay, to enjoy the peace they had earned.

"For a world without gods is a world without much to fear," said Corum.

"That is true," Jhary agreed.

"Then stay," said the Lady Rhalina.

"But," said Jhary, "I go to seek worlds where gods still rule, for I am not suited to any other. And," he added, "I would hate it if I came to blame myself for my misfortunes. That would not do at all! Gods—a sense of an ominiscience not far away—demons—destinies which cannot be denied—absolute evil—absolute good—I need it all."

Corum smiled. "Then go if you will and remember that we love you. But do not despair entirely of this world, Jhary. New gods can always be created."

This ends the third and final
Book of Corum